catching preeya

Fight, flight...or fall.

RISSA BRAHM

WANT MORE OF RISSA BRAHM'S PARADISE SOUTH—FOR FREE?

Hello Outrageous Readers of Romance!

Sign up for my newsletter and get a deleted scene from *Catching Preeya*—plus juicy extras from the entire Paradise South series—and lots more exclusive content…all for **free!**

Details can be found in the ***Author's Note*** at the end of *Catching Preeya*. So we'll meet up again post-HEA! See ya there, and enjoy the ride!

ISBN 978-1-944557-09-6 (print)

ISBN 978-1-944557-10-2 (epub)

ISBN 978-1-944557-11-9 (mobi)

Published by: *108 degrees*™

Brahm, Rissa (2016-04-01)

Illustrated Romance Cover design by: Damonza

Catching Preeya (Paradise South, Book 3)

TKA Distribution. Kindle Edition.

To Pre-Dawn from the past—a distance-gauge.
And to Dads.

CHAPTER 1

WITH HIS MESSENGER bag hiked high on his shoulder, Dr. Ben Trainer stood far from the cluster of frantic, pushy travelers lining the baggage claim carousel. He stood at the very end of the belt, alone and patient. An intelligent choice. A necessary choice. Stark civilization hit hard after being away for so many months. Hell, being back in the Western Hemisphere, in The States, in cloud-heavy Seattle, locked up his chest, knotted his neck, and tensed his shoulders, lower back and jaw.

He sighed as he spotted his battered duffel winding its lackadaisical way around the conveyor belt amidst the pricey and pristine luggage sets, the plutonium grey golf club bag, and the family of snow skis clothed in durable vinyl travel sleeves. He scoffed—the entire village he'd just returned from could be fed and clothed with the value of the clubs alone.

He yanked, then slung and strapped his heavy-duty canvas pack onto his back. He took a few long strides away from the carousel as a few college kids moved in, catching onto his end-of-the-belt idea, no doubt, when his phone pinged. It could only be one of two people, the only two he had left in the world. His sister and Stan, his longtime friend and attorney, the one who'd orchestrated this required visit to the Emerald City. Ben would answer it later, though. He just had to get out of there. The surrounding grimaces and frantic tones were getting to him fast. Cab, hotel, sleep—*stat*. Then a quick morning of hell at the hearing before flying away again. *Far away.*

He weaved his way outside to the taxi booth and grabbed his spot in line.

Then it hit him—or his shin more specifically. And it hit hard. A carry-on made of, God, titanium? Then it rolled over his foot, as if in slow motion. He fought the need to grab his leg as the flight attendant controlling—or not controlling—the culprit roller bag flicked her gaze up at him, and he caught it. Or, rather, her gaze caught him. Her eyes stunned and awed, even more than the bullet-proof bag had.

"I am so, so sorry." Her eyes—violet to blue to endless—apologized too, as she yanked her carry-on toward her like it was a misbehaved child.

His pulse spiked. "It's okay. Really." Any shin or foot pain, abolished. Airflow, vacuumed. All replaced by electricity, then a cloud of billowing guilt in his vise-gripped chest.

His phone rang from his messenger bag.

But he could only stare at her.

Ben.

It rang again, such an obnoxious jingle. The woman held his stare while her lip curled and one brow arched.

And again, the high-pitched electronic tune of horror.

She swallowed a giggle as her eyes shot down to their feet, her cheeks blushing—in sympathy, no doubt. But with her eyes' disconnect, her spell broken, he was able to unzip his bag with fumbling fingers while the ditty dittied another time. He dug for, then grabbed the cell and hit buttons without looking to stop the noise.

He swallowed as a new noise, a garbled voice met his ears. Coming from the phone. The screen showed Stanton's profile. He'd hit Accept, darn it. "Excuse me," Ben mumbled to the shin-slamming heart-pounding distraction in her formfitting navy-blue uniform. He pivoted a fraction. "Stan? Hey, man, just got in, got my bag, and—"

Screaming—no, shrieking. Overwhelming waves of it. Near-pandemonium.

"What is it?" Violet Eyes asked him or no one, craning her neck.

Ben towered above the crowd. A flock of frantic women followed one focal point, a man—tattooed, pierced, and brooding in chains and boots and leather—strolling in Ben's direction.

Were those video cameras on the guy's flanks?

"One second, Stan." He plugged his free ear, but it was no use. He couldn't hear Stan—let alone his own thoughts. And the plume of motion grew closer.

"God, what is it?" his alluring taxi line companion asked again, standing on her tiptoes.

He spotted a guitar case strapped across the celebrity's chest. Ben hiked the strap of his bag higher on his shoulder. "Some rock star, I guess?" Flying commercial? *Publicity hound.*

Phone still in his surgeon's grasp, Ben watched the chaos-maker stride ahead of the frenzied fans and paparazzi, sweeping by the shuttle van line, past the cluster of smokers outside Jetta Air, continuing toward the taxi line—where the clichéd rock sensation stopped short.

Is he looking at me?

"Josh?" Violet Eyes breathed—Ben keyed into her voice through the uproar.

The next instant, the rocker had Violet Eyes in his arms, swinging her around and around and—

Bam!

On the third rotation, Violet Eyes' swinging legs knocked Ben off balance. His cell phone and a bit of his pride flew from his grasp.

Recovered and steady a heartbeat later, he could only gawk at the flight attendant and the apparent celebrity in their continued revolving embrace. Any minute the guy would put her down and break into song, the next frame of this b-grade music video intro. As if on Ben's mental cue, the rock star set Violet Eyes' feet to the ground, but didn't stay to serenade her or the masses. No, the rocker pulled her out of line and escorted her and her naughty carry-on away through the still-shrieking she-wolves.

Ben shook his head and blinked hard to reground himself in reality, then sighed.

And shit, his phone!

Eyes to the sidewalk, no sight nor sound of it. *Damn!* He got down on hands and knees and spotted his phone a few pairs of high heels and loafers away. He scrambled for it, but got impeded by new sets of legs. *God, I'm just too old for this.* A full lifetime's worth of gravity had weighed him down since his young wife passed. He felt eighty, though he was half a century shy.

Waiting for a man in boots to step one way or another so he could go in for the rescue, his ears rang from the now-fading raucous. Distracted, he broke focus for an instant, and the phone went skidding while more shoes inadvertently kicked and tapped it along. He crawled forward a few feet. *Still just out of reach, damn it.* Then, a clearing. Risking limb and digits, he grabbed for it just as a fire-engine red high heel began its descent, as if targeting the ancient yet indispensable phone. Jamie had given him the antiquated device, and he wasn't ready to give it up yet. His fingertips made contact with the rubber antenna nub and pulled the cell toward him. Now cupped under his hand, he clutched it for dear life. A narrow save. He sighed, exploded to his feet, then phone to ear, he wondered if Stan had stayed on the call.

"Stanton, man…you there?" He switched ears again while scanning the sea of bobbing heads and camera phones competing for a last glimpse of the celebrity hand in hand with the ocean-eyed flight attendant before they disappeared around the bend.

"Yeah, you okay? What the hell happened?"

Ben shook his head. "My life flashed before my eyes, is all." He laughed and grabbed the handle of his duffel. "Some huge rock star took over the arrivals at Sea-Tac. I'm just standing in the taxi line and…well, someone bumped me." He snorted then swallowed as the flight attendant's twilight eyes floated through his mind. *Surreal.*

"Ben?"

"I'm here, I'm here…so yeah, my phone flew…with you on it. The durable thing's survived the third world a few times over, though. No harm done."

"Jesus, man. Only you."

Ben sucked in then released a long, measured breath. "Only me is right." Ben grabbed his duffel and moved up in line to close the gap. "And God, I have to be back here tomorrow."

"Quick in and out again, huh?"

"Yeah, man." *Thank God.*

"But hey, you should be fine. How often do you run into a rock star at a commercial airport, let alone run into 'em twice?" Stanton laughed.

"Exactly." A short snicker. "Hey, my turn's up and the cabbie's in a hurry—"

"You should've taken me up on the ride, Ben."

"Nah, don't want to put you out. But hey, see you at the hospital…eight a.m.?"

"Join Zoe and me for dinner, at least."

He nodded his thanks to the driver for taking his bag. "Jet lag, man." He switched ears so he could open the car door. "Gonna do room service then sleep, Stan. Another time."

"All right, Ben." A slight huff. "See you at eight…and have a good night."

"Will do. You, too."

He smirked and threw the phone into his messenger bag. *A good night, right.* Another one filled with utter quiet. He hated the quiet. It let his guilt's relentless screams fill his head. His heart. He preferred third-world chaos over that screaming any day of the week, any hour of the day, any second of every excruciating minute that his life ticked by. *Screaming guilt.*

CHAPTER 2

I T FELT LIKE just after midnight when Preeya woke up not knowing her place in the world, or rather, her location in it—an occupational given for a flight attendant. But when she looked around the dark, dank room and over at the sleeping beauty of a man next to her, she remembered where she'd landed. Like a punch in the face, she remembered.

Yesterday afternoon she'd arrived in Seattle for a longer-than-usual eighteen-hour stopover. Ah, the Emerald City—home of grunge-rock nostalgia wrapped in down-to-earth pipe dreams under a blanket of stratus-cloud gloom.

She'd planned to crash at Gigi's. She hadn't seen her best friend in way too long—God, since she'd turned down so-safe-and-sweet Evan, his marriage proposal having scared her shitless, scared her sprinting. Yet another dream crusher for her ever-dashed father. *But screw him.* Gigi was more *family* than her father ever was.

But she'd stood Gigi up. And had ignored Gigi's calls.

Why?

Jaw clenched, chest tight, she shook her head. *Karma.* Karma had had different plans. And Preeya Patel never passed up a meant-to-be opportunity. Gigi got that better than anyone. But then why didn't Preeya just answer Gigi's calls and texts, and explain? Preeya knew why. Or rather *who*—she looked over at *him* and frowned, feeling a new level of nausea.

Such a mistake. "No such thing," Preeya's mom had taught her. Preeya clung to her mother's other mantras, too—*just go with it...sky's the limit... fly free*—because Jenny Patel's hipster philosophy was all Preeya had left of the woman. Out of loyalty alone, Preeya's gut overruled all—like when it had told her to drop out of medical school to become an FA. Well...her gut and the deep desire to throw her father the finger. Killed two birds with one stone on that one, proving herself an *efficient* flake, at least.

Efficient—hah! She didn't know if it was day or night—or the day of the damn week, for that matter. Shivering cold and hangover-queasy, she slammed her hand down on the nightstand and groped unsuccessfully for her phone. She squinted, scanning the room. No clock. And *his* phone for a glimpse at the time? She'd heard it pinging incessantly from somewhere far off, probably the bathroom where he'd spent most of the night. But she didn't hear it now. Must've died, all that activity. No doubt a waiting list of groupies, ping by ego-crushing ping. Between that certainty and his cocaine-cocktail coma, she so needed to get the hell out of there. Wow, had this "fly by the seat of her skirt" kismet adventure yielded none of the magic and wonder that her mother had foretold.

Well-beyond the opposite.

Josh Bolte, the torrential, savage rocker, the lead singer of Carnal Knowledge—garage band gone global—had been her first, well...*everything*. Before he and the band took off—figuratively, literally, heart-crushingly—he'd been the one who'd fit her picture, her plan for unplanned ecstasy to the end of days, her potential partner in crime. He was wildfire and vibrancy and depth all wrapped up in a gorgeous package of heat and delectability.

Heat and delectability? She beheld the lump next to her. Nope. Not even close. Not anymore.

So what did that make her?

One hot mess with a nagging conscience.

Enough dwelling and move your ass, Pree.

But where to even begin? He lay curled up in a fetal position under all the covers, while her body lay next to his, stark naked and trembling, and from her hazy recollection, her clothes were scattered throughout the wreck of a room. Because last night when he'd carried her through his bandmate's guest room door, he'd torn her clothes off, then his, and tossed them. So damn hot. So carefree. So what she'd wanted…

The AC fan clicked on as an acidic burp bubbled up her throat. More rough reality mixed with hangover. But she wasn't nearly as bad off as he was. God, right when he'd offered her a line of his "white powder escape," she should've been out. Instead, too jet lagged to find her phone and clothes, and too embarrassed to call Gigi, she'd opted for vodka as an available—and legal—sleep aid while he rode his own wave alone.

She put one foot on the floor—perpendicular and immediately dizzy—then the other foot. "Oh gross!" She recoiled to the bed. Her toe had sunk into something cold and lumpy.

Josh growled.

She glared while frantically wiping her foot on the fitted sheet, holding back tears with all she had.

She sucked in a breath—along with the stench of the room, a sickening accord of vomit, spilled vodka, old pizza, and maybe sweaty socks? The putridity sparked a riotous headache in her skull while her heart sank to the pit of her stomach. She surrendered back onto the bed. He huffed then shifted. Wow, the man of her wildest dreams, this new and *unimproved* Josh Bolte, was so far from who she'd remembered.

"Seven years…" A desperate exhale, a plummeting hot-air balloon. "Have I not learned anything in seven damn years?"

Josh rolled to his back. "Shhhhh." His arm swung in from out of nowhere, his hand landing *almost* gently on her lips, mushing them to a hush. "Need. Quiet."

She took his hand off her mouth with the tips of her icy-cold fingers, as she would with someone else's dirty tissue, and let his arm drop with a thud on the other side of his body. She lay back flat on the unfriendly mattress as he shifted to his right side and tucked that shushing hand under his cheek. He faced her, still clinging hard to sleep. *Oblivious.*

A beat snored by, then he sighed, his breath raw and wretched, right in her face.

"Jeez-*us.*" More nausea.

He groaned.

She grabbed the top sheet he had twisted tight around his divine body—his empty shell of a body—and yanked. The thin sheet *sort of* soothed the goose pimples rippling up and down her bare body. Now she shivered from a deeper chill. An awareness.

A billion stabbing icicles of awareness.

"How did I think you were so—" She shook her head. "No. The real question," she whispered to anyone, to no one, "is how the hell did I end up here? Again? I should be years beyond…this. *You.*" His type. "But if not you"—she swallowed then sighed, shoulders hanging low and limp—"and not Evan, then who?"

Or what?

And goddamn it, when?

She shut her eyes tight. Hiding behind her eyelids for the moment seemed like the most immediate escape route. But the blank-slate nothingness inside her head offered no comfort. "Not better at all."

"Seriously…shut the fuck up…*pleeze*," Josh groaned, then turned his head the other way.

Oh, he wants quiet?

Well, screw that and screw him. She collected a lungful of oxygen fuel, shut all filters down. "Fuck you, Josh! How could I have fallen for your bullshit, even for one more night? Jesus, who am I?"

Yesterday, when he'd halted his confident stride, spotting Preeya in the taxi line, that long-ago look in his eyes—that same searing, soul-wrenching gaze—her heart had halted, too. And her breath had ceased. The raging fire rippling up her spine had not allowed her to do anything but return his maddening, core-clenching gaze. That's when she'd ignored Gigi's calls and bypassed that tall, uptight, and bumbling-but-sweet stranger who she'd shin-slammed with her carry-on—the man with the alluring yet sad amber eyes.

Sweet eyes.

Not like Josh's blazing eyes…that fizzled at the first hint of rain. *In Seattle, no less.*

Damn you, Josh. Intent, cocky, directed. He swooped her up and swung her around, sweeping her off her feet again.

And she'd *gone with it.* Gone with him. *Again.*

Damn it. And damn every pathetic daydream, night dream, vision, and fantasy of him.

"Because *this*…with this *you*…isn't *me*." She could've wrung her own neck realizing then that most of her quickie romances were with cheap imitations of *him*. "Except for Evan. He was different. Polar-opposite *different*." A quick puff of laughter at the insight morphed into near hysteria. Yes, she'd been ranting like a lunatic, but it felt too good to stop. Releasing, venting, *realizing*. "And you know what?"

Josh growled low in his chest through his pillow sandwich.

"Evan was my attempt at the status quo. Me trying to appease my dad, in place of med school." She sucked in her bottom lip and bit down. Then she snapped back, "But, hey, flight attendant training wasn't easy!" Her words barreled through the darkness as the AC kicked off, the rattling hum done for a time.

But she wasn't done. Not yet. "You've never met Dad, but take my word for it, you're a lot alike." She nodded, enjoying the comparison. "Yeah, you're both arrogant assholes with a god complex." She lay back again, then stared for a beat at the blackout drapes, unwavering in the now-static air. "And I'm nothing to him now because he can't tell his friends his kid's an airhead 'trolley dolly'. Well, fuck 'im. Travel and adventure and being true to my heart, that's goddamn important. Vital. My path!"

Josh gave a violent huff.

She huffed back. *Still not done.* Not even close. "Anyway, Evan was just too safe, too static. Then he proposed, with a ring…a real ring! I just flipped out and—"

"Hey…babe, listen." Josh opened one eye to a squint. "Enough with the fucking monologue. My pounding head can't take it." Said in the unsexiest rasp she'd ever heard.

And—*babe*?

Reduced to a *babe*. Another level of fury formed way down in her icy toes and shot to the tip of her *cute-as-a-fucking-button* nose.

Fucking *babe. Why not slap my ass like the rich pervs in business class do while you're at it?* And, hell, did he even remember her name? Who she was? Who she'd *been* to him? At least, so he'd said and written and sang. His muse, goddamn it.

Fired up now, she kneeled on the mattress and squared her shoulders. "Well, Mr. big-time lead singer who couldn't keep it up for more than a millisecond last night—"

"Hey, are you fucking done yet?" Both eyes had finally opened, his nostrils flaring.

"No, I'm not. And I wanted *you* done...done talking and ranting and singing your bullshit pseudo-deep lyrics and puking all night. And I wanted some just-deserts sex and closure, too. I wanted, *want*, a lot of things, Josh Bolte. But as one *real* rock legend sang, we don't always get what we want, now do we? Do we?"

*

Words, words, and more empty words. Tossed around like confetti.

Ben had never dealt well with bullshit, with red tape, with hoops to jump through. And he'd always hated muddy waters.

But here he was at the medical review hearing. In the middle of the gray zone. Sitting in the stifling conference room for the third time this year. Here nothing was black and white. And he needed black and white, now more than ever.

Ben had always been direct, principled, cut-and-dried, and too honest for most people, most of the time. As a kid, he'd gone to the extreme—rules were rules, and they absolutely *were not* made to be broken. He'd been the teacher's pet and class tattle tale until a fist to the nose in fifth grade made an impression—and so had the calm, cool, and collected surgeon who'd fixed him up. So although most had expected him to become a cop, a lawyer, or a judge, he'd become a surgeon, and a pediatric specialist, to boot.

But now his practice was lost, his local reputation destroyed. And until the medical board made its decision, Stanton had recommended that Ben take an extended leave of absence from the hospital. Doctors Without Borders had been Ben's saving grace for the past year, and he couldn't wait for his next mission, this time just south of the border.

For now, though, and without Jamie by his side, he'd have to suffer through. She'd been his perfect counterbalance, the gentle stream to his stubborn rock. He sighed and focused on the hovering clouds through the boardroom's skylights.

Stanton cleared his throat, pulling Ben back to the present, to the huge conference table, familiar faces staring back at him. His in-laws, in particular, glared more than they stared.

A snicker escaped Ben's lips. Stanton jabbed him in his ribs, but Ben ignored the reprimand and let his mind jump back in time to the looks on Jamie's folks' faces when he'd *told* them that he'd be marrying their daughter. "Yes, immediately after high school graduation." As always, no games—no tiptoeing or dancing around it. And he'd made it happen. Because he and Jamie had been meant to be. Forever.

Forever.

Well, even a doctor can be wrong.

But for a solid decade plus two years, he'd been right. No doubt in his mind, in his heart, or in his soul. He'd called it. They'd started a wonderful life together. And he'd do it all over again. To experience that level of depth and height with another person—yeah, he'd do it again.

All of it.

Even and especially now, damn it, with those vile words flying over and around his head from across the mahogany table, making him sick, his white-knuckled fists in plain sight on top of his notepad that was blank except for Stanton's scribbled warning to "Keep cool."

Fine, damn it. But he'd make them eat their words. Their vile accusations. The review board, the hospital directors, the legal teams, and his former in-laws—all of them. Because he knew their words were just colorless shreds of recycled paper floating on air with no hope of landing on solid ground.

*

Preeya's throat hurt from yelling, but her stomach had settled a bit.

"Everything okay in there?" a female voice, assertive yet muffled, piped through the door.

Preeya pulled the sheet she'd stolen back from Josh up to her chin.

Josh shoved his head farther under the pillow, then grumbled and belched at the same time.

Jesus, really? Like she needed any more convincing?

"Hey, Josh. You hear me?" From outside the door, not so muffled anymore.

"What the fuck is it, Dawn?" Josh shouted.

Dawn? A pissed-off girlfriend, or, holy crap, his wife? Was he married and didn't say? Oh, wouldn't that make this all so much better. Preeya shivered with dread.

Snoring resumed.

"Josh!" Preeya shook his shoulder. "Who the hell is the woman at the door?"

"Fucking band manager," he muttered. "Lesbian, hard ass, on my dick all the fucking time to keep me, you know, on it." His words, stifled but clear enough.

Bang, bang, bang.

"Hey! Answer me or I'm coming in. You remember what happened last time, Josh?"

Naked and sicker to her stomach now, Preeya really wanted to be gone before this stranger broke down the door. "What happened last time?" Preeya shot.

"I flushed his entire stash is what happened."

Jesus, was her ear to the door?

"Remember, Joshie boy? Cost you a good few grand or so, eh? You know I'll do it again. Don't give a shit if you have the shakes onstage, either."

Preeya watched Josh's nostrils flare between the pillows still tight around his chiseled cheekbones. But he didn't budge or grumble or speak.

"Fuck it, Josh. I'm coming in."

The door flew open. The hallway light streamed in.

"What the hell, man? It's the middle of the fucking night—*my* time," Josh barked.

Preeya squinted, adjusting her eyes to the scene. In the doorway stood a petite woman—like, child-size—in a thick leather jacket, buzz cut, gas station pants, clunky black army boots, and huge blue-gray eyes. *Angry eyes.*

Before Preeya could take a next breath of the room's putrid air, though she noted a slight difference since the door had opened, the little manager stormed into the room, kicking through the awful pigsty on the floor. She headed straight for the window while Preeya clung to the bedsheet, brought her knees to her chest and stared. At Josh—hiding. At the intruder—searching...for his stash? Then at the floor strewn with wads of paper, smashed beer cans, crumpled chip bags, and pizza leftovers she didn't recall set at her feet—the grossness she'd stepped in. Preeya surveyed the rest of the floor, with its piles of notebooks, Josh's opened guitar case, and strewn clothes—somewhere, *her* only wearable uniform—and then at the dead watch on her right wrist. Covering her tattoo. The tat that fit his, currently covered by the blankets he'd stolen. God, what a fucking joke. She raked her fingers through her long—oh God, so matted—hair as her thoughts rushed and the room spun, adding to her queasiness that wouldn't quit. If she could locate her carry-on or purse, she'd grab some *legal* form of pain pill, if she'd remembered to replenish her stock. She wasn't known for keeping track of, well, much of anything.

But the crunch of a beer can ripped Preeya from her daze. Hands on hips, the short, gruff intruder stood by the window. "*My* time, eh? Always *Josh Bolte* time, you selfish prick. Always making *my* time—my *job*—hell. You don't know your ass from your cock, right from left, day from night!" The little woman, Dawn with the unmistakable Canadian accent, whipped around to the window and flung open the curtains.

Merciless white glare tore through the uncovered window, Seattle's summer sun somewhere back behind the always-hovering cloud blanket.

Preeya squinted, swallowed hard, and gasped for breath as if the hatch to this underground prison had been pried open. Though blinding and even more clarifying as to the horrid state of her surroundings, there was hope outside the metaphorical dank dungeon. Her mistake of a night could be wiped away, burned away with the blinding and diffused light of a new day.

Day.

"Shit! No...*No!*" It couldn't be day. What time of day?

Preeya shot up, feet to floor just narrowly missing the cold pizza again, and hunted on and around the nightstand, kicking at piles, upending boots, flipping boxes. No fucking phone anywhere. *Timedaydateflight-fuck!* Out of the corner of her eye, something out of place.

Josh's leather jacket—*neatly* draped over a chair back? *Asshole.* She took one giant step over a puddle of something—*dear God*—and lifted the cherished article. And there on the seat cushion lay her phone, safe, sound... and silenced? *Fuck, Josh!* She snatched it up, hit power. A screen full of missed calls and alerts flashed to view...then the empty battery icon. *Dead.* Shit, she'd forgotten to charge it before the short-lived seduction-to-vodka bottle-to-bed. *Damn it.*

Timetimetime. She grabbed the device then scanned the room for her purse—for her charger—but it and her carry-on were still MIA, even in the full-on light of goddamn day.

Josh's charger, at his powder-white nightstand. She crawled onto the bed, reached over him, ignored his rapid-fire cursing, and yanked the cord from the wall. Returning to her side, she plugged it in behind her nightstand and connected her phone. Panting, waiting, praying—while not realizing that her makeshift toga had fallen to her middle in her mad rush, letting her right breast free. Her nipple pebbled with the cold room air—the damn AC again, right on cue.

And not realizing, too, that Miss Mini Manager was still present. Dawn's brow lifted, eyeing her bare tit. Preeya glared back at the woman while jerking the sheet up to her chin again and refocused on her phone. "Please, please, please."

"It's eight a.m. on Friday May 30th, sweetheart—"

"Eight? No."

"Yep. And my boy Josh here has a lineup of promo interviews in thirty minutes. Which"—Dawn turned to Josh and scowled—"I reminded him about a dozen times yesterday." Back to Preeya. "And although I love you little groupies taking the edge off for him—"

"Whoa." Preeya's eyes shot death darts at the woman. "I'm *not*...a *groupie*."

She wasn't. Not seven years ago, and not now. *Tell the woman, Josh. I'm Preeya. The* Preeya—from the guest room that summer, that *entire* magical summer. *I'm Preeya the muse, damn it.* The one who inspired the song.

The song.

And she was *the* one...before she *wasn't* the one.

But instead of Josh tuning in to her mental plea for justice—*manage your expectations much, Preeya?*—he only let out a low, guttural snore.

Oh God, it's worse. Now with a witness to her state of *pathetic*, it was so much worse. "Josh, damn it, tell her."

Josh lifted the top pillow. "Get the fuck out. Both of you." His rasp and words and, God, his breath again, made her guts twist tighter, her head spin faster, her heart pound harder in horrid told-me-so shame.

The pillow descended again on top of Josh's stunning face.

Asshole.

Get out? Preeya *wanted* to flee, to run, to fly—nothing in the world she wanted more. First the little intruder needed to make her goddamn exit so Preeya could find then throw on her clothes. And Josh needed to get up to drive her back to Sea-Tac.

She heaved a breath then froze. At the entire task. Not just because she was still at the brink of projectile vomiting, but also, she didn't know which insurmountable step to take first—Dawn out, clothing hunt, face and body presentable, Josh up and ready to drive—and she now had to recoup her totally vanquished pride. *A fucking groupie?*

First things first.

She jutted her chin out and filled her chest—when her phone finally booted up. She glanced at the screen. Twelve missed calls—*Geej, Dad, and fucking Aunt Champa?*—and three calendar alerts. She swiped them all away with a furious flick and faced Dawn to resume her ego's defense.

"For your information, I'm Josh's...old...an old..." *Fuck.* What was she?

An old groupie, Pree. You're an old repeat groupie who he'd called babe. "Babe," like he'd probably call any of his quick fucks. Yeah, just a twenty-five-year-old groupie in the center of a pathetic whirlwind of devastating reality.

God, living for the *now* had never felt so shitty.

"Am I just a stupid groupie whore?" she asked the room's apathetic peanut gallery.

Dawn cleared her throat. "Dude...what the fuck with the groupie shaming? Ever hear of women's right to sexual liberation and exploration and experience? Sex, drugs, and rock and roll for all, man." Dawn glared at Preeya then at Josh, then back to Preeya, a newer softness in her previously harsh expression. Then the woman cocked her head to the side. "But being *this* prick's groupie, that's another story." Dawn snorted. "He's just—"

"Awful." Preeya grimaced and shook her head as tears welled in her eyes. "But I remember him as...as someone else. And I was someone else...to him...I'd thought." Her tears, unstoppable now, assuredly carried yesterday's mascara with them down her cheeks, black streaks of shame. Chest tight, throat thick, and words hard to come by but not impossible, she sniffled then wiped her nose. "I'm a Josh Bolte groupie *has-been*."

More weeping.

Dawn sighed. And probably rolled her eyes.

"I'm pathetic." She couldn't stop, and didn't try.

Her shoulders sank low—her chin hit her chest.

Dawn cleared her throat. "Seriously, dude. I don't have time for this... and I thought you didn't, either."

Hah. "You know what's funny?" she sniveled. "I'm late for nine out of ten shifts. I can't even get this flight attendant gig right."

A triple-beat snore rolled from Josh's throat while Dawn just stared at her.

"Flight attendant, eh? So you really should watch the groupie slut shaming, dude. Flight attendants know how to party just as hard as groupies..."

Preeya rolled her eyes and sighed. *Is this a women's lib lecture now?* "I'm not...shaming anyone. I don't slut shame in general, as a matter of fact. I just...I just...*me-shame*," she said with a head jerk toward their common pain in the ass. It was true. She didn't judge anyone but herself—at least she didn't think she did. She kept strict lines at work—to limit awkward situations on the job—but a lot of her FA friends enjoyed themselves...a lot. And hey, power—and pleasure—to them...well, except for Denver-based Kelly who pretended she didn't have a husband and kids at home when she damn well did. Preeya hated cheaters, men or women. Betraying one's family just crossed the line. But, yeah, other than that, she didn't judge.

"Well, shaming yourself is just as bad, you know...you *groupie air hostess whore*." Dawn broke out laughing.

Preeya glared at the small woman until she keyed into the teasing glint in her eye. "Fine. Okay." Lips bunched, eyelids halved, waiting out the stranger's waves of enjoyment at Preeya's expense. "Funny." Preeya wet her parched lips and sighed through Dawn's continued laughter while the woman's earlier words echoed in Preeya's ears. *Shaming myself...just as bad?* No, the message wasn't lost on Preeya. It settled slow and soft in her heart like a lost piece of cloud falling to earth. *Fog.*

"So..." Dawn's laughter eased. "About you leaving?"

Preeya sucked in her bottom lip. *Keep it together.* "Right. *Leaving.* Well, first I need *you* to leave so I can get my stuff from around this hellhole without tripping over my...toga wrap, here, and"—she turned to Josh, sighed long and sad, and shook his hefty, muscular shoulder—"damn it, I need to get to the airport, Josh. Wake up."

Nothing.

"He's not going anywhere, dude. Well, not anywhere but to my lineup of interviews downtown."

Preeya ignored Dawn and shook Josh harder.

He whined and grunted while holding the top pillow down to his head harder now to block her out.

"Please, Josh."

"Please, what?" One eye squinted open through his white, fluffy hiding spot. "You're still here, for fuck's sake?"

Her back teeth gnashed so hard she shivered from the squeak. "I am until you get your ass up and drive me to my flight, my job."

He lifted his head, eyes open wide—he seemed suddenly conscious, aware, if just for that moment. She blinked with disbelief. Deep and familiar and nearly warm, his expression. "Yeah, no, babe. Sorry, I'm" —he shoved his head back under the pillow—"—in no shape to drive. No shape to be awake. Just, you know, cab it. Grab some cash on the nightstand." End mumble. Head hidden. Snoring resumed.

Huh. Cash? For a fucking cab?

And *babe*, a third time.

Before she could take one last rip into the sad excuse for a man, Dawn piped in.

"You're a real dick-fuck, Josh." Dawn threw a pair of jeans at him, one with a thick chain clipped to the belt loop. It made a thundering clank against the bedpost above Josh's head.

The enemy of my enemy?

He grunted then rolled over.

Preeya looked at Dawn then at her phone, plotting backward from her flight's departure time—ten thirty-five—while the screen alerts flashed again in her face. Swipe-swipe-*wait*. The last alert, a calendar item her meddlesome aunt, her dad's sister, had sent to her phone. Preeya's jaw locked down harder as she processed the details of the calendar item.

Her heart hit the pizza-laden floor.

"Holy hell, the wedding! Wedd-*ings*!" One wedding she had to be at, one she had to miss, and both she wanted to pretend-away and ignore, like they were never happening at all.

Get it together, Preeya, and just make. This. Flight.

CHAPTER 3

"JUST MORE OF the same," Stanton told Ben. "They'll review your testimony and come back with a verdict sometime next month. The fact that your medical license wasn't suspended, Ben…that's a huge sign. They're just going through the motions because of your in-laws' petition."

Speak of the devil. Jamie's parents came out through the heavy wooden doors and huffed as they walked past him, avoiding eye contact like their lives depended on it.

"God, all this for what? So they didn't get their way. It wasn't their way to have, damn it," Ben mumbled to himself more than to Stanton.

"It's always the case, Ben. Even though I make a living at it, the legal route's hardly ever a win-win for anyone. They may be trying to satisfy their egos…or mend the pain, but the real hole never gets filled, not through court, at least."

Ben sighed. Stanton knew. Thank God *someone* knew. Because the press and the review board and the hospital staff pretended to know, but behind their consoling words, their doubting eyes betrayed them. He could tell them all again and again how Jamie wanted to live her last days in peace, to end the chemo and to just let nature take its course. And that when nature did take its course, the cancer shot through her like a bullet train. And that his wife's folks just fought and fought. Hell, because Jamie "quit," they didn't even show up to her funeral. Her own parents. Their only child.

But it was all a waste of breath. He sensed the seed of suspicion in all of them.

Damn them. "They should be ashamed. And now they think crucifying me will kill the agony?"

Stan shook his head. "It's hurtful stuff, man. I don't envy you. Kick a man while he's down, it's just not good karma."

Ben rubbed his eyes, then his head, sighing through his underlying fury. And talking more on the matter wasn't helping. He wanted to get the heck out of there, but his in-laws were still at the elevator bank. With nowhere else to go right then, he just had to redirect or he'd put his fist through a wall. "How's Zoe, man?"

"Great. Yeah, we just came back from Vancouver, celebrated our tenth anniversary." Stanton froze, eyes wide. "Sorry, man…I—"

"What? The whole world stops because I lost my wife? Shut the hell up and tell me more." God, the tiptoeing and the constant oozing pity. Always hovering. As bad as the loneliness, if not worse.

"Right. Well, we'd both been so busy with work, we decided to tear away for the weekend. Used the anniversary as an excuse, and—" Stanton bit his lip and gave a short, quick sigh.

"And?"

Stanton glowed with joy—and unsubtle guilt. "Well, I need something from you…even though you're, you know, scared of kids." The man smirked.

"I'm a *pediatric* surgeon, for Christ's sake." Granted, his mentors had only demanded he go pediatric because of his "skills in the OR." *Steadiest hands, tiniest organs,* they'd said. But he'd admit, operating on an anesthetized kid doesn't mean he's good with one that's awake and talking.

Stanton pounded Ben's shoulder and widened his smile—the old, natural, ball-busting smile Ben faintly remembered. "I'm kidding, man—they flock to you like you're a walking, talking video game doused in sugar."

Also true. The harder he'd push kids away, the closer his niece or nephew or patients came climbing, crawling, chattering. It used to crack Jamie up.

"Anyway…" Stanton's grin had flatlined and he cleared his throat.

"You're gonna be a godparent, Ben. That's what Zoe and I wanted to tell you over dinner."

Ben's chest tightened like a vise. He tried to swallow, but couldn't.

Ben, speak.

"Wow…a kid?" His pulse spiked. "You guys are pregnant." Ben nodded, letting it sink in. His best friend, a dad. Like he'd almost been. He glanced at his friend, but Stanton's eyes had shifted to the floor, then to the bad art on the wall.

Again, tiptoe we go.

But…don't you ask for it? Honestly.

Quiet. "Great news, man." He pulled his friend in, slammed him on the back, wrapping him in a congratulatory hug. "So glad for you. Really, Stan. Heck, it's about time."

"Thanks, man." Stanton blew out a breath of pure relief and smiled. "And the godparent thing? We know it's been a shit time, Ben, but there's no one we'd feel more comfortable with…just as long as you settle stateside eventually." A snicker left Stanton's upturned mouth.

Ben swallowed back a knot of hard angst.

"Hey, man?" Stanton squeezed his shoulder. "You okay?"

"Yeah. Sure. Godparent, yes. I'd be honored." Robotic, at best.

Stanton nodded then shook his head. "I caught you off guard, man. I knew I should've waited for Zoe—I'm so bad at this shit."

"No, no." Ben shook out his daze then clapped his friend's shoulder. "Stan, it's good, really."

"But you're white as a—"

"I'm *fine*." Regret, immediate. He sighed. "Sorry, just…the jet lag, and I should probably eat something."

"Hey, brunch, my treat."

God, no. "Can't, man…sorry. Remember, I'm catchin' my flight in the next few hours. Have to grab a bite at the airport." He noticed the elevator area was finally clear, and started toward it. "Hoping Sea-Tac will be far less eventful than yesterday, right?" Violet Eyes flashed to mind, and he immediately blinked away her image along with a new round of guilt.

"Yes, right." Stan snickered. "Rock star mania…" Awkward silence ate his friend's polite laughter right up.

Ben hit the elevator call button, but it didn't illuminate. "Thanks, though, really." Then he pressed the button and held it hard with his thumb.

"Rain check."

"Absolutely, Stan. After the next hearing."

Stanton nodded. "Should be the *last* hearing."

"Right." And, strangely, Ben couldn't imagine the medical review hell *not* hanging over his head. "What the heck is with this elevator?" Jamie's folks had taken it…maybe they held it to screw with him. *Wouldn't put it past Edward.*

"Not sure, but it'll come." Stanton cleared his throat, gaze forward. "Hey, Ben…you ever need to talk, I'm here. You know that, right?"

"Of course. And I appreciate it, man." Ben's index finger punched the elevator call button a few times more. Hard.

"And watch your email for an update from me?"

"Sure." His mouth too dry for more words than that, Ben stared at the unlit numbers above the elevator. *Seriously, is the damn thing stuck?*

"And you'll respond to those emails?"

"Right." God, he needed water. "Just gotta work around the sporadic Internet cafés—all dial-up."

"I'll cc Stacy and leave a voicemail on that crappy old phone of yours." He grinned. "And hey, try sending a postcard this time? Like, to let us know you're alive and—"

A text buzzed Stan's phone and Ben's chest unlocked. A reprieve.

Stanton huffed. "Guess I'll be heading down to Olympia earlier than I thought." The man looked up from his smartphone. "My next hearing got bumped."

The elevator dinged its arrival. *Finally.* Doors slid open and Ben followed Stan into the car. "Hey, at least now I can take you to the airport on my way down to Olympia."

Ben's jaw tightened—just the thought of more talk time.

His friend sensed his reluctance. "Traffic's gonna be a bear. A second passenger gets me in the carpool lane…" Hopeful eyes.

Ben grabbed a breath, caving to social etiquette. "Right. Sure. That'll be great. Saves me the shuttle fare, at any rate."

Stanton snorted and gave him a strange look, like, *Why would you need to save money?*

Ben lifted his brows, but Stanton said nothing, just looked back down at his smartphone. Ben hadn't even told Stanton what he'd done with the *windfall* that was Jamie's life insurance policy—he'd anonymously donated half to cancer research, and the rest he'd put in trust for his heirs—Stacy's kids. His in-laws had made sure the insurance-funds topic remained another source of skepticism. But he kept the funds' destinations confidential—let them all think what they wanted, that Ben had a lifetime of financial freedom due to his wife's death. *Sick fucks.*

Ding. The lobby. The doors slid open and a few nurses slid by the men as they walked out.

Stan shoulder-bumped him. "Hey, don't pretend you didn't see the redhead scoping you out."

Ben glared at his friend, teeth gnashed. *Jesus.* "Which way's the car, Stanton?"

"This way, just past the hot receptionist." Stan laughed, but killed it when he met Ben's death stare which screamed silently, *No, I am not ready for it, Stanton. Not ready by a long shot.* When it came to other women, *tiptoeing* was permitted—no, it was goddamn required.

CHAPTER 4

S HE LEAPED OVER a pile of notebooks, Josh's boots, and...shattered glass? The vodka bottle. She remembered he'd thrown it against the wall for emphasis during the chorus of some bullshit rock ballad he'd "been working on."

"Watch it, there!" Miss Mini Manager pointed to a narrowly missed puddle of Josh's sickness.

"Oh, God!" Preeya halted, grimaced, and scrambled to the right as Dawn's self-control crumbled to the revolting floor, laughing again at Preeya's pain while Josh groaned in an escalating crescendo.

Preeya stood still for a second, scanning the rest of the floor for her clothes and strategizing so she'd avoid any other surprises. "This is such a joke."

"What's that you said?" Dawn asked through waning laughter.

"Nothing, it's just that—" She paused, having just spotted her flight attendant's scarf smack in the middle of yet another puddle. Preeya looked up at Dawn to be sure she wasn't imagining it.

No, she wasn't imagining anything. Dawn sighed, shrugged as if helpless, too, then placed her hands on her hips and wagged her head at Josh.

Ugh. Preeya hoped to God that it was the last gift he'd left on the small guest room floor before making it to the bathroom last night—instead of making love to her, or, at the very least, delivering her to the other side of an ultimate finger-gasm like he'd done years ago.

"Goes to show that coke and pills don't mix. Anyway, you were saying something…and collecting your clothes, because you really do have to go so I can get my lead singer up and at 'em," Dawn said with a slight apology in her smile…until she eyed something on the dresser. Preeya followed the woman's gaze. A tall water bottle. Full and sealed. Dawn smirked then looked at Preeya, motioned to the dresser with a nod, then winked.

Water? God, yes, she *was* thirsty.

Ohh, water! Not to drink. *To pour. To wake.*

"I couldn't find his stash to trash, so…wakey, wakey with a splash?" Dawn whispered so low the words were almost mouthed.

Preeya snickered. She could totally wait for rehydration—and her exit so she'd make her departure!—if it meant she'd get some fluid revenge. She smiled at Dawn without wasting thought or time in considering the repercussions. Because karma, opportunity…

Dawn waggled her brows.

"Last night *was* shittier than shit," Preeya said quietly, justifying her support of Dawn's scheme. "He just had to 'do a few lines first.' Then the pills."

"Which led to this puking mess—which he might think I'm cleaning up, being the grunt manager and all."

"A puking mess, indeed." *And a goddamn tease of a night.*

Preeya nodded along with Dawn as more counterproductive thoughts swarmed Preeya's brain. He'd had her in his arms and at his mercy, then thrown her on his bed with such passionate abandon. She'd been so ready for the natural heights that her nostalgic heart—and core—had replayed in her head, ready for the encore performance of his magic fingers and tongue and hands and, yes, his magic steel, too. How he'd grind and sweep and pluck and strum her like he did his beloved guitar under hot stage lights.

But instead, he'd rolled away for the condom, snorted who knows how many lines, and popped some number of pills—that were certainly not ED pills—and returned to her, a vacant shell. Greek-god-gone-flaccid, impotent, lost in his own world of self-declared greatness.

Preeya looked at the water bottle, all twenty-some ounces of it, then back to Dawn. Preeya's nostrils flared as she breathed out—as opposed to breathing in. The air quality was really getting to her.

And as if Dawn read her thoughts, "He's worse than any of the other guys in the band. Narcissist to the nth…constant cocaine and sex binges—rehab twice. Hell, I've had to fight statutory rape charges and squashed umpteen paternity claims for this prick."

He rolled over. Preeya and Dawn paused. He grunted, then snoring resumed the next second.

"Believe me, based on last night's experience…sex, paternity? Not an issue."

Dawn glanced up at her. "Well, since you didn't seem to get any perks out of the deal…" Dawn gave Preeya a final head nod toward the big bottle of crystal clear Washington spring water revenge. "You do the honors."

Preeya knew that time was wasting, but, hell, she wanted—no, needed—to do this. Preeya grinned, filled her lungs, and beelined for the water bottle. She untwisted the cap, but then paused where she stood. Only feet from the bed, her eyes zeroed in on Josh then shifted to Dawn. "Camera? Video? Or just mental record?"

"Oooh, I like you, *not-a-groupie*. I like you a lot." Dawn winked then reached into her thick leather jacket for her cell. "You wanna give me yours, too? I can handle two at a time." Another eyebrow waggle.

Ignoring the sexual innuendo, Preeya smiled but declined. She couldn't afford to lose or forget or, hell, incur damage to her phone in what might be a chaotic backlash after the water poured. "Mental record for me, thanks. You can email me what you get." Preeya refocused on the task at hand, taking a step closer toward the lump in the bed.

"Wait," Dawn said.

Josh groaned.

"What?" Preeya whispered, so close to her goal. She really didn't want him to wake up before she *woke* him up—cold, wet, and shocked.

"Maybe we should prep the escape before all hell breaks loose. He'll go insane…"

Shit, she was right. And her priority—her flight—had been totally overshadowed by the enticement and excitement of retaliation. She sighed. "He'll be up…but pissed and definitely won't drive me…and a cab at this point? I've got only two hours to get through Seattle traffic, security, and check-in. And the lead attendant hates me as it is." She sighed longer. "I can't be late. And, job or not, I really *can't* miss this flight."

"Right, weddings *plural*," Dawn said with a somewhat empathetic tone—empathizing with what, the little woman couldn't know.

No clue at all.

If Preeya missed this flight, she'd miss Amy's wedding. Her college roommate would never forgive her. And Amy'd ordered the bridesmaid dress, the hotel room, the works. Also, Preeya had promised. Preeya didn't break promises.

But, being honest, she hadn't made the promise to Amy out of selfless loyalty alone. Going to Amy's wedding became Preeya's alibi, so to speak. Assurance that she wouldn't fold and attend her father's wedding. A guarantee against her own potentially weak will, because the likelihood was high that her father's guilt trip and her aunt's shame-fest would beat her.

"But I'll sleep better if I do this!" Her voice lifted, eyeing the water bottle with enthusiasm.

Dawn snorted then turned to Preeya. "I'll take you. To the airport…" Dawn took a few steps closer to Preeya and leaned in to whisper, "I always buffer appointments for him with a three or four-hour window." Dawn stood up and gave her a proud wink and nod. "I've got my moped, so just, you know, get dressed and we'll go. There is no traffic with *my* ride…shoulders all the way."

Fly by the seat of her pants, yes, but a death wish? "Thanks, but…not in my uniform…and my carry-on bag? Wherever the hell it is…" She sighed, shook her head, and clutched the bedsheet toga tight to her chest. "I'll just cab it and pray…and…" She looked at her scarf on the floor. "Shit, I'll have to chuck that and borrow or buy one…or wing it. I'm good at that, at least."

Yeah, winging it was a talent to be proud of, right?

Preeya found a pencil-line smile for Dawn while Dawn just stared back at her and shrugged her leather-geared shoulders. "Okay, suit yourself. I have enough to deal with here, anyway."

Josh grunted and swore *not* under his breath.

Skip the payback and call a cab, Preeya…then shower and get the hell gone already!

No. Preeya's nostrils flared, eyes widened, throat thick.

Dawn kicked back through the beer cans and trash toward the door, seemingly done with the excitement of the grand water wake-up plan. "Come on."

Still, *no.* Preeya patted the water bottle in her hand like a football, then tilted her head at Josh. She moved to the bedside and lifted the covers, exposing Josh's naked midsection. As Preeya's lips lifted into a shit-eating grin, her arm—with the crystal clear liquid—lifted, too. She could hear Dawn's gasps of muted laughter as Preeya held the bottle over Josh's limp dick and bare ass, all tucked in tight to himself.

A tingle of joy sprinted up her spine as she began to tip the bottle—slow at first, just to get the water to the neck then to the opening, anticipating the reaction she'd relish and remember forever. Dawn appeared at the corner of her view, camera phone in hand.

"Ready," Dawn whispered, her shared zeal glowing.

Preeya inhaled, then flipped her wrist.

A fast flow of pure Washington State spring water splashed down on Josh's naked, ultra-defined and sought-after body, while Preeya's spirits soared.

*

Gasping, screaming, snarling, Josh Bolte bolted up and out of bed.

Finally, the king had risen.

Dawn rolled around on the putrid floor dying, camera phone still in hand, pointed up at a wet and naked Josh.

His eyes were wild, but thankfully focused on drying himself off, rather than finding the source of his rude awakening—Preeya, who cried harder now from hysterical laughter than she had from her earlier poor-me sulk-fest. And she just couldn't stop, which made Dawn laugh harder.

Josh—growling, shivering—reached for the jeans Dawn had thrown at him earlier. At one leg in, he keeled over, held his gut with one hand, his mouth with the other, then he ran—hopped, really—to the bathroom. He slammed the door then retched his guts out.

"What, no guest room floor?" Preeya asked Dawn with a lift of her brow.

"Thank God," Dawn blurted, patting Preeya on the arm, then made her way to the bathroom door and pounded it with her right fist. "Now get cleaned up, asshole!" she added for good measure while Preeya crushed the empty water bottle in her hands. The loud crinkling didn't overshadow Josh's cursing between heaves, but Preeya found him way easier to ignore now.

Dawn smiled. "Come on, Josh's...*old friend*. You can use one of the other showers."

"Thanks. God, do I need one—or five." She felt her hair again and then looked down at herself, still wrapped in the sheet. "I just have to find the rest of my things." She grimaced, then peeked under the bed.

"Right. I'll grab you a clean towel from Otto's room while you do that. Be right back."

"By the way, my name's Preeya. And...thanks."

Dawn nodded then disappeared while Josh still swore-spewed-flushed-repeated and Preeya hunted for her roller bag in the never-to-be-forgotten guest room.

*

She found her purse and carry-on in the corner of the room behind the closet door.

"*Preeya*," Dawn said as if to herself, standing in the doorway with a white fluffy towel. "Preeya?"

"Yeah. Preeya. It's East Indian."

Dawn studied her face, right eye squinting.

Preeya smiled, but she really didn't have time for games. "Preeya Patel." *What?*

"Are you *the* "Guest Room" Preeya? From the song?"

Preeya looked at Dawn, then lifted her unbelieving gaze to the ceiling. It seemed that Josh had, at some point in the past, spoken of her, of *them*—however, whenever, whatever. Preeya wanted to fall down on her knees laughing, but she was too tired and ill—*and too late*—to do anything but smirk. "Yes. That's me...or should I say, that *was* me."

"Well isn't this ironic?" Dawn said, slamming *the* guest room door—most definitely for Josh's benefit.

"Pretty ironic, yes." Preeya hadn't noted the déjà vu irony until now. The song inspired by their first night together in that very guest room seven years earlier.

"Hey, listen, when you're sick of dealing with disappointing dickheads," the petite drill sergeant said, examining Preeya up and down with no subtle appetite, then nodded with approval, "I'd be honored, Ms. Preeya 'Guest Room' Patel, to show you the other side. There are no flaccid cocks in my toy drawer, I can promise you that."

And with that invitation to lesbianism, Preeya crossed the threshold of the clean and pristine hallway bathroom with her roller bag in tow and her uniform bundled under her arm. She nodded her thanks and smiled. "I'm pretty sure, Dawn, that I'm stuck on men. What type of man? Hell if I know anymore...if I *ever* knew." Because from Wildfire Josh to Safe-and-Secure Evan—and every guy in between—she couldn't for the life of her say what the man of her wildest dreams looked like, who he'd turn out to be. Hell, she couldn't even say she knew who *she* was at this point. Preeya rolled her eyes. She only knew that she needed to make that flight to Puerto Vallarta. To that destination wedding. She'd have to figure the rest out from there.

Dawn nodded, accepting the gently put rejection. "Well, the offer stands if you change your mind."

Preeya smiled and blinked, then put her stuff on the counter—and got an unwelcome first glimpse of herself in the bathroom mirror. *Not* good. And being out of that guest room, she got an objective whiff of her hair. God, she needed a *scour*, not a shower. She glanced at her phone to see how much time she had for her hair and makeup before—*oh crap*. "The cab!" She hadn't even called for one yet.

"Already called one for you." Dawn winked as she reached for the doorknob.

Preeya's chest decompressed. "You're a lifesaver." Preeya could have kissed the woman.

"Nope. Just a band manager slash doormat." Dawn snorted. "I'll give you that privacy now."

The door closed, leaving Preeya alone in the new space with new sound—the streaming shower. The contrast lulled her…and agitated her at the same time. *Quiet and alone* was a thing. Not a good thing.

Relax, Pree.

She took a moment to adjust her breathing then dropped the sheet and kicked it into the corner.

Focus on moving your ass.

Right. She stepped into the steaming-hot shower and washed off, scrubbed off the past hours of regret and shame and embarrassment and disappointment—and all the past delusions, too. In a matter of hours, no more Seattle clouds—hello Vallarta sunshine.

*

Preeya sat on the front stoop, her knee bouncing as the next cab-less minute passed. Anxiety pinched the nerves in her neck. She just needed a distraction, company, something, someone—*always*. Short or long stints of solitary time, it didn't matter. Being on her own just freaked her the hell out. Ever since she could remember, Gigi had been the only solution. When her chest got tight to the point of panic, she'd call her best friend and Gigi's voice would carry her through.

Monophobia. Geej had looked it up. One remedy besides therapy she'd never tried: take ten slow, full breaths. Since she didn't have the balls to call Gigi yet, and the tightness in her chest was tightening, she began to count out her breaths and hoped like hell for the cab to appear.

But nothing. No cab, tighter chest.

And through the stupid breathing exercise she'd caught the lingering stench from the guest bedroom on her clothes, damn it. She reached into her purse for her 3.4-ounce bottle of coconut-lime body spray. *Good scent, good distraction.* She applied two squirts of faux freshness to her uniform, then slipped the sweet-scented spray back in her purse.

Back to solitary silence, she swallowed, sighed, then sat up straighter. Maybe her chest would fill if she threw her shoulders back and expanded her rib cage. But, *no. Shit.* Mildly frantic, she glanced at her phone for the time. She growled then chucked the phone back in her purse between her book and her zippered pouch of personal keepsakes.

Hmm. She knew one thing inside that pouch could distract her from her locked-up lungs, the late cab, the shadow of nausea from Josh-night, her job's possible end, and the real likelihood that she'd miss more than one wedding this weekend.

She smacked her lips and unzipped the plastic case. An essential scrapbook at her fingertips, with boarding pass stubs of international firsts, ticket stubs from favorite concerts—Carnal Knowledge not among them—smashed pennies, drawings from her kid sister, Prana, and photos. *Gigi, Prana, Amy, Amanda.* Ah, and the only pic of her and her mother—at the Free Tibet Fest when Preeya was six. She paused her fingers and closed her eyes. The recollected scent of sandalwood incense and fried dough drifted through her mind. Her lungs filled with one full intake of relief. Not the item she'd been focused on finding, but she already felt better.

She held up the photo and sighed, then put it back to continue the hunt while the image of her mom lingered. She hiccupped a laugh. Jenny Patel was the exact opposite of Preeya in appearance—too many times had people assumed that her mother was the nanny—until people noticed their eyes. The same color, shape, angle, depth, and placement. Otherwise, her father's East Indian genetics overrode all. But nothing more of her father would take hold in Preeya. *No goddamn way.*

"Still no cab?"

Preeya's hand flew to her chest as she turned to find Dawn standing behind her on the screened-in porch.

"Not yet." Back teeth gnashed, Preeya forced herself to keep calm. At least she was no longer alone, right?

"Memory lane while you wait, eh?" Dawn opened the screen door and plopped down next to Preeya on the porch steps. "What's that?" Dawn reached for the folded sheet of paper, the next item in the pouch, but Preeya grabbed it and grinned semi-politely.

"Uh, a picture my little sister drew for me." From the last time Preeya was down at SafeHaven. She pulled out the page and opened it, sensing Dawn would hover there until Preeya showed her. Staring up from the page, two stick figures on a rainbow holding hands. Preeya let out a laugh—her sister, Prana, loved drawing Preeya with a humongous heart near her stick-figure chest, always far bigger than Preeya's head.

"Are those wings on your legs?"

Preeya chuckled. "Full-body wings, I guess. She only understands that I fly for my job." She swallowed back the knot moving up her throat. "She's in a special needs facility in Northern Cali. She's pretty literal, delayed processes and all. She's seventeen now, but on a first-grade level…" *And declining.* Preeya smiled with her mouth, not her eyes, outlining the wings with her index finger. Funny, her sister had drawn Preeya with wings well before she'd begun flying for a living.

"Wings like an angel," Dawn said, eyes on the page.

"Hmm." Strange, from a stranger.

Weirder was the knot in Preeya's throat. It morphed into a fast surge of guilt that cascaded down to Preeya's stomach. She'd been anything but an angel lately, anything but worthy of the brand of pure, unconditional love her sweet sister gifted her with. Since leaving Berkeley, leaving med school, becoming an FA, Preeya's visits to her sister were less and less frequent. And with their mother gone, their father self-absorbed, her sister was truly alone down there.

"Sweet picture." Dawn nodded, then pulled out a cigarette and offered Preeya one.

"No, thanks. I don't smoke and, uh, if you don't mind…the uniform already smells…*interesting.*"

"Right, sorry." Dawn put the cigarette behind her ear and the pack in her pocket. "Your sis—"

Buzz. Preeya's cell phone. "Sorry." She glanced at the screen. Her father. She hit Decline without a thought. Nothing would deter her from *Amy's* wedding. Not a word, not a guilt trip. *Nothing.* Her father replacing her mother with one of his superficial, cosmetically enhanced gold diggers—she meant patients—God, it made her feel *more* nauseous than she'd been in the guest room.

"Ignoring someone?"

"Yeah, er, no."

"Sorry. Not my business."

"It's not that." *Well, yes it is.* "I just don't want to think about anything except for catching my flight."

Silence. Dawn sighed as Preeya pinched the bridge of her nose to relieve the headache between her eyes.

"So, who was that pretty lady in the Free Tibet pic?"

What happened to none of your business? "Uh…"

"Sorry, too personal?"

Preeya narrowed her eyes at the woman. "Dawn, how long had you been standing behind me?"

"Not long, and I actually wasn't standing. I was sitting in the porch swing—needed a breather from the fumes inside."

Preeya couldn't blame the woman on that count. But, wow, weird vibes, no boundary lines. *But it seems the norm of the day?*

Preeya could be a bitch, rake the woman over for, well, kind of snooping and sort of hitting on her despite Preeya's man-only proclamation—or she could *just go with it.* "My mother. It was my mother."

"*Was?* So when did she skip out on you?"

"What?"

"Your mom…when did she ditch you?"

Preeya choked on a gulp of air stuck in her parched throat. "How do you know she left? What if she'd…died?"

"Nah, she didn't die. Hating your dad for marrying someone new when you're, you know, an *adult*...you would *want* your dad to move on if she'd died. But you're pissed. You feel he's betraying her and, therefore, he's betraying you. Yeah, I'm pretty sure she's alive and well...somewhere?"

"Wait." Preeya's eyes narrowed, darting. "How do you know I'm pissed at my father? How do you know anything about...anything? *Me?*"

Her chest heaved, her pulse raced. *What the hell?*

She was accustomed to Gigi's sixth-sense intuition, but it was too rare to expect from anyone else. So that meant this chick had been—what?—digging in her stuff? She'd already barged in on her and Josh—a good thing in the end, but still—then snuck up on her, looking over her shoulder for who-knows-how-long from the porch swing, and finger-diving into her zipper pouch of keepsakes. Why would the woman be above, well, anything sleazy? After all, she was an acquaintance of Josh's, right?

"Sorry. I'm a nosy bitch," Dawn said, laughing. "But if you'll just cool your tits for a second—"

"Excuse me?"

"Listen, I'm a band manager of five very dysfunctional men. I don't have a line anymore when it comes to...you know—"

"Privacy? Etiquette? Manners? Hell, aren't you Canadian?"

"Yes to all of the above." Dawn just shrugged as her laughter faded. "Hey, I've saved the band more times than I can count with my alternative methods." She cracked up again. "Talk to me when you've seen a six-foot-five tattooed monster cry like a baby because of my digging—Otto...abandonment issues. But if it gets them up onstage, it's gotta be done."

Preeya gritted her back teeth and tried to chill. This woman had backed her up with Josh, called her a cab—wherever the hell it was—and when it came right down to it, Dawn's unsolicited analysis of Preeya's family matters was, well...right.

Right. On. Point.

Damn it. Was she that transparent?

Preeya swallowed in surrender. "How did you do that?"

"Two and two, dude, two and two. The 'weddings, plural' and the way you got all emotional over your mother's picture...then you declined a call from a Dr. Indra Patel. His tiny screen icon clued me in—he's definitely your father."

Preeya grimaced.

"Except for the eyes, of course. Those are obviously your mom's and they're out of this world. Unbelievable, really. Violet, like in the song." The woman looked closer, harder, almost like…like Dawn wanted to kiss her. Preeya pulled away to put some space between them because, yes, the vibe had definitely gone there.

While ignoring the compliment and Dawn's second attempt at sexual-preference conversion, Preeya lifted a brow at the woman. "Seriously?"

Dawn cracked up. "Just fucking with you."

"You can stop then. Not much for jokes right now." She grabbed a frustration-clearing breath. "And they're not *violet*. They're *near* violet. Deep blue, really." Preeya never liked the attention she got for her eyes, the stares.

"Okay…well, while I *don't* look deep into those near-violet eyes of yours, tell me, am I right? About your mom? I usually am. It's a thing."

Preeya stared at Dawn for a long moment then sighed. She hated talking about her mother, but here she was, stuck on this porch step waiting for the slowest cab in history. "She left to live on an ashram in India when I was seven. Gave up her name, her possessions, everything for—"

"Wait. You're fucking with me. She gave up her possessions, like, her CDs and her clothes, and…her fucking kids?"

Preeya rolled her eyes, but before she could get a word in edgewise—

"That's from some movie. No mom leaves her family to feed the starving children of—"

"That's exactly what she did."

"That shit's fucked. Totally fucked-to-the-wall fucked. I mean, she pulled a Mother Teresa with a family-abandonment twist?"

Preeya scoffed. The standard reaction, though she thought or hoped that a near-midget lesbian might have a broader perspective than most. "I get that you, well, *don't* get it." Gigi was maybe the only one in the world who didn't make her defend her mother. "But my mom's, like, a saint. And I'm proud of her. For her to leave us, my sister and me and my dad…it's what she felt she had to do. She's helping hundreds of children, mothers, people every day."

"Still…it's crazy! As strange as it goddamn gets." Dawn squinted at Preeya then searched her face.

Preeya met her eyes with apathy.

Dawn tilted her head. "Well, I guess…just because I haven't heard of anyone in my entire life doing something so insane doesn't mean it's not…a good…selfless thing. A pretty huge thing, I guess? A humanitarian thing?"

Preeya snorted at the pleasant surprise, while Dawn had started out sounding like Preeya's aunt Champa. She smiled then blinked, almost wishing Dawn had continued on the attack. Strange, Preeya knew, but she felt particularly defensive of her mom today, the day before her father planned to officially replace Jenny Patel in his life—Preeya really could have used the outlet. "Yeah, my mother *is* pretty unbelievable. It looks like I'm miles from being like her, though. She's rare and vast and selfless while I'm, well…I'm here." She motioned with her chin toward the house, Josh in the front guest room. "Here, escaping *that*."

"Don't beat yourself up, man. Josh is…*Josh*. And hell, you meant something more than the rest of his lays at some point in time. Millions of chicks across the planet would die to be you. I know—the fan site gathers some pretty vocal crazies. And no one else inspired a number one hit, woman! Come to think of it, you should be getting royalties."

"Oh, please."

"Seriously, if I were CK's manager back when Josh wrote 'Guest Room,' when you inspired it, I would've probably insisted." Dawn nudged Preeya with her shoulder.

"Right. Well, yeah, I think I'll focus on reality, like the cab pulling up." *God, anytime now.* Preeya grinned.

Dawn patted the pockets of her thick jacket. "Let me run inside for my phone and call 'em again."

A crash from inside startled Preeya and brought Dawn exploding to her feet. "Grrr…these assholes couldn't wipe their own asses without me." Dawn marched into the house and slammed the porch screen door behind her. "For fuck's sakes, what now?"

Preeya refocused on the lack of traffic on the road in front of her.

"Oh, hey…" Dawn poked her head back out. "If the cab comes before I get back out, email me and I'll shoot you the water-pouring video." She winked at Preeya. "My email's on the CK website. And let me know how it all goes down…you know, the weddings, the hunt for your man or for yourself or whatever—" Another clang and a string of *fuckfuckfuck*s interrupted Dawn's good-bye. "Fuck!" And she was gone.

Preeya laughed then sighed. "Thanks, Dawn," she whispered to herself. "And bye."

*

The men got out to the parking lot. Fresh air filled Ben's lungs. "Hey, can we swing by the hotel for my duffel?"

"Sure."

They slid into Stanton's sleek, black two-seater. "Car seat friendly, I see?" A sarcastic smile.

"I'm getting rid of it Friday, before Zoe asks me to."

"Surprised she hasn't yet."

"She has, in her head. You know…marital ESP?" Stan shot him an awkward grin.

Well, you asked him to be candid, didn't you?

Ben nodded and found a fine-line smile that led to the billionth thick silence. Jesus, this was going to be a long drive, and if Ben remembered correctly, heavy traffic or not, flashy sports car or not, Stanton drove like a sloth.

The engine roared to a start. "So where's the mission this time? I don't think you said."

"Central Mexico."

"Jesus." Stan looked both ways—four times—before rolling out of the parking lot. "With all the cartel news cropping up? Ben, do you have a death wish, for God's sake?" Stanton sped up a bit on the straightaway, then glared at him.

But Ben only stared at the road ahead.

Stanton scoffed. "Listen, I get it. You need to do what you need to do… to get back to living…but first Nepal, then West Africa…it's like you're picking riskier locales each trip. People vanish in Mexico, Ben. You're starting to scare us, man."

First, thank God, Stan *did not* "get it." The man had no clue whatsoever. Second, Ben scared himself enough for the both of them. "Next left." Ben pointed. Third, he needed riskier, louder, more souls in need, each one a milli-fraction of his penance.

Stan grunted, "Thanks," then threw Ben a look—nostalgic, sad. He could tell his friend missed the old Ben, the high-intensity, driven Ben who used to plan his future—his and his amazing wife's future—far, far out… and down to the very nanosecond all at the same time. But that guy was long gone. Now, sheer self-apathy flooded his veins. And it made people nervous. It made Stanton nervous, and there was nothing he could do about it—but to be the hell away from them all.

At least act human, Ben—be nice, a voice said in his head—not his usual mental narrator. Ben gave an imperceptible head shake and cleared his throat. "It's just been good to get away, Stan. I go where the people need help."

At the hotel's main entrance, Stan threw it into Park and let his lip curl. "Yeah, man. Sure." He nodded and gripped Ben's shoulder. "Again, this review will wrap next month and you can finally settle down again. Clean slate, right? Maybe, even, well, in time…start dating? Zoe's sister—"

"I'm good alone," Ben snapped, out of the vehicle the next instant. Just about to slam the car door in the man's face for such an asinine fucking suggestion, Ben paused—*be nice*—and exhaled hard. Eyes targeted on the hotel's automatic sliding doors, he cleared his throat. "Thanks, though. Be right back."

*

"Three minutes, Preeya. They promise." Dawn yelled through the screen door, startling Preeya again. Then she vanished back inside. From the sound of things, all hell had broken loose—glass-shattering harmony, violent-shouting melody. Josh's voice definitely took lead.

Glad to be outside—*for three more minutes, God willing.* Or else she really might miss this flight. She'd already set her mind for the onslaught she'd get from her father and his family for missing *that* wedding. But *Amy's,* she didn't want to disappoint Amy. And she couldn't pretend that another warning from the airline didn't make her neck muscles spasm. *So much for "flying by the seat of your pants," Pree.* Maybe she wasn't made to live like her mother. But her father's path turned her stomach.

She swallowed a knot of disgust and refocused on the unzipped pouch still in her lap. She should close it up and put it away. Abandon her hunt for that one thing.

A motorcycle whizzed by, then another—still no cab. She struggled to zip the pouch, the photos and postcards all brimming above the zipper's horizon. She tamped the pouch down on her lap, then gave a pat to the top of the collected crap, and as she did the pouch contents parted in the middle, like the damn Red Sea—and there it was, the thing she'd been looking for, staring up at her.

A love letter, mocking her in perfect silence.

Josh had given it to her just before he'd left her and Seattle so long ago. The letter-slash-poem that he'd made into song lyrics. The song that, as of just a year or so ago, played around the clock, around the world. The damn thing drove her insane. "Sun and Moon in the Guest Room." God, if only Dawn *had* been with the band back then. She laughed out loud. "If muses got royalties…" She'd have the money issue off her plate, facing harder times since refusing her dad's guilt funding.

She exhaled. Royalties or not, the paper at her fingertips was probably worth something. But no, she'd never have sold it. It had been priceless. *Had been.* She'd always hung on to the stupid letter along with the stupid fantasy attached to it. "Close old doors and bigger ones will open," Mom had always said. Looking at the letter, she hadn't heeded her mother's advice on this one. In fact, not only had she kept the note—pitifully enough—but she'd read it from time to time. Hell, being honest, she'd memorized the letter and lyrics over the years, way before the song got played-out on the radio. But she'd always been a believer, a dreamer, a goddamn romantic.

And a tad bit of a masochist, too.

She looked down at the paper in her hands.

As if on autopilot, she found herself opening the quarter-folded paper with the reverence reserved for an ancient scripture just discovered. Smooth paper stock with worn, frayed edges. A delicate relic, a whole seven years old.

"You, my muse," and "my angel-savior with soft, mocha skin. Oh, violet eyes, where have you been?" Blah, blah, bullshit, blah. A few more *always* and *in all ways* and *forevers*, it read. And then the best part, the chorus: "Your sun, my moon, entwined in the guest room."

For fuck's sake.

Preeya rolled her eyes and willed a huge breath into her lungs. Then she held the paper up to her face, blocking the sudden glimmer of easterly sunshine breaking through the clouds. Her fingertips slipped along the top edge, spreading out the page of handwritten crap and lofty promises.

She blinked. A slow blink.

Then, pinkies up, she tore. Straight down. Right in half.

Rotating the rectangle remnants in her determined fingers, she tore again.

She let out the breath she hadn't realized she'd held through the ceremonious shredding. She then wadded and crushed the four pieces of Josh's love letter into a small tight ball of never-gonna-be.

Not with anyone, maybe. The torrential romantic love and adventure she craved in a man—in life, in herself—might not exist. Period. Anywhere.

And she had to accept it.

She pulled her arm back behind her ear and threw the paper ball with all her silly and naive delusions—her past—as far out as she could, out toward Lake Washington for the damn thing to sink and drown and die.

But the wind picked up and carried the wad in the other direction. It landed on the road. Right on the center yellow line of Sandpoint Way.

Her arm dropped. So did her shoulders. She swallowed back brimming tears.

A tear fell just as the yellow cab drove up the road with its turn signal on.

But as if in slow motion, like the most perfect and poetic lyrics to a song, the cab—late by twenty-three minutes—ran right over Josh's lyrical love letter, smashing it with old, weathered tires into the tar-black street.

In her heart, a bit of levity. In her head, the cabbie was forgiven for his tardiness. In her soul, a hope, a spark, that something other than deep disappointment awaited her today. Starting by making her friggin' flight. Then she could be done, again, with these heavy-hanging, weep-me-a-damn-ocean clouds. *Seattle.*

CHAPTER 5

H
E THANKED STANTON with a wave and sighed, glad he'd soon
be no-one-at-all in Sea-Tac's blur of travelers.

"Be safe, you hear?"

Ben nodded and waved again as Stan drove off. He glanced at his watch.
Early enough for check in, food and a nap at the gate. *Good.*

With a new and relative spring to his long stride, he headed inside. He
put his bag down to use its wheels feature, popped the handle up, then rolled
forward a step while searching for the Jetta Air counter. His hand rubbed
his head—freshly shaved—which Jamie had always said he did when he was
anxious. He definitely rubbed his head more often these days.

Another step—and a near collision. He froze there, letting his pulse settle and the train of travelers pass. There were just so many people, a cluster
of busy, busy people living and breathing and worrying and hoping their
lives away. God, he just couldn't wait to get to the middle of nowhere again.
Where real people—raw, basic human beings—waited for him. Needed him.
And he needed them right back.

He found and got into the fairly long line for check-in, but realized he
had not a thing to worry about, it being two hours before boarding. He
inhaled, exhaled, then loosened up his shoulders. *Much better...*

Until the bickering behind him entered his sound-space. A loud and animated family—*definitely not from here*—fought over who'd made them late
for their flight home to New York.

"Please, folks, go on ahead of me." He took his duffel handle and stepped aside. "I'm extremely early."

"Seriously, man?"

"Yes, of course." Ben nodded, glad to help, and glad to regain some peace during his wait in line.

"Thanks so much, sir," the heavy set patriarch said, ushering his family of six ahead.

Then a set of older couples gave him an imploring look.

"Sure, sure. I have time." And after a snowball of tardy Northeasterners cut in front of him—thick Seattle traffic often threw tourists for a loop—he thought about the hectic insanity at arrivals yesterday. The entourage and fans milling around that arrogant jerk. He grumbled the recollection away, then glanced at his itinerary. His first-class window seat would make everything—

Wham! A large object slammed him square in the back, forcing him to lurch forward. *Seriously?* He caught himself by planting his left foot, then turned. A female soldier had just heaved her large green duffel onto her shoulder. She apologized to him profusely while he regained his composure.

"Honestly, no worries," he told the woman with her fifty-pound bag on her shoulder moving up in line a few steps. He noticed her top hand had a terrible burn scar across her knuckles.

"Bomb detonated. Wrong wire. But hey, on that one, we all survived." A slight smile revealed itself behind the all-too-serious stories-upon-stories clinging to those few words. Her eyes. Her steady and deadly tone. "You look like you've seen a few war zones yourself." She searched his face. He shifted his stance, swallowed slowly, radiantly uncomfortable all of a sudden. What had she seen in him to say such a thing? Instead of the pride he might have felt at her comment, one that might have established common ground between them—an NGO doctor and a true combat hero—he felt only a torrent of that seething drug he'd gotten so used to, even hooked on—guilt. It tore through him now in a wave. He'd seen stuff, yes, but he felt more like an onlooker, an observer. A lazy goddamn couch potato in life. First watching Jamie, watching the meds, the decisions, the oncologists, the time. Then the consoling faces. Those haunting, pitying faces. And the accusing ones, too.

Then he'd traded one immense daze for another. Paperwork and airplanes and caravans and dust and hungry, happy, dirty faces that were just glad to have a meal or a moment's relief from an infected bug bite. He saw it all. Interacted with it all. A war zone, though? No. Not a war zone like this soldier's bomb-blasting, hidden-sniper, death-around-the-corner war zone. No, he didn't possess the real balls, the real courage, the real gumption that this soldier had in spades. Going to defend her country. His country.

He wasn't a fighter. Not for his country, not for his morals, not for himself. Worst of all, he hadn't fought for Jamie. He hadn't fought for his own love, his own wife. Not really. He'd *insisted* on upholding Jamie's desire to die in peace versus his in-laws' wishes. But he hadn't fought like he should've fought long before it ever got to that point. He should've been able to do something more. Fight cancer, fight death, fight her pain and life-draining sorrow.

"Your shirt and badge."

"What's that?"

"You look shocked, like you're wondering how I'd figured…"

"How you figured…? I'm sorry. Running on too little sleep." He laughed at his own confusion, sucked into his ever-void.

She smiled and gave him a subtle nod, as if she genuinely understood that it wasn't lack of sleep that he suffered from. He suffered from an endless and jumbled game of connect the vacuous dots playing out inside him—dots that never made a coherent picture. "You're with Doctors Without Borders. Your shirt and badge…" She referenced the lanyard hanging around his neck.

"Right, yes." He kept his grip on his duffel's handle while his other hand moved to close his jacket over his chest. "Been traveling with the organization for the past year. I've gotten far more than I've given."

"A year's a long time. Good of you."

Was that sarcasm? He met her eyes then he shifted his focus to the speckled tile floor and sighed. No, she'd been totally genuine. He let the corners of his mouth curl a bit just to act somewhat socialized. "Again, it's been better for me than I've been for them."

"Other way around for me, I think." She pulled her phone out of her pocket and held it up. "Missed two birthdays for each one of my babies." The screen shot of her freckled little girl and her toothless little boy made him wince behind a forced smile.

More kids he'd never have. "Cute. Must've been hard to be away."

"I shouldn't complain. Other than the hand, I'm back with my limbs, life, liberty, right? And it was an honor to serve. Made my family proud."

He smiled at her. She was tough, confident, glazed with a motherly softness, this soldier wasting her breath and words on him. "You live in Houston, or are you continuing on?"

"Central Florida." Her low, mellow rasp soothed him. But it seemed the thought of her final destination didn't soothe her. "You? Where's home?"

Home? *Nowhere anymore.* "Here, Seattle..." He shifted his feet. "I'm heading to Puerto Vallarta, where my sister and her kids live. Then off to Central Mexico for my next mission."

"Next in line, please," a Jetta Air agent called with a listless wave.

"Safe trip home." He nodded and extended his hand. They shook.

"Safe trip...away. And sorry again for the fifty-pound jolt."

He watched her head up to the agent and, rejecting the help of the two luggage handlers behind the counter, she tossed the long green duffel on the scale.

He sighed then tucked his badge into his shirt—no conversation starters. He'd pull it out again to get through security faster, but for now he was ready to *not speak* to anyone. Sleeping his way to Houston would definitely be the plan.

*

After check-in, he headed toward the security line, always easy and quick for him with his badge.

Minus the default anxiety of checking in and making the flight—and yesterday's unusual celebrity chaos—Ben loved airports. As of late, going somewhere that wasn't Seattle for starters. But mostly, the people-watching. Jamie had gotten him stuck on the distraction. Walking, talking stories, every airport wanderer.

"Sir, please." The TSA officer waved him forward, looked closely at the medical badge around his neck, then at his passport. "Very good, Doctor. Be safe."

"Thank you." Ben rolled his bag straight through to the faster pre-check lane. No shoe removal, no electronics out. Smooth and easy.

A middle-aged couple eyed him from the regular security line as they unlaced, unbelted, and stripped off their jackets, her hair clip, his watch, and a laptop each. Ben smiled then dodged their uninhibited glares. Jamie called people like them "grumpy gremlins." And just as he thought it, the woman's scowl deepened, like she'd read his mind. But it didn't matter. Guilt wasn't a factor for Ben in this context. No, no. His perks at the airport were appreciated and justified. He was heading to the heat, dust, and grime of the third world where tents over rocky ground replaced cushy hotel rooms. Mosquito nets and ground holes for toilets and ice-cold bucket showers were considered perks to the locals. *Ah, relativity.*

So he ignored their evil eyes as he went through the scanner and came out the other side with a smile for the TSA agent awaiting him with her wand. "Sir, please. This way."

Huh? He cocked his head then found a patient smile for the woman as he moved to the side as he was told.

"Is there a pocket knife in your murse, sir?" She pulled his messenger bag from the belt.

He tried to hide his slow-blink frustration. *Murse?* He cleared his throat. "Yes, my pocket utility combo…I've had that thing with me for my last several medical excursions. I'm an MD with Doctors Without Borders and I need certain tools for—"

"Tools? Knives are not permitted on board, sir."

Doctor. "Of course, but—"

"I don't believe a pocket knife is considered a medical tool, sir."

Ben formed a tight-lipped smile and pulled the thing out of his bag. *Damn it.* All past TSA officers had let him keep it.

But not this one, not even with a soft, imploring smile.

Fine. "Can I mail it to myself?"

"Certainly, sir."

Doctor.

"Over there." She pointed to a small postage counter. He stepped toward the stand in an invisible huff and pulled out his pen from his shirt pocket.

He'd just finished writing his name when the sound of light jeering met his ears. The disgruntled couple had made it through before him. *Well, good for them.* May they have each other's "grumpy gremlin" asses for a long time to come.

"Nice, right?"

He looked up from his almost-completed self-addressed envelope. A female flight attendant with her shirt partially untucked—emitting a strange and overpowering scent of coconut-lime and…vodka?—had stopped and bent over in front of him, fighting with her carry-on handle. Only her back and her bottom—in a wrinkled formfitting skirt—faced him.

He swallowed. Was she speaking to him?

"TSA pre-check."

Yes, she had spoken to him, *sort of.* But still committed to keeping to himself for the remainder of his travel day, Ben dropped his self-addressed envelope into the mail slot and tried to ignore her.

"It's the best." She yanked her roller bag handle up with such force she almost stumbled backward into him, but right before impact she planted her right foot—her shoeless, burgundy toenail-polished foot—hard to the floor and caught herself, then began a new fight with the enemy bag, the front zipper pocket.

Still looking at the floor—at her delicate, shapely foot—he cleared his throat and returned his pen to his shirt pocket. "Sorry? The best?" he asked, glad the woman was still distracted with her bag—no eye contact, no unnecessary conversation, no hassle. While he didn't wait for her answer to the exchange she'd begun, he pulled out his boarding pass to check his gate assignment. And as he glanced up at the gate signage, she looked over her shoulder.

"Pre-check, heaven on earth. Saves my ass every time."

Violet Eyes.

She tilted her head, definite recognition. And her eyes held that same smiling glow inside their depths.

Of course they glowed, Ben. Her world had probably been "rocked" by that cocky asshole, the rock star. He shook his head. *How cliché?*

Don't be a judgmental prick, Ben. The woman had known the guy's name.

Every woman at the airport knew the guy's name.

You know what I mean. They obviously knew each other.

Fine. She might not be a fuck-around-with-just-*anyone* kind of flight attendant, but—

She swallowed, then broke their gaze, yanking him out of his thoughts.

"Okay… Gotta run. Safe flight."

And she was off, heels in hand, carry-on in tow, snug skirt not hindering her legs from tiptoe-running through the terminal. The hot-mess of a beauty was gone before he could blink.

He shook her image out of his head and snickered. A mirage—or a second mirage. Too crazy of a coincidence. Maybe his mind had finally gone there—insane, cracked. His heart was there, splintered to hell, so why not his head? He took a deep breath and folded his first-class boarding pass in half—not along the perforation—then slid it into his back pocket with a sigh and moved toward his gate.

*

Preeya had sprinted to—and through—security, heels in hand so she could run without tripping or breaking a shoe. And somehow—and as usual—she made it to her gate in time, sort of. No thanks to that second run-in with Golden Eyes again…however crazy it was. Because kismet or not, she had to stay focused. On what, she wasn't sure…but not. On. Men. For the time being.

"Why do you do this to yourself, Preeya? And to me?" Amanda gave Preeya a half smile with an all-too-familiar glower. Preeya's longtime flight mate always covered for her, saving her ass more times than she could count.

"It was seriously the traffic this time." She kissed Amanda's cheek and whispered her thanks. "I need to grab a real coffee, though…rough night. Can I run?"

Grumble. "Go. Fast."

Yeah, sometimes Preeya took advantage, but she'd pay Amanda back with her exhilarating company. Amanda had sought this job—glamour waitress of the skies—for some extra income for her family and extra adventure away from her family. Preeya *was* Amanda's excitement. They were layover buddies, complementing each other perfectly. Compared to many FAs, Preeya was considered pretty tame, just wild enough for Amanda. And Amanda played the mother figure—she drew and kept her lines. Through Preeya, Amanda got to cross those lines without actually crossing them.

Preeya scurried away from the gate in search of the nearest triple-shot grande mocha with extra whip. She'd grab a muffin for Amanda, too—and one to fill the hole in her own liquor-lined gut. God, she was glad to be anywhere but back in that room with Josh. *Here* and *now*, she could breathe. In fact, a familiar thud-thump bumped the inner walls of her breastbone—she was glad to be back in her domain, an airport. She looked up at the vaulted ceilings, the skylights, the expansive windows running alongside the grand terminal of gates and shops and people. A gazillion hectic people. And as she weaved in and out of the variety of those travelers in her path—from her fellow lost souls, to determined go-getters, and all the newbies and death-wishers and life-clingers and high-flyers in between—she felt at home. In an airport, she felt at home.

She laughed out loud. Maybe she'd become an FA not only to freak her dad the hell out and to secretly—and deplorably—run into Josh Bolte or whoever/whatever the hell he represented. Also, maybe, she had just known there was more to life, and the epitome of a vibrant life could be observed—if not found—in an airport. Any airport, really. Large hubs or small connector sites, the movement of walking, talking landmarks of time, to Preeya, was a thing to behold. An airport had a heartbeat, a vibration, a bravado bigger than her. Bigger than anyone.

And her craving for adventure, the new and different faces and stories and options. Infinite options. And time. Her travel-centered job had definitely given her options and the time to find the person, place, or thing that might sate the super-deep blank spot inside her.

And now, maybe because of the Josh wake-up call, the liberating note-tearing ceremony, and Dawn's freaky-honest analysis, something new stirred in her. A slight spark of exhilaration with a soft touch of hope. Between her eyes and at the base of her spine.

A nagging anxiety had lifted.

Everything had worked out despite the despicable and surreal past twelve hours. She had made it to Sea-Tac in time for her flight, Amanda had her task list covered, she'd make it to Amy's wedding, no problem, and the Josh-nightmare was behind her…

…and in front of her? The future ahead?

Her destination coffee spot.

Not quite what she'd meant, but just ahead was the sight and scent of Java Lava. Of course, the line was more than ten people deep. She sighed, but instead of cursing and checking the time again, she repeated the usual mantra, *go with it*. And with Seattle's rare sun rays peeking down at her from the skylights, *the sky's the limit.*

Yes, damn it, the sky is the limit.

*

Her phone rang and startled her as she struggled to balance her drink while shoving her credit card back into her purse so she could free a hand to get her earbuds in before missing the call.

She didn't have to look at her screen to know. *Gigi.*

"Where the hell have you been?" Sisterly wrath emanated.

"Shouldn't you know, Geej?" *Don't be snarky, Preeya.* "Sorry…I'm a bitch and it's a long story—"

"*Long story*, my ass. You had me worried sick. You were supposed to be at my place by six last night. Just so happens that Rod stayed over and you'd have been on the sofa, but that's not the point. So *not* cool, Pree—not cool at all. I mean, how many of my calls did you flat-out ignore?"

"I guess I take it for granted that you know I'm safe, you know?"

"Bullshit. You know that other than pregnancies and deaths, I see only cloudy, blurry shit—nothing concrete. If you've just hung up with your evil bitch of an aunt...or, God forbid, you're being raped, I can't distinguish between the two other than knowing down to my bones that you're in pain."

"Geej, I'm sorr—"

"No, you let me finish! I sensed that you were more than distressed last night—for the entire night and through to this morning. So after I called the airline to be sure you landed, and that you were on the damn flight from Tampa in the first place, I almost called my dad." Detective Donlow, Seattle PD. Like a father to Preeya, he would've been more than pissed, too, if Gigi had gotten him involved and it had been nothing serious. But a brief flicker of delight hit her heart while picturing Josh in handcuffs, arrested for possession. *That may have just been worth it.*

Gigi's rant brought Preeya back to the present. "You hear me? How selfish can you be, Preeya? Then I had a moronic thought to check your chat status online. And the stupid happy emoticon pulled me back from red alert. So fuck you—updating your online status and not texting me. And now, explain, goddamn it! Because 'smiley face' still didn't match the vibe I was getting."

Preeya's shame and guilt sank to the pit of her stomach along with her heart. Yeah, in the ride from the airport with Josh, she'd posted a gleeful emoji to mark the unbelievable serendipity of it all. *How stupid.* She swallowed then cleared her throat in order to answer her furious friend, but the cracking embarrassment in her voice was unavoidable. "Josh." *In a word.*

"Josh...Josh Bolte? Your first...*Josh Bolte?*"

"The same." Barely a whisper

"Enough of the clips of info, Pree, because seriously...I'm gonna flip out in a second."

Preeya inhaled then blew out the details. "Carnal Knowledge is playing Seattle, apparently. I was in the airport's cab line and he just swooped me up."

"Josh Bolte flies commercial?"

Preeya snickered. That struck her yesterday, too—for a nanosecond. But in retrospect, wow, had it made perfect sense. The desperate asshole need-ing all the fawning groupie-love he could get. "Yeah, but that's, like, the least-weird part of the entire situation, believe it or not."

"I believe it. And now I'm glad for *whatever* you got last night, stand-ing me up for that dick wad. And making me worry." Gigi blew out her remaining fury into the phone mic. "But, shit, tell me everything. I need to hear details."

Preeya laughed then looked down at the coffee calling to her. Her own brand of drug, much needed, but she held off. "I felt like a total asshole, Geej. Just pathetic."

"Hey, hindsight, love. I'm stuck in the game, too, right? How many times have I gone back to Rod?"

"Yeah. That's pathetic, too." Preeya smiled then broke down and took a sip of her mocha.

"Hey!"

"Sorry. It is, though."

Gigi huffed. "I guess, but screw off. Life's complicated. Love's fuck-ing complicated."

"Well, I know I'm *not* in love with Josh Bolte."

"Infatuated, though."

Yes, okay...she had been. "Well, that infatuation's now ironed into Sandpoint Way."

"Huh?"

"Nothing...just that I'm so over him and that pipe dream, Geej."

"Good news. I always said he was a flaming asshole, like that stupid tat-too." Gigi scoffed.

"It's a flaming sun, Geej, not an *asshole*." The fiery sun on his wrist aligned with the bright blue moon tat on hers. Together, a total eclipse. *I really should get the damn thing removed.* "But anyway, yes, *he* is an asshole, and I'm an ass for going with—whoa, whoa. Geej, hold on a sec."

Preeya caught the monitor hovering above the coffee menu, the local morning news. *Evan?* With his cheesy-yet-super-sweet face, now with a new something added. Yes, an unmistakable glint of pride.

"Pree, you there?"

"Sorry, sorry. Yeah. It's just…Ev. He's on anchor desk, Channel 4 News." Preeya pushed out a quick breath and shook her head. Production assistant reporting the news? In only a month? "Amazing. Maybe ending *us* opened more doors for him, after all? My Aunt Champa always said my flightiness was contagious. So now without *me*, he can focus and actually move up in his career, huh?"

Clean slate, Pree. Again, sky's the limit.

"Listen, love, your fucking 'flightiness' isn't contagious…your vibrant energy is. And yes, good for Evan, but you are going places, too. Places you can't even imagine yet."

"So…you do know something?"

"Damn it, Preeya."

"Kidding. Just kidding."

"All I know is that I know *you*. And that I love you and all your *crazy*, too. Your fucked-up family can project their bullshit on you all they want because they're blind to your dynamic charisma, your brilliance, and your too-big heart. You are going far, my friend. I know it in my gut."

"Yeah, hopefully to *Puerto Vallarta, Mexico* far, if I make it in time," she said, ungluing her gaze from the TV and moving her ass back toward the gate through the terminal's maze of people.

"But before you board, bitch, tell me about Josh already!"

"Well, the first thing you'd appreciate knowing"—she stole a few sips of coffee so she could be done with it before seeing Leena—"is that I officially have Josh Bolte and any and all representations of him and his type out of my system. Oh and…I got hit on by a lesbian. A pretty cool chick, too."

Gigi gasped then giggled and said something that got swallowed up in an announcement that clobbered Preeya's ears. "Preeya Patel, please. Preeya Patel to Gate S10. Preeya Patel to gate S10 now, please."

Leena. "Shit." She slammed the rest of the mocha in five hard gulps. "Geej, I gotta get on board before they leave me, then fire me." The flight couldn't really leave without her, but she couldn't ignore how replaceable she was.

"You're killin' me, Pree. When you land, then. I mean, chick-love *and* Josh Bolte!"

"Gigi, I'll call you. When I land."

"Wait, Pree. You're okay, though? Josh—he didn't hurt you or anything? And you're remembering your pill for God's sake!"

No, she was horrible about taking her birth control, but it hadn't turned out to matter, had it? "Geej, he didn't hurt me—except for the pain in my throbbing, completely unsatiated clit. But, I'm fine and good…and covered. But I'll call ya during my layover in Houston with more."

*

Ben sat in a far-off corner until boarding. Only five more minutes or so. Then sleep.

Until then, he thought he'd people-watch some more, that is, if sleep didn't take him first. God, he was so tired. The hearing was an early one, but it wouldn't have mattered. The review board, his in-laws—or rather, former in-laws—their attorney, and even Stanton, were all so draining. His lids felt so heavy, iron and nimbus-cloud heavy. God, weren't they supposed to be boarding now? A minute ago even? But he couldn't fight the exhaustion, the gravity, not even for another…his head nodded, chin to chest—

A loudspeaker announcement rocked his eardrums. He gasped awake.

Preeya Patel please, to gate S10.

His eyes open now, dry and wide, he refocused on the scene around him. By the window, his nameless soldier friend was on her phone, only twenty feet away. She paced then faced the window, frozen, her back to him. His heart still raced from the shock of the loudspeaker, but that and his new distraction on the phone had conquered his drowsy spell, at least.

The soldier, however mellow and calm she'd been while in line with him at check-in, seemed anything but right then. He couldn't make out her words, but her gestures were animated, staccato and sharp. Her head shook back and forth then tipped up to the ceiling in what he imagined to be some kind of prayer or request for an out-of-body answer. When she wasn't gesturing, she'd sigh, her shoulders lifting high then falling low. In total, he sensed a level of desperation in her that sent chills up his spine.

He shifted in the hard curve of the plastic chair.

Not your problem, Ben.

He looked down at his feet.

Avoidance is key, Ben.

Clank.

His gaze shot up, following the sound. His soldier friend had thrown something at the window? She crouched down then stood up the next second, holding a gold ring between her thumb and forefinger. He immediately moved his hand to his chest, to his gold chain under his shirt which held his wedding band. No longer appropriate to wear on his hand, he kept it all that much closer to his heart. He watched the soldier slide her retrieved ring onto her left ring finger. She stepped closer to the window, hand soothing the glass—feeling for damage?—then she shoved her phone into her pants pocket and dragged her duffel to a chair a few rows away from him and sank into a seat. Good. She didn't see him there. *All good.*

But not all good. Not for his nameless line mate. Returning home from war to what—a fight with her husband? He rubbed his head and sighed. Although he'd do anything to have contact, any contact, with his Jamie again—even a fight of epic proportions would do—he did not envy the woman. She seemed defeated, drained.

Odd, though. A fight with a spouse, a loved one, produces heaving fumes of raw emotion, real blood-rushing life. Not so with Unnamed Soldier. A thick quiet with a resonating emptiness came off her like the silent devastation after a land mine detonates—the one travesty he'd witnessed on his very last mission. Anyway, her leftover void was palpable.

Like his void was palpable.

He couldn't just sit there and ignore her pain. No, he had to do something.

He looked at his boarding pass, Group 1 First Class, just as a flight attendant—*Violet Eyes!*—sprinted past the podium, chucked a coffee cup into the trash, and rushed through the boarding door while onlookers grumbled and booed. Then she was gone again, a flash of energy. He returned his focus to his solemn soldier. Then to his boarding pass. *That's it.* He'd give her his seat. Yes, that's what he'd do. But from their brief exchange earlier, he knew she wouldn't take it, not willingly. Too much pride. He had to do it anonymously. He'd go through Violet Eyes or one of the other flight attendants. Yes, he'd board first and arrange it. His much-desired sleep would be had, or attempted to be had, in coach class. He'd managed sleep standing up in desert heat on past missions. Coach would be fine. He realized that a first-class seat for Unnamed Soldier might be a useless bandage over the deepest of heart wounds, but it was something, right? It would be a brief comfort, a sign of appreciation. And it wasn't even a unique gesture, as he'd seen it done before, by vets or patriots or guilty souls like him, but again, it was something. Something for someone who seemed to be devoured by a similar nothingness.

And having an excuse to speak to Violet Eyes…that was not a motivation in the slightest.

CHAPTER 6

PREEYA TOSSED A guilty smile at Leena on her way back to coach.
"Glad you could make it, Preeya."

"Thanks, Leena. Me, too. And in case I hadn't told you before, you really are the best," she called over her shoulder with her most professional-yet-cheeky tone. Leena had turned the other cheek at Preeya's punctuality issues too many times to count. And although it was done with an air of superiority that caught Preeya in the chest each time, she owed the woman a lot.

"You've told me. But it's gettin' really old," Leena yelled. "So is covering your ass, Preeya."

As of that morning, Preeya knew a lot had gotten old, and she also knew that actions, not words, were needed to start changing things.

She scurried back to put her purse under her jump seat but kept her cell in her skirt pocket. On her way to check the overheads with Amanda, she stuck her head in the restroom to tidy her hair, check her makeup, and tuck in her stupid blouse. A bit better, passable.

She moved up the aisle and slid by Amanda, pinching her ass as she did. Her loyal friend shot her a look of mock rebuke. Preeya giggled and blew it off with a sweet-as-sugar smile as she checked the first of the overheads, engaging her calf muscles to reach all the way back to be sure they were all empty.

"You get the rest, Pree...I've gotta pee before the lovelies board."

"I have some extra pillows and blankets up here, Preeya. Come and get them, would you?" Leena called.

Amanda rolled her eyes.

"Go pee. I got this *and* Leena." She waved Amanda on. "Sure thing, Leena!" Preeya rushed through the rest of the overhead compartments within arm's reach, adjusted a safety card in the pocket at row four, then made her way up to Leena.

She smiled wide at her superior as she reached for the stack.

"And hey, you owe Amanda a break so you're on beverages and cleanup." Leena's brows raised but a smirk betrayed the subtle reprimand. Preeya knew Leena liked her despite her shortcomings, and she knew it kept her employed, sad to say. Was that the charisma Gigi spoke of?

"Preeya, did you hear me?"

"Sure, of course, Leena," she said as she squeezed down on the slippery plastic-wrapped stack of comfort amenities while wearing a sweet smile for the first of the elite-class passengers. One after another they entered the tight confines of the airplane cabin, with its recycled air and the slight stench of toilet and hand sanitizer.

Ready to head back to her section, she nodded at Leena and swiveled her feet when someone caught her eye. *No.*

Yes.

The man towering over Leena. *Golden Eyes.*

Her breath halted, just stuck there in her throat.

And her heart beat in her ears.

In her memory, the one thing her father agreed with her mother on—there's no such thing as coincidence.

She watched him, awestruck, while he made his way row by row, his head awkwardly skimming the cabin ceiling. It surprised her how calm and cool he seemed, more than used to his above-it-all vantage point. But not cocky. *Kind.* Yet totally confident. Even with his chin nearly touching his chest as he made his way—and his shoulder bag, only slightly less ridiculous than a fanny pack—his confident air made the beating in her ears freight-train down to her stomach. Then lower still. Her cheeks heated and her eyes darted down to the floor. Not that he was looking at her face or reading her thoughts or gauging her spike in body temperature to know the sudden whirling feeling below her belly. No, he was reading, with sharp focus, the seat plaques lining the bulkhead.

And as his eyes scrutinized the next seat number, she brought the pile of pillows in her arms a bit higher up her body, up to her nose, then peeked over them. She could still see his face, a gentle yet strong face. With those soft, tired but dazzling eyes now checking his seat assignment stub with great scrutiny. It made her giggle low in her chest, how OCD he was being about his seat number in contrast with that unmistakable confidence—that tall, towering poise. The routine continued, him checking the stub in hand against the seat plaques, the stub to the next plaque, and on with each next step down the aisle he took until he looked farther down the rows.

Right at her.

With those eyes.

He'd forgiven her with those eyes when she'd slammed him in the leg with her bag yesterday. And she'd not forgotten that he'd taken her breath away then, too. And during their brief security run-in when he'd been too busy to notice her until it was too late. Until she had to run.

But, well, here he was. With those warm-as-honey eyes. On her flight.

He continued toward her, down the aisle.

And, God, with the bright fluorescent cabin lights, those eyes of his just sucked her in and burned her up. They were a bright, golden-wheat hue accented by flecks of copper and bronze. Light, glowing eyes.

But they possessed a solemn something behind them.

His gaze held hers in its grip. Magnetic. Eyes narrowed but smiling. Because he absolutely recognized her, too.

He dropped his gaze that instant and all she could see was the top of his clean-shaven head. Was he embarrassed she'd caught him staring at her? Like she'd been mortified a moment ago when she'd felt that twinge of pulsating heat at her core? *Oh God.* She squeezed the armful of comfort amenities tight to her chest to refocus her attention to the task at hand, her paid task, and as she took a step back toward coach, the entire pile—each and every pillow and blanket—spewed like a waterfall to the cabin floor.

Shit. Preeya couldn't ignore Leena's glare before the woman turned to the next oncoming passenger to deflect and distract from Preeya's ridiculous fuck up. "Hello, folks, welcome. Welcome aboard Jetta Air."

And Preeya, heat flooding her cheeks even more now, knelt down to clean up her mess of sleep amenities.

CHAPTER 7

"EXCUSE ME?" GOLDEN Eyes knelt down to help her pick up the strewn recycled flannel blankets and hypoallergenic pillows.

"Oh, thank you. But, really, there's no need," she said, trying like hell not to look him in the face as she scrambled to clean up her spill. *No time for distraction.* Sweet-meets-unknowingly-sexy or otherwise, she needed to keep focused on her job, getting to Amy's wedding, *then* life choices. *Her very own,* albeit long-winded, mantra.

"Um, here." He handed her another felt blanket. "And, uh, I do have a quick question for you."

Shit. His voice was like the color of his eyes—smooth melted honey—and it coated her insides. *No, damn it.* No time for chitchat or pick-up lines or, God, those eyes, the very cause of her pillow spill. He should find his seat and ask *Leena* his question.

She tried to hide her impending huff, then grinned. "Yes, sir." Her eyes hard-focused on the remaining few pillows at her feet. "What can I answer for you?"

He leaned into her slightly and whispered, "Actually, I was hoping you could do me a favor?"

Damn it. Eye contact. Several shared blinks followed until she forced her eyes down his face. To his lips, red and moist and curled up at the corners, mesmerizing dimples she hadn't noticed before, now on dreadful display.

He placed a pillow on her stack and cleared his throat.

Oh God. Still unable to break the spell, she forced a smile.

Preeya. "Sorry, sir." She swallowed without success, her mouth too dry to dislodge the embarrassment from her throat. "What favor is that?"

But he, too, seemed paused, frozen. With no items left to collect from the floor, he narrowed his eyes, tilted his head, and studied her. God, was she doing this to him a second ago? How awkward. And breathtaking.

Leena's voice reached her ears then. "Hi, folks, how are you? Traffic jam ahead. It won't be but a moment…"

Preeya swallowed as she stood up with the tower of pillows and blankets firmly in hand this time. He stood up with her.

"Sir, what was it…that you needed?"

"Oh, God, sorry…I'm, um…" He blinked hard and slow. "It's just your eyes…they're so rare. You've probably heard that a million—"

"Excuse me, Preeya, dear, but these passengers are ready to come through," Leena stated over the tall man's shoulder, though Preeya couldn't actually see Leena behind him. And standing only a few inches from her, the towering helper with a favor was overwhelming her senses.

"Terribly sorry. Yes, let me just move out of the way," she said as she stepped into a row of seats while balancing her reacquired stack. That was easy. Harder was shaking off Golden Eyes' reaction to her.

And her reaction to him.

*

"What did you need, sir?" she repeated with an accommodating smile in her renewed rush to get back to coach class.

He could only stare. Disheveled or not, rock star…*fodder* or not, vodka-laced perfume or not, he was captivated. Against his better judgment and, heck, his chest full of guilt, she'd snatched his attention. *Again.*

Yesterday in line, before the chaos took her away, he thought her a mirage, with something behind her eyes—sweet depth, wild dreams, passion. Then seeing her the second time at security, that struck him as strange. Now, here, on his flight, inches from him, well, he just couldn't figure out what to think, how to act—what to do with his gaze. Look her in the eyes?

Those purple-indigo enigmas, illuminating dusk or lavender fields or purple haze in the silvery moonlight over a placid lake.

Framed by black-as-ink lashes.

Okay Poet Ben.

Fine, stare at the mile-high stack of synthetic blankets in her arms.

No, back to the eyes. Just look at her and ask her your damn question already.

He targeted her eyes, batting at him.

Waiting for him to speak.

Speak, damn it.

"Preeya?" *The first-class attendant again.*

Preeya. Perfect Preeya.

Hurry up, Ben.

"Right, real quick…so you can get back to work. I saw a military servicewoman waiting to board. I hoped to give her my first-class seat." He handed Preeya his boarding pass stub, which she pinched with the only free fingers she had.

She nodded and smiled from behind her stack of comfort stuffs. "Certainly, sir. That's…very nice of you." She cleared her throat and took a step toward coach while he got caught by her eyes again. Damn those piercing, stunning, soul-deep eyes. "I'll just put these items down and then I'll—"

She paused. The head of a lanky kid with a huge backpack strapped to his shoulders blocked their view. The teenager, earbuds stuffed in his ears and hands stuffed deep in his pockets, lumbered past them. Slowly. An adorable little girl followed close behind with her own roller bag, which nailed Ben in his Achilles' heel. He grimaced, bit his bottom lip to redirect the pain, then exhaled. At least it wasn't a second hit to his shin, which had bruised overnight.

The path cleared. "I'll meet you back here so we can find her to know her seat number."

"Well, actually," he said, rubbing his ankle with his other leg while speaking in a hurried and hushed tone. God, he hoped she didn't think he was trying to sound seductive, because that would've been even more awkward after all his gawking.

But why the hell would she think he was hitting on her? *You're arranging a seat exchange with someone, Ben…not a threesome, for God's sake.*

Oh Lord. His face burned, throat thickened. He brought his hand up to the top of his head and rubbed, resetting his thoughts to continue, then swallowed to find his voice. "I'd like to give her my seat anonymously, or she might decline it…if she has someone to decline it from, you know?" He also really didn't want any attention from the deed. He'd had enough attention over the past several months and years. He was definitely done with the spotlight.

But *her* attention made his heart crash against his chest. When she opened her mouth to respond, he found himself interrupting her with nervous, annoying chatter, but he just couldn't contain himself. "Because in the terminal earlier, she bumped me, the soldier did, and I of course dismissed it, but she'll remember me, and definitely decline and—"

"Sir." She threw him a pseudo-polite smile, which he couldn't blame her for—the lead flight attendant's impatience radiated from only a few rows away.

Dumbass, let the woman do her job. "Right. When you're free…"

"Yes, sir, of course. Maybe go to the rear of the plane and wait for me there?"

"Sure, yes. I'll just…stand in the back…in coach and wait…for you."

"Yes. Fine." A warm, only slightly fake smile lifted her face. She waited. "Please, after you, sir. Just head all the way back."

"Right, yes." He nodded then slipped by her, his front grazing her back. And, Jesus, the sensations that blasted through him, up and down him, weren't warranted, not at all. And his uncontrolled reaction to her body pushing right up against his, his hard and unmistakable response, could not have been ignored.

Oh Jesus.

Violet Eyes—Preeya, rather, *Pretty Preeya*—sighed then coughed.

Move, man! He took one more large sidestep, and he found himself safe on the other side of her—safe and mortified and flooding with burning-hot shame.

"That way, sir. Just wait for me by the restrooms—" Her brows lifted, "at the end of the aisle, sir."

Man did he want to run, sprint, fly down the aisle. Away from her. But not. He couldn't even look at her again, but he also couldn't move his feet.

"Sir, would you please take your seat?" the first-class attendant called back to him over Preeya's head.

He lifted his hand, an apologetic wave. Then to Preeya as he backpedaled a few steps—movement in the right direction, at least. "Thanks again... for arranging the seat swap for me."

She flashed a final smile and nodded, then turned her attention—her stunning eyes—to the coach passengers awaiting the pillows and blankets in her arms.

*

Preeya headed back to her seat hoping no one else needed anything from her. After the pillow disaster, it had only gone downhill. There was Leena's passive aggression, pushing and pulling her in all directions—fair retribution, Preeya guessed, but...wow. Then, between handling the first-class seat swap, a diaper emergency, the leg-room upgrade complaint in 13A, and the child in 6B who was too cute to deny crayons and an extra blanket to, not to mention the doom-and-gloom in 20C, Preeya's hangover headache had been shoved over the edge. And she still needed time to send her ritual text to her sister.

She closed bulkheads on her way back to get the safety demo seat belt and oxygen mask, and when she finally got to her jump seat, out appeared Golden Eyes.

Right. How could she have forgotten? She hadn't, not really, and couldn't even if she'd tried. When he'd brushed by her earlier, bodies mashed together in the tight aisle, he'd left quite the impression.

Hard to forget, for sure.

Preeya—Jesus. He's a passenger. And again, she had her lines—no things or flings with passengers, pilots, or crew. And her new *focus.* There were to be no flings of any kind. Not until she figured out who the hell she was, and then what she wanted.

A polite cough from nearly a foot above pulled her from her zone.

"Sorry, sir, to have kept you waiting."

While avoiding his sunlit eyes, she took out the seat-assignment stubs—Kyla Ruiz Allen and Benjamin Trainer—while hoping this interaction moved along faster than before, because the doors had already closed and she needed to do the safety demo. And Preeya sensed Leena's glare thirty-five rows away.

"You were right about the soldier's modesty. She declined right away... but I convinced her. She was very appreciative and thanked you."

"But...you didn't tell her it was me...my name, right?"

"No, Mr. Trainer, I did not tell her your name." She flashed him a reassuring smile.

He held out his hand. "It's actually *Dr.* Benjamin Trainer...but please, call me Ben."

A sharp, hot surge of disgust hit her between the eyes.

Doctor.

Her headache raged.

How was it possible that Mr. Tall, Sweet, Somewhat Solemn and Too Serious but Subtly Sexy could turn into Dr. Arrogant Prick Good Samaritan in a single, solitary instant?

Chill out, Pree. He hadn't stated his title in a snooty tone, but, wow, had her perception of him done a one-eighty.

But Kyla Ruiz Allen hadn't corrected her when she'd missed the *Sergeant* title on the soldier's uniform name tag. Though the woman had every right to. Did this guy really need to shove *his* title in her ear?

Give him a break. Maybe it was for safety's sake? Letting her know he was an MD in case of emergency?

Here in the twenty-first century, a PA announcement sufficed in finding a medical doctor on board, if need be. Had this guy ever flown before or seen a movie? She swallowed back the thick knot that had lodged itself in her throat. "Your seat, *Doctor*, is in the seventh row, letter *B* for *Bravo*." She smiled, showing no teeth, trying like hell to hide her surfaced disdain—his enticing confidence from earlier had morphed into an air of cocky superiority she just couldn't stomach.

"Thanks so much for doing that for—"

"Good morning, everyone, this is your captain speaking. Jetta Air welcomes…" the loudspeaker announcement began.

"You'd better take your seat now…*Doctor*." Yeah, she went *there* again.

Preeya! You're being a bitch.

Damn it, fine. "And have a nice flight."

He smiled and lingered and swallowed and nodded while she said nothing, only offering her perfect FA-trained smile, hands folded neatly in front of her. Then, finally getting the hint, he walked his tall, cocky doctor-self down the aisle to his seat.

"He's *not* gonna have a very nice flight, I can tell you that," Preeya whispered to Amanda as her friend gathered the items for the safety demo that Preeya was supposed to have started already. "The guy's six foot something—he'll be hella cramped in his new economy seat."

"God, I hope he's okay. You just don't find sweethearts like that, like… ever." Amanda scooted by Preeya and raised the sample seat belt buckle above her head as the prerecorded safety spiel began.

"Yeah. I guess," Preeya mumbled then sat in her jump seat and buckled up. While she waited the minute for Amanda to come back, she took out her cell, swiped through more VM alerts and missed calls—Aunt Champa and Dad—and slammed out a text to her sister. *Seattle to Houston to Pto. Vallarta. Love ya, little sister, Pree.* Then she followed the text with a wide-smiling selfie. *Totally fake smile…Prana will know it.* Her sister was developmentally delayed but more intuitive than even Gigi most times.

Amanda plopped down beside her. "Hey, you sent your text out?"

"Yeah…you?"

"Yeah. But I wonder if my youngest would be better off not knowing the whens and wheres?" Amanda pursed her lips. "On my last off days, she snuck into bed with us—nightmares of me…not coming home."

"Yeah, it's hard when you're little." Preeya hid the chills shimmying up her back, then cleared her throat.

"It's hard for my oldest baby, too—"

"Renee?"

"No, she's fifteen—could care less. I mean Brad. He's getting fed up with my being gone. Beyond his cock and the kids, I think he genuinely misses me." Amanda's brows danced, then transitioned into an empathetic smile.

Marriage was not a topic she grasped, so Preeya steered back around. "Prana doesn't really get what I do, just that I'm not with *her*." A different rippling chill hit her chest.

Guilt again.

Amanda patted Preeya's leg. "Hey, that tall and super-sexy doctor...you know he's with Doctors Without Borders? Modest as hell, too. I had to yank it out of him while he was standing back here...waiting for *you*." Brows waggled with unwarranted excitement.

Preeya rolled her eyes. "How *humanitarian* of him..." Her annoyance level shot up a few more degrees.

"Wow, Pree. Bitter much? What's your deal?"

"First off, did you see the way he was looking at me? Now I get it...hungry for the easy flight attendant before his stint in the third world?"

"I didn't get that vibe from him at all—he even referred to you as the 'beautiful attendant with the violet eyes.' And he'd already let on that he knew your name. *Preeya* rolled off his tongue like a perfect tide...while he made love to you on the beach of his dreams."

Preeya huffed at her friend and grit her teeth.

Amanda cracked up and slapped Preeya's arm. "Seriously, though, Pree, he didn't even tell me he was a doctor until five minutes into our obligatory chat while...he waited for you, *Violet Eyes*." Amanda smirked.

"Yeah, I'm intentionally ignoring you now." Preeya glanced at her phone—but she was unable to hold her tongue. "You know *I* know *doctors*. Between med school, Prana's specialists, my dad—they're all money-driven god complexes. This one"—she motioned up the aisle—"our tall MD in 7B"—with the eyes of damned sunset and liquid gold—"is the worst kind. The kind that doesn't admit his true nature."

Amanda shook her head.

"What?"

"You're such a cynic, Pree." Amanda laughed. "Not all of them can be bad. So your dad pays the bills by doing tits-and-ass enhancements." Amanda flipped the page of her gossip magazine. "And plenty of doctors do good without money being their primary focus."

Preeya leaned into Amanda, gawking at the gossip rag on her lap, and nudged Amanda with her shoulder. "See all those celebs—enhancements galore. Not just a few doctors make a shit-ton of money off of 'em. Hell, my dad's even marrying one of those…those wax jobs. Tomorrow!"

Amanda sighed. "Oh, Preeya…" Which meant, "Accept it and move on."

Amanda was right. She should accept her father's oh-so-selfless path, and remember that she was her mother's daughter—or, at least, aimed to be.

She sighed and put her attention back on her phone.

Her aunt's voice message awaited.

"By the way," Amanda piped up again, lifting her head from the rag, "where did you run off to last night? We missed you in the lobby lounge."

"Oh, God, don't ask." She got goose bumps up and down her arms and rubbed them away as fast as they'd come. "Just really, don't even ask." And resumed her last-minute phone message retrieval.

"If you ask me, being done with Evan has got you nowhere fast, sweetie. Empty sex isn't gonna fill the hole. Well, not figuratively, at least." Amanda slapped her leg at her own joke. "We're just not like the other girls, Pree, and we're better for it…"

Funny. That Amanda thought Preeya'd gone wild after ending it with Evan. The opposite was true. She hadn't slept with anyone after rejecting the ring. Except now, with Josh, and again, that wild attempt failed wildly. And just because Amanda had a husband waiting at home didn't mean that an anchor was necessary to keep Preeya grounded, sexually speaking. Anyway, like Dawn had pointed out that morning, the double standard shouldn't be a thing anymore. But it was to Amanda, and Preeya didn't feel she had to change anyone's perspective or explain herself—well, except *to* herself.

"Well, I don't believe that I did ask you." She winked at Amanda and put her phone to her ear to listen to her first voice message before takeoff. "But for the record, last night was supposed to be…different and—"

"Hey, miss. Miss! I thought no cell phones allowed after the plane leaves the gate?" a paper-thin brunette with a neon-pink lipsticked scowl whined while attempting to pull the bathroom door open, though it clearly read Push.

"Excuse me, ma'am," Amanda cut in. "Please do return to your seat immediately and buckle up. You'll have to wait to use the restroom until after we reach cruising altitude and the captain has turned—"

"A buncha hypocrites, all of you," the woman grumbled, and moseyed back to her seat several rows up.

"Why? Why do we do this job again?" Amanda asked.

"Because…" Preeya pressed the number eight on her phone to repeat the message she'd missed. "We love flying these here *friendly skies*."

*

Two voice mail messages.

Amy had left an excited, near-hyperventilating report on "the absolute perfection" of the bridesmaid dresses, the weather in Vallarta, and of Darren, Amy's soon-to-be-husband. Yes, the straitlaced, sweet-as-pie Darren James. Preeya smiled. Though she still had a small glint of angst over attending the event, she was absolutely glad for her friend.

But now on to the second voice mail. Aunt Champa.

Preeya sneered through the entire guilt-saddled discourse for not having yet arrived in Berkeley for the "rehearsal brunch."

Amanda tapped her leg again. "Hey, you okay?"

The plane picked up speed for takeoff and she quickly powered down her phone. "Yeah, of course." She shrugged and smiled. "I'm fine."

Totally fine.

Family. Priorities. Disappointment. Just more of the same BS.

Aunt Champa had raised her since age seven. Which was when Preeya's mother left, only months after Prana was born. Preeya's father had to go into private practice—full-time to afford SafeHaven for Prana—which meant he had no time or energy to raise a growing seven-year-old.

So Preeya had been left with a replacement mother while her father all but vacated—he'd visit her on holidays and birthdays. *Thanks so much, Dad.*

And Aunt Champa? A wonderful mother figure—to her own damn daughter. Preeya's cousin Asha was the same age as Preeya. Growing up, her aunt had done a pretty pathetic job at hiding her preference. The woman's disdain for Preeya had been palpable, even—or especially—to a child.

But Preeya found ways around it. Mainly fleeing to the across-the-street neighbor's house. *Gigi.* And her then-weekly visits to SafeHaven, to see Prana. She cringed at the memory, having to depend on *Gigi's* father to take her to see her sister because Aunt Champa had been too busy—with Asha—to make the trip but once a month. She inhaled the cabin's recycled air deep into her limited lungs in an attempt to filter out the limitless guilt—her sister, her baby sister, had been the forsaken soul here, the deserted one. Not Preeya.

She rubbed a kink from her shoulder, as if that would clear her thoughts, her shadows. She knew full well that seeing her sister, being there for her, was the only solution. She'd visit Berkeley next month. Then she'd read to Prana her favorite book, Shel Silverstein's *The Giving Tree*, for the millionth time. She sighed into the slight relief settling into her shoulders and neck. Reading that book to her sister, seeing the like-new excitement in Prana's eyes, always filled Preeya's heart to the brim. That look Prana gave her, like everything her sister gave her, was exponentially more than Preeya could ever give back in return.

The plane lifted off. Mount Rainier showed her magnificence through the tiny cabin crew window, and Preeya nodded. A good final sight of Seattle. She pulled her book from her purse, the bookmark holding her place was a lilac envelope which held another picture Prana had drawn her. She slid it carefully to a back page and sighed as she began chapter four, entitled "Family Matters." Yes, family matters, indeed.

CHAPTER 8

IN THE AIR twenty minutes, Leena rang. And Preeya answered.

"I'm ready for service. You?"

"Yes, Leena, we're all set," Preeya said, just having finished going over the beverage stock on her cart.

"Before you take the cart out, do offer a real drink to that doctor who switched with the servicewoman. Courtesy of the airline."

"Sure thing," Preeya said hiding the grimace from her reply. Yes, she was being admittedly judgmental of the man, but with her asshole father on her brain, her less-than-kind attitude toward the *good doctor* crept up her spine.

She smiled and nodded her way up the aisle. Seventh row. Seat B. Yup, his knees were so high he couldn't even put his tray table down. God, that sucked.

"Sorry to bother you, Dr. Trainer..."

"Oh, hello...Ben, Ben please..."

"Okay, *Ben.* Well, the airline would be honored if you'd accept an in-flight beverage—wine, champagne, a mixed drink?" She handed him a menu. "Whatever you'd like. A small *thank you* for your kind and noble gesture." She laid it on thick, as thick as artery-clogging butter, but the alternative, quite the opposite, wouldn't have been what Leena intended.

"Thank you so much, but no, I'd prefer not to drink any alcohol. The whole doctor-on-board thing. Just...safer."

Of course. "How responsible." *And self-important.* "Then may I offer you a special meal instead? The sergeant will still get your first-class meal, but we always have additional elite guest meals. Today's salmon or shrimp options are actually quite delicious," she lied.

"Sure, yes, please. That would be nice…thanks so much, Preeya."

She forced a polite grin at hearing her name from his lips then nodded. "I'll have it for you shortly, then." As she spun to leave him, the voice of the tween-aged boy—backpack interrupter in the next row—cracked to a start. "Ma, is there really no meal service on this flight? I'm seriously starving."

"I told you to eat at the airport, but you didn't listen. Now sit tight and watch your sister," the mother said in a harsh whisper, then got up from her seat and moved into the aisle. "Excuse me, miss? May I use the restroom quickly before the drinks cart blocks the way?"

"Of course ma'am. And…go ahead to the one in first class. The ones in the back are taken." Preeya let the woman by, then made her way through first class—smiling and nodding—to grab the very special meal for the very special passenger in 7B.

*

He watched her shimmy through first class. *Preeya*—a freeing, breathing name to match such a woman. *Preeya.* She was of either Middle Eastern or East Indian descent, he thought. Exotic, stunning…and slightly snarky. He whispered to himself through a subtle smile. "Preeya."

And the thoughts sweeping through him brought with them a next round of guilt. Looking at another woman at all—just deplorable. Even though it'd been a year. It just felt…wrong.

What did it matter? He wouldn't act on the surge of heat she'd ignited. *No chance.*

And since their brief and official introduction in the back of coach class, he had a strong sense that she wouldn't act on anything, either—he'd noted the sudden change in her disposition the moment he'd mentioned his title, which he did on every flight he took to make sure some crew member knew in case of emergency. Maybe she thought him conceited or arrogant by doing so? Not his intention, of course. Not by any means. So even if he'd felt some kind of two-way connection at the earlier pillow-crash site, it had vanished since.

He sighed then shoved his feet flat on the ground to see if his high knees would drop any lower. Nope. So he'd be dining on his lap today.

A minute past and Preeya was back. He tried hard to contain himself—his too-wide smile and jackhammering pulse—as she handed him the concise tray of shrimp with a colorful pilaf, crisp-looking broccoli with a glistening roll on the side. He heard the boy in front of him huff then turn to see his meal through the seat crack. Ben nodded at the peeking boy, then at Preeya. "Thank you. It looks delicious." He lifted his brows then smirked, noting Preeya's awareness of the envious passenger in front of him.

Preeya lightened some, her lip curling into a softer smile. "You're quite welcome. Any regular beverage with that?"

"Water, please. Just water. Oh, and with lemon and no ice?" *Shut up, Ben. Aiming to prove her theory right?* Or maybe he was a stuck-up asshole pretending not to be.

"Sure. No problem."

He did not miss the eye roll she worked hard to hide. As an air hostess, he figured she must get the most obnoxious requests from passengers and hate it. And he's just another passenger. *Lemon, no ice.* He shook his head while his eyes followed her form back up to first class.

Eat, Ben. Just eat.

He looked at the first-class cuisine on the tray teetering on his knees, then a few inches higher at his audience—the boy's peering eye maintained its steady focus.

He smiled and sighed then unclipped his seat belt. Holding the tray of elegant sustenance, he stood up. He was tall enough to easily bring the tray up, over, and down onto the lap of the boy in front of him. As he sat back down and buckled up, a gasp of happiness floated up and over the sixth row.

"Wow, mister. Thank you!" One shrimp already in hand, near his mouth. "Thanks so much!"

"Don't mention it, bud. Enjoy."

Ben reclined into his economy-class seat with its semi-flexible pleather headrest that cradled his…neck, then adjusted his smashed kneecaps against the hard plastic of the folded tray table, and let his eyelids close. He sighed into attempted sleep.

*

Preeya returned to *Doctor Ben* with the water—*lemon, no ice*—but…he'd dozed off?

"Miss!" 9F waved at her and without giving Preeya a chance to tell the woman she'd be right with her—so she could figure out where the finished first-class food tray had vanished to—the woman called her again. Preeya played dumb; the woman could wait. Was the doctor's tray under his seat? She didn't see anything under those long legs of his. Maybe Leena or Amanda had come by? She screwed her face at the man, peaceful and calm despite, God, how incredibly uncomfortable he looked. She couldn't help but smirk but then scolded herself just as 9B tapped her on the shoulder. How bad she wanted to give the cup of water in her hand—Ben's water—to that woman, Josh Bolte style.

"Ma'am?"

"Water. I need water to take my blood pressure medicine. Extra ice."

Of course. Extra ice, no extra manners. None at all, in fact.

Gnashing her back teeth, Preeya glided to the rear of the cabin for the extra ice—and to take an extra long, clearing breath, then to vent to Amanda. Once at the economy crew area, she caught a moan of pain from Amanda as her friend lifted a heavy tray from a bottom fridge drawer. Without a second thought, Preeya put 9B's ice request on hold to help Amanda restock the cart.

"Thanks, Pree. Lower back's really getting to me these days."

"Maybe that masseuse we like will be in the crew lounge today."

"He's in Dallas, Pree, not Houston."

"You're right. Hey, can you hand me a cup of ice from the—"

Ping. The always-magical sound of some passenger's call button. Amanda glanced down the aisle and sighed. "6C. God, do they have us running today, or what?"

"You're not kidding," Preeya said with her head behind the mini-fridge door.

"After 6C, can you take the cart, Pree? I left off at row twenty-three. I'll meet you there in a minute, just gotta pee again…sooo bad."

"Sure thing."

Amanda pulled the restroom door closed and Preeya moved into the aisle when the back intercom buzzed. *Leena*—but Preeya had already turned her attention to 6B…and saw Dr. Ben Trainer crouching down in the aisle.

Sudden and jagged screaming from the panicked mother. *Shit.*

Preeya grabbed the Medibox to her left, pulled it from its wall clasps, then flew down to row six.

Leena got there at the same time.

The boy, the lanky tween with earbuds, was gasping for air, one hand at his throat, one on his chest, eyes wild with fear, wheezing and hissing and terrified.

Dr. Ben Trainer looked up at Preeya from his crouching position in the aisle. "No known allergies, according to the mother. This is a first-time occurrence." He refocused on the boy, offering him soothing sweeps of comfort with words and questions and instructions while he looked in his mouth, checked his pulse, scrutinized his pupils, all almost simultaneously. That is, until the boy made a hard, raspy grab for air, then his eyes rolled back in his head and he lost consciousness.

As if in slow motion, the boy began falling sideways, limp like a rag doll, but Ben caught him and situated him upright in the seat. He held him there while checking his carotid pulse again, and without looking away from the boy, he uttered a directive. "Epinephrine…for anaphylaxis—now, Preeya. Now."

She had already knelt beside him, med kit beside her, the snap-clasps flung up with both thumbs. She hunted, found, grabbed the epinephrine pens.

The mother began to shriek. Shivers scurried like a thousand spiders up Preeya's spine. Leena tried to calm the woman, her hands stroking the mother's arms, but the woman's panic only worsened and made her other child—the little girl Preeya'd given crayons to earlier—sob and wail. The surrounding passengers were fast on their way to frantic, too. The contagion was hard to contain—even Leena was getting frazzled. And where the hell was Amanda? Still in the bathroom?

Ben, somehow still mellow yet supremely focused, locked eyes with Preeya as she unwrapped the first of the two adrenaline auto-injectors.

"His chest is still lifting." A breathing boy, a good sign.

"And if we can stop the rapid throat swelling, it'll continue to. So, Preeya, listen. I need three things. I need calm, I need the captain to land at a major metro, and...I need those two epi auto-injectors at the ready—"

She slapped the first one in his hand and began ripping open the second auto-injector while his other directives registered. She gathered all the air she could into her boa-constricted chest and prepared her announcement deep and loud, ignoring her own light-headedness. "Please, everyone," she said as she watched him slam the pen into the boy's thigh, but no response, "stay seated, seat belts buckled, and, for the doctor, you must remain calm and quiet."

She handed him the second injector.

But he handed it back. "We wait five minutes." He checked his watch. "Now, while I've got a hold of him, punch these armrests up. I need him flat."

She did as he asked. Locating the hidden latch on the underside of the aisle armrest, she lifted it, then slammed the other two up hard and quick, while calling to her superior who was now trembling in the throes of the mother's fit. "Debrief the captain, Leena. We need to land. Major metro. Now."

"Right." Leena sniffled, took a huge breath, then waved Amanda up.

Amanda appeared the next second and took the mother's arm.

But the mother balked. "Why isn't he doing CPR? Why isn't he helping him breathe? My boy!"

Preeya stood up to help Ben lay the boy out, head at the window, feet hanging in the aisle, and then turned to the woman. "Your son is in good hands, ma'am, but the doctor needs calm." She looked deep into the woman's eyes—such horrified, helpless eyes. Eyes, she imagined, of a mother who thought she might very possibly outlive her child. "Go with Amanda so your daughter isn't seeing this. Then come back when you're calm...and bring back some water for your son." Preeya touched the woman's arm with a soft graze. "He should be revived by then, and he'll need his mother, and that water. Go now."

Amanda took the panic-stricken woman away from the scene and down the aisle, leaving Preeya to help Ben to help the near-breathless boy who had begun turning a ghostly shade of blue.

She put her hand on Ben's shoulder. "Okay. Ready."

But Leena still stood there staring.

"Go, Leena." Preeya snapped. *What the hell?* Leena spun around in the direction of the cockpit.

"And get the AEDs," Ben called.

The AEDs? Preeya swallowed hard and nearly choked on the dryness in her throat. *Please don't need the defib pads for this boy. This child.*

Ben's hand met hers, as if sensing her terror. "Probably won't need 'em; it's just in case. Second epi shot, please."

While he checked the boy's carotid again, she placed the injector in his free hand.

"Pulse and breathing are slowing." He held the shot up to his face and checked the injector's dosage. "Another point-three milligrams...here we go." He slammed it hard into the boy's other thigh.

They both stared at the child. At his eyes and face, his throat, his chest... which had ceased any and all movement. The boy's breath had stopped.

"Okay, buddy, let's do this." Ben glanced at his watch to note the time again, then rose up on his knees and began CPR.

"The pads, now?" Preeya asked from the floor while holding Ben's waist to balance him through a rough patch of turbulence.

Between counts, "No, not yet."

Ben finished two swift breaths into the boy's mouth, now purple lips. Still nothing. "Yes—two, three, four—the pads." Breath, breath. "But, Jesus, a defibrillator on this age heart..."

Shit, was Ben getting concerned?

"I'm going to grab the AEDs myself—Leena's taking too long." She spun toward first class to go, but Ben grabbed her wrist before she took a step.

Ben couldn't say a word to follow up his touch before she heard it. *A gasp.*

A gasp from heaven, that's what met her ears.

The boy jolted, his torso suddenly perpendicular to his legs, clutching his neck in his hands, air flooding into his shocked and oxygen-deprived body. The lanky and frail twelve-year-old body, now sitting up with life. *Alive, thank God.*

His mother came running up the aisle toward them and knelt at her boy's feet. Ben slid behind the boy at the window end of the row and let the child rest on Ben's chest while the child continued to oxygenate.

Preeya's heart racked her rib cage and, officially dizzy from adrenaline and pure fear, she let her body slide to the floor then surrender back onto her calves. She swallowed back the emotion, held it at the brink. Oh God, that mother's terror. Dear Jesus, the weight of the mere thought of losing a child made her never, ever want kids. Thoughts of losing Prana, her baby sister, swept in but Preeya blew them out again with a violent gust as quick as they'd come. *No, not ever.*

Leena was there the next second, heaving with relief. "Oh God, thank you."

"Landing…?" Ben asked of Leena.

"Boise. Seven minutes out."

"With this type of allergic event, we don't know if there will be another episode. Have an ambulance standing by. And two more injections at the ready."

Preeya got up from the floor. "The kit in the front has two more. I'll get 'em. And waters…" The boy's mother brought one back for her son as Preeya had instructed. "I'll bring back a few more bottles."

"Yes. Please," Ben said, his head leaning against the hard window shade, the boy still panting, eyes closed, weak, wilted against Ben's sweat-drenched and heaving chest.

Preeya started down the aisle, but looked back over her shoulder.

At Dr. Ben Trainer.

How'd he do it? Moment by moment, breath by breath, he'd pushed life back into the *lifeless*. He literally breathed a second chance into that near-dead boy, that hardly-lived-yet son of that mother, that gasping-and-grasping child, the brother to that wailing little girl. To keep it down, all of the erupting *near-death* and *too-close*, Preeya bit her bottom lip. Hard. So hard it might've drawn blood—she didn't know or care. But the sharp pain did its job. No tears. *Breathe, and no tears.*

It had been just way too much *life and death*. Perhaps she'd stumbled upon yet another subconscious reason for having dropped out of medical school. *Life and death*. Not for her.

CHAPTER 9

THEY LANDED IN Boise, Idaho, without another anaphylactic episode, and the twelve-year-old was off-loaded quickly and safely. His trip to Puerto Vallarta, Mexico, would be for another time, apparently. As would Preeya's.

She'd most definitely arrive in Vallarta some time *after* Amy's wedding ceremony—and she'd probably miss the celebration, too. She was the flight attendant with the least seniority, the most medical training, the most favors owed to her associates, and the one who'd been most present during the entire medical ordeal in-flight, so she was required to stay grounded until all the mandatory medical and liability paperwork for the airline and FTA was finished.

In Boise.

"I'll be back, say, in two hours for the forms?" the Jetta Air rep asked... *but didn't ask.*

Preeya inhaled, rallying patience and calm. "Sure thing. And when's my flight out?"

"Tomorrow, the two p.m. to Houston."

Two p.m. Three and a half hours to Houston, a minimum one-hour layover, a three-hour flight to Vallarta...*if there's a non-stop.* She'd get to Amy no earlier than, *shit,* 8:00 p.m.?

Preeya procrastinated making the call to Amy. An image of her friend's far-off fist wringing out Preeya's heart muscle in her chest made it hard to catch a full breath. And honestly, she was strangely disappointed. Amy's extravagant shindig—and the perfect distraction from her father's matrimonial joke—might have even been fun. Reuniting with college friends, laughing, dancing, and drinking—which she'd have kept *light*, the mere thought of vodka in the guest room sent shivers up her spine. She sighed then pinched the bridge of her nose.

And shit. It dawned on her that she now had her time-off request solidified, flights set. Three days in Mexico with no one there she'd know when she arrived. Amy and Darren would be on their honeymoon cruise already, and everyone else would also be long gone. She'd have to hit the beautiful beaches and sites on her own. *Solo.* Chills drifted up her neck.

She swallowed and looked across the lobby of the oh-so-glamorous Boise Inn.

Where she was *not* alone.

The Jetta Air representative stood there grinning from ear to ear, a proud glimmer in her eye—what a happy little delegator.

And sitting at Preeya's three o'clock with a different kind of pride—yes, a justified yet modest, subdued pride—was Dr. Ben Trainer. He'd also been asked to stay in Boise—the airline would compensate him with a few travel vouchers for the future as thanks—as his input and medical sign-off were both necessary for the liability report.

So Boise and *Doctor* Ben—who she might just have been wrong about, but probably not. She sighed for the tenth time and bit her bottom lip. *Bright sides?* She wasn't all alone, and she wasn't in a guest room in Seattle or at a wedding in Berkeley. Yeah, there's always got to be a bright side. More of her mother's wisdom that had stuck.

Preeya zoned out the window, but from her side view caught the good doctor's smile and his simple, sweet gaze to match. She ventured a look his way, but he flicked his attention to the enormous pile of forms.

Yes, best focus on the paperwork.

Because they had only two hours. For the mountain of paperwork. And after that absurd and completely unrealistic deadline? Twenty-four hours of nothing in the nation's great potato capital.

Stick to the silver lining, Preeya, and just go with it.

Go with it, right. Go help the man get through the paperwork and then…talk to him. Like a human being. What else is there to do?

Preeya swallowed then sat forward on her seat. "Are you—"

"—so should…"

They both snickered at their simultaneous attempts, then immediately threw their gazes elsewhere. Until she felt his blazing eyes on her neck, and her checks burned. She turned her head and caught him. And he didn't flinch. He only keyed in to her gaze harder. Unrelenting.

Moments slinked by; neither looked away. Not awkward, and not necessarily hot, though something in her stomach fluttered. No, it was something else. Something lighter. A relief. One that only two people who had saved a life together seven miles above the earth could understand, know, share.

And so this was it. Just her and him, the dynamic duo, stuck in the invigorating city—*town*—of Boise, Idaho. Together for the next twenty-four hours.

*

She pulled a breath to quiet the deafening pulse in her ears—God, what was with the nerves?—then gave him a thin-lined smile. "So, starting the paperwork…"

"Yes, we should…" He took out a pair of glasses from his man-bag—she swallowed her giggle—then felt her phone at her fingertips.

Wait—what about Amy? And Gigi, especially after this morning's lecture. "Um, you know, though…I should send a few 'I'm okay' texts to family first. Who knows if this little detour made the news…then I'm all yours."

His brows floated high on his forehead and his cheeks blushed—*Jesus, all yours?* She shook her head, positive her cheeks were redder than his, while he cleared his throat and, blinking his eyes long and slow, he rubbed the top of his head. A beat passed, then he snickered, effectively breaking the *awkward*. "Yeah, good idea. Let's, uh, get our phone calls out of the way and then…get to this pile."

Preeya nodded and tore her eyes from his—again. *Text Gigi.* Yes, do that. She keyed with lightning-fast thumbs—*I'm fine. In Boise, detour. Will call you tomorrow.* Still under the man's well-maintained gaze, her pulse now in her neck, maybe even visible to her one-man audience, she was all-and-only thumbs—she watched the autocorrect's necessary magic as she tried to slow her breathing down, if only a bit.

She shifted her gaze up at him as he snapped his down—to his phone. He was now actively texting, too.

Okay—back to her device—*next, Amy.* A call, not a text. Necessary for this level of news. She shifted in her seat, squared off to the window so her voice wouldn't carry, and sighed into making her dreaded phone call.

It rang and rang and rang—not unexpected. Amy and the rest of the bridal party would be getting ready for the rehearsal dinner—until the voice mail greeting took the baton.

"Hi! This is Amy Rine, soon-to-be Mrs. Amy James." Cue the high-pitched squeals and giggles, and Preeya's eye roll then accepting grin. "Please leave a message and I'll try to get back to you before the honeymoon. Otherwise…catch ya after the fifteenth!" *Beep.*

"*Ame*, it's Pree. Just…call me back as soon as you get this. Love ya." *Love.* Knowing Amy, neither love nor a thirty-five-thousand-foot-high near-death emergency would soften the blow. Preeya pictured Amy smothered by her horrid sister slash maid of honor, and her equally horrible mother, and sighed with her eyes. A connection that Amy and Preeya shared—horrendous family members—made this detour all the worse. Preeya should have buffered her trip by an extra day at least. If she had thought about—

"So, the potato capital of the world, huh?"

Preeya looked up from her phone while her thumbs paused at her virtual keyboard, unsure what to type as a follow-up text to Amy, anyway.

"Yes, right." She licked her extremely dry lips and cracked a smile. "Potato capital."

"And when we get done with this…crap…" Ben nodded at the pile, "I hear the Annual Potato Conference is going on in town. That's why they stuck us here, at the *elegant*…Boise Inn. The real hotels are all full." He puffed out a laugh then swallowed as awkward silence ensued.

She smiled. "I guess every great root vegetable deserves a big annual celebration?"

"Right. So, after we tear through this pile, we can maybe check it out… or…" He glanced at the papers then looked over his shoulder, "we could check out the bar instead. Maybe even before we hit the pile? A quick decompressing drink?"

Preeya raised her brows at him and tilted her head. *Who's this?*

"I mean…I'm glad I skipped the drink on the plane…but I'd say that at least one drink is medically necessary at this point." He leaned forward and looked over the paper pile's horizon. "I tell ya, I've been in the middle of an Ebola epidemic in West Africa and a malaria scare in Nepal…but having an anaphylactic kid some thirty thousand feet up somehow trumped it for me. My nerves don't rattle easily, but right now a shot of alcohol is doctor ordered."

Huh. The good doctor might really be human after all…

She shifted, both heels now on the swirly brown-and-green lobby carpet. "Truth?" She leaned in too. "I was scared shitless up there. And I've had a few incidents in the air. None involving a child, though. And that mother…I was terrified for that poor woman."

He nodded and sighed as his hands moved to the top of his clean-shaven head again, as if rubbing away the anxiety of the flight—stress she'd sworn hadn't hit him at all. Then he returned his hands to his lap. "You know, it wouldn't have gone down as well without you there, by my side."

"Thanks. That's nice of you to say…but it's a fact—that the boy *wouldn't* be okay if you weren't on that flight."

"The episode might not have happened at all if *I* wasn't on that flight… I'm the one who gave the kid my shrimp dinner—without the mother being present. It was stupid of me. Absolutely moronic."

Though it was probably not the smartest move, it was well meaning. *He* seemed well meaning, all the way around. Maybe he hadn't been out to impress? A true Good Samaritan? "Well, the mother did say it had never happened before, so she would've probably said yes if she *had* been there. And…I didn't serve it to anyone else. Neither did Leena—she said there were only beef and chicken takers in first class. So maybe the shrimp was bad…in which case, it falls on the airline."

"Possible. But it wasn't his stomach. But I noticed Leena saved the shrimp leftovers in a bag for the authorities, so it'll be examined anyway."

"Right." She shifted her focus to the papers. "So…though a drink sounds good, we've still got this to deal with in now less than two hours' time." She motioned to the stack. "Should probably crush it out before the great Boise Inn bar, huh?"

He smirked and nodded, then shook his head. "Can't. I'm king of paperwork, but not even I can get through this stack without a little liquid relaxation. Not after that."

He took his glasses off—God, she hadn't realized how hot he looked with or without…*hush, Pree!*—and then he rubbed his eyes. She licked her lips again as he returned the dark frames to his face.

A handsome, regal, kind face. *And subtly sexy.*

He slapped his hands to his thighs, knocking her out of her not-subtle daze, flaring her cheeks up to wildfire temps. He seemed to graciously ignore her auto response by redirecting his gorgeous amber gaze to the infamous papers again, and then scooted forward on the chair in preparation to stand. But before he rose, he paused a beat. "Seriously, though, Preeya, I predict I'd need not just one glass but an entire bottle of something strong if you weren't with me up there. You really do have a head for emergency situations. The kid wouldn't have made it"—he retargeted her eyes with dire sincerity—"if it were just me, alone up there. Leena, Amanda…" He shook his head. "There's not a doubt in my mind." He gave a solid nod for emphasis while holding her gaze for another beat, then he stood up, steady, strong, towering over her while she stayed seated.

She licked her lips as a flood of deep…something—maybe pride?—filled and warmed her chest. His sincere words and soft smile froze her up. Speechless. And his arrogance all gone—melted away like black ice on a city street, unsure if it had even been there to start with.

He cleared his throat and held his hand out to her. "One drink. Join me. Then the forms. Please? Drinking alone…it just isn't my style."

She licked her cracked, dried lips a third time. A drink—and absolutely nothing else—was justified. Her shoulders, tight, her neck, cramped. Yes, she could for sure use some liquid relaxation. And a toast between them, maybe? Not to celebrate the Great Potato, but a shared victory in the sky.

She nodded as she collected her things. "If you're buying…okay." She snickered and took his hand. And it took her aback, how big and rough his hand was for a doctor, and how firm and dry and warm. She swallowed as she stood with his help. Meeting his gaze, she blinked a thanks, then pulled her hand away…to grasp the unruly handle of her roller bag. "It *has* been a rough, well, twenty-four hours, really."

"A rough twenty-four, huh?" he asked with a wink in his voice as he collected the huge pile of papers in his arms and then turned toward the "bar."

She nodded, remembering he'd been witness to her exit with Josh in the taxi line, but she gave him no reply. They'd be fellow saviors decompressing together, but nothing more, no need to share backstories. She *needed* to keep focused. On herself. By herself. For the foreseeable future. Searing amber eyes aside.

CHAPTER 10

S HE WAS READY to hit the bar when a phone buzzed. Her heart
sank. *Amy.*

But her screen showed blank. It was his phone from that awesome
murse of his.

He grunted and put the papers back down on the table. He grabbed
then glanced at his old-as-dirt flip phone. "Hey, I'll just be a minute. It's my
sister," he explained without her asking. "Meet you inside?"

"Sure thing." But as her words left her lips, a skeptical surge shot up
her back.

Sister, right. Why it mattered, she didn't know, but the warmth in her
chest had cooled a bit, and fast.

A drink. Get the drink. But get the papers first.

She spun around, grabbed the pile without him noticing, and left him
there in the lobby to start without him at the bar.

*

Stacy kept him on the call for too long, insisting on hearing the entire
in-flight saga.

He didn't cut her off, wasn't about to tell her he had someone waiting
for him. *A woman.* No, he couldn't say the words out loud, even. An innocent drink or not, he wasn't even going there with his sister. Stacy's response

would've made him run away from the bar as fast as his long-ass legs would carry him.

He cleared his throat as he went to gather up the papers. *Gone?* Pretty sure they were the only two souls in the hotel, he shrugged and headed to meet Preeya and assumedly the paperwork at the pathetic excuse for a bar.

He laughed out loud as he entered the rustic little lounge—Preeya was on a bar stool waving wildly. She called his name to be sure he saw her, even with no one else around except for the bartender. The three empty shot glasses in front of her—and the pile of forms on a table behind her—helped explain the shift in his in-flight medical assistant's mood. She *was* petite but muscular—no skinny waif, for certain. Still, one shot would animate someone her size in that short a time, let alone three shots.

He nodded and continued toward her.

"Dr. Ben, over here!" *Okay, got it.* "Ben!" He smirked at the bartender and waved at them both.

Ben. Hmm. How strange it was to hear his first name spoken out loud. Beyond the brief conversations with Stanton and his sister, he hadn't had anyone call him Ben in just over a year. He was Dr. Trainer abroad and to staff and patients. And he liked the clinical objectivity. He liked not being "Ben" to anyone for a while.

Also strange and out of character for him was that he'd made it a point to this stranger—even before she assisted him in saving a life today—that she call him *Ben.*

"Earth to Ben…or more like *Boise* to Ben." She laughed. "Did you?"

"Sorry. Did I…what?"

"Want a double or just a wimpy single shot, good doctor?"

He smiled then looked at the bartender instead of at her damned bewitching eyes. "A double, please." Then he mustered the strength to return her gaze. "Why not? I'm game. Back in the day, I passed my exams on no sleep *and* a case of beer," he lied. Her disbelieving glance and single raised brow said she saw right through him. "Okay, so no, I haven't ever done that." He shook his head and laughed. "But I can sure as hell finish this small stack of documentation on a double shot. Well…pretty damn sure." He winked at her. *Jesus, man…what is with you?*

"I actually finished most of the pile while you were on your call. There are a few I can't do—medical professionals only—but the rest wasn't too bad at all."

Huh—gorgeous and diligent.

Ben, man, stop. And keep cool.

Right. He swallowed then grabbed the pile, checked for surface spillage on the bar top, and seeing none, plopped the papers down and hopped up onto a stool.

"Wow, you really attacked this. Was my call that long?" he asked, thumbing through the stack as the bartender set a double shot in front of him.

"Yeah, or I work fast. Or both," she said through a giggle and a wink. "I hadn't realized how bad I needed a drink…which I used as the carrot to finish the papers. But sorry I didn't wait for you."

He nodded and raised his drink to her. "No worries, and cheers," then he threw it back and grunted as the icy-hot vodka poured through him.

She giggled, a next shot in her hand, gotten as if by magic. She lifted her glass. "To shrimp safety!" then pounded the drink back.

He cracked up then, his laugh deeper and louder than he'd heard it in… so long. The drink, the flight, the outlet…the company. "Yes, to safe shrimp."

Then she broke out laughing, for certain from the fourth shot hitting her already saturated bloodstream, because what he said just wasn't that funny. But it didn't matter. *This*, whatever this was, felt really…good.

Preeya wound down then grinned, wide-eyed. *God, those eyes, just too much.* "So, how's the…sister?"

"Oh, she's fine, thanks. Your family?"

She scoffed. "*My family…*" She pulled out a fast, wide smile—but her sarcasm and sadness weren't missed. "They're all good. Thanks."

A buzzing noise from the bar counter stole their attentions.

Her phone this time.

"Gotta take this."

He nodded. "Of course."

He couldn't help but follow her with his eyes until she was out of sight. He shook his head, then refocused on the paperwork that needed his signatures. Which he needed to do before drinking another drop. He moved off the bar stool and took the papers back down to the clean two-top table.

And, God, what had he even been thinking? Official medical papers at a bar counter? *Jesus.* He couldn't risk anything at this point. Any signature he put down professionally should be from a clean and sober state. The last thing he needed was for this woman, as beautiful and as sweet as she seemed, to make mention that he'd downed a double shot at 4:00 p.m. He really shouldn't even be in the bar with the documents—he could've done them in the lobby.

The bartender cleared his throat. "Another double for you, Doctor?"

The loose and limber feeling taking over his body felt awesome. And yes, he wanted another double—more loose and slack and ease.

But maybe it wasn't the shot that he craved. "In a few minutes, I think. Just gotta get through these signatures."

*

"I'm so sorry. God, can you believe the timing of this shit?" she said to Amy over the semi-clear connection.

"Come on, Pree! There's not even some four-connection flight you can catch?"

"No, sweetie. I tried everything, believe me. The soonest I can get out of here is tomorrow afternoon. By the time I get into PV, you'll have already left for your honeymoon cruise."

Silence. Then a whimper. "Well," she sniveled, no longer holding back tears, "at least the boy's okay. I guess if my main bridesmaid's gonna miss my wedding, it better be to save some kid's life." Amy laughed through her emotion.

"Hey, I can already picture how dream-come-true perfect you'll be tomorrow, going down that aisle, and since I'm picturing it, it's like I'm already there. Always, right?"

"Always..." she blubbered into the phone.

"I love you, *Ame*. Just focus on your day, your wedding, and your honeymoon!" she said, trying to lighten the mood.

"Okay, Pree. Love you, too."

"Call if you need. I'm stuck here in hell, I mean, in Boise," she said through her forced laughter, though it was turning out to be not so hellish at all. "Need to vent or bitch about your sister, your mother, whoever, whatever, I'm here—your remote bridesmaid service...okay?"

"Yes, okay. Bye, Pree," Amy whispered, then ended the call.

Preeya sighed. Amy'd been more understanding, yet more disappointed than angry—which kind of hurt worse—than Preeya had expected. Her heart sunk. But she knew Amy'd be fine. No one was more supportive than Darren. She'd be in good hands. *Amy's in very good hands.*

And that thought sent a tinge of regret up her neck. Maybe some jealousy to go with it? She could have had that steady support. With Evan. If she hadn't backed out, quit him for the possibility of someone or something better. *Better?* Like quick-time Josh? *Jesus.*

She quickly shoved *that* entire topic back down deep. She couldn't even think on it. She'd do as she'd planned, put it all off until she got down to Vallarta, to the sun and beach.

Oh, God...alone.

But not alone yet. Ben and more shots—tequila, not Josh-night vodka—awaited her. A safe-enough distraction to pass the time. Yeah, she could work with Dr. Ben for the next few hours, then she'd crash hard in an adequate bed in a semi-decent hotel room in this Boise Inn. Worlds better than last night. She shuddered. Yeah, she'd have no trouble falling asleep tonight. Adding today's adrenaline rush from the flight and the start to a good tequila buzz, she'd crash good and hard, no doubt.

*

He looked up from signing the last form, and there she was.

"Ready? Shots are waiting," she said anxiously.

He smiled. "Yeah, almost." He scratched out his signature at the bottom of the current page and flipped to the next. "Hey, so, out of curiosity, how extensive is a flight attendant's medical training, really?" Leena, the head flight attendant, had been so flustered it just made him wonder. While on the other hand, Preeya had been so grounded, focused, capable, "on it."

"The basics, of course. And annual re-certs. But, you know, we don't have medical incidents too often." She knocked on the wooden bar counter. "Take Leena. She's been an FA for some twenty years, and this was her first major incident." She paused in thought. "And here I thought I was getting into the most chill and fun job ever." She snorted. "After pre-med undergrad and then a year in the MD Program at Stanford, I dropped out. Just too much *serious* for me."

"Wow." He nodded slowly while processing this new information. A new side to this intriguing woman. "Huh." He collected the forms from the table. "And now…a flight attendant?"

No answer. Just a quick glance before she turned to the bar for her next shot, which had actually been *his* next shot, and without waiting for him to join her, she shrugged and slammed the liquid back.

The sudden shift in her mood, undeniable.

Maybe from his question?

Yes, dumbass.

Noted.

"It's four thirty and the Jetta Air rep will be back at five. Let me go bring these docs to the front desk, then I'll resume the shot-a-thon." He pushed his chair back and stood, holding the pile of papers to his chest. Keeping the clear separation between the docs and the liquor—while giving Preeya some space and time to unwind again—were both good ideas.

He glanced at her and smirked as she brought yet another shot to her lips.

She jutted out her chin. "Hey, I'm not on the clock," she blurted defensively.

"I'm not…saying anything. I'll, uh, be back to join you…if there's any left."

Through his teasing laughter she glared at him for a beat, then pursed her lips. He'd surprised her with his flippant comment. She clearly didn't know how to take him. "You know flight attendants only get paid when the doors are closed and the plane engines are on?"

"I did *not* know that." She was getting sloshed.

And he was getting anxious and hot and excited and short of breath. "Be back."

*

He made his way to the front desk counter where the young clerk stood smiling—a wide, toothy smile. Was she eyeing him? God, she must have been no older than twenty. Maybe younger? Before he'd left his private practice after Jamie got sick, he'd had pediatric patients in this girl's demographic. "May I have a large envelope, miss?"

"Sure," she said, licking her light-pink lip-glossed lips at him. "Here you are." She slipped him a brown envelope and tilted her head as if waiting for more.

"Thank you." Avoiding eye contact, he quickly put the forms inside, clasped it, and asked, "Clear tape?"

"Here you go." Her right eye twitched.

Was that an attempted wink? *Ugh.*

She placed a tape dispenser on the counter, keeping her hand on it so that when he pulled it to him, their fingers touched. Her brows lifted while his furrowed. And his hand retreated that instant.

"Uh, excuse me, please. I'll be right back…thanks." And he beelined to the bar.

Preeya's back was to him as he approached. "Hey…"

She turned to him, the back of her hand moving across her mouth. "Sorry, I had to do it. But you'll catch up," she said, then smiled with a glint of mischief in her eyes.

He shook his head at her, then got to his point. "Here. I need you to take this to the front desk. Please."

"But you were just there…"

"Yeah, but it's safer if you do it."

She squinted at him, obviously wanting more detail.

"The desk clerk...she's a baby. And she's absolutely hitting on me. Just go for me, explain who's picking it up, and when. I'm literally nauseous right now. I can't have a prepubescent girl giving me any type of looks...*God.*" Even though there were no other guests in the place to play witness, he was sure there were cameras in the hotel lobby. Yes, the court case had made him more than paranoid, but his medical license was already on the line and he couldn't possibly handle any more scandal.

She smirked, then took the envelope. "Okay, but wait for me on that drink."

"Oh, like you waited for me?" he busted her back. Where was his bold new attitude coming from? The prior shots?

In a blink, Preeya had gone and come back again. "She *is* a pretty little thing."

"God, please." He shook his head. He raised his double shot high in the air. "Cheers, to young lives saved."

"To young lives." They clinked their doubles and threw them down their throats.

*

She counted the glasses in front of them for damage control. Three doubles in for him. Four for her. "Do you think the agent came for the papers yet?" he asked, his speech only slightly slurred. But he was too tall to be affected that fast, right? She snickered in disbelief.

She looked at her watch, shook her head at herself—*stupid watch, again*—and then pulled out her cell phone. "Four fifty-eight. No, not yet," she said. "You don't drink often, do you?"

"No. On my excursions, crazy homemade moonshine-type stuff is just too risky. Gut-sickening or not, though, I'm on the straight and narrow most of the time. I feel like, well, I'm always *on*, you know. What if...what if someone needs me?"

She smirked at him. "Do you like to be needed?" she asked, her head cocked to the side.

"Not like that. I just, well, I feel responsible. Hell, what if I'd taken that drink you'd offered me on the plane?"

"True." But God, one drink? He was like a human tree. "But if you drank more, your tolerance would go up. And the rod stuck up your ass would probably, you know, come down...and out...I think." She broke out laughing at his expense, almost hysterically.

"Hold on now. I do *not* have a pole up my ass!"

"I said a rod, not a pole. But either way, don't you? You even walk like you do. So serious, so—"

"On duty?"

"Yeah! On duty."

"Well, I just told you...I am. I always feel like I'm *on duty!*"

"That's *exactly* why I left med school. Well, one reason, at least. I couldn't waste my precious moments on earth living like that."

"Oh, precious time on earth spent helping people is a waste?"

She paused. And glared. Then a beat passed, until the Jetta Air representative approached. And cleared her throat. "Hello there…"

Ben turned on his stool and blinked slowly. "Hello." Preeya thought he sounded very composed, doctor-like. "We'd left the envelope at the front desk for you. Did you get it?"

"Yes, thank you. Just wanted to hand you your boarding passes for tomorrow afternoon's flight, and your future travel vouchers, Dr. Trainer. Thanks again from Jetta Air."

"Not a problem, really," he said, taking the items from the woman's hand.

"Preeya, please watch your intranet email for any follow-up questions we or the authorities may have."

"Yes, of course," she answered dutifully, covering her mouth, her breath, with her hand. But why the hell did she care what this woman thought? She was twenty-five years old. And had helped save a life today. Why didn't she deserve a damn drink or so? And again, not on the clock.

"Good, then...safe flights tomorrow," the agent said with a wave and left them.

Ben eyed the bartender nodding at his empty glass and resumed their conversation. "So, anyway, you're a flight attendant now. Helping people that way?"

She grunted. "Yeah, I wanted to take life less seriously. What's wrong with that? You only live once. And I still do get to make a difference, like today…" She'd caught the judgment in his tone.

"And you're waiting for, what, a certain age to start the serious portion of your life? When you get to help people not by accident, not on a fluke, but for real?"

"Maybe." She looked down at her empty glass. "I just want to be completely ready if or when I ever choose to…settle." Because, God, what she feared more than anything was settling.

"Settle?"

Not in the mood for an argument, she revised. "I meant *settling down.* Planting myself somewhere." She felt a hard knot gather in her throat.

"Huh…interesting. So, in other words, you're saying you may never be ready to take life seriously?" His amber eyes were piercing hers with too much force. Too much intensity. And too much glaring truth.

Wow, things were just getting too damn serious. Third-degree-from-Dad serious, even though Ben's delivery was a drunken ramble. Who the hell did he think he was?

She slammed another shot back that she hadn't even realized the bartender had filled for her. Then she looked at Ben hard—his deep worry lines between his eyebrows, around his eyes; the peppered gray in his gruff—and yes, sexy-as-hell—five o'clock shadow. He couldn't have been beyond his mid-thirties.

"Hey, Ben…how old are you, anyway?"

"How old am I? Is this sheer avoidance, or…"

"Just, how old are you? You're acting like my father, so I think I should know just how many years of wisdom you've got over me or under him to be taking such a lofty stance. This line of questioning is bordering on daddy déjà vu," she said, punctuating the last words with raised brows for dagger-like emphasis.

"First off, I'm thirty-two. And second, I am *not* trying to be your father—"

"Oh, you don't wanna be my daddy?" She smirked, a flintiness that surprised even her. She was solid mush—her ninth and tenth ounce of vodka just hitting her gut—and, damn it, consequential shock waves hitting her core. And while he stared at her in awe, she couldn't stop her mouth from running on. "Hey, do you shave your head because you're losing your hair? When did it start...and was it from stress? Or was it genetic...from your maternal grandfather's side, I think? I remember that's the dominant gene for male-pattern baldness...right?"

She watched his face turn grim. He looked down at his empty glass just as the bartender came to fill it up again. "Thanks, man."

Then Ben cleared his throat and turned his head to look her square in the face. A glower that made her breathing halt. "I shave it. Easier for me to manage in the field." He slammed his drink back. "Sorry if I'm not more like your *daddy*."

A direct hit.

*

Had she felt the icy tidal wave? Goddamn good if she had. He'd shaved his head when Jamie went through her first round of chemo. And he kept it that way all the way through. Now it was a ritual he relied on. To honor her. To keep her memory close.

The next double he downed made the room spin. Hot, delicious, floating relief. He spun on his stool, or was he stationary but his mind whirled? Or the Boise bar? B.B. Boise bar. He laughed, twirling, spiraling around the room with Preeya inches away. She was in his face asking him something over and over again. Until an urge spiked up his spine to stop the spinning and kiss her.

What the hell? How many shots had he actually had?

Her hands took hold of his face. Was she going to kiss *him*?

"Are you okay, though? Seriously." The blue-to-violet-eyed beauty spoke slow and clear, her words poignant. And loud. Her breath, vodka and sweetness. "Ben, come on, tell me...are you?"

"Yes, Preeya. I am okay. Are you...Middle Eastern, East Indian, or...

maybe Nepalese? I went to Nepal. *Are* you Nepalese? That's my guess. Either way, you're like a princess, that's what you are. A *kumari*. An Asian princess. From the sky."

"Oh, man, are *you* gone. Can I get a bottled water please, John?"

The bartender tapped the counter. "Right away."

How'd she know his name? Did she guess? He didn't look like a John. *But I don't look like a Benji.* That's what Jamie used to call him. He had hated it. But missed the hell out of it now. *Benji.*

"No, Benji's not *gone*, Preeya and John. I'm really here. Right here in front of you." He felt like his words were clear, although slightly slow in falling from his mouth. "But water sounds good, too. So, what are you then?"

"What am I?"

"Your ancestry, your background?"

"Oh, um, my mother was—"

"Was? Did she die?"

"No, or, actually…I don't really know." He watched her eyes glance up to the ceiling in thought. "Whatever, um, she was or is a European mutt? And my father is FOB Indian, some thirty years ago. He's actually an MD, and an asshole. No offense."

"None taken. Wait, why would *I* take offense?"

"Because he's an asshole doctor."

"Are they mutuallistically exclusive?"

"Do you mean *mutually*?"

"That's what I said: mutualintrinsically executive."

"Yes?"

"Yes? You're asking? Or yes, they are. They go hand in hand or not?" His voice turned serious. He could hear his near-harsh tone, but he was trying to get down to logic. And he seriously didn't want to lose his train of thought, because God, it—the thought train—was flying by at a thousand miles a minute.

"Yes, they are linked, interdependent. He is a money-grubbing asshole doctor."

"Not possible. There are too many types of doctors, and people. What does he practice?"

"Cosmetic surgery. Tits, asses, lips."

"Oh."

"Yeah, I told you…asshole doctor."

"Come on, Preeya…you know that not all doctors, not even all plastic surgeons, are scum. Many help burn victims, cleft palates. I am…*was* a pediatric surgeon. Now I can't be an asshole and work with kids, right?"

"Actually…you can. I've not met a doctor who isn't a greedy, unfeeling prick. My dad's just the worst of them," she said sighing into her hands. Then she picked her head up to look at him. "Wait, you *were* a pediatric surgeon?"

"Long story. Gave up my practice…needed a change, so I've been with Doctors Without Borders for the past year. But my point is, there are plenty of assholes who aren't…aren't…shit, I forgot my train!"

"Your train?" Her eyes brightened. "Are you sure it's your train you're missing? Or could it be your plane?" She laughed at her quip and slapped his arm. Hey, whatever made her mood flip back to fun, because, God it felt amazing to be…silly. Silly and stupid and happy. He hadn't had anything but *solemn* and *serious* for ages—decades, maybe.

No, Ben, just a couple of years.

Two impossibly intense years.

Snap out of it, Ben.

Okay. He tapped his empty glass and the very attentive hotel bartender quickly appeased him. No risk of patrons driving drunk, Ben guessed.

Ben pounded the shot.

"Wait, I remember!"

"What?" Preeya tilted her head at him. So goddamn gorgeous.

He shook his head to re-remember. "*Assholes*! Assholes who aren't doctors and doctors who aren't—"

"Pilots!" she yelled, flinging pretzels—from a bowl she'd apparently been hogging—all over the floor and counter.

They both cracked up, Ben almost sliding off his bar stool while watching Preeya pluck up each pretzel on the bar and shove them into her mouth.

"Not sanitary—at all!"

She rolled her eyes at him with her cheeks full and lumpy. God, she was too exquisite and adorable…and judgmental as hell. The doctor bias, in particular, he aimed to abolish.

"You do know what I'm saying, right? About doctors?"

She nodded and mumbled something impossible to make out.

"You know that *I'm* a doctor who *isn't* an asshole, right?"

She nodded again, this time with her eyes lit up, glowing almost. Then, as a giggle built up in her chest, she covered her mouth so pretzel crumbs wouldn't fly out. But he got her answer. He knew she understood.

He also knew that behind her drunken laughter and glowing eyes, he saw real and raw pain. What had her father done to hurt her so badly? What sharp thorn lay festering inside the heart of this bright and vigorous woman?

But the thought vanished the next moment when his stomach twisted in a tight knot then morphed into floating, airy, nausea. He held his torso to anchor himself.

"Here"—she opened the water the bartender had handed her and held it up to his lips—"drink."

Her hand was hardly steady and she laughed—some drops dribbled out the corner of his mouth until he grabbed the bottle from her and finished the entire thing in one long swig.

"Wow."

"Yeah. I needed that." Then he belched. "Oh, excuse me."

She giggled, shaking her head at him. "You really just don't let loose, do you?"

"And you really don't know how smart and stunning and sexy you are." His cheeks burned up. And he didn't care. He burped again, excused himself, and then groaned as the floaty feeling returned, flooding his gut. "I, uh, think I need a bed," he said, sliding off his bar stool.

But she wedged herself under his arm before his imminent crumble to the floor. "Hold on there," she said with a grunt, obviously unable to hold him. She helped him square his feet and stood him up straight. All the while, he stared at her and didn't try to hide it.

He knew he needed *sleep* in a bed, but God, he wanted her. With him. For more than company. But did she want that, too? With him? And how would he ask her? How did this work? It had been so long. Before Jamie. *Jamie*. What exactly did he think he was doing?

Then a smile spread across her brilliant face, her head tilted slightly to one side. "I'm just gonna help you up to your room. Come on, Dr. Ben, let's go."

CHAPTER 11

HE'D HEARD RUMORS of how forward—hell, how aggressive and promiscuous and forward—air hostesses were, but he'd never come face-to-beautiful-face with one. Like this. In all his travels. Three countries in a year.

But then again, he most definitely had not been looking.

Or was he reading into things? Maybe she was only helping him walk to his hotel room, like she'd said?

But what if she wasn't *just* walking him? What if she was coming inside with him? Helping him to bed. And joining him.

A wave of nausea and guilt tsunamied in his gut.

Chill out, Ben. You're just drunk. And queasy. And nervous.

A lump had formed in his throat, keeping him from swallowing successfully. His palms were sweaty; did she feel that? Because she was holding one of his clammy hands in hers, guiding him. God, she must've.

What would happen when they got to the room? Damn it, he got married so young. Jamie, and only Jamie. Fuck, what was the etiquette? The *how* of *this*?

She took the key from his other clammy hand. Okay, she's just going to help him with the key.

Right? Or no?

Was she staying? Because he wanted that. For her to stay. So badly he wanted that.

But as they got closer to the room, he didn't. He couldn't. The guilt had crossed the threshold to code-red status. He didn't deserve pleasure. He deserved nothing.

But, God, he could use the release. How long had he been so uptight, so visibly tense, even to the blunt assessment of this stunning stranger who knew nothing of his history, his loss?

His loss. How could he do this? To Jamie, to her memory? But she'd made him promise to move on. To live. And this woman holding his sweaty, quaking hand was leading him. He probably wouldn't have been able to walk without her.

Shit, would he even be able to perform if he couldn't handle walking one foot in front of the other? He'd been out of practice for so long—being intimate, not walking…well, walking drunk, too. Anyway, it had been more than two years since he'd been intimate. Two fucking years.

Two years since he'd made love to his wife.

As soon as she'd been diagnosed, all the way up to now. Nothing.

What the fuck was he thinking? That he could swing this? Getting off with his right hand a few times a month wasn't near enough to be ready for this woman. This *caliber* woman. Preeya, with the celestial eyes.

"I'm feeling a little—" He paused to hold his stomach again with his one free hand. And…because he swore he'd heard a soft whisper and it freaked him the hell out. Then that hushed voice became a shout as quick as a switch. He glanced at Preeya who definitely hadn't heard it. She just continued leading him down the long, depressingly brown-and-green carpeted Boise hotel corridor.

Boise? He had never been to Boise.

Man the hell up—the voice again, stern, sharp. The quality and tone, not *his*. It was low, and it was positively…female. Familiar. From that morning, with Stanton. But closer this time. And loud. Ear-jamming loud.

Then, *Buck up, Ben!*

Jesus…*Jamie?*

He looked at Preeya again.

He could tell she hadn't heard it. She still focused on the hall ahead. Not on him and his internal *crazy*. *Thank God.*

And when she stopped short—they'd apparently reached his room—she looked up at him with those eyes, lavender and deep and somehow softer and sadder and sweeter than they'd been since the taxi line, then security, then pillows…

And now he was certain her eyes were also most definitely wanting.

*

He leaned down as his free hand moved up from his stomach to her face. He slowly let his lips meet hers. Only his lips, though. And they pressed into hers, holding back the internal, desperate, screaming need for more. And reining in the same heightened level of guilt, restraining it with all his might, he inhaled her essence.

Then he pulled back. To look at her. To be sure she still had that look in her eyes. That desire.

And, yes. It was unmistakable.

So he moved in again with his parched, unsure lips, so thirsty for hers. Her moist and tender lips—lush, sensual, waiting.

Welcoming. Her hand reached up to the nape of his neck, returning his kiss, gently dragging and caressing her lips over his. In his head and heart he felt a fluttering sense of relief and warmth and, God, the very beginnings of bliss.

Then her tongue swept in, immediately electrifying his senses. It had been such a long, sad, hopeless time.

But now, after an agonizing past, he was on fire.

While refusing to let his lips leave hers, he snagged the key card from her hand, blindly opened the door, and pulled her inside. Kissing and caressing her still, he never wanted it to end.

Firm, directed, he pulled her to him and lifted her off the floor, her toes hovering, floating across the room. Bed found, he laid her down. As if he'd just returned to his body from a long journey away, back from a black hole in space, his entire body pulsed with the energy of this woman.

"Wait."

"What? Are you all right?"

"Condom, in my purse. It's by the door."

How the hell could he have forgotten?

Because he was two years—no, fifteen years—out of that line of think-ing. And drunk off his ass. But thank the Lord that this gorgeous, fiery, intel-ligent, and forward-thinking creature had a condom in her purse. If she was a little philandering, at least she was safe about it. But he didn't want to think of her with another man. No. Now, she was with him. Only him.

He looked at her, ready and waiting for him, lying on top of the tight white duvet cover, smiling at him coyly, like a cat waving its sly tail for him to come to her. To take her.

And he was hard as steel for her.

Grab the condom and take her, then.

He swallowed back the last remnant of anxiety sticking in his throat and went to her purse. He secretly hoped that she had two condoms in it. If not more.

Woozy and sweating hot, he crouched down at her bag, nearly falling over, when his necklace, with his wedding ring, fell out from under his shirt.

It dangled. He stared.

Do it, Ben. It's okay. It is. The voice.

He swallowed and slammed his eyes shut. Up and over his head came the chain, quick, like a bandage. He clutched the chain with his gold wed-ding band in his hand, then stood—God, too fast—took three steps toward his messenger bag and slowly placed the chain into the innermost pocket. And zipped it. And exhaled hard.

Condom. Go.

Damn she was demanding, and that's just one thing he fucking loved about his wife. His late wife. And for Jamie, and really only for Jamie, had he always done what he'd been told. He stumbled back to the purse. Of Preeya's. The vibrant and amazing woman waiting for him on the hotel room bed.

*

She could kick herself for breaking her new rule—self-focus only. But his pure, unadulterated focus on pleasuring her was just...unreal. Yes, she could justify this—a doctor-prescribed and customized therapy session of cathartic self-focus.

Then add the good doctor's stamina—and he was sloppy drunk, too. Men under the influence, in her experience, usually took forever to come, if they even came at all before surrendering to sleep, and all the while she could have been a hole in a wall for all they knew, pounding and thrusting away.

But not Dr. Ben. He was there. All there. And detail-oriented. Masterfully precise in his direction, his pacing and positioning. Like a good, attentive doctor, he cared for her, all the way in and out of her. His fine, throbbing length, and what he did with it, took her breath away. Over and over and over again.

And adding the other things he did to her while pumping her to the peak again and again—she was undone. The twirling and pressing of her sensitive bud, and the caressing of her slick lips with his surgeon hands.

This man, she thought, could take as long as he damn well pleased. Because five orgasms to none—none yet, though she intended to make him wail by the end—she was in ecstatic bliss and was inhumanly ready for more. Not sore, not tired or spent, just energized and delirious with...*something*.

Was it joy?

Joy was the only word that fit.

And God, how *he* fit. So fucking well, he fit in her.

"So, the flight's at two?" he panted, moving his mouth down her bodice.

"Yeah, in the afternoon," she added, writhing under his delicious control.

"Oh, God, that's good. Just so, so damn good," he said as he nibbled above her hipbone, making her squeal. "We can do this all the way to noon p.m., then."

She laughed at his totally drunken state as she went to look at her wrist for the time, but caught herself—and her phone was too far away. Her eyes scanned the room. The neon-red alarm clock on the other nightstand read 1:00 a.m. "You can go for fourteen hours? I mean, one to noon...nine, no ten hours. Hell, whatever, I'm game."

"I feel like I could go nine or ten or fourteen hours." He looked at her face from between her thighs. "It's been...a good long while for me...doing *this*." He sucked the soft part of her inner thigh just below—and so close to—her aching core. "I'd say I've got some catching up to do." He smiled, then refocused on her tensed thigh, giving her the most sensual and sweet plowing of kisses she'd felt—maybe ever. "But I'll need to maybe...break. To eat," he said, smiling up at her again before switching to her other thigh, again teasing her to the edge of madness.

She threw her head back in total elation.

How was he doing it? Making her forget everyone and everything. No Josh, no Evan, no fucked-up family or flights or failures or fears.

There was only Dr. Ben Trainer and his powerful focus on pleasing her. His energy and attention. His ravenous hunger for her, and for at least right now, only for her.

*

The experience in her, with her, over her, was so different, so immensely, amazingly different, that the guilt had just subsided, drifted away. He felt freer than maybe ever before.

For what seemed like hours, they moved together in perfect rhythm, like ocean waves brewing before-then-during-then-after a storm. Again and again—crashing pleasure with easing calm in between.

He hardly knew this woman, this exquisite being, but their bodies were intimate and in such sync—as if they'd known each other for all time.

He recognized something in her, a deep-seated need that he was all too familiar with. The same need to flee, to fly, to run—to escape at all costs. Medical school to...flight attendant training? Why? She was so bright and strong and grounded. What the hell was she running from? What had caused that lingering pain he'd spotted behind her ocean-deep eyes?

He swept her hair away from her face and kissed her cheek, her bare shoulder, then the crook of her neck. She lay tight against the length of his body, her deep and sated breath soothing him to join her in half sleep. His top arm ran along her curves, his fingertips drawing figure eights on the soft, taught skin of her hip. His other arm went under, up, and around her, draped across her middle like a sash, her breasts spilling over his forearm, creating a spectacular tangle of mocha and cream. Such contrast and complement at once. He breathed her in while sinking deeper into the bed, into the pillow, and into the fit of their bodies.

The euphoria from their sensual dance maintained its vibrancy even after the buzz from the liquor had worn off. And with the radiance of their connection came a sense of clarity. He could now let it all sink in. That this was the first time since his wife's passing that he'd stopped running. Paused for a breath. His own life's marathon had become a compulsion, one that had taken over without him realizing.

He took her top hand and brought it to his lips. He kissed her knuckles one at a time through a muted laugh. How strange and lucky and good for him and for her—two marathon escape artists in peak escapist condition and form—to crash into each other, head-long, on a flight to Houston, Texas, via Boise, Idaho, the Great American Potato Capital of the World.

He pressed her hand to his cheek. "Glad we skipped the potato conference," he whispered.

Through her half sleep she hummed in response.

He didn't aim to wake her but, well, yes, he did. No longer under the influence of anything but the raw energy and comfort between them—the *fit* of them—he began a new round of kisses, one to each finger, then down the length of her hand, her wrist.

She moaned.

He parted his lips, his teeth, his mouth, and took her thumb in, surrounding and sucking and nibbling it.

He heard her swallow then sigh long and sweet.

His cock became solid hard desire again.

He closed his eyes, relishing her taste, her scent and sound. And when he opened his eyes again, she was facing him, eyes wide. Needy again, too.

*

Sleep had been conquered by limitless desire. True desire. No more alcohol buzzing through her now, just pure and unadulterated want. *Want* for this man.

And she sensed his raw, unaffected need, too. His soft caress and tight hold of her, his warm breath and rolling vibe, his solid steel pulsating against her thigh—God, her heart and head and core were ready to burst. "I want more, Doctor Ben."

He growled deep down in his throat and gave her a wicked smile. "*I* want more, Preeya Patel." His eyes locked on to hers with unrelenting angst, he slid his hand up her cheek, down her throat, across her collarbone to her shoulder. "All of you." He pushed her shoulder down to the bed, flat on her back, then moved over and down her. "Every last drop of you." Her anguishing arousal clenched and pooled with need for him. Ready to give him everything, every last drop. Like he wanted.

And so the master surgeon got back to working his miracles. He and his delectable tongue whirled and sucked and spun her into a river of release she'd never dared to imagine before.

"Be in me. Come with me, Ben."

"Not yet." He dipped his tongue deep into her sex and pressed into a hot point. Her hips thrust up hard. He moaned with pleasure—God, that got her so much wetter—then he lifted his head. "See, I've got a lot of work to do down here before I leave the operating theater," he said in a British accent.

She laughed and heaved and wriggled as he did what he wanted to her. What she apparently needed, so said her doctor.

And round after torrential round, his fingers, his lips and tongue, and finally his magic, maneuvering steel dipping in and out of her, too—yet still insistent on his own delayed gratification—brought her to higher and higher peaks. Loftier peaks meant farther and deeper falls into endless bliss. God, he drove her to the brink and back again.

After countless releases—she felt so goddamn selfish—she had nothing left in her to release—no tension, no worry, no question. All that remained was that same joy he'd injected her with when their lovemaking had begun hours ago. Her body seemed to permanently hover at that joyous peak now.

But there was more pleasure to be had. *His* pleasure. She needed him to explode and shake inside her again. She craved his satisfaction—satisfaction gotten by her, from her, in her.

*

Their eyes were locked—their bodies, too—and as she rode him, rocked him hard and deep from above, he went to a new realm, a new stratosphere.

"You like this, Doctor? Or…" She slowed her rolling hips and brought her breasts topped with her dark-cherry nipples, down to his chest then mouth while sliding back and forth along his solid and trembling length.

"Oh God, yes. Like that. Slow like that." Long and slow and forever.

But he couldn't hold on *forever*, though he'd give anything to work that miracle. "I'm coming, Preeya." He gripped her ass so hard she squealed. He grunted and grunted again, and again with each constricting, convulsing release. Inside her, surrounded and devoured by her tight, hot embrace.

*

His eyelids showed heavy after they'd flowed together a third and *maybe* final time for the night. *Maybe.* She looked at him and giggled, not quite believing the level he'd taken her to, she'd taken him to, they'd taken each other to.

It shocked her when she looked up at the red neon clock. 3:00 a.m. Two hours had gone by in a fantastic, dreamlike blink of an eye.

And now Ben held her in his arms. He didn't make it fourteen hours, but he definitely made her night—no, her year. Who was she kidding? He'd blown her decade—her entire sexual lifespan was rocked by this man. Practically a stranger, but too familiar for her to put into words.

Words. At the bar. Words and judgments had been spoken and made and unleashed, and all very likely true. Brave, true words from this *doctor*, this tall stranger, this man with the forever-sun in his eyes.

CHAPTER 12

S HE COULDN'T SEE the clock in her current and extremely delectable position—spooning and safe in Ben's grasp. And even though the soft sunlight creeping under the blackout drapes gave her a general gauge, well, based on yesterday's guest room surprise, she needed to check just in case. She shifted only slightly as not to wake him. But the neon digital numbers were still halved from her vantage point. She lifted up onto her elbow so she could see over Ben, onto his nightstand. 10:00 a.m.

Okay, plenty of time.

Her eyelids sank back down like a cozy blanket, her body still entwined with his, at home in a hotel room, as if they had been there forever.

He stirred then smiled, a slight hum escaping his lips.

"*Mmmm,* Jamie—I could lie here for days and days with you in my arms."

Jamie?

A quivering scowl swallowed her smile as her heart rammed her rib cage.

Mmm-hmm, his "sister." *Right.*

Goddamn prick.

And fuck me! Too good to be true usually was. Her chest heaved with silent regret and disdain and more sinking disappointment. To let herself go wild about this man. Ugh, she could just strangle herself.

How had she let this happen? A married man? A married *passenger* man.

And a doctor? *The* doctor from *her flight*! Medical report cosigners. She'd crossed so many lines she could hardly count—or breathe.

Too much and too depressing.

She rolled out of the bed, sly and stealthy, and threw on just enough clothing for the quick escape to her hotel room down the hall. She found her room key, tucked her panties, bra, and shoes under her arm, and slid out, shutting his hotel room door behind her with the quietest, most anticlimactic click of the latch.

*

Brushing his teeth, he *didn't* go over it again in his head for the fifth time that morning—her leaving his arms, his bed, his room before he woke. And after eating breakfast alone in the barren bar, he didn't analyze the *why* or *what* behind the lack of handwritten message on the pillow, the counter, the bathroom mirror, or…maybe in his shoe? And no answer when he knocked at her door or called her room.

But by noon when she wasn't down in the lobby to catch the minivan to the mini airport, he wasn't angry or self-conscious that she'd left him cold. No, he was worried for her, that she'd miss the flight. And maybe that he'd done something, said something, or hadn't?

But they'd connected. In his gut he knew they'd connected. So something had to have happened. She left some message or note of explanation at the front desk. No doubt.

Reluctant but compelled, he went to the front desk clerk with the dangerously flirty eyes. She leaned forward as he approached, her cleavage too pronounced for his comfort. *Jesus, this generation…*

"Yes, hello. Can you try calling room one twenty-three? Preeya Patel should be down here by now for the airport shuttle."

"Ms. Patel has already checked out, sir." The girl's voice was too breathy for the context.

What the hell? Had the airline rerouted her? Yes, that must've been it, and she just didn't want to wake him. And now he knew he'd missed a note with her phone number somewhere in his room, or maybe even with

Miss Young Thing here, and she was withholding Preeya's message, playing with him.

"What time did she check out?"

The girl looked at her screen. "At ten thirty, it says here, sir."

"Any messages left by her, for me? I'm in room—"

"One eighteen. Yes, sir, I mean Dr. Trainer, I know," she said with a wink. God, this was bordering on awkward. She started typing, shaking her head from side to side. "No, Doctor. No messages. But is there anything I can get for you?" Head tilted, lashes batting.

He heard a car pull up to the automatic entrance doors, which slid open on cue. "No. Thank you, though." He placed his room key card on the counter and sighed. "Take care, now." He took himself and his roller bag out to the shuttle, confused and fighting disappointment. No message. No number. What the hell? What the hell had he missed?

*

When her flight team arrived, a proud smirk took over her face.

"Kell!" Jess from San Diego called over her shoulder. "Do you see what I see?"

"I'm not sure, Jess. It looks like Preeya beat us here, and seems to be done with seats, carts, and, Jesus, bulkheads, too? But, you know, I had a crazy night with John from Atlanta—it could be all that leftover adrenaline flowin' through me, making me see things," Denver Kelly teased. Preeya had worked with the two enough times over her FA stint for the expected reaction.

"I can get here on time! Even early! It's not unheard of," Preeya defended with a light huff.

"Preeya, love, it really *is* unheard of. But yes, you've always been *able* to." Kelly cracked up. The tall, slender blonde swayed her narrow hips down the aisle toward her and kissed her cheek. "Good to see you, girlfriend. And thanks for hitting the check sheet for us."

True motivation be told, Preeya had done everything possible to avoid the main concourse, and the plane served as the ultimate hideout. Plus, busywork took her mind off her fury.

When she'd gotten to the airport way early, she'd had no cover at all to escape a run-in with Ben. There was no Jetta Air lounge in damned Boise, Idaho. For a couple of long hours she hid behind her book while tucked away at a back booth in the airport's one bar, figuring that he'd never gravitate to it—*if* he came looking for her, which he wouldn't because he'd already gotten what he'd wanted. So yeah, the bar was a safe bet—he'd probably revert back to *rigid and responsible* as soon as he stepped out of the hotel. Into the real world. The world where he's married or involved or whatever the fuck. *Asshole.*

Dr. Ben Trainer, just another damn cliché.

Which made *her* into yet *another* cliché. Dropout, trolley dolly, flaky fiancée, has-been groupie. *Ugh.* Now Dr. Ben's on-flight medical assistant turned off-flight side fuck.

Just, *no!*

Hey, Pree, no regrets. And live and learn—another mom-ism.

Okay, fine…learn then! Stop making the same fucking mistakes, and learn!

She'd gnashed her teeth hard realizing that waiting until Vallarta to begin her whole self-focus *thing* had been a stall tactic. *No more waiting, no more excuses.* That's when she'd stopped thinking and started moving. Through the terminal at top speed-walk-in-heels *speed.* Long before the ninety-minute mark for her shift's check-in, she'd rolled her little carry-on to her gate while praying that the aircraft would be early.

And it had been, thankfully.

So she got on board early, before the entire crew. A good start to her anti-procrastination and pro self-focus campaign.

She and Jess handled last-minute coach-class items in the back—Preeya taking an extra second to check the medi kit—while Kelly finalized her first-class preparations up front.

Dr. Ben Trainer would be in first class to Houston—if he didn't pull another Mr. Nice Guy seat swap—and so as long as Preeya kept to her section, she'd never have to see him again. Yeah, she'd be in coach while the selfless doctor, selfless lover—*selfless,* her ass—would live it up or sleep in cozy comfort after an exhilarating and exhausting night of heart-pounding, mind-blowing sex.

Chills sprinted through her, shivers exponential in degree to those from her disastrous night with Josh. She tried to shake it off, but the vibrations ran too deep. So much for Gigi's theory of the "dynamism and charisma of Preeya Patel." And so much for the existence of instinct and intuition. She really should have fucking known.

She sat in her jump seat out of view from the aisle, texted Prana, *Boring Boise, Idaho, to Houston, Texas, Love Pree*, and then hunted for her book to hide behind again.

Pulling the novel from her purse, she smiled at the bookmark, slid it to the back page, then found her spot—*Chapter 6, Her Name Matters*. Hilarious and perfect. Because no, in fact, her name didn't. Her name hadn't mattered worth a damn. *Jamie's* did.

*

"Is there a Preeya Patel on this flight? A flight attendant? Near-violet eyes?"

A few people behind him cleared their throats to move him along.

But screw them.

The tall blond attendant smiled then glanced at his boarding pass. "Yes, in fact, she is on duty in coach class. But if you could kindly take your seat now, right there in 3A, I can bring you a refreshment?"

"Um, sure, but I—"

"Please, Dr. Trainer," she whispered, her hot breath tickling his ear, "there are several guests waiting behind you."

He sighed and moved to his seat, clearing the aisle for the backup he'd created.

But how did that woman know he was *Dr.* Trainer? No title was noted on his boarding pass. Had Preeya told the flight attendant about him? And *what* about him?

Who cared? More irritating to him was that if she was on this flight, then why the early departure from the hotel? Giving her the benefit of the doubt just expired.

And denying his anger had only made it escalate in absolute value. They'd undoubtedly connected last night. Deeply. For hours. And he knew she'd stayed in his arms until at least 6:00 a.m., when he drifted awake and watched her sleep for a while before falling away again into a dream—with her in it.

The cluster of first-class folks had cleared and the flight attendant, Kelly—so read her tag—approached him. "What can I offer you to drink, Doctor?"

He smiled. "May I ask, how do you know I'm a doctor?"

"The entire Jetta Air crew knows what happened yesterday. You saved that boy's life. So amazing. Hopefully this flight will be much less dramatic." She winked and patted his hand. "So what can I get you to start this flight off right?" Wink.

Well, actually, if you can switch my seat with anyone in the back row of coach so I can talk to Preeya and find out what the fuck? "A large bottle of water will be fine," he said, needing further remedy for his underlying hangover. "And I know Preeya must be very busy, but if there is downtime for her, would you mind asking her to…well, just please ask her if…that I need to speak with her about…the medical forms we had completed yesterday."

"Sure, Doctor. I will pass along the message. But if she can't catch you on board, after we land in Houston you can grab her…if your connection isn't too tight," she said. Then she glanced at his itinerary on his tray table. "But you should be fine, as it seems you have a hefty three-hour layover there. And Preeya is part of the Puerto Vallarta crew as well. You'll have ample time to connect. If not in Vallarta, at the latest."

"Thanks very much." She'd be going to Vallarta, too? His pulse spiked in the center of his chest. Yes, he'd catch her. He had to. He'd find out what the deal was, without a doubt.

Kelly came back, placed a napkin down, then the perspiring bottle of water. But he slipped the napkin out first. "Thank you, Kelly, and…" He quickly pulled the pen from his shirt pocket, jotted his cell number down, and handed the wispy textured square to the woman, "would you please give this to Preeya just in case we somehow miss each other? It's really very important."

"Of course I will." Her lip curled at one corner while looking him up and down, then she winked again. He cringed, the front desk clerk at the Boise Inn coming to mind. He wondered if the woman would give the napkin to Preeya like he'd asked, or keep his number for herself? "Right away, Doctor."

CHAPTER 13

IN THREE MORE hours, she'd be safe on a flight to Vallarta. Until then, Houston had a lounge. Crappy food, but a lounge to hide in nonetheless.

She offered to finish Jessica and Kelly's breakdown so Ben would be long gone from the D concourse. But she'd still have to lie low. Doctors Without Borders...that meant he might be heading to the international gates, too. But at least she could be certain he wasn't heading to Puerto Vallarta, one of the richest hubs for international expats and vacationers in Mexico. No, he'd probably be heading on to somewhere decrepit and needy—whatever made him feel important and righteous. Then he'd play that righteous role to get some other pathetic soul into bed.

Whatever. Hey, maybe she had nothing to worry about; maybe he was at baggage claim already. His girlfriend or wife *Jamie* texting that she had the minivan parked outside baggage claim with their two and a half kids. And the dog.

And his wedding ring was probably in that super-organized man-purse of his. Yeah, that black leather *murse* she'd forgotten to make fun of last night at the bar. A fucking murse. *Jesus.*

But why would he be gone out of country for a year if he had kids? Even to "do good"?

Hello, Preeya. Her own mother had left her and her sister "to do good"—permanently.

What did it matter, anyway? She was just lucky that the asshole clued her in before she got taken. Oh God, like Hannah, who she'd met in FA school then flew with her for a year before Hannah quit altogether. That girl was so sweet, fell for this guy she'd met on a red-eye to Philly. A year of pretend later, she found her doting dream man at the baggage claim. Greeted by a wife and in-laws.

Yeah, Preeya was super lucky Ben hadn't made it twelve hours before his truth leaked out.

Because the way he'd been with her at the bar, in the hotel room—all night long—she could have been deeply taken. Easily. Maybe worse than Hannah. And worse than Preeya'd ever been taken before, by Josh all those years ago, or by any other person, place, or thing, for that matter.

Her phone buzzed her back to the present. *Gigi.*

Her heart warmed. "Hey, Geej."

"You made it, then. To Houston?"

"Yeah, finally in Houston."

"Weird vibes last night…like superhuman good ones…"

"Yes, well, I *did* have an amazing night," Preeya said, completely unsurprised that Gigi felt it—it was that damn powerful. "But it was shattered with unkind reality by morning." Preeya adjusted the earbud in her left ear, then grabbed her roller bag's handle and began walking toward the Jetta Air lounge.

"Again?" Gigi asked. "You're having a good few days, Pree."

"Yes, again, and yes, a really good string of days and bad clichés. This morning's beat all, though. He called me by another woman's name, Geej."

"Ouch, sweetie…I'm sorry. But hey, did you at least get your kicks?" That's Gigi, silver-lining sleuth to the core.

And yes, she had—she had gotten her night *kicks*—incredible waves of kicks…followed by a huge kick to the ego in the morning. "Yeah, Geej, but that's so far from enough anymore. So not enough, by light-years."

"I know, Pree, I know. And you deserve more," she said, then giggled, not matching the context of their conversation at all.

"What are you laughing about?"

"Sorry, it's just…stop! Rod is tickling my feet. Stop it!"

Preeya closed her eyes. She pictured her best friend on a couch in front of a TV, having her doting, attentive boyfriend rubbing and tickling her toes. Like Evan used to do, which at the time she'd hated. *Then*. God, she was an idiot, wasn't she?

But she loved hearing Gigi happy. "Tell him hey for me, Geej."

"Preeya says hi. He's waving back." Gigi giggled again then sighed. "So, Pree, what next? On to Vallarta?"

"Yeah, but since I'm missing the wedding"—she looked at her phone for the time—"as we speak, and the airline already gave me the vacation days, I'll have a few forced days of alone time."

"I know you hate that, sweetie."

"I do, but it'll be…good…for me. Right? Won't it be good for me?"

"Yes. Yes, of course. And when you get sick of yourself, I'm here. As usual. Call anytime, always…oh shut up, Rod…yes, anytime." Preeya heard Rod's muffled exclamation of pain—Gigi probably hit him hard in the arm.

Preeya smiled. Gigi was her rock, always and forever. "I will probably cave and call you at hour two of my solo-cation," she said, pausing to read the overhead signs to get her bearings—*destination Jetta Air lounge*—because more recently, all of the larger international hub layouts merged together in her brain. She squinted at the large sign's possibilities, then, finding her target and following the arrow, the Jetta Air crew lounge was only some fifty feet away.

"Pree, you there?"

"Yeah, I'm here, Geej, sorry." She veered right and weaved her way toward her next safe haven. "I'm just—"

A hand took her wrist.

She spun around, half ready to knock someone in the shins with a big swing of her carry-on, and half ready to greet some pilot or FA she'd worked with. Either way, any and all words escaped her, so she looked at the large hand clutching her wrist and then up at the owner's face. In awe.

Why was she so shocked? *The largest airport hub in the world can't circumvent fate, Preeya.*

"What the hell happened to you, Preeya?"

She narrowed her eyes at Dr. Ben Trainer, then glared at his hand. Still on her goddamn wrist. Yanking her arm from his clutches, she knocked her roller back over, the hard casing made a loud thud against the tile floor.

They both bent down to grab the bag and its extended handle until she growled low and deep. "I got it." *Because first off, fuck karma, fate, Mom—all of it.*

Second, did he think she was a total fucking idiot? *What happened?*

Through her phone at her ear, a muffled but escalating voice. "Preeya? What have you got, Pree?"

"Geej, gotta go." She ended the call and stared at her phone screen. Thinking. *Damn it.* Just a matter of feet before the lounge entrance, too. She stole a deep breath. *He's not even worth getting heated up over. Just keep cool.*

Composed and calm, she peered at him, focusing on his nose—not his eyes, not his lips—just the very tip of his nose. She cleared her throat and hunted for a mellow-sounding intonation. "What do you mean?" *Too shaky, Pree. And lower.* She let her primo FA smile surface. "I'm taking my break before my next leg." *Because, asshole, the flight is work for me, not a leisurely stroll through the clouds, you know?* "Did you have a nice flight?" Sweet as saccharine.

"Preeya, come on…what's the damn deal?" Then he moved a step closer. "Why'd you sneak out? No word…nothing. We had such an amazing time last night. Really…something…"

God, she was not going there. Before opening her mouth in reply, Jessica and Kelly strolled past, tilted their heads, then whispered among themselves all the way into the lounge. "I had *thought* so." *Don't, Preeya.* She just needed to end it there. "But you gotta know, it was the alcohol talking…working. It was just the drinks, nothing more."

"The hell it was!" he yelled.

Whoa. "Shhh. Jesus, Ben. Yes. It was. You don't get out a lot, I understand. But it was just a one-nighter, a fling. We socialized folks sometimes have them…" Even though, again, she rarely did. Well, again, except for the prior two-night string. *Ugh.* Cue hot acid reflux.

He glowered at her, his right eye a tad smaller than his left, while he began rubbing the top of his head. His expression, confused—a desperate question hovering in those golden spheres of his. "That is *not* what it was."

She turned, realizing this would be an endless circle to nowhere. And her feet really did hurt. She needed to sit, eat, and relax for the half hour before checking in again.

But he took her hand gently and urged her around to face him.

Damn it. More than hating that he was still in her face, she despised her body's reaction to his touch. The hot spark in her core he'd ignited last night had simmered, but since he'd grabbed her wrist, it had spread like wildfire. Hell, his general fucking presence killed her slowly, forcing up those warm, rolling memories of *them* from only hours earlier—in heaven, before "Jamie."

"If you didn't feel the energy between us, then I need to see a psychiatrist—I must have been hallucinating. Clinically insane."

She had felt the electricity. And was driven crazy-insane by it. But the bucket of ice-cold wake-up had already been dumped over her head. Yeah, that fine-burning fire was out.

Put out cold!

"No. It's just relativity, Ben. You're a dime a dozen and I guess I am, too…"

"How dare you take this so lightly!"

"Please lower…your voice."

Back to a whisper. "I put everything out there last night, and you…you blow it off like it's nothing?"

"It wasn't me who blew it off."

"I don't know what the hell that means, but maybe it's true what they say: flight attendants really do fuck-flee-repeat! Off to screw the next fool, right? Another brooding rock star? I'll leave you to it."

*

He couldn't believe his words after they'd left his mouth.

Maybe they were from the years of pent-up…everything, but it shocked him, and from her facial expression, it shocked her far worse.

It took her several seconds to get her bearings. And then to speak. "What the fuck did you just say to me?"

"I—"

"You…you can go *fuck* yourself!" she yelled, apparently uncaring anymore about decibel levels. Then she stormed off.

And he couldn't utter a sound, a syllable to try to stop her. He knew better than to follow her—nothing would come of it. He screwed up royally, and damn it, had he even deserved a night or more with someone like her in the first place?

No was the answer. Definitely not.

He walked toward his connection, head down, hangover headache ramped up to full force, and another rush of guilt flooding his veins. God, that guilt—it might just drown him from the inside out.

CHAPTER 14

SHE'D FIND SOLACE in the airline lounge, a place to decompress. Her blinding rage already forced to a simmer, if only to keep up appearances around her coworkers.

Like Kelly and Jessica.

They were at the bar flirting with a pair of pilots. Before they caught sight of her, she ducked into a corner chair facing the window. She sighed then shook her head. At least hiding spots were coming her way.

She situated her bag, sunk into the plush red armchair, and then stared at the floor. Empty time went by while all-encompassing whooshes and zooms of arrivals and departures rattled her bones. And during that stretch of time, her fury at Ben, and at herself for letting it all happen, morphed into sheer apathy, a detachment she'd never known before.

And it felt good. Nice. Empty peace and ease.

But on the other hand, though she loathed admitting it, what she'd experienced last night, that level of liberation, that degree of true joy, couldn't be had if she chose *apathy*.

But even that "true joy" wasn't real, Preeya.

A reminder that ran rampant through her boiling veins. She squeezed her fists tight. Ben was just a romp, a fucking roll in a bed in a hotel in east bumble.

Low expectations, an objective outlook. That had to be the way now. The status quo. Hey, after taking a bit of time to self-focus—learn to be alone for five minutes without having a panic attack—maybe *Evan* was the way of her future? Maybe *that* was the best it could get?

"Preeya...hey, Preeya?" Kelly stood in front of her for who knew how long, wearing an expression of concern mixed with confusion. "You okay? Did you drop something on the floor?"

Preeya blinked out of her zone. "Hey. Oh, no. Just thinking...and tired. I guess the whole thing with the boy on yesterday's flight...it was a lot. And I didn't sleep well."

"Right, that's what kept you up...that whole episode with the boy... and the doctor and all." She winked, holding out a beverage napkin for her to take. "He wanted me to give this to you. I'd almost forgotten...but then I saw you both together outside the lounge, and then you in here..."

Preeya took the napkin, glanced at it long enough to see ten digits, and decided not to rip it to shreds like she wanted to. She wouldn't be gossip fuel for the Jetta Air girls. It was enough that she knew they'd caught Ben's hand on her wrist, but hopefully none of the yelling. "Thanks. Probably more questions on the paperwork. It was a pile a mile high."

"Sure, yeah, a mile high. Well, we're off to Tampa in a while. Have a safe one to PV, and I guess, see ya when we see ya?"

"Thanks, Kelly. Yeah, safe flight."

The tall blonde smiled then twirled toward the bar.

But the woman didn't make it three steps before spinning back around on her heels, and hip-shook her way back to Preeya's side. "Hey, when you talk to the doctor next and...you know, if he ever happens to ask about me, maybe just text me his number, or give him mine? I thought he was so yummy—clean-cut, tall, and a *doctor*. I would've called him myself, but I didn't wanna freak him out, calling outright with no reason or excuse other than...you know, because..." She giggled. "Well, he didn't strike me as the pick-me-up, ready-to-play type, which makes him that much yummier." She licked her lips and waggled her brows.

Jesus.

"Well, as it turns out, Kelly," Preeya died to say, *"he is that type."* And, God,

would they go too well together, both married with children and pets and hidden rings.

You don't know that.

I've seen pictures of Kelly's model fam.

And Ben?

I sense it with Ben.

Maybe Gigi's "powers" are starting to rub off on you.

Shut up. In her gut she sensed it. Though she hadn't sensed anything but pure bliss when she'd felt his cock's pulse and rippling release and length and girth and power in her last night.

Or when she'd been swimming in his arms.

She suppressed a growl and through gritted teeth pasted on her friendliest FA-to-FA smile. "Yeah, Kell, sure thing. I'll try to put a word in for you." And try not to cram the damn napkin with Ben's blessed fucking number on it, down Kelly's ultra-deep, well-used throat...to choke on!

Preeya! Blow job, Ben, last night. *Judgy bitch.*

Fine, I'm a slight hypocrite. All fueled up about Ben again and taking it out on Kelly... *Though she is a cheating—*

Stop. Just stop.

Preeya sighed, her internal back and forth ending in exhaustion.

As she watched Kelly shuffle back to her men in waiting, she let the remnant anger ripple through her, down her, and out her toes. No more thoughts about the dickhead who'd obviously fucked around enough to have some other woman's name on his lips. Some *Jamie.* A fucking *Jamie.*

Had to call his sister.

Exhale bad, inhale good.

And no more thoughts about him tricking her into believing she was *all* he had on his mind. All that mattered in his damn world. For the night, at least.

She looked down at her purse, where the napkin with Ben's number lay, which she'd inadvertently crunched up into a tight, sweaty ball when Kelly wiggled away from her corner of the lounge. She chuckled—wadding up men's written messages of bullshit was getting to be a thing.

But her smirk fast became a frown. Severing ties, sitting there on her own, alone. *Alone time* was coming, and coming fast. Her lungs were already constricting, whispering their hatred of the idea of landing in Vallarta *solo*. For three whole days. She swallowed the fast-developing ball of angst with no success as she reached for her phone.

Call someone. For distraction. Gigi for sure wanted to know why and what ended their last call so abruptly. *Nuh-uh.* She couldn't rehash that right now. She'd splinter into tears. Instead she tapped out a quick *Call ya when land. All okay,* and then went back to brainstorming while her breathing became shallower still.

Amy? Not Amy. God, her college roommate was already married by this time, throwing a fucking bouquet or dancing drunk with cake on her nose and about to get on with her honeymoon cruise and the rest of her perfect marital life.

Her family was of course out, except for Prana—Prana always made her smile—but it was too late to call SafeHaven. God, she missed her sister. Always loyal, always lit up to see her. She should've rerouted herself to northern Cali for an extra visit this month. That's what she should've done.

But it had already been too late. She was scheduled to work this leg. And two days off wouldn't give her enough time to *possibly* catch a standby flight and drive to SafeHaven.

She powered up her phone screen to think. Some missed calls from her aunt and from her cousin, Asha. Oh God, don't think about *that* wedding. She winced, went to shut down the phone…when a text rolled in.

From Evan?

Hope you're good, just thinking about you. No need to reply. Just wanted you to know. Ev.

She looked out the window. Still sweet as sugar. Even after she'd dashed his life plans. *Their* life plans.

She remembered her words to him that day, a month ago. She'd told him she needed to venture out. "To really get to know myself," she'd said.

God, she talked a lot about getting to know herself, and did not a damn thing about it.

You are now, Pree. This trip.

Yes, this trip. Here she was stressing over the next three days she'd be alone in paradise. By herself. No company, no distraction. And it terrified her.

Pathetic.

More pathetic were the words of truth that she could never formulate in her head, let alone say to her almost-fiancé: "I don't love you, Evan. Never have. Just didn't want to be alone…" God, it would have murdered his heart, and just because she hadn't loved him enough to marry him, or even to stay with him another day, didn't mean she wanted to hurt him like that. Evan was a good, sweet man. Eager to please her. Eager to love her.

While she, well, just wasn't ever satisfied. With anything. So maybe there was truth to the breakup words she had spouted to him. She did need to venture out. And she definitely needed to find out who the hell she was. Because although she had no fucking clue what she was seeking—what she wanted—she knew in her heart what she didn't want. And that, at least, was a start, right?

Her phone buzzed again, the same text, still marked as unanswered.

She hit Reply. *Hey, saw you on anchor desk. Congrats, Ev, you so deserve it! TYL.*

She sighed, picturing him signing off the news desk every morning at 11:00 a.m. sharp. Every single morning. "Make it a great one, Seattle," or whatever phrase or tag he'd snagged for himself. Yeah, she was really glad for him, proud of him, and impressed with him. He'd carried on without her, moved on for the better. And she wouldn't have had it any other way.

She stood up, threw her phone in her purse, jerked her carry-on handle up, and strode to her gate. She'd kind of liked the adrenaline rush of being early on her last leg, getting the checklist done before the other girls arrived. And she liked surprising the hell out of Jessica and Kelly. She liked that a lot. Because, *screw them.*

*

Ben sat in the extremely uncomfortable seats at the gate and closed his eyes—with only four hours of solid sleep because of the vodka-induced sex-fest all-nighter after the adrenaline-rush emergency after the hearing, and now the crash-and-burn with Preeya—it all finally hit him. He fell into a light doze. Deeper and deeper he drifted, despite the chair, the PA's random announcements from some far off gate, and the obnoxious video game music from the teenager behind him. His exhaustion conquered it all. And when Preeya's eyes floated through his mind, her expression sweet and sensual, the same look she'd given him at his hotel room door last night, he knew he was officially out and dreaming.

Until a child pulled on his pant leg, shocking him awake. The next second, the toddler's mother issued a slew of apologies in Spanish. He rubbed his eyes to focus, then told her not to worry and gave the kid his famous— but just scary enough—thumb-disappearing trick, which sent the kid back to stay with his mother for good. He felt a little bad because there it was, his disconnect with kids. Ben sighed, then caught the child watching him from afar. To make it right, Ben held up his hands and wiggled all ten digits, proving everything was in working order. The child, in awe, giggled and ran behind his mother again. Ben laughed, winked at the toddler, then giving up on the nap— or maybe escaping Preeya's inevitable in-dream gaze—he turned on his phone to call his sister, Stacy, to tell her he was due in at 9:30 p.m.

"Looks like the flight's on time."

"The kids are excited—they get my famous mac and cheese every time Uncle Ben comes home."

"You turn me into a damn kid on Christmas morning when you bring up your mac and cheese!" He grinned hearing his sister laugh, fake modesty mingling in between her chuckles.

Then the first-class boarding announcement met his ears.

"That's me, Stace—see you in a few hours."

"Wait, how long are you staying, Ben?"

"For three days. Then I travel with the vaccination team through to Tula, an hour north of Mexico City."

"God, I hate that you're doing this. Puerto Vallarta is safe, a paradise, but a *Gringo Americano* crossing the damn country, I just—"

"I'm taking precautions, Stacy. Listen, I've really got to go. You can play mom when I see you in a few hours, okay?"

"Fine. Fine. Oh, customs takes forever. Have a protein bar with you!"

"Got it. No worries," he said, fingering not a protein bar but his DWB badge—that magic ticket through the short line. "I love you. See you soon."

He hung up smiling, glad now for her nurturing ways. It hadn't always been that way. But age and time had made him appreciative of the only family he had. When Jamie died, Stacy had never been more vital to his well-being and to his sanity. She was solid, unconditional—always. Even while raising two kids on her own, she never let him down.

He handed his boarding pass and passport to the male flight attendant at the podium, got and gave the obligatory smiles, and headed down the ramp. He knew Preeya would be on board, but had decided not to bother her.

Though he really wanted to make things right, damn it.

Just sleep; focus on seeing Stacy and the kids. Then on to the Central Mexico mission. For more soul-cleansing work.

When he boarded the plane he spotted Preeya immediately, there in the first row of coach. She stood on her tiptoes, helping a passenger push, more like shove, a bag into the overhead compartment. Her long, jet-black ponytail highlighted the curve of her back, her hips, her bottom. He felt an uncontrollable shiver shoot up his spine.

But he sat quickly to shake it off. "It's done, Ben. All done."

He sighed, closed his lids gently over his eyes, and hoped that his pre-tend sleep would become real sleep as soon as humanly possible.

*

When she turned to answer Bobby, the flight's lead host in first class, she spotted those damn illuminating amber eyes as Ben turned to sit in his cozy first-class seat.

Had he followed her, maybe even changed his flight? No, not likely. *I mean, get over yourself, Preeya.*

But such a coincidence? *Nice try. There are no coincidences, Pree!*

And was it really that crazy? How many connections did Jetta Air have from Houston, anyway? Like, five? A twenty-percent chance wasn't all that mystifying.

Either way, she was safe in coach again, and by the time they'd land, he'd deplane and be stuck in customs for an hour or more, and she'd shoot through the express crew lane and she wouldn't have to face Dr. Ben Trainer ever again.

She took out her phone to send Prana the ritual takeoff text and then power down, but a new message stared up at her, one that was too all-caps-angry to ignore.

THE GALL, MISSING YOUR FATHER'S WEDDING. Your father is crushed. So is Sylvia, your stepmother. Right, *Sylvia*—her father's goddamn tit-enhanced patient? God, how cliché?

But the worst part of her aunt's message made her gut wretch. *The one most crushed by your absence is Prana.*

What—they'd gotten her sister from SafeHaven?

Screw Champa. The hell with all of them. Using Prana. Like they knew her sister from a stranger on the street. To people like Champa, her sister was a burden, an alien, a leper.

This was nothing out of the ordinary for her aunt. Or her father. Maybe an East Indian thing, the tool of guilt? Convenient and at no cost to the user.

She flung her phone in her purse, then clicked her seat belt buckle with unnecessary force. She inhaled a lungful of recycled air. *Puerto Vallarta. Alone. Here I come.*

CHAPTER 15

AFTER CUSTOMS AND immigration, she walked with the other flight attendants through to the exit. And there he was waiting. For her? Damn it, she hoped not. And how did he get through so fast?

"Hey, I'll catch up to you guys…seven sharp, in the lobby," she said to Bobby and Janet, glad that at least for tonight she wouldn't be eating alone.

"Isn't that the doctor from yesterday's flight?" Bobby asked her of Ben, who leaned against the wall in a casual, totally out of character pose just past the time-share hawkers.

"Yeah, but how did you know that?"

"The company intranet had a photo of you and him with the boy at the ambulance yesterday."

"Oh." God, she hoped it hadn't spread beyond that. "Well, he must have a question for me about the medical reports we filled out," she told him, again keeping her business to herself.

She waved to them and veered reluctantly over to where Ben stood. His eyes were narrowed, searching hers, but not drawn to hers like the past looks he'd given her. Not even raising his eyebrows as she approached. Not even standing taller. Was he even waiting for her at all?

A spark of some leftover rage tore through her then. And a touch of embarrassment, a pinch of insecurity. But she was already a few feet from him and couldn't turn away now.

"Were you wanting to speak to me again?" *To say some fucked-up, judgmental generalizations that don't apply to me because you don't know me from Bobby or Jan or Jessica or fucking Kelly?*

"I'm actually waiting for my sister, but I am glad to see you... I want to apologize." He shifted his stance and stood taller. "I am sorry, you know, for what I said. To you. I was angry. It was uncalled for."

She was listening.

"You were just so flippant about...us and...well, I hadn't been with another woman since—"

"Since who? Jamie?"

"How did—"

"You called me Jamie this morning...when I woke up in your fucking arms."

"Jesus!"

"That's right, you actually said 'Jesus, Jamie.' That's exactly what you said."

Ben sighed and shook his head, cheeks flushed like he'd seen a ghost. "I am so, so sorry. Listen, Preeya...Jamie—"

"Don't bother, Ben. I'm totally over it."

"She is, *was*...shit! Jamie is my late wife, Preeya. She passed away a year ago...from cancer."

She swallowed, but with her heart lodged in her throat beating triple time, she felt like she was choking, impending death by airlessness and horrifying stupidity.

"I should've told you, but...the mood, the timing." He stepped closer to her, as if he wanted to take her hands, but instead he shoved them in his pockets and lowered his chin to his chest. "Anyway, you're the first woman I've been with." Eyes down at the floor, cheeks now hot red, he was a man in the net of embarrassment, like a teenage virgin in the locker room with his all-too-experienced buddies.

Preeya was struck in the heart. And sick to her stomach at the same time. Like she had the sudden weight of the world on her shoulders. She'd been cruel, left him at the hotel without a word. Raked him over the coals in Houston.

And she'd taken the re-virginity of a goddamn widower! Fuck, he should have really said something, right? Because she couldn't have known. He was too damn confident, diligent, masterful with her body—and with his body—in bed. For God's sake, she would never have known. She was led to the peak of pleasure too many times to think such vulnerability existed in this man.

Now she felt ill. *She* had become a landmark in time for this man, this good-hearted, well-meaning, perfect-soul of a man. A doctor. Without borders. Who'd lost his fucking wife.

Wait, wasn't he too young to have lost a wife, for God's sake?

She just stood there and shook her head. Speechless.

"Again, I apologize for saying what I said to you...it was screwed up...just not okay."

She believed his apology. It was disgustingly authentic. Gut-wrenching.

She was the asshole. And he was the saint.

Damn it. She had even sensed—and ignored—his immediate regretful look when he'd spat those words at her in Houston, when the shock in his wide eyes stared back at her even before she shot her biting words back at him and stormed into the crew lounge. His words didn't even fit his mellow, professional albeit slightly arrogant doctor persona. Even the newer addition of swear words to the man's vocabulary was almost too weird for her to hear. But it was also refreshing. More real. Like he was admitting he was less perfect than maybe he was. *But hardly imperfect at all.*

"It's fine," Preeya said. "I mean, I get that you were pissed. I understand now. And I assumed something about you *first*. I was the one who was totally off base. The whole thing, a crazy mess of assumptions...which I started." She looked down, almost too embarrassed to meet those eyes again.

"Preeya, it's okay. Really," he said while leaning into her as if to make sure she caught his follow up smile backing up his words.

She nodded and gave him a half grin back. "You know...what you said about flight attendants, well, although I don't sleep around..." Yes, she wanted him to know that, "I have plenty of female FA friends who definitely, you know, are out to have a good time. Just like plenty of guys are—no matter their professions. And except for one or two FAs I know who cheat to play"—she paused to sigh, thinking solely of Denver Kelly—"why shouldn't women who work their asses off and travel for their jobs get to explore and enjoy?"

She nodded, proud of her stance. Dawn from the guest room would've been proud, too.

He nodded back. Like he understood. "Fair enough." He cleared his throat and shuffled his right foot. "Still, nice to know I wasn't one of an army."

She met his eyes and smiled. "No. You were anything but."

More like one of a kind.

The next moments of lingering silence could have been awkward, but they weren't. Pensive or mind-clearing, but not awkward. She laughed to herself—maybe she and Ben both just needed to get out of their own tiny boxes, away from their habitual assumption-forming, line-drawing, and judgment-making.

"Anyway, I'm sorry again about skipping out on you…I'll blame it on a bad past few days, but hell, my whole life is 'a bad past few days' times a thousand…million." She scoffed then shook her head, eyes sighing from the reality hit.

He smiled at her with something like empathy in his gaze. Then he cleared his throat. "Listen, I'm staying with my sister, and she's made dinner. I don't know if you get much home cooking…but her mac and cheese is out of this world." He punctuated his sweet offer by literally licking his lips.

She almost laughed out loud, but held back, defaulting to a one-sided grin that silently shouted *I want to but shouldn't.*

"Come on, join us." His hand left his pocket and touched her elbow—a gentle nudge—which she pretended not to notice.

But she noticed. And her heart muscle noticed.

"You can strengthen up, overcome your bad-days streak with some of Stacy's motherly-love-infused cooking—my sister's kind of…well, you'll see, if you accept the invite?" A smile slid over his face, brightening his eyes.

God, those eyes—she looked away like a shot.

"Doctor's orders?" he added sweetly, almost innocently.

She didn't know. Out of the blue, this altruistic and life-saving doctor, out-of-this-world lover, mourning widower. God, she didn't even deserve to be in his company, let alone become his dinner guest.

But real food? Real people? His *real* sister? No agenda? It seemed innocent enough. Maybe just a person being kind. It could be the most real interaction with people other than Gigi and her sister that she'd had in who knew how long. If not ever.

But... "Thank you. I'll pass, though. I have dinner plans with the other whore FAs." She winked. "Another time, maybe?" she said, and started to walk away from him toward the cab line.

"Wait." There he was again. With his deep honey eyes, their slight sorrow hidden by a glaze of confident control.

He slipped a business card into her hand. "Just take this. I have an international cell plan, so call anytime. Really, anytime at all."

Even though she already had his number on a napkin crumpled up deep in her purse because something stopped her from trashing it, she took the card from him with a nod of thanks. Then his eyes shifted to a woman waving at him across the crowd of handlers, drivers, and scrambling tourists. The excited woman had eyes of melting honey too, with a warm smile to match. She was most definitely the sister who had home-cooked food ready for him.

*

Hugging his sister, he felt home. This visit was a long-overdue and much-needed respite. A breath of fresh air after the third medical review trial, and the year of third-world travel. Family was the best medicine now. At least for the next three days.

While he put his passport in a secure zipper pocket in his messenger bag, Stacy caught him up about the kids. Then she started quizzing him on his upcoming medical expedition—when a hand touched his forearm.

"I changed my mind, if that's okay?" Preeya's voice was somewhat meek, at least in contrast to her brash, outspoken tone he'd come to know over the past day and a half. Her long-lashed violet-infused eyes smiled at him. And he felt a twinge of the similar resurgent hope he'd felt the entire night before, when they were together.

"Yes. Good. Perfect. Um, Stacy, this is Preeya. Preeya Patel, the flight attendant who assisted me with the boy in-flight yesterday."

CHAPTER 16

HIS SISTER HAD just moved to a rented tri-level overlooking the Bay of Banderas. The view was mesmerizing. He could tell Preeya agreed—her eyes lit up, her hands grasped the balcony rail with excitement mixed with caution, and her chest lifted with the intake of fresh sea air. For him, his peripheral view was more captivating than the tropical expanse in front of them. Yes, Preeya hopelessly captivated him.

His niece, Beth, and nephew, Peter, came running out to greet him. They were both a head taller since he'd seen them last, and each had sharp and spry looks in their eyes, too. And as always, they were all about their Uncle Ben.

Until they met Preeya.

The kids had always loved hearing Ben's medical tales, even before he'd visited far-off places this past year…but this time their dinner guest and her flights of fancy and crazy high-in-the-sky stories trumped all. Ben no longer existed. He loved it, though, her role as storyteller and entertainer to the nine and eleven-year-olds. It fit Preeya too well for words—her connection with the kids. With Stacy, too. He couldn't remember his sister laughing like that. A gift with people, a cool head in chaos, and such intelligence in general, what a waste, Preeya quitting medical school, not specialized in something pediatric. But it wasn't any of his business. At least not yet.

Stop fantasizing, Ben. Stop thinking at all.

He shut off his brain and listened, then joined in the laughter erupting over the world's greatest mac and cheese.

After dinner, the kids dragged Preeya off to show her their rooms while Ben snuck to the kitchen sink to start the cleanup before Stacy the Martyr finished the entire job herself.

"Benjamin Trainer," Stacy whispered in his ear from behind, "I haven't seen that look in your eyes since…" She paused and cleared her throat, catching herself—*tiptoeing*.

He sighed, just realizing that Stacy hadn't uttered Jamie's name since the funeral.

Maybe he'd given off a certain vibe—and maybe it was time to stop. "Since Jamie?" he asked, giving her permission to broach the delicate subject while he stared at the sudsy sponge in his hands.

A nervous laugh tumbled from her mouth as she began packing the leftovers. "Yes, since Jamie, Ben. And maybe with a new person in your life, you'd stop going on these dangerous expeditions." She squeezed his shoulder on the way to the fridge with the containers. "I worry, Ben. I want you happy and…not…dead!"

"Stacy, please." He put the sponge down to give her his full attention. "First off, they won't give me the dangerous missions yet." Though he'd kept on the coordinator as his year mark approached for more impactful projects. "So you need to keep the whole mothering-your-adult-kid-brother at bay." His brows lifted to drive home his point.

He didn't blame her for falling into the default role—she'd been his rock and only constant since their parents passed when he was only a toddler, being shuffled between relatives thereafter. And now, a single mother to Beth and Peter—yeah, he understood her pattern. Still, he'd outgrown it by about two decades of action-packed life.

"And, my dear sister and best friend, you're reading into things here." He flicked his eyes toward the kitchen door, to wherever Preeya had been smuggled off to by the kids. He needed to keep an even head about Preeya, and didn't want Stacy's excitement to tip him over the edge, because, God, after last night, then today—and *now*—he was too close to *there* all on his own.

"*My ass* am I reading into things," she shot back. If nothing else, his sister was fiery. And he both hated and loved that about her. "No, no, brother, it's not just *your* gazes at her. Oh no. That beauty you brought home, sharp as a tack I might add, is not keeping her eyes off of you, either—"

The kitchen door swung open. Preeya entered first, the kids in tow behind her.

"So, I got to see some awesome shell collections and surfing awards." Preeya winked at the kids. "But now I'm ready to work. How can I help here?" That's when Beth and Peter magically disappeared from the kitchen.

Stacy shook her head and sighed. "I should give those two some direction. If not toward *this* mess, then toward bed," she said, waggling her brows. Stacy flashed a grin then exited as quickly as the kids had.

Preeya was at Ben's side the next second, her hand on his arm, motioning with a head nod to let her help. Electricity and dishwater—not the safest...but Jesus, her heat.

His throat went dry, mind went blank.

Get it together, Ben.

He cleared his throat then smiled at her as he hunted for his voice—words, composure. "You don't have to help with dishes. You're the guest—and you were literally on your feet serving hundreds of crabby people all day. Please...sit and relax."

"No, I really want to be here with you...*to help*." Her near-bashful smile dimpled her blushing cheeks.

He nodded, chest tingling—*here with him? Really?* He moved to the center island to pick up where Stacy'd left off, packing the rest of the mac and cheese. But again he had no reply. Like a damn teenager—though not the teenager he'd been. He'd always said what he'd wanted, and then taken it. With Jamie, with everything. What the hell had happened to *that* Ben?

"The kids and your sister are wonderful. What a sweet family. I never had anything like this."

He sighed and grinned, relaxing into her sweet words and voice. "My sister practically raised me." He got back to packing the last of the baked dish. "I broke her in for those kids. So their successes are really mine," he said through a snicker. Then he paused. "You know, you're really terrific with them."

"Oh, thanks. I, uh, have a younger sister myself," she said over her shoulder. "Prana. She's got Down's syndrome and its...ancillary issues. Anyway," she said, turning back to the dish in her hand, "I've had years of practice communicating with a brilliant yet childlike mind. Patience is Prana's biggest lesson and best gift to me...oh, and true love."

His breath left him like a sudden vacuum. Knowing this other side to her, it made his heart flip. She was an enigma. *Okay, but stop staring and speak.* "I'm sure. Of course." He licked his dry, cracked lips, weird for how humid it was in Vallarta and in that kitchen. "You know, many of my patients during residency had debilitating and diminishing diseases. It must be so hard for you and your family. Over the years, with little to no progress, it wears on you, yes?"

She nodded but kept silent. It wasn't quite an uncomfortable silence, but he sensed her pain. No, he felt it. It paused him. The last words he'd spoken—*years, no progress, wearing*—replayed in his head. They were equally applicable to what he'd endured with Jamie. And God, it had been his worst nightmare come true.

He looked up from the container he was filling, Preeya's attention focused hard on him.

She had turned from the sink, hands white with suds. "You have a gift. With how you truly empathize with people...like, with me...just now. *You* lost your wife, yet you feel for me? While my sister is alive?" She took a step closer to the kitchen island and placed her wet, soapy hand over his. "Ben, I'm so sorry for your loss. It must have been horrible. It must still be horrible. For you. Yet you're so strong, and so giving."

He shook his head, closed his eyes, and moved his hand to his chest, to feel the wedding band he wore around his neck. That he'd taken off last night. In Boise, with Preeya. A new surge of guilt shot through him, made him dizzy, while Preeya's words whirled around his head. Then they hit his heart.

And something changed.

Preeya's words, her soft and gentle, humble and sweet sentiment, settled in like a child's head sinking into a pillow at bedtime. Her words weren't rejected like some foreign organ implant, the donor being too unrelated or false. His donor now, Preeya—Preeya and her genuine words—had been accepted by his ever-combative heart. This time his body rejected the guilt, the shame.

His heart pounded with relief and heat and promise.

He felt flushed. How had this stranger penetrated him like this? Plenty of others had tried to broach the subject, but had all failed. Miserably. They'd just managed to increase the pain. And even though he knew his heartache was not unique, it of course felt singular to him. Somehow Preeya Patel had just made him feel...okay about that. Not even his loyal-to-the-end sister ever managed such a feat since Jamie passed.

Words didn't seem an appropriate response back to Preeya: her genuine tenderness, this landmark, deserved more. So much more. He swallowed back a knot of emotion in his throat, while refusing to remove his eyes from hers. God, he wanted to take the two steps toward her, take her in his arms. Be taken in hers.

But the kitchen door swung open—Beth needing her new friend as badly as he did, it seemed.

"Preeya, Preeya! Come see," his niece said, bouncing up and down. "Peter's got an iguana to show you!"

She nodded at Beth, smiled with a slow, sweet blink at Ben as she lifted her soft, soapy hand from his. "I'll be right back?"

He gave her a nod, then Preeya followed Beth out just as Stacy came in, brushing by Preeya and giving their guest a warm smile. Had Stacy been standing outside the door? He wouldn't put it past her.

But he couldn't care less. He felt dizzy and light yet anchored at the same time.

"Oh, God, Stacy..." He shook his head, searching for words.

"Do you believe me now? She's into you, and it's good. It's really good." She smiled, then turned away from him, taking over dish duty.

He hoped to God his sister was right. That Preeya was "into" him. *Into him*—God, he felt old. He snorted then sighed. *Wait.* What if his sister was off, just seeing what she wanted to see? What if he was just a charity case in Preeya's eyes?

No, Ben. From the way she touched his hand, no. It was real. It was too real. But…

"I just don't know. I'm so far out of the game, Stace. I can't see home plate. I'm not even in the nosebleeds. I'm like, across the damn street. Hunting for a parking spot in the ninth inning."

"Not according to her—I promise you that. Not according to her, little brother."

She kept silent for a while, attacking the dishes full force while her words resonated in his head.

"I want to take her to the beach, to the Marietas, maybe. Tomorrow."

His sister paused, turned, and smiled at him. "You should. You absolutely should. The Marietas are perfect—a good boat ride—swim, relax, hike. Weather's supposed to be perfect. You'll need lots of sunscreen…"

"Yes, Mom," he scoffed, realizing some things would never change.

He looked back down at the center counter and reached for the rag to wipe it down. "I'll ask her tonight. For tomorrow."

"Good," she encouraged.

"Yeah. I'll just, you know, ask her."

*

"You sure I can't drive you to your hotel? It's really not far."

"Thanks, but no. I shouldn't take any more of your time and your family's kindness. Really." She smiled. He had done so much in just forgiving her for skipping out on him, then giving her a slice of a different and sweet reality; a home and a family for the evening. He couldn't possibly know how special that was.

Then the trust he'd given her the night before, putting his heart on the line. His first intimate experience since his wife had passed. Preeya still shivered from the thought, the weight, the depth of that notion.

And she, of course, couldn't forget the incredible sensations he'd gifted her with. The vibrations still rang through her body, now more apparent since her mistaken fury had been diffused and his kindness had brought her heart to a new version of open.

No, she'd taken enough from him. "I'll just take a cab and let you be with your family. You said you were only here for what, two or three days?"

"Yes, then on to a vaccination project."

She smiled at him. He was so intriguing, giving, calming. "So, I guess…"

"Tomorrow," he blurted.

"Oh, you're leaving tomorrow?"

"No, no. I mean, tomorrow…let me take you to this place I love. The Marietas. They're islands, a forty-minute boat ride from shore. At the opening of the bay. There's a hidden beach, it's just amazing. It's my favorite place here. I want to take you, that is, if you have no plans?"

Plans? The only plan she had was to procrastinate her forced-upon R & R with herself. "But don't Stacy and the kids want to spend time with you?"

"The kids are in school every day and Stacy is a writer—when the kids are out, she's in her zone and nothing and no one exists. So I'm on my own here. That is, except for dinnertimes. Otherwise, I get no attention, no love," he said with a puppy-dog sadness in his eyes, then he smiled at her like he had last night. In the midst of their sensual play in the Boise hotel room, where he'd transported her to another place, another world.

And to have that again, God, it was so tempting.

But she just wasn't sure. To drag this out…was it fair? What of her mandated alone time? Because she was so damn lost, and getting down to the problem and the solution—assuredly *her* and *her*, respectively—was so overdue. And based on Evan's recent success after she'd left him, proof positive that her issues seemed contagious. And Ben was just too good of a man. Another day together—possibly a heavenly, unmatched day—wouldn't it just be a painful tease? For them both? *And…and…and.*

His smile vanished during her mental deliberation. "I've gone by myself before, to the Marietas. No obligation, Preeya, really." A polite grin followed.

He thought she didn't *want* to go with him?

No, no. That wasn't it.

But before she could form words from thought, he took a step back. "The islands are a great place to think, reflect…I recommend you do go, whenever you can. You'll be here two days, you said?"

"No, I mean, yes, two days, but no, I wouldn't want to go on my own. That's not it," she said, trying to drill into him her intended meaning with her eyes, because, *damn it*, her words were just not doing it. "I just feel—" *Screw it.* She said she wanted to venture, to gain new experiences and possibilities—to really live, right? "Yes. I would love to go with you. Tomorrow sounds wonderful."

"Oh, great…yes, good." He glowed, nodding, grinning, gazing. "Okay, so the boat leaves early, when it's cooler…say I pick you up at eight?"

"Eight it is."

"And I'll bring the sunscreen."

She laughed out loud. "Yes, sunscreen is important, *Doctor.*"

He blushed. "God, I do sound like a doctor. The funny thing is, I was only regurgitating what my mother hen of a sister said a few minutes ago." He blushed more.

"What's funnier is that, if you hadn't noticed," she said and smiled while striking a pose, "I'm 'dark mocha' as it is—I don't really worry about burning."

"Okay, okay, hold it. Now I need to play doctor. No matter how dark your natural skin tone, your skin still needs protection. And…we're only, like, twenty degrees from the earth's equator here. I've seen some of the worst cases of melanoma in darker-skinned people and—"

She leaned into Ben and kissed him on the cheek. "I'll wear it for you, Dr. Ben." Then she turned to walk up the house steps toward where the cab would pick her up.

"Have a good night. See you tomorrow at eight."

"I'm at the Airington!" she called over her shoulder, getting her final fill of his bright sunset eyes before he was out of her view for the evening.

"Hey, text me when you're safe at the hotel."

"Will do." He was too damn sweet for words.

CHAPTER 17

S HE SLID INTO the cab and sank into the seat, exhaustion hitting her all at once.

The cabbie stopped singing some happy tune, an English pop hit—*Radio Inglés*, who knew?—and shared a wide smile as he lowered the volume. "*A dónde vas, senorita?* Where to?"

"Oh, yes, um, to the Airington, *por favor?*"

"*Si, si, senorita.*" He put the cab into Reverse to get right with the incredibly steep hill that led down to the main town road, and turned up the volume of the radio again.

Your sun, my moon, entwined in the guest room.

Violet orbs, absorbed in my love,

See no one but me, my angel from above.

In Mexico? *Jesus Christ, you're kidding me.* She wanted to laugh and cry and scream all at the same time. "Oh, please, sir…"

He couldn't hear her—he was singing too loudly with Josh Bolte's cheesy-ass words. *Please, God.* "Senor! Would you mind turning the station? Um, *cambio, por favor?*"

He still couldn't hear her, not over the belted chorus of ridiculous bullshit.

She tapped his shoulder. He looked at her in the rearview and lowered the volume—*thank you!*—and just as she opened her mouth to ask him to please, for the love of Mother Mary, change the radio station, well, just then, the song, Josh's song with his pseudo-deep lyrics, ended.

"Yes, *senorita*, did you need something?"

She shook her head and smiled, holding back a strange urge to laugh hysterically. "No, sorry, nothing. I'm fine."

She shifted in the seat to look out the open window. Yes, she *did* feel fine. Really good, in fact.

She relished the sea air rushing in at her face as Josh Bolte's stupid lyrics left her mind—scattered to the wind. She felt good and free and calm, and thought to text Gigi to tell her so. She turned on her phone, but her finger hit the power button again the very next second. *Just be here, Preeya. Just be.*

She took in a big breath and blew it out in what turned into a half laugh. On her own and relaxed? Preeya Patel? Yes. She was alone and happy as she watched the Vallarta landscape zoom by as the star-filled sky illuminated the coastal town. She loved this, the scent of night jasmine and sea salt. And the feel of the bay's trade winds blowing in through the window. She laughed as her long hair whipped up and into her face. Her fingers raked her silky strands back, but more of her hair would come lashing, in her eyes and mouth and tickling her neck.

The sound of her laughter filled the backseat of the cab; even the cabbie looked up at her in the rearview, obviously intrigued by her hysterical commotion. And the onslaught of her hair and her continued giggling made her laugh harder—she hadn't laughed like that, all alone, to herself, and so wholly, for ages.

God…not since she was a little girl.

An image of rainbow pajamas came to mind. Sick, home from school, her mother only one room away, Preeya had been watching television. Yes, *I Love Lucy*, the chocolate factory episode. Lucy and the relentless conveyor belt of chocolates. Preeya had laughed so hard her stomach ached. A deep-in-the-belly, tears-falling kind of laugh. In that room, like in the cab's backseat now, it was just her and her deep, resonating, wholehearted happiness.

*

Preeya's airline cohorts were all at the Tara Lux, but since Amy had already booked and paid for a room for Preeya at the elegant Airington where Amy's wedding had been held, Preeya *had* to stay there. The beach access and pool alone were too much to turn down, even though she'd know no one.

Yes, really all alone.

Her breathing hitched and her mouth went dry as the cab pulled under the portico.

Relax. Ben's coming for you in the morning.

Yes, that's right. She'd hit the bed now, and 8:00 a.m. would come in a blink.

Or she *could* just call Bobby or Jan for a bit of company. No, they'd be out and about by this time.

She could shout to Geej. Her rock. *Again—no, Pree.* What if Gigi was busy with Rod or, God forbid, she didn't have Gigi at all anymore.

Her heart rammed her ribs and pulsed up her neck. And the next image in her head—*Ben.*

Widowed. So young. She saw in his eyes how lonesome he was, by no choice of his own. Waking up next to someone every day, planning for *forever* with someone, then *poof.* All gone. She wouldn't be able to bear it. Her heart ached for him.

No, you know what? She'd go straight to her room and try to get through without a crutch, without distraction. Like Ben was forced to do now. She's a grown woman, for God's sake. She could damn well do this.

And as soon as it was decided, she noticed how horribly empty the luxurious lobby was. No line at the registration desk, not even a person behind the counter to greet her. It was slow season in Vallarta, but this was eerie.

She dinged the little bell at the barren counter and out came a nice-enough clerk. Preeya got checked in, got her key, and made her way to the elevator. Still no sight nor sound of another soul, just deafening silence. Even with the humidity thick in the air, all the way up to her room, icy chills swept up her neck.

She unlocked her sixth-floor room door and rolled her bag across the threshold into the darkness. The stark quiet of her large suite, alarming.

"So, this is it." She could swear her voice echoed.

Lights. Her hands hunted for the light switch. *Ahh.* Modern, gleaming emptiness stared her in the face. Ultra contemporary design: decor, furniture, carpet, and duvet. Clean, fresh smelling, a step up from the Boise Inn, for sure—and a mountain up from Josh's bandmate's guest room. *This is a good start.*

She dropped her purse on the front counter, dug out her phone and charger to juice it up—ready to call Geej if she absolutely needed to—and then, so she wouldn't trip, she rolled her bag across the room to the large standing closet. The wheels made a cushy scrolling sound through the plush carpet. The carpet caught her eye; its swirls and dots of soft tropical hues soothed her, in contrast to the hard, stylized angles of the modern desk, headboard, closet, dresser, TV stand. Everything, really, had sharp, crisp edges. Even the lamp shades. But the soft, cushy, swirly carpet, she couldn't wait to walk barefoot.

And no puke puddles. She laughed out loud, then swallowed back hard—something was different here than in the cab when she relished the feel and sound of her laughter, when the wind kissed her face. This no-distraction thing in this static and now almost too-clean room was going to pose a challenge.

Breathe and get busy with something, Preeya.

TV? *No, too easy an escape.*

She could get undressed, unpack, hang up her civilian clothes, prep her uniforms for dry cleaning. *Yes, good idea.*

She kicked off her heels and wiggled, stretched and cracked her toes against the soft, thick carpet. Freeing her feet from her heels after a long flight was equal to taking off her bra before bed. *Heaven.* She took a breath—*this wouldn't be so bad*—laid her carry-on flat on the floor, and unzipped it.

She breathed evenly, felt good so far. *Keep going then.*

Okay, unpacking. She pulled out *The Giving Tree*, her sandals, and her toiletry pouch. What remained? A bag of *dirty* and a balled-up and assuredly wrinkled mess of *clean.* Wow, she really needed to start folding her things. She sighed. Hanging the stuff might help, but doubtful. She stood up, faced the closet doors, then paused.

Froze, really.

Her reflection in the gleaming white laminate, her image muted but clear, halted her breath. She tilted her head. Her eyes, masked by the usual and required FA-thick makeup, stared back at her like a stupid puppy. A bizarre feeling—déjà vu?—filled her chest. Her eyes in the reflection looked familiar—*of course they were familiar*—but from a long-ago time. And unlike her exhausted body—her back, her neck and shoulders, her knees and feet—her eyes were wide open, wide awake, wide with…fear.

Raw, childlike fear.

And she thought she'd been doing so well. But the stark dread gazing back at her now was someone else's.

Someone else's.

Her heart racked her rib cage, her lungs screamed shut.

In a flash of moving memory, she was seven again.

Seven-year-old Preeya. When she'd…she'd run to her mother's closet.

That one morning…

Preeya jumped back, a full length away now from the glossy white doors and her carry-on bag and from her surreal, long-ago reflection.

The same doors. *Fuck.* The same exact reflective laminate. In her parents' bedroom. Not white, but light gray. Storm-cloud gray.

And like a crashing wave dragging her down—and back—her baby sister's wailing filled her being. Prana, only weeks old, on the other side of the house. *Why so far from Mom and Dad's room?* Preeya had woken up to the tiny screams, and after some minutes, she wondered why her sister wasn't being lulled or fed or rocked, burped, changed, something? Her dad had left for surgery—before dawn as usual. She'd seen his headlights hours before through a sleepy haze.

What day was it? No school…*Sunday*. Right. A snuggle-up and sleep-in day.

But no, not while the baby kept on. Sometimes they'd let Prana cry… to teach independence, she'd overheard them say. But this crying spell was longer, louder.

Preeya ran to the baby's room. No Mom asleep in the rocking chair, or anywhere in the pink plaid nursery. Preeya reached over the side of the basinet to give her sister the pacifier—quiet came instantly. A moment's peace. She knew Prana would spit out the milkless plug in a minute's time.

Was her mom still asleep in bed? She had been super tired since coming home from the hospital. Preeya tiptoed to her parents' room. No one in bed. The bathroom? Empty. Her mother's bathrobe hung on the wall hook.

Huffing from her nostrils as the crying began again like she'd predicted, Preeya ran to the spare room, the playroom, then darted barefoot down to the kitchen, sure Mom would be on the phone and cooking with that loud overhead fan whirling, sucking away the Indian spices, and Prana's baby cries with them.

But no. No Mom.

In the office paying bills? No. Dining or living room? No one. Powder room? Empty. Preeya checked every room and space and nook in between. The house was too huge—Daddy had bought them a mansion, which she'd thought she'd loved. But no more. Now she hated it.

Preeya began calling, then screaming, "Mommy! Where are you?" over Prana's baby howls, which had by that time filled every part of the house and Preeya's head and heart.

Preeya's hand clutched the knob to the mudroom out to the garage. Okay, if Mommy's car is there…she stepped out. *Her car's here! So Mom's home.* But where?

Trembling, she peered inside the car's tinted windows in case. *No Mom. No relief.*

In fact, just the opposite.

Her first squeezing heart-pain episode. The first of a billion.

Her airways closed in the dank garage of that humongous house, with its walls shrinking around her and her baby sister who lay screaming upstairs in the frilly, lacy pale-pink basinet. Crying her little baby lungs out.

Preeya's chest-tightening escalated from there. With every passing second, with every magnified baby-scream, each one like a pair of scissors stabbing Preeya's seven-year-old ears, Preeya's chest constricted. Her thoughts were clobbered by possibilities: Had Mommy been taken by a bad guy? Or by aliens like in the shows her babysitter hadn't stopped her from watching?

Preeya wanted to crawl up in a ball and hide.

Hide!

The bedroom closet. A few times since Prana was born, Preeya had found Mommy sitting at the bottom of the huge bedroom closet, humming, rocking, and counting her silken scarves.

Mommy had explained she was just hiding.

"Like, hide and seek?"

"Yes, love. I'm playing hide and seek."

Well, it *was* the perfect hiding place.

A game of hide and seek, then.

She sprinted up to her parents' sunlit bedroom again, straight for her mom's glorious clothes closet. Doorknobs in hand, little lungs filled, Preeya shut her eyes tight and pulled open the gray and glossy doors. Her mom's flowy dresses, skirts and jumpers, shirts and scarves and hats, shoes and belts, were all there.

But no Mom.

Maybe she *was* taken.

Preeya's heart cracked from the earthquake inside her chest. The fear of life without her mom…

But hope is relentless. Her mom wasn't inside.

She must be outside. In the garden.

Mom's watering the flowers before it gets too hot out, of course.

Preeya remembered how hard and fast and free she ran down and out to and through the vacant front yard around to the back, barefoot and uncaring of the jagged-sharp landscape rocks because—sun and stars!—she'd solved the puzzle. She'd find her mom—gorgeous, tender, and calm—in some floral flowing dress watering their garden of vibrant flowers. Whispering to them, singing to them.

Panting, she got to the garden, the lonely little flower bed…

Where a ten-ton train landed on Preeya's heaving little chest. *No Mommy.*

She looked around to be sure her mom wasn't crouching at the base of a needy morning glory or pruning the low-lying baby blue eyes she and her mom had planted together. Shallow breath led to another round of panic as

Preeya spun around and around, hearing and seeing no one—not a soul at the pool, the lanai, the flower garden again. Around and around she spun. Dizzy. No one. *No one.*

She and Prana were officially all alone.

The memory blurred then in her head.

She gulped for air, now back in the hotel room. Alone.

She needed to call Gigi. Fast. *Now.*

No. No calls to anyone. Keep looking. At yourself. In the closet doors. *Remember, goddamn it.*

Fuck you!—she remembered. Everything. Running inside, to the kitchen, the fridge door, the emergency numbers. She'd called and paged her dad, the hospital, the office. The man had been in surgery.

She remembered *not* dialing 911. She'd get in trouble for dragging the police or an ambulance there. *Nobody's bleeding. Everybody's breathing—sort of.* The issue: *her mommy's gone!*

"Mommmmmy!" she'd shrieked so loud. Prana's cries became hiccups then, gasps for air. Preeya remembered taking the cordless phone and sprinting up the stairs for her sister. And on her way up, she'd hit the only labeled speed dial as she went.

Her Aunt Champa.

That's right, yes, she'd called her aunt.

And then grabbed and comforted Prana, and wouldn't let her go. Not for anything. Not until her dad came home so many hours later.

And God, those hours had felt like years.

*

Preeya willed her eyes to zoom out of the depths of the reflection in the white laminate closet doors of her hotel suite. She caught a breath, then four more, chest heaving. She was back to the present, though robotic and chilled with remnants of that childhood trepidation flooding through her from top to toe and back again.

With a long, stoic sigh, she slowly reached for the door's handles and opened the glossy white closet.

Except for hangers swaying from the doors' movement and the one plastic laundry bag, the closet was stark empty.

Empty.

She treaded backward and hit the king size bed with a jolt, forcing her to sit.

Staring ahead, chest heaving, mouth desert-dry, mind blank, she waited. Unsure for what.

She shut her eyes. *Slow your breathing, Pree.* Slow, calm…

Too calm. Her father's long ago explanation, spoken too calmly, too accepting, too *okay*.

Damn her father. He'd finally come home after work that day, and after overhearing him whisper to her aunt about some voice mail, Preeya remembered him kneeling at her feet—her baby sister still clutched tight to Preeya's chest.

"You know how big Mommy's heart and spirit are, Preeya, *bitay*. And how strong she knows you are. Well, Preeya"—he'd held her shoulders tight but did not look in her eyes; she remembered that part well—"your mother left us to be a mother to many, many little girls and boys who need her more than even you and your sister do. In India. Many, many children are starving. She left everything and everyone to follow her heart. We should be very proud."

Why would she think I don't need her? I do need her! We need her!

Distraught fury and confusion had raged through her—she felt it now, the memory was so vivid—but Preeya nodded obediently while repeating her father's words to herself: *Be strong like Mom says you are, Preeya. Be strong, be proud.*

And you still have Daddy. And Prana.

Sometime during her mental processing, her heart's processing, her father had taken the baby out of Preeya's grasp, and then looking through her, he'd said, "Your mom is a tremendous soul. Leaving you girls was the hardest thing she ever had to do. Remember that, Preeya. Remember how hard it was for her."

And no words about her mother were ever spoken again.

So in her little-girl logic, Preeya had become a humanitarian by proxy. She gave up her mom to children who needed her far more than she and Prana had.

But a week later, her father left Preeya, too. With Champa. And Prana went to SafeHaven.

Preeya scoffed through clenched teeth and slammed her fists on the plush white comforter. So instead of her father's love, focus, attention—and maybe some much-needed therapy?—her doctor dad instead prescribed a healthy regimen of abandonment after abandonment.

And she couldn't believe she'd never made the connection. Her day-and-night terrors of being alone *of course* stemmed from that life-altering day, and the solitary days to follow.

But that's in the past, Pree.

Now, to be whole. On her own—*whole.*

She could do this.

*

She looked around the room, willing herself to stay calm. Alone and calm. Shake it off and find something to distract, something to do. Because fuck her father!

She began biting her nails, a nervous start to a panic episode. *Relax.*

Then Ben and his amber eyes flooded her mind. And soothed her.

Ben Trainer. A surprise. Not only wasn't he a playboy or an adulterer, but he wasn't the cocky, arrogant doctor playing world-savior she'd thought, either. He was sweet and real and somehow even empathetic to her life's low. Without condescension.

And damn hotter every minute they'd been near each other, forget about the out-of-body sex from the night before. Which she couldn't, even if she tried.

She closed her eyes to recall the ebb and flow of his movement over her. Then, with a pulsing in her core, she opened her eyes again. There, staring at her, was the grand Jacuzzi tub. In the loud silence of the empty room, it was practically calling her name.

Her clothes were bunched on the floor and her hair was down the next instant. She moved across the cool terra-cotta tile like an aimless cloud to the tub's edge. Adjusting the water temperature, she found herself smiling without control. Ready to relax and pamper herself like a woman on her own in the movies—she'd soak and lather and just *be*.

CHAPTER 18

H E COULDN'T SLEEP. *Preeya.*

Every time he shut his eyes, her violet gaze stared back at him, through him. Something in his veins, like oozing liquid heat. Mercury. Lava. Bliss.

And the thought of her made him rock-hard, ravenous.

But not an ounce of guilt surfaced—dare he think it.

The windows were open. Warm sea air from hundreds of feet below his sister's hilltop home drifted in, meeting his face, his mouth, his nose. He inhaled deep and long, then threw his head back onto the feather pillow. He was sweating, burning up. He kicked off the bedsheets. His bare chest filled with flash floods of Preeya, images of her writhing, her silken-smooth body rocking above him. He worked to fill his lungs with the Vallarta trade winds as his hand slid down his torso to his steel-hard cock. God, what she did to him. What Preeya Patel did to him.

*

Yes, this was something positive to do alone.

She'd found the perfect temperature—just short of scalding—and too tempted by the clear-liquid heaven, she got in while the tub filled. Her body melted into the water while the parts of her that remained uncovered became chilled in comparison. She huddled closer to the faucet, needing the hot water, letting it hit her knees then run down her legs while splashing her face, her shoulders, her breasts, her pebbled nipples.

She focused on the waterline rising—slow, gradual, and even—helping her breath follow suit. When the water level reached her hip bone, she let her legs fold open, her calves, knees, and thighs now satiated by the liquid warmth. Another round of goose pimples dominoed over her upper body, still prey to the cool air currents of the room. While she waited for the large tub to fill, she hugged herself and rubbed her pruning fingers up and down her arms. Up and up the hot, placid pool crept until finally it covered her navel. She exhaled as she slid her body down and laid her head back into the welcoming water, her hair and scalp getting a subtle and seeping massage.

Her entire body was now encapsulated by hot-fluid comfort but her breasts. She marveled at the contrasting stimuli igniting her senses—scalding heat and breezy cool, the sound of rushing water into the tub's silent stillness, tensed muscles above the water line and loose below, lips dry and toes wet.

And letting it all cancel out, she found herself floating in absolute peace.

Her focus had never been so keen, so sharp. Sharp like her nipples, the only part of her that hovered above the waterline, tight with the remnant chill moving over her and seemingly more sensitive than usual. Maybe from the detailed attention they'd received the night before. *Ben.*

She inhaled deeply, his name on her lips, his amber eyes in her thoughts, his body over hers in her waking dream. She sank lower, her legs in lotus position at the very bottom of the bath, the faucet's stream hammering down on her sensitive juncture, igniting her, arousing her deepest desires—her mental image of Ben fanning the flame.

She'd never in her life been alone by choice, and also had never, by choice, indulged in pleasuring herself.

She swallowed back against the tingling energy sprinting up her body. Her hips and ass shifted to keep the hot stream of water directed, focused. And her mind focused. Focused on being in Ben's powerful arms. She moaned, an involuntary sound that shot fire to her cheeks. *But no one's here, Preeya. Just you.* She inhaled, pleasure not panic, then exhaled, pure relief and calm, and sparks of sensational dynamite.

Oh, God. The hot water's steady, delicious pressure poured over her delicate bud, turning her innate sensory button to *on—so* on—and made her hips slowly rise and fall, as if she were meeting Ben's body, pressing into his strength. His boundless manhood. And the waterfall kept sensitizing her wide-open flower which pulsed and clenched with each passing moment. *Oh God, Ben.*

The water level rose, now threating to swallow up her pebbled nipples, like impending kisses. Ben's kisses. She blew out a stream of more contrasting cool air which hit the tips of her hardened nipples, and it was almost too much. If only the warm, wet, firm pressure of Ben's tongue was there to give and take the painful ecstasy of it, just like he had the night before.

She lifted her head to look at her tensed stomach muscles and curled toes and her hips lifting higher and higher to reach her image of Ben. Then she arched her back, increasing the length of her body so the impending dam of energy that waited at the gate of her heaven had longer and farther to travel. An infinite and limitless flood of pleasure just waiting to rush over her. Faster and higher her hips lifted, meeting the solid stream of water from the faucet…

Until she met her peak. *Ben. I'm coming, Ben. Oh God. I am. Coming.*

CHAPTER 19

SELF-INDUCED ORGASM ASIDE, he hardly slept at all. He was too excited. When the sun rose, so did he, excited to be awake, and strangely not tired at all.

He laughed to himself.

After Jamie passed, he had to find ways to trick his brain just to get his two feet on the floor most mornings. Coffee, the paper, the news, a run—or a damn doughnut? While recouping at his sister's after the funeral, not even a glorious Vallarta sunrise had enticed him. Because, Jesus, what could he tell his mind to look forward to if it wasn't Jamie by his side, or in the kitchen making coffee, or in the shower, or in the car waiting for him? No, instead of his wife, his love, all he'd had was the emptiness, the shame, the logistical nightmare of his medical license surrounding him. That was what awaited him each and every day since Jamie left him.

It had been a few months of downward spiral when a colleague told him about Doctors Without Borders, and he jumped on it. He needed such an extreme to move him forward. To keep him going. With life. To see *raw reality* and *struggle* worse than his own, and to see a difference he could affect. It was the only thing that made his void manageable. Or the illusion of. But it didn't fill it, not really. Not at all, in fact. It just kind of hid it from view. From his view.

But none of that mattered today. The clock showed 5:00 a.m.; his feet were firmly planted on the floor and there were only three more hours until he got to see Preeya again. Three hours before he got to talk to her. Laugh with her. Swim in her near-violet eyes. Hear more about her past and present. And what she wanted for her future. What did she really want in future? In life? He craved more direct knowledge of her being. What drove her on? The intrigue was almost killing him.

Just three more hours.

*

"Yes, I had a good night, Geej," she said, blushing from three thousand miles away. Glad her friend saw only vague vibes of happenings, for the most part. "I relaxed, took a bath, watched some TV, and fell asleep. Alone," she added, a little pride leaking through, knowing Gigi understood what a triumph that was for her.

"Well, I will tell you what, my friend, you had me awake all night for *somethin'*. I couldn't get this crazy swirling sunshine image out of my damn brain. All night long! Finally I had to wake Rod just to get the energy out of my system. He wasn't complaining any, but I am exhausted this morning, that's for sure."

Okay, so on a subconscious level, Gigi knew…but Preeya wasn't going to dignify her best friend's digging with any confirmation of her bathtub activity. She'd finally enjoyed herself—alone—and didn't want to dilute its magic by speaking of it. Even to Gigi. But she would give her a tidbit of something to get her friend sated. "Well, I am going to a secret hidden beach today with Ben. The doctor."

"The doctor? What doctor?"

"From the other night. From Boise."

"Boise…wait, wrong-name guy?"

"Yeah, that one."

"So…you're going desperate on me now?"

"No, Gigi. Turns out that I'm the ass. He's a widower. I was the first woman he'd been with since, you know, his wife died."

"That's a pretty heavy lie if it is one." Gigi sighed, a huff of cynicism. "Seriously, Pree, that would be one sick fucker if it isn't true."

"It's true, Geej. His sister had me over for dinner last night. It's all legit. He lost his wife over a year ago."

"Dinner at the sister's? Okay." Gigi paused to process. "How old is this guy, Preeya?"

"Early thirties. Look, his wife died of cancer and, well, he's just a guy…a sweet, super-intelligent, and, God, so tall and…so sexy. But at the same time, an old soul, you know?" She paused and pictured him. "Not my type, really…but not like *Evan* not my type, more like…*out-of-my-league* not my type."

Too-good-for-me not my type.

She worked to catch a fuller breath. Ben's lack of fear, his ability to adapt, move, risk, change, keep calm in the face of chaos—life-or-death chaos—it all hit her in the face and forced another hunt for air. "He's actually a bit OCD, ultra cautious and serious, though he's showing signs of loosening up." Preeya snorted and her pulse began to race at the running thought of him: Ben casually waiting for her at the airport exit, sitting across from her at dinner, opening up in the kitchen, saying good-bye outside. *But then the sunscreen.* She laughed out.

Gigi ignored the outburst. *Talk about serious.* "A doctor, Pree. You hate doctors."

Preeya cleared her throat rather than get defensive. Then consciously quiet, "He's different, Geej."

Then Gigi cleared her throat. No words followed.

"Yes, I can be wrong. Not *all* doctors suck…I guess I need to start being more specific. I hate greedy, superficial plastic surgeons who abandon their kids—that's my revised criteria. Anyway, he's an MD and a humanitarian. He travels the damn globe helping the devastated third-world, Geej…"

"Ahh, your adventurous-man check box can be, well, checked."

Preeya sighed. "I like 'im, Geej."

"Sounds too good to be—"

"I know, I know. Hell, I'm not marrying the guy, but God, he's really… real. And sweet. And the sex was, well, *unbelievable* is an understatement. We clicked, we fit, and that's what screwed with me most when I thought he'd just used me, that I had been so wrong about how in-sync we were. Because, God, it was like we'd been together before." *Or forever.* "Geej, I can sense your eyes rolling. Maybe I don't have your 'magical intuition,' but I think going with *this* is good. It feels right. So stop being so skeptical. I'm trusting my gut, and it does. It feels right."

"Can't help it. I love you. I'm protective."

"Look, I missed the wedding, I'm here alone, so what have I got to lose? Shit, Geej, this is just a new path to explore, like you said when I left Evan: 'Explore new paths!'" Gigi had hated Evan because she'd thought Preeya had totally settled. When Preeya rejected the ring, Gigi threw her a surprise party.

"Right, yes. I did say that. But a widower is some heavy shit. What's his name? I've gotta try to tune in to this one."

That *was* who Gigi had tuned into last night...Ben, Preeya's masturbation muse. "Ben, his name is Ben Trainer, but Geej, really. I'm good. Don't waste your energy. I'm just having a good time. An innocent time. He's leaving in two days; I'm leaving in two days. It's all fine."

"Fine, Pree. If you say so. You just be careful. Seriously. You are ultra-sensitive and have your own special brand of daddy and mommy issues."

God, how did I ever become best friends with such a psychoanalytical freak? Who always happens to be right!

"Hey, I sensed that shit!" Gigi shot.

"What?"

"Something...not nice...about me."

"Did you hear me think that you're always right, which is the only thing I hate about you?" Preeya threw back in mock exasperation.

"Well, that's true." Gigi sighed hard into the phone. "Listen, just don't get all defensive and closed up, Pree. I watch out for you 'cause no one else does."

"Hey, I'm working on opening up and, you know, conquering my demons. Just last night I...I handled myself—all alone—so there!"

"What do you mean *handled*?"

"Clitoris-ly handled."

"I knew it! The sexual energy was too crazy-high and un-muddied!"

"Un-muddied—not a word, Geej."

"Whatever! You got yourself off! Good for you, Pree! So proud...welcome to womanhood!"

"You're welcoming me to womanhood, Geej? You still sleep on a futon with that teddy bear, the one with the striped sleeping cap."

"Hey, don't rag on Sleepyhead. He still has my mom's scent, and the futon mattress is good for my back. Anyway, bitch, I'm just excited for you, rockin' the finger!"

"The bath faucet, actually."

"Oooh, nice...so spa-like." Gigi inhaled as if picturing herself in the same glorious state, then sighed herself back into seriousness. "Preeya, I just want you to be happy. And to stay happy. As long as you're taking this doctor guy at face value, go and have an awesome day. And maybe just, you know, sleep tonight. Give me a break from all the sexual energy in the ethers, would ya?" She laughed, but Preeya knew she was dead serious.

"I can't promise anything about tonight, Geej, but I will have an awesome day." Of that she was certain. In-her-gut certain.

CHAPTER 20

THE MARINA PARKING lot was nearly empty, it being low season, and not too many tourists headed out this early in the day anyway. Ben opened the car door for Preeya, helped her out, and then handed her a package wrapped in purple tissue paper. "This is for you."

Nose scrunched, she squared her stance and shook her head as she opened it. "You really shouldn't have gotten me anything."

"It's a Thai sarong. From the Bangkok airport. I had a layover there." Then he willed himself to shut the hell up.

"It's gorgeous. Thank you. But"—she laughed out loud—"you hadn't met me yet...when you bought it? And it's so perfect..." She fingered the thin fabric, her face all lit up.

He nodded and gave her a tight-lipped grin. "Honestly, I had brought it back for Beth, but when I gave it to her last night she insisted I give it to you instead. 'To go with your eyes' were her exact words. So I guess it's a gift from Beth, really."

The tilt of her head made him melt.

"That's really sweet of her. And of her uncle." She winked as she flicked off her sandals, holding his forearm for balance. "I love it so much, I'm puttin' it on right now." A smile of sweetness laced with spice took over her face.

Which made him slow blink in disbelief at how unbelievably stunning she was, and then that she was going to strip down. There. In the public parking lot. He flung his gaze down her body, then back to her eyes.

"Don't worry, Ben. I have my suit on under this."

"Right, of course." But the small groups of carwash guys scanning the parking lot for business all had ample time to watch her slide, wriggle, and bend out of her clothes and down to her swim suit. And the sensations that the mere *thought* of her undressing brought out in him—every amazing square millimeter of her body that he'd devoured a day and a half ago—he realized that he should have given her the sarong in the car. So she could have changed in the car.

Really, Ben?

He swallowed and shook his head to stop his gawking and thinking and overheating, and then stood in front of her to block her from view while blowing out a long, calming breath.

"Hey, hold this for me, would ya?" She handed him her purse, freeing up her hands to unbutton then shimmy out of her jeans shorts, revealing— *oh God*—her black-and-silver bikini bottoms. He sighed and rolled his eyes. She then wrapped the sarong tight around her curvy hips and voluptuous behind. Yeah, he needed to bite down on something, and *not* picture biting down on her.

Because she was just too much for him. An overload for the senses. The other night's torrent, then last night's sweet surreality—her with him and his family—and *hell*, every minute of his own torturous questioning and fantasizing and analyzing up to now.

And just when he thought she was done, her arms crossed in front of her, and her thin white tank came up and over her head. Her bikini top held and lifted her breasts perfectly.

Damn, this was hard.

And now he was hard. Rock hard. He lowered her purse a few inches, to cover his auto-reaction.

"Hey, so, where's *your* purse today?" Her brows danced with pride at her playful dig, then not a moment later, she keeled over laughing, taking his wrist to keep herself steady.

Though he'd craved her touch, God, since he'd picked her up from the hotel, he still had some defending to do. He cocked his head and narrowed his eyes. "If you must know, I left my *messenger* bag—"

"Your *murse*, you mean…" More hysterical giggles. "AKA, man purse."

"Oh, that's it." He swung her purse onto his shoulder, lifted her up from her bent-over laughing fit, and pulled her into him and his very well-maintained hard-on.

Her laughter halted. Her eyes widened then showed a glint of surprise-to-heat-to-need.

"As you can see, or rather *feel*, I'm plenty man enough to carry a 'murse'—aka 'man purse', if you'd prefer to—"

Her mouth cut off his words, her lips and tongue taking what they wanted from him as she pressed her purple sarong-wrapped center hard into him.

Holy hell.

His pulse pounding through him, he groaned into the depth of their kiss, completely unable to keep his hands in one place. Her face then neck, her shoulder blades, her graspable ass then silken arms and around to the smooth center dip of her spine… If only he could touch all of her all at once. Because damn, he wanted all of her, *this*, all the time.

From the strength of her hold, the caress of her lips, it seemed so did she, which sent relief and more ecstasy rocketing through him as their early morning lip lock continued. Her sudden need danced with his…until whooping and hollering from the loitering car washers broke through their bubble, their little corner of parking-lot paradise.

Between the guys' applause, Preeya's resumed giggles, and his racing heartbeat, he found it hard to hear or focus or breathe. But when her hand went to his chest, over his heart, and her gaze met his, he found his grounding.

He kissed the top of her head. "Our audience got their fill for the day, I think."

"Yeah, I think so." A puff of laughter, then she licked her lips. "Here, I can take my purse back now."

He hiked her purse strap up higher on his shoulder—and shifted his stance to adjust his now extremely snug-fitting shorts—proudly. "No, no. I'm good. I felt naked without my *murse*, anyway." He winked while she shook her head at him and sighed. "But, hey, I did bring the sunscreen." He reached into the car and pulled out a travel size bottle. "And my special waterproof phone-and-wallet pouch." He tugged on the lanyard around his neck, the pouch under his shirt.

"So very prepared, Doctor."

"That, I am. However, I have nothing to carry the sunscreen *in*. Gosh, if only I had brought my *bag*, I wouldn't have to ask you to carry this in yours."

"Touché. Now, gimme the lotion." She took the small bottle and tied a triple knot around its neck with her brand new sarong. "How's that?"

"Perfect." *Perfect Preeya.*

"Anything else I should tie on here?"

"Nope. And…I'll lock your purse in the trunk if that's cool?"

"Sure."

"Need anything from it first? Your phone…though I don't think it would even fit in my handy water-proof pouch…"

She took a second to think. "You know what…it's my solo-cation. It would be good to be off the grid for a bit…and anyway, you have your phone in case of emergency."

"Which won't happen because, damn it, we had enough emergency the other day to last us a lifetime."

"Definitely." Preeya shook her head and flicked her eyes to the sky.

"So…I think we're all set."

She took his hand, laced her fingers in his, and smiled at him with her eyes. Those eyes. "All set."

"You know those eyes will be the death of me, Preeya Patel." He squeezed her hand as he led her to the marina entrance.

She blushed and squeezed his hand back.

"I need to ask, does anyone else in your family have the same violet hue?"

She glanced up at him, then out to the bay ahead of them. "My mother." Her voice got thick. "I have my mother's eyes—and her flightiness, too, so says my aunt."

His breath paused a beat as he studied her. That deep sea of surfacing sadness flooded her heart, and now his. "You okay?"

She met his gaze again. "Sorry…yeah, I'm good." The corner of her lips crept up. "No, I'm really good."

He sighed then smiled. "Me, too. I'm really good, too. And God, Preeya, you're gonna love the island. And the falls. They're pure magic." He leaned in and kissed her lips. "Sadness-stripping magic."

His secret spot, the one he'd found after Jamie died. He'd gone back there each and every day for a week blinking mental snapshots of the cascading falls with his grief-stricken lenses. Trying to stop time, and then maybe trying to rewind it?

But today, to his relief and to his enthrallment, he wanted the water—and time—to move forward. He wanted to move forward. Maybe he wanted to move forward with this woman?

Ben, don't jump so far ahead. Right over that waterfall's edge.

The Vallarta Adventures guide came into view, waving to them from the dock.

"Okay, ready for our adventure?"

"Absolutely, Dr. Trainer. I'm so, so ready."

*

He held her around the waist the entire boat ride out to the Marietas. A firm, protective hold. And although it was ninety degrees by 9:00 a.m., the brisk stream of ocean air chilled her to the bone. He somehow knew it and held her closer to him.

The group on the boat was pretty small. Beside Ben and her were Pedro the guide, his assistant, Surfer Dude Ted—he'd actually introduced himself that way—and two retired couples from Canada—so said their hats, bags, and other touristy paraphernalia branded from their home country.

The two couples were funny, Preeya thought. She nudged Ben to witness the hilarity. The two silver-haired men, one thin as a rail and the other with a healthy beer gut, spoke to each other, while the cute older ladies chatted away together like little clucking hens. Occasionally the respective husbands did a kind of grunt-and-nod to their wives when they needed something. Sunscreen, or a snack or what have you. And in response the respective wives would grimace at their husbands, but would then provide the requested item. Disgruntled, but fulfilling the need nonetheless.

Ben just shook his head and laughed. He leaned in to her. "It gets that way pretty fast." The whispered comment, just loud enough to compete with the boat motor and ocean wind, sounded like it came from experience. She laughed to herself. She would have thought Ben and his late wife too young to have gotten to such a state of grumpy telepathy. But she couldn't possibly know.

Ben sat back, pulling away from her ear, and shifted so his arm supported her back better. Now square and centered in their seats, she and Ben both faced their boat mates. To find four pairs of eyes staring at them. A common wonder—no, pure awe—had come over both couples' faces. The ladies' frowns had morphed into wide grins while each reached a hand to their longtime partners. And the men each returned close-lipped smiles and patted their respective wives on the backs of their hands.

"Are you newlyweds?" the thinner man asked.

"Us? Oh God," Preeya laughed, looking at Ben with a total loss for words, the spotlight being just too much for her.

"Is it that obvious?" Ben answered confidently, taking Preeya's hand, bringing it to his lips, and kissing it sweetly.

"You make a lovely couple. Don't they, Charles? Don't they make a lovely couple...can you remember when we were that in love?"

"I can't remember what I ate for breakfast, dear. But I'm sure it was delicious, since you made it for me," the rounder man answered his wife.

"Oh, Charles, we went *out* to eat this morning," she scoffed, slapping his hand lovingly with a hint of what might have been a very standard frustration.

"You have an extraordinary time together, you hear? And make every second count," the lady with the sun hat interrupted her friend. "Because it goes fast, I'll tell ya." She winked, then she shot up to her feet. "Dolphins!"

She pointed a sun-spotted arm out toward the front of the boat. "John, get the camera. Get the camera!"

And the four older folks rushed to attend to their necessary proof-recording devices, while Preeya, still in shock at the interaction, tilted her head at Ben. "You are something else…"

"What? It made them so happy. Why not just go along with their hopeful version? And give them a little vicarious…good stuff."

"Is that what we have here?" She motioned between their bodies, huddled tight together. "Good stuff?"

"Yeah. Good stuff." He nodded and smiled, holding her gaze in his. "And it's not too far off base, is it?"

Her heartbeat blocked her ability to swallow. Or to talk. She could only nod.

He took her chin in his grasp, stopping her head from nodding and her thoughts from rushing. "We're in public, Ben," she whispered. "The elderly."

"I know. But we're newlyweds, Preeya." He leaned in to kiss her, and placed a light peck on her cheek, then one light touch of his lips to hers. He followed the sweet kisses with a whispering of words at her ear, but she couldn't make them out over the boat motor, the *oohs* and *ahhs* from the dolphin sighting, and the rushing wind.

She looked at him and his wide amber eyes so deep and soft and warm and…waiting for a response from her. God, he was so sweet and so were his whispered words, she imagined. She tilted her head at him just as the old folks' excitement peaked—something about a baby dolphin.

And then Preeya could not contain herself any longer. An explosion of laughter—out of the blue, ill-timed and unstoppable. She patted Ben's thigh and shook her head, trying to tell him through her uncontrollable outburst that she wasn't laughing at him. That it was the entire scene, the comedic play they'd been cast in, more hilarious than the murse episode, funnier than even her favorite *Lucy* clip from childhood. This, she thought, was priceless.

And as Ben waited patiently for her to rein in her laughter, she put her hand to his face. She calmed down, composed herself, and found air and words. "I'm sorry, it was just that I didn't hear you. I didn't hear what you whispered. Over all this…" Her other hand swept across their airspace, presenting the bay and the people and all.

He shook his head, took a deep breath of sea air, and then just went for it. Loudly. "I said that I love being here with you, and I am as happy as I can remember!" Which paused Pedro and Surfer Dude Ted and the old folks, too, distracting them from their dolphin experience for an interim chorus of "aww" from the women and nostalgic nods from the men.

Ben grimaced, sighed with his eyes, then leaned closer to her. "It isn't too far of a stretch though, is it, Preeya Patel? Being happy together. For at least the moment?"

He pulled back to look in her face. As if wanting confirmation. Searching her eyes.

In awe of him, of *them*, she felt like her answer to his question radiated from her. No words needed. And none were even possible. Her heart had leaped higher into her throat, choking her with kinetic joy.

He must have known, understood, seen, because he took her hands. "And this moment." He met her forehead with his. "And this one." He brought his lips to hers. Another light feather of a kiss. A dusting of snow on the first day of winter. "And this one here." The tip of his nose brushed hers as he angled his face and moved his mouth toward hers again, pulling her top lip with his full, moist lips, gently and sweetly sucking, holding. And he lingered there for a heartbeat. And another.

Until she felt him disengage. Her chest sank as the space between them filled with bay breeze and sea spray. But she kept her eyes closed, softly, as if she could keep their prior moment alive, lasting, frozen in time.

And he must have known her need. Because he leaned in again. Warming her again. At her ear now. And completely in his zone, in tune, she could hear his breath and nothing else. Then he whispered, "I am so fucking happy being here with you, Preeya Patel." Every syllable was clear as the seawater they raced over. And as clear as the blue sky floating overhead. Just crystal clear and real.

She turned to face him. Her mouth at his. Her lips on his. Her breath and thoughts and words, his. *Me, too, Ben Trainer. Me, too.*

Thirty minutes later, she caught sight of their destination—dots growing into spots growing into fuzzy mounds—while she reveled in the afterglow of Ben's sweet care.

She hadn't been a recipient to such open and honest affection. Not ever before.

And it felt amazing. Absolutely breathtaking. But scary and unreal as hell. Because now that it had moved beyond "too good to be true" into "really damn good," the worry now was that it would become "as good as it gets" or "anything worth having goes away." Well, the last one she'd made up on the fly.

Stop dreaming up worries, Preeya, and just go with it.

Like Ben was doing. Brilliantly, she'd say. God, so perfectly. Going with the flow. And to her credit, to her surprise, they were flowing damn well together, in the *now*. Yeah, she was here with him. Creating and catching real-live glimmers of joy.

And then, like a wave had come up and over the boat, a sense of relief or forgiveness or easing washed over her, and with it came a stark realization. Being here with Ben was only possible because she'd been honest with herself, and with Evan, ending their stint of complacency. Because if she hadn't done that, she'd never, ever have known such sweet, attentive warmth here, now, with this man holding her tight in his grasp. So her family thought she was crazy for closing a door to a steady, solid life—probably scared shitless that she really was like her mother, with a taste for the unknown, for life's dynamic and endless possibilities. But right now she had every confirmation that she'd made the right call. Freeing Evan from her forever-wondering mind, but more, freeing herself to seek out—and maybe just catch—the possibilities that awaited her. Like the possibility sitting next to her on this speedboat to some paradisiacal hidden beach off the Pacific Coast of Mexico. She sighed and glanced at Ben. This kind, bright, sensitive, humble, funny, and sensual man was *not* a rock star. He was better. So much better. And real. Here. Happening. Now.

And it definitely would not have been. This, their pretend honeymoon, would not have been.

Ben Trainer, where the hell did you come from?

*

The dolphins followed behind the boat the entire way to the magical Marietas, and even a humpback whale showed her flare, heaving herself out of the water and crashing down again with a mammoth splash. They got drenched, absolutely soaked. Ben wiped her face with the bottom of his shirt, and she almost couldn't stop herself from sliding her hands over his exposed skin, feeling his firm abs, around to his hips, then pressing her body into his.

But she didn't do that. God, of course she didn't. But holy hell, she wanted to.

Instead, she had wrung out her ponytail on his head, and began to laugh hysterically. Ocean water dripped down his nose and over his lips, which curled up into a coy smile. "You'll get yours, Preeya Patel. Oh, you'll get yours."

She hoped to God that was a promise.

At that point, the sweet older lady in the sun hat was being less than subtle about photographing them and their water play. Preeya just laughed and pressed her cheek against his rough and so-sexy stubble, filling the newlywed role. Ben played along happily—he pulled her close, kissed her cheek, her neck. Once the onlookers got their fill of photos, the pretend Dr. and Mrs. Ben Trainer soaked in the essence of the beautiful bay.

CHAPTER 21

THE SCORCHING SUN had dried and warmed them both by the time the motor clipped to a halt. They were there. At this place Ben Trainer loved so much.

Pedro announced that it was time to jump in the water and swim to where he pointed, a short, cavernous arch in a lush, green-covered landmass some two hundred feet away. "That way is the hidden beach, *mi amigos.*"

So much for getting dry. She stood up, tightened her new sarong—and sunscreen—tighter around her waist, adjusted her bikini underneath, clicked the life vest closed, then dove in. Ben followed right behind her, meeting her in the water, the palm of his hand on her bare back, as if to tell her he was right there with her.

Their fellow boat mates took a good while longer, their bickering from the boat about who and what was going when and where could be heard from a hundred feet away as Preeya and Ben swam together in the shallow, turquoise waters. They looked at each other and laughed when they finally heard the far-off splashes of their older friends entering the water.

"When we're old and gray, *sweetie*, I hope we're still doing this sort of thing, even if we're slower and grumpier then." She winked at him then splashed him in the face with her hand.

He laughed then disappeared under the water.

She looked around her, pulse ramping up a notch—were there sharks and jellyfish in here? Because she thought she'd heard...

A hand slid along the back of her neck, down her back, and snapped the strap of her bikini top.

He popped up, laughing.

"Hey there, buddy."

"Sorry, but slower and grumpier isn't my style, Mrs. Trainer," he teased, then he took a few faster strokes and waited for her to catch up, or rather, to catch *him*. The playful chase was making her hot in that cool, crisp water. Hot, thirsty, and wanting.

She swam after him and caught him around the waist with her legs. She squeezed for a moment, then pushed herself off before his long, thick arms could bring her in. Yes, she liked this play. She liked this picture of *them* in general. And thinking back to the ultra-serious, righteous, and slightly cocky doctor she'd met on her flight only nights before—*God*, how wrong she'd been. And *wow*, she really, really liked this man.

They continued their swim together, now more or less side by side. Ben had been there before and obviously knew the way, so they didn't need to stop and wait for Pedro at the opening to the arching entrance of the island. They swam on. The water was so crystal clear to the bottom that she could see small schools of fluorescent fish darting this way and that. They made their way through the watery tunnel to the hidden beach, like two magnets unable to keep from touching each other somehow, some way. And she liked it. A lot.

As they got to the shallower water of the inside portion of the site, her hand was in his—strange but as natural as could be. She laughed to herself, unsure of when he took her hand. Or was it she who took his? What did it matter? It felt right. Righter than right.

She smiled at him as he helped her out of the water onto the white sandy beach.

"Stand here and look up." She did as he told her while he unclipped her life vest and tossed it on the ground.

The scene had captivated her speechless. Her toes wiggled in the silky white powder with escalating excitement. *No words at all.*

She tore her eyes from the view hovering over her and looked at him.

Still no words available. She reached up on her tiptoes, slid her hands around his neck, and kissed him on the mouth, a deep, delirious kiss. Then she backed away from him almost giggling—*glee*, that's what ballooned in her chest—and began to spin around and around and around, eyes up to the earthen crater above them, which opened to a perfectly blue circle of wide-open forever-sky.

*

"Pedro thinks you're beautiful," Ben said while she continued her spinning dance of awe. "He was going to ask you out but I told him to wait until after our honeymoon's over."

"Well, Pedro *is* kinda cute…maybe he can take me on a honeymoon tomorrow."

"Yeah…or if you prefer, we can call our honeymoon day over here and now and I'll go hook up with Sun Hat and Charles over there. They look like they'd be into a threesome."

She paused, stunned to laughter by his out-of-character comment, and, too dizzy to function, she fell to her knees. The two older couples were just making their way through the archway toward them, their back-and-forth grumblings echoed throughout the cavern. Imagining Ben and the couple not *operating* on them but *operating on them* made her nearly pee her pants, or bikini bottoms, as it were.

Since she'd already made it to the so-soft sand, she crawled on her hands and knees to a perfect sunny spot while her laugh attack simmered. She squinted up at Ben with a raised brow and patted the spot next to her. "Get over here, hubby, and let's get some sun. Because, man, do you need it." She smirked at him standing there so sweetly proud and tall, his lean, long, and athletic build making his statement for him. "Sweetie," she said for the benefit of their older friends and, well, the game of pretend had become fun, "you're gonna blind someone with that gleaming white torso of yours." She reached for his ankle to pull him down to join her already. "That is, if you don't scare someone to death with those farmer's-tanned arms first."

He gave her a narrowed stare then flicked his eyes away in mock anger.

"I meant those *lean, muscular* farmer's-tanned arms, *hun.*" Again, for their audience. "They're totally sexy. Hot red sexy." Another laughing outburst covered up her preoccupation with the head-to-toe and inside-out tingling sensation shooting through her. It was the total recall of those arms—his strong, sinewy arms—holding her down, flipping her over, squeezing, wrapping, and maneuvering her, any way he wanted—only two nights ago. *Too long ago now.*

She lay back on the warm, wet sand and patted the spot next to her again, then untied the sunscreen from her sarong. "Here, I'll lather you up."

But Ben didn't speak or budge. He just stood over her, still and tall and pensive. Was he soaking her in with that golden gaze of his—she adjusted her bikini in case—or was he planning how to cook her up and eat her?

No clue.

Then, without a word, he nodded to her—or someone farther off?—turned on his heels and disappeared. *Even stranger.* And the sudden and ultra-strong glare from the sun streaming through the overhead crater practically blinded her so she also had no clue where he'd gone.

So mysterious.

A half minute later he was back with waters for them both. Or not mysterious, but really sweet. And hydration-conscious. She smiled a thank-you as he sat down next to her, hip to hip. She was glad to be in closer proximity to him again.

"So, while we wait, do you wanna hear the background of this place?" He pointed up at the hovering crater, which cast an ethereal shadow around the outskirts of the über-romantic and mystical beach.

"Yes, please…but while we wait for what?"

He smirked, waggled his brows, and took a large gulp of his water.

She gave his arm a light shake, impatient with the game, though she liked the game very much, and she liked the playful Ben very much. "Wait for what, Ben?"

"You'll have to *wait* for what we're waiting for. Now, for your history lesson…get ready to get your bubble burst…"

She cocked her head, eyes narrowed, unsure if there was innuendo in there or what. "Okaaay?"

"This massive hole above us was created by bomb tests performed by the Mexican government decades ago."

She frowned like a child whose bubble had just literally been burst.

He touched her chin and began to laugh without pause.

"Stop laughing at me," she mock-whined and slapped his arm.

"Sorry, sorry…" But he couldn't stop his laughing fit. "It's just…you… look like I ruined Santa, the Easter Bunny, and the Tooth Fairy all at once." He leaned into her. "You're even gorgeous when you pout, Preeya Patel." He placed a kiss on her earlobe, then on her neck just under her jawline. He dragged his lips down and over her shoulder, then down her arm while she followed his trail of grazes with her eyes. "Mmm, you taste salty-sweet." He leaned back again, dug his elbows into the sand, and gazed at her.

She rolled her eyes playfully and lay back to join him. Breathing in the sea air and his scent, a mix of sea salt and musk, she felt high. His hand at her side brushed her leg; she laced her fingers through his and squeezed. Then they both looked up above them.

The backstory of the locale—aka, their mystifying pretend honeymoon spot—didn't do any damage to how splendid and breathtaking the place was. Or the day. And the moment. With Ben by her side.

*

He squeezed her hand back, then brought both of his arms above his head and settled all the way back onto the white silken sand. "Nap with me a while," he said. "We still have a bit of a wait for—uhp, I almost slipped."

"Oh just tell me, already. Please, Ben?"

But he'd already closed his eyes, pretend-snoring away.

She huffed and tightened her grip on his hand, then settled down into the sand to wait patiently. The ocean's tide outside the cavern lulled her, but she didn't want to close her eyes. She was still too in-awe of the thin shell of earth hovering over them. "This is like another world…"

With his eyes still shut, he broke his fake-sleep silence. "You wanna see another world that *was* made by Mother Nature herself?"

"Definitely…"

"Good," he said as a tall shadow appeared on the sand in front of them. "My man Pedro is here to take us." Ben grinned at her with a twinkle in his eye, like a little boy about to show her his secret tree house.

He helped her up and then kept one of her hands in his, then nodded at Pedro to lead the way.

CHAPTER 22

THIRTY MINUTES LATER they were at his spot. Pedro plopped himself down on a rock by the far side of the falls, placed his cap over his eyes, and wasn't shy about his intent to doze off. Maybe he was just being awesome, giving them some privacy. *Good man.*

He glanced up at Preeya, wanting to stare at nothing else all day. Her attention was set firmly on the waterfall cascading down the natural rock cliff into the pristine lagoon, an endless oasis. God, her dark-lashed eyes couldn't get any wider, he thought.

And he understood why. To him, this place was heaven on earth.

But now being here with Preeya, it had elevated to something else, something more.

He looked hard at Preeya then touched her arm to grab her attention. "Strip."

"Excuse me?"

"Take your clothes off. The water's perfect."

"Wow. Okay, Mr. Forward," she said with one brow raised.

He smiled and lifted a brow back. She liked him this way, he could tell. And *he* liked him this way. His true, no bullshit self.

"Chop, chop." He tilted his head expectantly, then he softened. "I promise, Preeya Patel, you'll thank me."

"Maybe, but you go first, Doctor Benjamin Trainer."

He gave her a wicked grin as he'd already started untying the drawstring of his swim trunks. Way ahead of her. "I'll meet you in there, slowpoke."

Completely naked and in up to his ankles the next moment, he dove in the rest of the way. "God, this is as perfect as I remember!" The temperature was bathwater warm.

When he dunked his head and came up again, Preeya was moving toward him, her sweat-kissed skin practically sparkling in the sun. Her breasts were full, chest out, nipples—*oh Lord*—pebbled and perfect, maybe from the temperature contrast between the incredibly humid air and the water's perfection. But maybe for want of him, need of his attention, his detailed tending and care like he'd given her the other night. He'd passed that test, thankfully. And was so ready to give her more. So much more.

And she continued toward him, slightly bashful but not shy enough to move too quickly or to hide herself. No, she glided into the natural pool slowly, seductively. And he could only admire. And anticipate.

Once the water hovered just below her nipples, she sank suddenly, then bobbed back up. "There's a drop-off!" she yelled. He laughed, swimming over to her. "I didn't know there was a drop-off." She spit out a stream of water and coughed, but then began laughing which made her cough more. When he got to her, she wrapped her arms around him, her smooth skin rubbing against his making him spark to life. He swallowed hard, trying to keep focus on *her*, not on *having* her.

"You're okay," he told her. "It's only ten feet down at this point. But come." He let his hands slide down her arms, ready to pull her toward the water cascade. "I want to show you what's under the falls. It's magic on earth. You'll see."

*

She couldn't stop where things were going. Neither could he, it seemed. It was a force of nature starting with a deep kiss behind a torrential wall of water.

She wasn't sure if she'd ever made love before. But hidden from the world on that perfectly molded bolder behind that impenetrable sheet of deafening water, that protective curtain rushing down between them and the outside world, she was undoubtedly made love to. No question in her heart. No question in her soul.

Their connection had all of the out-of-body passion they'd shared the first night they were together in Boise, Idaho, but she was anything but out of her body now. She was so present, so in the moment with Ben, she couldn't help but feel like it was a dream. Like there was no *before*, no *after*, just them, *together*, writhing in perfect harmony, the gentle vapor from the falls gracing both their bodies. A magical mist. Pure magic, like Ben had said. His kisses and their connection, also perfect. Unforgettably perfect. She didn't want to wake up from the *now* he'd brought her to.

But they had to leave the enclave eventually. And when they swam out, she was thankful for his constant touch. There wasn't a second when his finger or his hand wasn't in contact with her skin. And she needed that, any remnant of his spark, or else she thought she might just evaporate, become part of the waterfall crashing down in front of her. And simply mist away. Up and away.

CHAPTER 23

ONCE THEY GOT back to Vallarta, Preeya felt like a year had gone by since morning. And she didn't want their yearlong day, their mock honeymoon, to end.

When he called his sister to let her know he wouldn't be home for dinner, she felt a tinge of guilt for keeping him from his family, but a wave of relief and excitement for his choice, choosing her.

He brought her to a very nice seafood restaurant—swimsuits and flip-flops in Vallarta's best establishments were the norm, he said. The place was *on* the river, the Rio Cuale, that fed into the bay. The flowing water splashed up to tickle her toes and legs she was so close to the bank. Vibrant overhead lanterns of blues and golds reflected in the water as dusk turned to twilight. "Are you positive you don't want to invite Stacy and the kids to join us?"

He gave her a look. "Absolutely positive. I don't want to share you with a soul."

*

Is this happening right now? In reality—not another stupid pipe dream of hers, not a waking dream?

And as if he'd read her thoughts, he reached for her hand from across the small, intimate table for two and locked his fingers with hers. She inhaled the evening air deep into her lungs to slow her pulse reverberating throughout her chest.

It's happening, Pree. And don't get too excited about it. She had to enjoy *now* and worry about nothing else.

She took a sip of the wine he'd ordered to attempt to do just that. It was a rich and fruity pinot noir, he'd said, one that he'd thought she'd enjoy very much. And she did—the taste and warmth and heaviness on her tongue—but more, the sophisticated association of the act of drinking wine. With a man, this man, at this fine dining gem on a river in Puerto Vallarta. She hadn't much experience with wine and fine dining and men, a real man—all what she'd considered more *adult* pleasures. A giggle escaped her at the mental reference. *Being* an adult. Yeah, twenty-five, it was time. She sighed and smiled at Ben who'd been watching her throughout her cerebral wanderings.

"Do you like the wine?"

"I do. I really do."

"It will go perfectly with the tuna steaks I'll order for us. This place is famous for their tuna, confirmed by yours truly. I need you to experience it." He winked then lifted his glass to hers and sipped.

She nodded and took another pull from her glass. It felt a bit strange, his choosing their meal, ordering for her—a bit presumptuous. But as the wine and the light rush of the river and Ben's gaze penetrated her senses, she let the concern go. She'd enjoy the experience, trust it. Trust him and his desire to make her as happy as he'd done all day long.

*

Dinner was divine, but she'd been too taken by Ben to have enjoyed it as thoroughly as he'd intended. He'd really have to blame himself, topping the meal with his own general effervescence—his questions and answers and stories and ideas made her forget all else.

And anyway, living for the now takes practice, she guessed.

"So, your opinion of your honeymoon day?"

"You are the ultimate pretend husband, Doctor Trainer, and the ultimate guide." To save herself from blushing, she held back her comment on what else he'd been *ultimate* at—her entire body still hummed from their love-making behind the falls.

He nodded; a sweet warmth resonated from him. Again, like he'd read her thoughts.

"You know...since...the funeral..." He swallowed hard, his Adam's apple lifting and falling with his suddenly tightened shoulders, "...I've used Vallarta. To hide away, to isolate myself from...myself. And from my past life." His face lowered, focused and pensive, his fingers fidgeting with his fork and knife. "But I will tell you something..." With slow and controlled intent, he brought his eyes up to meet hers.

"What's that?" she asked, now swimming in his eyes of sunset.

"Today, with you...I feel like myself again. This place has felt like a deserted tropical island to me over the last year-plus, but now...I'm here to enjoy it. Like, I'm really *here*. It's a paradise again to me. With you."

She smiled at him, melted for him. His foot met hers under the table. And her hand found his above it.

"I've been meaning to ask you," he said, his thumb stroking her wrist, her tattoo peeking out from under her ever-dead watch. "What is *this* exactly—what does it represent?"

"My blue moon," she said, half smiling.

"Is it your sad blue moon?"

"No, it's not *that* blue." She laughed. "It's just rare. You know, the full moon that appears a second time within the same month?"

He smiled and shrugged. "Us doctors definitely don't know everything." He winked.

"Well, I got the tattoo with my teen-hood boyfriend...total rebel rocker type."

Ben's head cocked to the side.

"Shit, yes, at Sea-Tac that day. Josh Bolte."

"Wow."

"Yeah...wow. Total pipe dream turned...pipe head." She shook her head. "Fell into the life, you know?"

"So you and he...that night..."

"Did nothing. Well, that's not true. He snorted, and I slept—with the help of half a liter of vodka."

Ben nodded, relief spreading a smile over his mouth. "The guy was pretty…intense."

"That's the one consistent thing about him. Not always into the bad shit, but always intense. God, back in the day we—or, *I*— thought our 'love' was so special, so rare and, yes, intense." She rolled her eyes and sighed, then chuckled at her own expense. "*So* damn special that he left me cold. Skipped out with no warning. But hey, he left a note—it wasn't a text, right?"

Ben blinked and smiled at her. "I thought you were going to say he left you for another hot girl, not that I can imagine anyone hotter than you." He waggled his brows, as if racking up points.

She shook her head as her face heated to scorching. "No, it wasn't as dramatic as another woman, though I can't say for sure there weren't others." She scoffed. There likely were. "Anyway, it hurt maybe as bad as catching him with someone else. *I hate cheaters.*" She couldn't help but think of her father then, marrying another woman. Although her mother had left *them*, Preeya had an image of marriage—idealistic as it may seem, *whatever.* Like *Legends of the Fall*, forever should be forever. *And it wasn't like Mom left them for another man, another family.* But still, her dad moved on. With *Sylvia.* Silicone-sexy Sylvia.

"Preeya…you okay?"

"Oh yeah." She shut her eyes to reset herself. "Sorry, got sidetracked… *anyway*, here's the entertaining part. That good-bye note that Josh had left me…"

Ben nodded, all attention.

"Well, it included song lyrics that I'd supposedly *inspired*…and now he's a gazillionaire. Ever hear 'Sun and Moon in the Guest Room'?"

Ben shook his head, then smirked. "Off the grid for the better part of the year. But wow, that's insane. Too bad muses don't get residuals."

She laughed. "That's what…a friend of mine said. Anyway, I heard the damn song last night in the cab. It makes me cringe every damn time."

"Teen love. Oh so deep, yes?"

"Yeah, right."

"Well, my teen love"—he moved his hand to his chest, to the lanyard around his neck, then dropping his hand back down to the table, he cleared his throat—"became my wife." He shook his head and sighed, then dug up a thin smile. "Shit, I'm sorry." But neither his expression nor his apology did a thing to hide the lingering sadness in his eyes.

She could've cried a river for him. "It's fine, Ben, really—"

"No. It isn't. We had such an amazing day. And"—he slid his hand out across the table, nearly knocking over his wine glass, and grabbed her hand—"you're amazing, Preeya. Fucking unbelievable to me."

The heat in her cheeks and the warmth in her chest got her light headed. "Ben." She looked down at their hands, then laced her fingers with his and slid her other hand on top. Venturing to meet his eyes, she found intensity and something else…and it was almost too much.

Topic change, Preeya. She had to get them back to the light side before she broke into sobs of *crazy.* Because, damn it, she also had loved the day, and the sweet—and sensual—focus on *them.* And she wanted that back now. For him…and for her. No downers allowed on such a day.

On her fake honeymoon.

She smiled…then untangled their hands to grab the dessert menu. "So, hey, do you, um, want to share a slice of triple-chocolate cheesecake? I have such a craving after our crazy energy-output today." She gave him a super-seductive glimmer.

But her suggestion was met with a *super*-awkward silence.

Then he squinted his eyes at her, swallowed, and disengaged his eye-lock. With the loss of his gaze went his warmth and their vibe. Ben had left the table, though his body still sat in the chair across from her.

She squirmed in her seat. *Shit, Preeya.* Bad segue.

She'd been insensitive—no, she'd offended him. Or worse, she'd *hurt* him. And now she couldn't overcome the heat stroke that had taken her by the throat on its sprint up to her face.

As she fought the tightening in her chest, that old panic as if she were all alone, her phone rang from somewhere in her purse—and there went any hope for resuming their kinetic connection. She closed her eyes and wished that a slow-motion blink would rewind and undo the past minute.

But it did nothing.

And the phone just kept buzzing.

"So sorry." She reached for the phone in her bag to at least stop the obnoxious noise. Then she glanced at the screen, probably deepening the offensive-factor, but as it turned out, the call was from SafeHaven. Which she'd just missed.

Not the usual ringtone, though.

"Shit."

"What is it?"

"It's, um, not sure. My sister's facility…but, damn it, um…let me go to the front and call, okay?" And without catching his reply, she'd placed full attention on her phone screen and gotten up from her chair.

She weaved through the maze of tables. Four missed calls from Aunt Champa and three others from SafeHaven? *Fuck.*

Why had she left her cell in her purse and her purse in the car all day?

So she could fully experience and enjoy the excursion away from the world. With Ben.

Screw enjoyment. Experience. Missing a call from SafeHaven—several calls—*damn it.* The surge of quaking guilt moved her legs and feet and pulse fast, late-to-a-flight fast. Short of breath, she came upon the slew of people milling about the restaurant's front lobby and vestibule. She worked for a full breath, then continued out to the parking lot when she pressed the number.

CHAPTER 24

"THIS IS PREEYA Patel. I just missed a call from—"

"Yes, hold the line, please."

"But is everything all right with Prana? Prana Patel, my sister."

"Yes, Prana Patel is…fine, but, oh goodness, hold a moment, please…"

Hold? What the hell? Was Prana fine or was she now *not fine?*

"Preeya Patel. How selfish can one person be? You miss your father's wedding and don't bother to call? Aside from all that I have done for you, young lady, you should really know what your father, my brother, has done for you. It's about damn time."

"Aunt Champa? What's going on? Is Prana okay? Tell me"—*you horrid witch!*—"is everything all right with my sister?"

"Oh, so you care about Prana? But you abandon her at this family function. The nerve…really, the nerve of you!"

Like their father's wedding had a damn thing to do with either of his precious daughters. He'd abandoned her and her sister. And Champa had the nerve to put it on Preeya?

Wait, had they brought Prana to the stupid wedding as bait? Or as the ultimate guilt trip? Or so her father could save face and look like he's father of the fucking year? Have at least one daughter present. And bonus points for having the disabled one there. *Fucking prick.* Hell, it was probably all of the above.

Focus, Pree. On what matters.

"Is she all right, Champa? Please, just tell me that. Is Prana okay?"

"Yes. But your father's not. He's devastated. And humiliated."

"Like I give a shit if he's embarrassed. Don't you see that? *I...we* were *left* by my parents—"

"Whoa, whoa, whoa—"

"No. You let me finish. I was stuck with you, my aunt, treated like an outcast, always put down just to bring your own daughter up. I thought family was...was unconditional. I had no goddamn mother, for Christ's sake. And you had to go and remind me that I wasn't *your* damn kid every fucking day I lived in your house. I never even felt like your niece..." She paused, out of breath and suddenly light-headed. "I hardly felt like a damn stranger!"

"Are you done, Cinderella?"

Silence. Preeya had no more words, just fumes, her chest heaving.

"First off, your father *did not* abandon you. Your mother, on the other hand, *did*."

"My mother left us for a cause; my father left us for fear and greed. Left us to the wolves, Prana and I—left to the fucking wolves."

"I am no wolf, my dear, and I hope to God you never go to India to know what preying animals *really* look like. But, no, you are wrong—dead-wrong about my brother. He saved your sister's life. And yours. And you're wrong about your mother, too."

"What the fuck are you talking about?" Then Ben came up behind her and asked with his eyes if he should stay there with her—worried compassion in his face. She nodded. *Because please, for the love of God, someone stay with me through this insanity.*

"Your mother left...because of your sister. A month after giving birth—*she left*. Not for some charitable mission in India, Preeya. Not for anyone but herself. She didn't want the *burden* of raising Prana. And so the coward left. She left Prana and you *and* my brother. She abandoned all three of you because of her selfish heart, her lazy, love-lacking heart."

"I don't believe you. I don't! Why would my father lie to me?" Her head swam, heart shook. "You just want to demonize her, is all. Because you got stuck with me. She sacrificed raising her own children to go and help hundreds. Thousands by now. You wish you had a molecule of that selfless-ness in you."

"Oh, you think raising your sister, with all her issues, wouldn't have scared her off? Her entire life would have been *on duty*. Prana is seven-teen years old now and she can't even use the restroom on her own. That child would've cut into your mother's perfect life. No more 'everything-to-the-wind'! That free-spirit got off scot-free, that's for sure."

Preeya went silent in her desperate attempt to find oxygen. But nothing. She could only muster a shallow half-breath through her shock.

"Preeya, your father lied to you for the same selfless reason he does any-thing. He didn't want you to blame Prana. And so you wouldn't think bad of your mother and then project her ills on yourself. But honestly, I think that's exactly who you turned out to be, Preeya Patel. Just like your selfish witch of a mother. And nothing like your father. If only..."

Preeya blinked her eyes. She took another attempt at air, but now hav-ing been stabbed in the chest by someone who dared call herself flesh and blood—her guardian—she couldn't for the life of her snag a breath. And if her gasping had pulled any oxygen into her lungs, it all must've leaked out those dagger holes in her heart, because the next instant she only saw a blurry version of Ben through hazy eyes. She blinked desperately for clarity, but things only got blurrier. And foggier. Then darkness.

CHAPTER 25

H E SLID HIS hand from her cheek to her neck and checked her carotid pulse. It was racing, but not in the red zone, and her breathing, shallow but even. He'd thankfully caught her when her knees gave out—God, a head injury would've meant half a night in a Mexican ER if you were lucky.

Her phone, though, he hadn't caught. It now lay at his feet. He shifted Preeya's weight in his arms so he could hold her and open the car door without her falling. Ben slid her into the front seat, situated her legs and head, then bent down to grab her phone from the ground.

It wasn't shattered, just dinged on a corner. The call minutes still ticked away—he heard a shrill voice coming through the tiny speaker. He put the phone to his ear, but the call ended. He hit End a few times to clear it before slipping the device into his pocket and refocused on Preeya.

He kneeled at her side, took her wrist to feel her pulse again, and to feel her warmth. He waited twenty seconds then multiplied—her pulse felt fast still, but nothing to be concerned about. He brushed a loose strand of hair from her face. So drained, so calm, so damn gorgeous and sweet and smart.

He sighed. God, what had upset her so badly?

She moaned, as if in a dream.

"I'm right here, Preeya. You're okay and I'm right—"

A buzz sounded from his pants pocket. Just in case it was whomever she'd been speaking to—her sister's doctor maybe?—he glanced at the screen.

Thnx Pree, and FYI, I can't stop thinking about you. Always, Ev.

From Evan Chambers, date, time, et cetera.

Evan? Can't stop thinking about her?

Hey. None of your business, Ben.

Right.

He shoved the phone back in his pocket and the lingering thoughts—*Evan?*—down deeper in his mind.

"Preeya. Hey, Preeya…it's me, Ben," he whispered in her ear. Her eyelids fluttered, then stuttered open.

"Hey, back," she murmured, looking around slowly in an obvious daze.

"You're sitting in my car. You just passed out."

"Huh. Right. Yeah, I…I remember…things going fuzzy."

He wouldn't dare ask what had upset her unless she wanted to tell him, but…"You're staying with us tonight."

"No, no. Just take me to the hotel. I'll be okay."

"You're staying. And I'll postpone my departure. So I can be here for you."

But her head just kept shaking from side to side. As if she was against something more than what he was saying. "No. No, no. I want to go with you, Ben. On your excursion. I want to go with you, to help."

Had he heard her right? Yes, but she was delirious. "I would love that, but you are not in any shape to make that call right now." And what of her job? Where was this coming from?

Her eyes widened and darted at him with a sternness he hadn't seen from her in the short—yet extremely intense—time he'd known her. "I am in fine shape. Perfectly sound. Never more clear-headed. Really. I want to come. I want to help. With you."

He smiled at her, though still taken aback. "We have another day and a half to think, talk, plan. Until then, let's get you home, comfortable, rested."

"I need Wi-Fi. Gotta video-call Prana, my sister. See that she's okay."

"Stacy has Wi-Fi."

"Your sister's house is fine, then. Let's go."

Ben moved to stand, but her hand took his arm. "Wait. I…I want to stay with you tonight. *With you*, with you. That wouldn't be…appropriate, though. At your sister's, with the kids there…"

His pulse ratcheted up a few hundred RPMs—her intensity, her insistence, her focused need, it was like a shot to his heart. "Your hotel has Wi-Fi, right?"

She gave him a frantic nod. God, that call had shaken her up and made her downright impulsive. "Yes. The hotel. To the hotel."

He swept a few more loose wisps of her black-as-night hair from her panic-stricken face and shook his head, unsure if this was happening in real life, real time. "Okay, so…I'll stay with you tonight."

"Yes."

"I'll call Stacy and let her know."

"Yes."

"You really should have a doctor close by in case, you know, you faint again." He sighed then winked—this was happening.

"Yes, Ben. I need you…close by." But her expression wasn't suggestive or seductive. It was still fear-stricken and stunned. His hand moved to her cheek, brushing it with his thumb. "I'll stay with you, Preeya," he whispered. "I'm here and I'm not going anywhere."

*

Just as he inserted the key into the ignition she took his hand and nuzzled her cheek into his palm. How drained she seemed. How vitally spent.

"Thank you. And, Ben, I'm sorry…for earlier. At the table. When you were trying to talk about your wife. And then *us*…I was—"

His finger at her lips halted her words. "You're fine, Preeya Patel. You owe me no apology. If anything, I owe you an—"

"No."

"Yes. It's hard to know…what to say around me. I still don't control… my emotions, my reactions." He shook his head then took her hand. "And honestly, since, you know Jamie's passing, I haven't felt like myself…the real me, until now, until *you*. So for that, I should thank—"

A loud ringing interruption came from his pants pocket.

"It could be SafeHaven…"

He shifted to grab then hand the phone to Preeya. "Just…keep it short," he suggested, not wanting her upset again. And not wanting it to be that Evan again.

"It's Amy…from her honeymoon cruise? There's gotta be something wrong. Hello?"

*

Amy's frantic ramble overwhelmed Preeya, so she put it on speakerphone so Ben could grasp anything she missed.

"They just got Wi-Fi restored on the ship, and we saw the missed calls from Darren's mother. It apparently happened Sunday morning. The doctors say it's a miracle his brother's even alive." Amy spoke through her sobs. "If he'll ever function again, they can't say. They can't even say if or when he'll come out of the coma. Darren is sick over it. His brother all but raised him, Pree. And there's no way for us to get there—no port stop for another day and a half…"

"God, Ame, I'm so sorry. What can I do?" She hated that tragedy hit her friend at all, but especially during her honeymoon. *Jesus.*

"My sister and mother are the only ones there from my side, and, well, they're fucking crazy. And Darren's mom is, of course, a wreck. I want to know how he is through trusted eyes, to put Darren at ease, if that's remotely possible. Can you just go to the hospital, check, give us the real deal? And give Elaine a little company, too."

"Of course." She motioned to Ben for a pen and paper. "Which hospital?"

"Santa Maria Hospital, ICU, room 515."

"I'll go now," she said while Ben nodded to her. "The friend I'm with, he's a doctor. He'll take me and we'll get the facts. Watch your phone and email, okay?"

"Right, okay. Thank you, Pree. Really, thank you." And the call disconnected with the last remnants of a whimper from Amy Rine, or rather, Amy James.

CHAPTER 26

THEY HEADED BACK into the restaurant to pay, to pee, and to check for Wi-Fi so they could skip her hotel for now and get to the hospital for Amy. But she needed to reach out to her sister before anything or anyone else.

"Watch your step here," Ben said, his hand at her lower back. His delicate touch sent warm waves over her skin.

"Thank you."

"God, when it rains, it pours, huh?" he went on, holding the door open for her.

"You aren't kidding." Her phone call with Aunt Champa flashed to mind, and the brash awakening to an opposite reality replaced the warmth of Ben's touch with a rush of icy chills up her spine. "I think I need water…"

"Of course. Sit here. I'll get a bottle and the Wi-Fi code…if they have a hotspot."

She plopped down on the long, cushioned bench in the restaurant's lobby and watched Ben's long strides to the hostess stand.

What if Ben hadn't been there? What if she'd been alone to hear her aunt's rant? Alone and completely off guard. And in contrast to last night, when she'd found a new piece of herself, a version of *her* where she could be on her own, and be okay. More than okay. Not lonely, but strong and alone, by choice. Like she was a worthy-enough person to be alone *with*.

But if she had been alone to hear what her asshole aunt had told her, she would have broken. Cracked in half.

To hear about her mother, a complete coward? Abandoning her and her little sister? And her father is, what now, a savior? And God, the possibility, the potential within her, according to Aunt Champa, to be just like her mother, a goddamn escape artist of the most pathetic, unnatural sort. Leaving her babies? Not for selflessness. God, what insanity! Not for the poor children of the world? And she had been so proud of the woman, the whole-hearted seeker of truth, love, spiritual fucking liberation. It had justified the sacrifice, the lovelessness, the loneliness. But now the veil had lifted and left Preeya blind in the glaring, raw and fucked-up truth of it all.

"Jesus, you're more pale than when I left you." Ben unscrewed the water bottle and handed it to her, scrutinizing her with his narrowed stare. The doctor, the lover, the friend—his look of concern made her chest swell and her cheeks heat, easing the angst in her throat formed from her family bullshit.

She sipped the water, and again, then handed it back to him. "Thank you."

"Better?" Still staring at her like she was a dandelion at risk of losing her wisps with one quick breath of a wishful child. And it seemed that not even her tornado of a family could destroy her so...

"Yeah, I'm fine. Or I'll *be* fine..." She sighed then pulled out her phone. "Here, sit with me." She laced her arm through his, then opened her video chat. "I'll introduce you to Prana. She'll like meeting you."

"Take another drink first." Like she did to him at the bar the other night. She smiled and took a pull of water per the doctor's orders.

*

She called the main number first, which she had to do anyway so they could help Prana set up at the computer. But this time she wanted to know what the hell Champa was pulling.

"Maicey Anton, please?"

The unit director. She'd been caring for Prana since the start. The woman answered warmly and began explaining the situation. It turned out Champa had been bluffing. They didn't take Prana to the wedding. But when Preeya wouldn't call her aunt or father back, Champa apparently drove the hour to SafeHaven under the guise of a visit—after not seeing Preeya's sister for how many years?—and insisted on making an outgoing call from their internal phone system. Aunt Champa knew Preeya would never ignore a call from SafeHaven. Irony of ironies, her phone had been in Ben's trunk all day. Hey, at least the witch had to wait a bunch of hours to get her rant-on.

"Is Prana okay, though? Did my aunt upset her at all?"

"No, hun, Prana's fine. Your aunt gave her a coloring book…stayed with her in her room for less than five minutes. Then, like I said, she fumed in the lobby for the rest of the time."

Preeya sighed with relief and calm. "Thank God. Well, even though I'll be up in a few weeks, is it too close to bedtime for me to video chat with her?"

"Not at all. I'll connect you. And Preeya, no worries. We wouldn't let any family friction or chaos touch your sister."

"Of course, Maicey. Thanks. Really, thank you."

While she waited, her thoughts ran rampant. *Aunt Champa.* That heartless, egocentric bitch. Playing Preeya like that. "But at least," she said to Ben, "Prana's okay." Even though she hadn't filled Ben in at all—about her family drama—and he didn't ask, didn't push. He just sat beside her, his hand stroking her back. Not hovering, just a strong pillar for her to lean on.

The picture-in-picture came up black on her screen, then her sister's face appeared. "Prana, sweetie. Hey, there. How ya doin', little sister?"

Her sister blinked and looked up to the right. That was a *meh*—just okay.

Damn it, Champa. "Me, too. But now that I see your sweet face, I'm doing way better. Hey, you're getting my chat-messages from the airplane?"

Prana replied with an excited nod and a wide smile.

"There's my girl."

With a crimped index finger, Prana pointed at the screen.

"Oh, this? This is my new friend, Dr. Ben."

Prana's smile got wider.

"Nice to meet you, Prana Patel," Ben said on cue with his deep and tender voice. "You have a pretty cool room there. I can see the poster of Shel Silverstein behind you. He's my favorite."

Prana's head began nodding rapidly, her gasping breath echoing in the mic.

"Oh, does *she* like *you*..." Preeya said to Ben, then squeezed his hand. "So, Prana, sweetheart, did you have a visit from Aunt Champa today?"

A nod and a scowl. Then a moan with furrowed eyebrows.

"Maicey said it was short, though, yes?"

A nod.

"And Champa brought you something? A coloring book?"

Prana glared, then cradled her arms and rocked them back and forth.

"Too babyish?" Preeya laughed. "Well, it's the thought that counts, right? Maybe you can give it to a little kid in the children's wing. Either way, Champa won't be back for a while, I'm sure. So, tell me what else is doing?"

Prana looked down then held up a photo of their father—a man Preeya'd apparently never really known, at least according to Champa. In the picture that her aunt must've brought—*eye roll*—he stood hugging a woman Preeya'd never seen before. His new wife, no doubt. Well, the woman had a nice enough smile. She was thin, almost gaunt-looking. Not cheek-and-tit-enhanced like she'd pictured. But Preeya couldn't really focus on her father or her new *stepmother* right now. It was all too much of a whirlwind to wrap her brain around. Her heart around.

Prana grunted.

"What's up, sweetie?"

Prana grunted again and lifted her eyebrows—waiting.

Ben laughed. "She's got your insistence, I think," he whispered. "What does she want?"

"My sister wants me to read our special book to her...but, Prana, sweetie, I don't have it with me. It's back at my hotel room. How 'bout I call you in the morning to read it to you. Okay?"

Her sister shook her head violently.

"That's a big no," Ben whispered to Preeya.

She nudged him with her elbow. "I know you want it now, sweetie, but before you know it, morning will be here. I'll call you at nine a.m., after you come back from breakfast."

Prana's breath got short and her eyes got wild. The on-duty attendant in the room had to settle her down, and Ben didn't flinch, like it was no big deal. Preeya liked that she didn't have to explain the situation to him. She could wait it out, knowing the drill by heart. After the attendant's soothing words, like clockwork, the deal for the morning reading of *The Giving Tree* was struck.

"So sleep tight, sweetie, and I'll video call at nine a.m. sharp."

Prana gave a surrendered nod to Preeya, but a wild wave and a huge, almost flirtatious smile to Ben.

Preeya cracked up, her heart leaping, while Ben waved back to her totally glowing sister. "Nice meeting you Prana Patel."

"Okay, then. I love you, Pran, and sleep tight." And she ended the video call.

"Wow," Ben said, his eyes studying hers. "That was unbelievable. The way you understood each other." Ben stared a few beats longer, shaking his head.

She smiled back at him, feeling safe and held in his gaze.

Wait…his eyes, were they damp? She leaned in an inch. They were.

The next instant his hand was cradling the nape of her neck, and he was kissing her lips with the sweetest tenderness. Caressing, dragging, dusting. Then he pulled back to meet her eyes.

"Not much shocks me anymore. Not much at all. But here *you* are." He smiled, then cocked his head, and glared at her. "And you dropped out of medical school? God, I could strangle you right now."

She got the underlying compliment, but…*no*. She couldn't touch the med school topic without falling apart. Not with the new perspective of her mother and of her father—of her whole nurture-and-nature composition in question. With the world as she'd known it flipped upside down, the last goddamn thing she needed to do was to discuss her fucking career path. So she swallowed, inhaled to capacity, then blew out a slow, calming breath. "Not going there 'right now' Ben." *If ever.*

"Fine, but to be continued—a conversation for another time." His lifted brow punctuated his sincerity.

She glared back—*fat chance*, without the words.

He took her hand—and she let him—as the deep lines set between his furrowed brows softened. "Come on." He stood, pulled her up with him and kissed her neck.

Her chest loosened, her heart eased. "Oh, my bag—"

"No, allow me." He grabbed her purse and slid it up on his shoulder with a wink.

She tilted her head and sighed a light laugh, letting go the rest of her agitation over the med school topic.

"What you need is rest." He led her out of the restaurant into the thick Vallarta night. "Let's do the hospital visit already so we can get you to bed that much quicker."

Mmmm, bed. With Ben. She looked up at him as a soft then hungry smile took over her mouth. "Whatever you say, Doctor." Because bed with Ben sounded like pure heaven. She squeezed his hand in hers as they neared his car. "And I'll be a good patient, I promise."

He unlocked then opened her door and helped her in. "You should know, Preeya Patel, that I find it near impossible to keep my hands off you right now. And my mind off you. You're getting your hooks into me, I think. Your big plan, is it?"

She sputtered a giggle as she clicked her seat belt. "I'm not much of a *planner*, but yes, I think…I think I could learn to think ahead a bit." Because *thinking ahead* with this man in her mind's eye didn't sound bad…not bad at all.

CHAPTER 27

T HEY'D MANAGED TO find the waiting room of the ICU where Amy's brother-in-law was being treated, despite the signage, *Solo Español.*

Preeya had dreaded seeing Amy's mother and sister, hating the idea of having to pull out her fakest FA smile for the catty women. So she was relieved to find only a young local family in one corner of the room and an older lady in the other. The older woman had to be Elaine. With frazzled gray hair pulled up in a straggling bun, and sad, solemn, vacant eyes, she screamed *fear for her child.* It was the same helpless look that the mother wore on the flight to Houston.

Elaine stared at the wall ahead of her and gently rocked her body back and forth. Those eyes, they were the shape and shade of Darren's. Unmistakably Darren's mother. She knew from Amy that the woman was sweet to the core and had a tendency toward deep depression.

"Pardon me," Preeya spoke quietly so as not to startle the woman, "but are you Darren and Zack's mother, Elaine James?"

"Yes?"

"I'm Amy's friend, Preeya. Her college roommate. And this is my... friend, Doctor Ben Trainer."

Slightly confused, out of sorts for sure, Elaine nodded with a kind smile. "Nice to meet you both."

"Amy called me an hour ago, from the cruise. We're here to give you some company, and maybe help decipher what the doctors are saying?"

"Oh, thank you." Pure relief. "The doctors don't tell me a lot, that's true."

Ben nodded. "It might be that there is nothing to tell just yet. Probably a good sign. But would you like to walk me to the nurses' station and I can see what more I can find out?" Ben held out his hand to help the woman up.

"While you do that, I'll go down to the cafeteria and grab you something, Elaine. Like a coffee, a sandwich?" Preeya offered, well rehearsed during her two-year stint in the skies—but this time, she'd made the offer from her heart. The poor woman looked withered, like a dried meadow flower in a summer drought.

"Oh no, I'm really fine."

"Elaine…may I call you Elaine?"

"Of course."

"Elaine, as a doctor and"—Ben swallowed hard, then cleared his throat and touched the woman's elbow—"and as a widower who's just lost his wife to a yearlong fight with cancer, I know firsthand how hard it is to watch your loved one hurt…with all the unknowns." He looked at Preeya—like he needed a quick shot of strength—then back at Elaine. "So, doctor's orders—you need to take care of yourself to be able to take care of your son. Keep strong, fueled. That is the best way to help Zack right now."

The woman nodded her surrender. "Please, an apple, and maybe a turkey sandwich. No coffee. I get too jittery on the stuff. Thank you, dear." She patted Preeya's hand, and then gave Ben her arm and showed him to the nurses' station.

*

Preeya got back a half hour later to find Ben and Elaine in the waiting room chatting.

"Sorry, long line. Late dinners here in Mexico, I guess," she said, placing the food items on a side table for Elaine.

"Thank you, dear."

Preeya sat down on the other side of Elaine and patted her hand. "You're so welcome. And how are we looking inside?"

"Well, I got a full report from Doctor Acharya and will write it all down so you can debrief Amy and Darren. But really, it's a big waiting game, sorry to say."

"After seeing him, do you think he's in pain right now? And when he does wake up, will he be hurting then?" the worried mother asked.

Ben sighed, then visibly clenched his jaw and swallowed hard. Preeya watched as he froze over, his gaze now glued to the floor.

"Ben?" She reached for his hand but he pulled away and stood before she could take it.

"I'm so sorry. If you'll…just excuse me for a moment. I"—he cleared his throat, treading backwards as if he'd seen a ghost—"I have to…make a phone call…that I forgot about earlier. So sorry." And he disappeared around the corner to the elevators.

CHAPTER 28

H E SAT WITH his face in his hands on a hard wooden bench outside the main entrance.

He couldn't get Jamie's pleading eyes out of his head, just staring him in the face. Her big brown eyes, backed by a yellowed veil and strewn with thin red veins, bloodshot from vomiting over and over and over again. "Please. Just do it. Give them to me and let me go," she'd implored him.

That plea. Her once-vivacious voice turned into a raspy, desperate beggar's.

Jamie had been through three rounds of chemo, all against her will, really. Between her oncologist, her parents, and frankly, Ben himself at the time of diagnosis, they had kept the hopeful pressure on. A few of his own young patients had entered his operating room for necessary surgeries resulting from the ravaging disease, and many had gone on to live long and well. But Jamie, by round three, had wasted away to half her weight and more than three quarters of her days were spent in excruciating pain—the other quarter was spent sleeping with the intermittent rotation of fevers then sweats then chills which shocked her awake.

They'd had plans. Dreams. And the loss of the baby, well, that murdered both their hearts. Any question he'd had about his fatherly instinct, or lack thereof, had been doused with kerosene and lit on fire with the news. But it took only minutes for Ben to view the miscarriage as a blessing in disguise, dare he admit it out loud. *Ever*. But God, to have a child by Jamie without Jamie. A piece of her in an animate, sparkling child.

But no. The failed pregnancy was replaced by the diagnosis of a malignant tumor in her left ovary. One year from that point, instead of them nursing a newborn, he was nursing his young wife.

And the catch of all catches: the state of Washington was a right-to-die-state, if, that was, the diagnosis declared the patient had six months or less to live. Her oncologist had given her nine months. And even though her tumor had metastasized exponentially, the man wouldn't adjust it—thanks to Ben's meddling former in-laws who doubled as big-time donors to the hospital.

Damn them. Ben was her husband, for Christ's sakes. And an MD himself.

But they just wouldn't hear their daughter's wishes. "No quitting. Just hang on," her father had told Jamie. Even though it was killing her soul to stay alive. Every passing minute pained her. Every breath. *Agony*.

So Ben was pushed into a corner. That day, in their home, her frail body nearly too weak to speak, her eyes cried for him to help her end it, and he couldn't take it anymore. He just couldn't say no. Not to his love. She prayed for liberation, screeched for it with her silent screams. And he wouldn't, couldn't deny her anymore.

He put the pills in her hand, then gave her the glass of water and straw to wash them down. Knowing exactly how the pills would respond with the morphine drip hanging above her head—the morphine, which did nothing—made him, in his heart, a murderer. Whether Stanton disagreed and worked his ass off to convince the review board that Ben's actions were within the confines of the law and hospital policy, Ben felt what he felt.

And, God, it haunted him.

He remembered the next details like it had happened a minute ago. Because, deep down and always, the scene replayed itself. Over and over and over again.

He had crawled into bed next to her and took her hand to his lips. The soft, silken skin of the top of her hand soothed him. She'd always managed to soothe him, even when she'd been the one anguishing.

To keep his tears at bay, he'd hummed. *Their* song. Her mouth and eyes smiled—so slight but so pure, but she couldn't hope to halt her tears. She'd been too weak to even try. Still humming—*don't stop humming*—he placed light kisses, a billion brush strokes, all over her thin, delicate hand. He'd kissed each fingertip, each joint, each knuckle. And he'd kept on humming. He'd turned her hand over to kiss her palm, each deep line and crevice, pressing into her his wholehearted devotion and gratitude and longing for the forever they wouldn't have. He kissed his undying love into her—each kiss, each sweep, each soft swipe and caress from his quivering lips, he injected himself—his heart and soul, his hopes and dreams. All of him, everything.

A whispered word. From *her* lips. It floated for him, to him, just as her eyelids slid the window of her life shut.

Love.

She'd said *love* and then left him.

His Jamie, his love, was in pain no more—he'd kissed and loved and cherished her to death. Like she'd asked him to.

*

Before leaving Elaine at the hospital to endure the waiting game on her own, Preeya gave Amy's mother-in-law her cell number and Ben's just in case the kind woman needed anything. She offered one last comforting embrace—though there'd be no true comfort until the woman's son was in the clear—then she waved goodbye and entered the elevator.

She took a huge breath in, then let it out in measured spurts of relief. But what relief? Another distraught mother, the second in one week. Not to mention the newfound truth about her own mother—her own mother *who'd left.*

She felt sick.

A panic attack?

No. No tightness in her chest. Though she was all alone in the elevator and wondered—then stopped wondering—why she didn't feel panicked.

Anyway, this *sick* was head-rush-meets-eruptive-gut *sick.*

Oh God, and it was threatening.

Sliding down the cold metal wall of the hydraulic elevator car, she swallowed and swallowed again to try to control her queasiness. She sank down until her ass met the tile, then she pulled from her purse the water bottle Ben had gotten her at the beach.

Clear liquid, clear mind. Now breathe.

Yes, breathe. Breathe and count and focus.

She took another sip of water, then focused on each floor's digital number, decreasing with the car's slow, sleek descent. She matched her breaths in and out with the gleaming red digits and started to feel relief.

*

Ten floors came and went, and by the time the elevator arrived at the main level, her stomach and head and everything in between had somehow settled. Settled and calmed—she'd handled it. She'd handled it on her own.

The elevator doors slid open, delivering her to the lobby. *Find Ben.* She was sure Ben had escaped down there to make his sudden and strangely timed phone call, or, as she suspected, to take a much-needed breather. He probably'd had enough of hospitals in his recent past, doctor or not.

She turned the corner to find Ben trying to buy a water from the extremely well-lit vending machine.

"Damn it."

She took a deep breath, still shocked at how that bout of nausea had vanished, then she squinted from the glare of the machine as she approached. "Just give it a little kick," she said, coming up beside him and demonstrating in real-time. "And voilà." The machine spat out a small and very overpriced bottle of ice-cold spring water. Huh, in Mexico? *But Puerto Vallarta, Mexico.*

He grabbed it and gave her a faint smile.

"You okay?" she asked.

"I am. Well, now I am," he said, reaching for her, pulling her into his arms. He squeezed her tight, like he didn't intend to let her go. "I'm okay now," he whispered in her ear.

She moved her hand up to his neck, then to his head. "So soft. Velvety now. Are you growing your hair back, because, although I like this," she said, rubbing his peach fuzz while still wrapped in his embrace, "I like the distinguished and sexy near-bald thing you had going on, too."

"I'm not sure what I'm doing," he whispered, still holding her tight. "Let's go back to your room. To rest…"

"Yes, that sounds good."

CHAPTER 29

FIVE DAYS HAD passed in what he considered to be heaven. In-her-hotel-at-the-bay, Preeya-heaven.

Ben had postponed his departure for one week. He used a few different excuses—Preeya's fainting episode, Elaine needing added support, and Stacy's worries—in hopes he could convince Preeya to change her mind about joining him, however dream-like it would be working together, making a difference together—hell, anything *together* with Preeya was a dream.

The DWB excursions were rough, but nothing Preeya couldn't handle. She was amazing—resilient, hungry for new things, new people, new adventures, brilliant under pressure. But beyond Stacy's safety concerns about the vaccine mission, he had his own—apprehensions that neither Preeya nor Stacy knew the half of. Yeah, Central Mexico, the cartel activity, the reports direct from the NGO, were pretty detailed. And he couldn't, wouldn't risk Preeya's well-being. Especially now that he'd found her, his second chance at love this life. Completely unforeseen. Unfathomable, really.

He felt her foot slide up his leg, over his shin as she shifted in her sleep. He tittered, his Preeya-inflicted bruise hardly tender anymore. Practically healed. As was his heart muscle—seemingly healed, or getting there. She'd done that. She'd effected that change in him.

And she'd changed too. She'd played the free-spirit card hot and heavy since he'd met her in the taxi line, but there'd been a thick underlying angst behind it. Now with him, throughout their time in paradise, she'd surrendered a bit...to the *real* Preeya.

And he was falling for her. Falling fast, falling hard.

Maybe so was she? Falling for him?

He wouldn't dare jinx it—he shoved the question down deep. For now, he took it as a great sign that she'd taken more time off from the airline to be with him, and she was so impassioned about this expedition, like she *needed* to go. Since that phone call the night of their pretend honeymoon. He still hadn't asked and she hadn't told him what that had been about, but he knew when she was ready, she'd bring it up.

For now, she was just laser-focused on going with him on this trip, while just over a week ago, her life had been a blank slate, pure limbo. Maybe this humanitarian route was her decided path? Relentless and excited, she pressured him every other minute to agree to her coming, and to help her collect the necessary camping gear she'd need. Yeah, she seemed ready to commit to something, to a set future. And although her zeal made it near-impossible to dissuade her from going and therefore, hard as hell to protect her—he now admitted to waiting for fate to help him out and play a card here—he was definitely glad to see her find a passion. A shared passion. He saw that she had so much to offer—too much...to be doing what she had been doing, which in his opinion, was just letting time fly by.

In the meantime, being with her each day and night in Vallarta had been pure bliss. They'd stayed in bed all day one day, then had gone dancing all night. Ben, dancing. Stacy couldn't believe it. Then out to the best of the best in seafood markets with Stacy and the kids, and zip-lining in the jungle. Beach time, spa time, *them* time. It had been surreal, really, when just a week ago he'd been in his dismal hell.

The sun leaking through the curtains nudged his eyes open, and when he caught sight of her lying next to him, the sheet across her brilliant breasts, the rest of her free for his absorption, he was too happy for words or thoughts.

They'd been naked in each other's tangled limbs and parts all night—kissing, caressing, talking about nothing and everything.

And that was all.

And that was perfect. He didn't even need the release last night, although she'd eyed his arousal, played and stroked and teased him during the hours before they were both too tired to keep awake.

He reached out his arm to touch her flowing black hair. Black as a starless, moonless night—a cool, calming night, though. One with a cleansing breeze. A night where fear, and worry of the unknown had no place. Because she was there with him, and he'd begun to know that with her, a bright next day would come.

He stretched the sleep out of his limbs, both feet on the hotel room floor. He went to the curtains to open them.

Yes, a new day is here.

*

He'd called for room service. The surprise breakfast in bed made her giggle.

"I've never had anything like this before." Her cheeks burned, chest swelled.

"Stick with me, kid…"

"I think I will." She smiled, and could definitely picture it, more and more every day. "Here, take a bite of this." She placed a strawberry at his lips—and he snapped his teeth shut, scaring her three inches off the pillow-top mattress. She laughed and laughed, almost spilling the entire tray of food.

He kissed her hand and got up from the bed—naked and delicious—and strode to grab the newspaper that had just been slipped under the door.

She heard him grunt then scoff as he made his way back to her. "So, Preeya Patel, you really wanna come with me on this thing. This trip through the dangerous jungles of Mexico?"

"You know I do." She'd go damn it. She'd wear him down once and for all, in the last day she had to do so.

He sat down beside her with the newspaper. And placed it at her side. "Seriously, Preeya, it's risky. Really risky." His finger pointed to the top half of the paper. The headline read, Cartel Crosses State Lines, then a photo of Mexican State Patrol clashing with masked gunmen.

Sudden angst lodged in her throat, a shock after so many days of total peace, ease, ecstasy. She swallowed hard, but the stubborn fear stood its ground.

"Puerto Vallarta is a safe haven. Cancun and Cabo, too. They're off limits to these kinds of things...government alliances." He placed his hand on her thigh and squeezed. "But I need you to triple-think this."

Her pulse filled her ears. "Shit, Ben. Maybe you need to triple-think this. Helping people is one thing, but dying in the crossfire isn't gonna help anyone. I don't think *you* should do this." Her brows furrowed, breathing shallowed. "Let's maybe...find something else, Ben."

*

Relief flooded his lungs. Thank God she didn't need him to argue her into reason. Crazy to think about, but until meeting Preeya, he'd welcomed the danger. The stoic sacrifice. What if he did die in the field? Who would care, beside Stace and the kids? But at least the pain would be over. Like Jamie's pain was over.

But now this woman, Preeya Patel, had crash-landed into his life and took his breath away in the process. "If you don't want me to go, then I won't. *We* won't go."

The relief in her eyes was confirmation enough of her feelings. For him. For *them*.

God, he was so deep into her.

And now he was ready to tell her. Tell her everything. Unleash his secrets. Let go of his guilt-ridden past. He slid his hand up her cheek then outlined her jawline.

"I want to tell you so much, Preeya." He swallowed, then forced his gaze deep into hers. "I literally put myself at risk, you know, on these expeditions, because...well, in the back of my mind, after Jamie, I was okay to go. I mean, well, I wanted...to die. I had no reason to live. I mean, I wanted to help people, but I didn't mind if I died doing it. These trips had become more of a hope for death...until now. Until you."

She leaned back against the bed and studied him. As if to weigh the magnitude of his words, his declaration, with what was possible. Like no one had ever wanted to live for her? For the amazing spark of light that he knew her to be.

"There's more, Preeya. I have to tell you more. And I don't want you to think differently of me. That's my biggest fear right now."

"I don't think there's anything you could tell me that would change my opinion of you." She placed her hand on his chest. "Tell me. Anything…" She kissed him, a slow feather of a kiss, then leaned away.

He sighed and brushed his thumb down her arm. Stalling.

"Ben, it's okay." Her head notched, eyes sweet, patient.

"My guilt, Preeya. I've been running away from it, trying to escape it in the far corners of the third world. But it keeps following me. Because the problem is *me*. But I won't let it drag me down anymore."

He moved the food tray off the bed, then took both her hands in his and studied their interwoven fingers while preparing words. The right words. "Preeya, I couldn't take it anymore, her pain—Jamie's—watching it devour her. Watching my wife fade into oblivion. In such agony. After the fifty billionth time she'd asked me to help her…end it, I…I just couldn't say no again. I helped Jamie die, Preeya. I helped my first love leave this earth." He shook his head hard and slammed his eyes shut to reset himself. "That's the guilt, the burden, I carry." He moved his gaze from their interlocked hands to her radiant face, her eyes—now sharp, otherworldly daggers against white fire.

She pulled her hands away and tucked her knees to her chest. And froze there. "How?" She spat the word, a demanding whisper.

He swallowed, not expecting the recoil, her sudden fear. But he'd begun, so he had to finish it. "I gave her the combination of pills. I handed her the water to wash them down. I held her while she fell away."

Nostrils flaring, she angled her head. "No." She shifted, her eyes shifted, her breath quick and ramping. "How could you? End a life? Jesus Christ, Ben. Because *you* couldn't take the pain?" Her expression showed pure disgust. "You're not a doctor with a god complex, Ben…you're a coward. A weak, goddamn coward!" She rolled away from him, out of the bed from the other side, the bedsheet now clutched to her chest, like a barrier to her heart. The heart that was so open to him only seconds before.

He was in shock. Her response sliced him open. His guilt more real now than it ever had been. But more permanent, like concrete. And it weighed as much. He felt the hardening cement in his veins.

"I loved her, Preeya. I did it *for* her. To see so much suffering in someone you love, someone you cherish?" He moved toward her, but she threatened him with an even harder glare.

"Cherish? In sickness and in health, Ben. Those are the usual vows, right? And you used your medical knowledge to make your life easier...better. That's what the guilt's about. You're a smart guy, Ben, and you damn well knew all along why your guilt was so thick. And then you use me as a damn confessional?"

"Jesus, Preeya. Would you just put yourself in my shoes for a minute?"

"Never! My goddamn mother took that road, the easy fucking road—" But she cut off there. "You're not worth the words. Just go. Just get the hell out of here."

"Wait a minute, Preeya...what if your sister met a threshold of pain so horrendous, so—"

"Would I end her life?" She shook her head, contempt oozing from her. "You need to go now, damn it. I mean it, Ben," she said, reaching for the desk phone.

"Fine. I'll go, Preeya. I'm leaving. In fact, I'm leaving early, like tomorrow. For the excursion. What the hell was I thinking, choosing...choosing good...sex over good works, over helping people!"

A hard decorative hotel pillow came whizzing past his head. "Fucking asshole!"

He ducked out of the room, crashing the door shut behind him.

CHAPTER 30

H E STOOD IN the hallway outside her door, chest and brain ready to explode with fury. And with raw disappointment.

Betrayed. After finally saying the words out loud, she turned around and threw them back at him. Like battery acid, her words fucking burned.

Betrayed. By this woman who he'd found a new, different, stunning connection with.

And she accused him of taking the easy road? Drop out of fucking medical school to become an air hostess? Two damn years of "tea or coffee?" What a goddamn joke.

And her mother left? Okay. Left her and her sister. That's fucked up, certainly. But hasn't she followed in her mother's footsteps just as closely? She video calls or visits her sister once a month? She's doing the bare minimum there. She has no clue what it takes to be a true caregiver.

Like he had been to Jamie.

Then there's Preeya's "evil" father, the superficial greed-monger of a *doctor*. He works his ass off to pay for a facility like SafeHaven—Ben knew the cost of that place. Preeya's dad made the tough call, it seemed to him. While Preeya boo-hoos about "Daddy the miser," when in reality Ben bet that every pretty penny went to the top-notch care for his youngest daughter...and medical school for his oldest, which Preeya had tossed away like yesterday's trash.

His chest heaved.

Damn it, though. Was it Preeya's fault? Really?

If he saw the other side, the abandoned daughter's side. Had she been the recipient of all the collateral damage? Shoved off by both parents. Maybe in her mind, all adults take the shortcut, especially when it comes to her. Why wouldn't she do the same in life? And why wouldn't she lash out at Ben, the one person she pegged as different.

But she had to see that the easy way for him wasn't the route he'd chosen for Jamie. Yes, it killed him to watch her suffer, but caring for her day after day, that's what he had chosen for his livelihood, his role and purpose in life—there had been no greater honor than to use his medical knowledge and experience to tend to his wife. His first love. At that time, his only love. He would have gladly cared for Jamie to the end of days.

If her quality of life had been at all bearable for her.

But the tumor, it took over like an oil spill in a clear aqua sea. And that is what he told the medical review board. The truth. That the medical regimen couldn't keep up, could never keep up with the growth.

But none of that mattered. What Jamie's parents thought, what the review board said, or what Preeya believed.

Because the day he'd given in—when his wife's eyelids fell and he could no longer see life in her huge brown eyes, it felt like he had fallen off a tall, jagged cliff.

And he still hadn't really landed.

Although he thought Preeya had come into his life to catch him.

He was wrong.

CHAPTER 31

ANOTHER DAY IN Vallarta would be insane. Pointless.

She should go. See her sister. Face her father. Get at the two-decade lie he'd let her live.

And Aunt Champa. She'd tear her apart for her cruelty. Her crass words. That woman was as bad as her mother, if not worse. At least her mother ran, branding herself a no-good coward. But Champa, she was just a pretender. Acted the loving sister to Preeya's father, but treated his child like a second-class citizen. Fuck her.

Fuck her twice. To accuse Preeya of selfishness? For not showing up to her father's wedding? The man had been absent all her life. No one let her in on the big family secret, of how goddamn *selfless* the man was, yet holding back his love, his attention, his presence. With such a cover-up, where the fuck would they expect her to put the blame?

But now she knew her mother's transgressions. And she couldn't allow herself to think on it. Champa's words rang too true. What if she was just a selfish, aimless coward like her mother? Constantly taking the shortcut, missing her purpose altogether.

And then there was Ben, who she'd thought was so damn different.

But he rivaled her mother. Hiding behind the ever-selfless doctor shtick. The Good Samaritan, putting his wife out of her misery! Just another pretender. Freeing himself of burden like her mother had done. Just kill off the pain. Cut out the pain. Run from the pain.

Yeah, that's how to do it—*Jesus*, his own wife?

She looked around the room. The walls felt miles away while squeezing in on her at the same time. And in the armchair by the window lay the purple sarong he'd given her, the one he'd removed from her body when they'd been together at the falls a week ago.

And then his words. At the hospital. To Elaine James. Those words, his voice echoed in her head. The torture in his tone, in his expression. Of needing to be strong for "your loved one." To really be there. *Out-of-self* be there.

Then she recalled his other words. To Preeya. Concerning her sister. What if—or really, *when*—Prana runs down her clock here on earth, her sister's poor body done with the fight. They'd said age fifteen, so Prana was already living on borrowed time. Just held up in that place. Waiting for her big sister to read and reread *The Giving Tree* to her. What kind of life?

Then Preeya recalled those assholes—the SafeHaven doctors—detailing her baby sister's demise. It had been four years ago. They hadn't known Preeya was there behind the door waiting for Prana to come back from PT. And how fucking flippant and clinical they'd been. Disgust raged up her spine just hearing their dialogue replaying in her head. With their charts and files and X-rays in hand, they'd discussed how Prana's body would fold in on itself from the inside out—her cells, her organs, everything.

And she'd blocked it from her mind.

She wouldn't wish such an end on her worst enemy.

And for her sweet Prana? Such a glowing, giving, tender girl. Preeya could think of no *end* worthy of such a soul.

She'd stopped breathing some moments before, only known to her by the rush of air flooding her lungs like a hot, high-pressure back draft. She threw herself on the bed. Tears from forever fell in a torrent and, all alone and unraveling fast, she didn't know how to stop them.

*

Ben went to Stacy's to pack for the expedition. He knew Stacy could tell something was wrong—and that he wanted space. But what he wanted and what she thought he *needed* were often two different things.

"Can I drive you tomorrow?"

"No, thanks. I'm good."

"When will you be back?"

"Two weeks. Three tops," he lied. He couldn't deal with her worry, not now.

"Any news from the attorney for the final hearing?"

"Shit," he said, then rummaged through his saddlebag for his phone. "Stanton said he'd email me the date and leave a voice mail." He scrolled through messages and found nothing. "I guess I should call him tonight since I'll be out of range."

"So, you really think it's still a good idea to go? Crossing through those central states, Ben? It scares me."

He knew and felt badly for worrying her. But he couldn't defeat the disappointment and anger fueling his decision. "I'm going, Stace. Doctors are needed there, and I'm a doctor. And I've delayed them a week. Anyway, I'm especially obliged since I've got no family to speak of."

"Oh, really? No family? You know, you can be a real prick sometimes, Ben Trainer. A real goddamn prick."

"You know what I meant."

"Doesn't negate the fact that you're continuously heading into dangerous territory and…" She got tearful then, "…and it would crush me if anything happened to you."

He left his packing for the moment and pulled his sister into him. "Shhh. It's all gonna be fine."

"You don't know that! No one knows—"

"Exactly, Stace. But I need to do this. And"—he pulled away to gain eye contact—"that's really not what I meant, about having no family," he whispered, then hugged her tighter.

CHAPTER 32

PREEYA WOKE UP fully dressed in yesterday's clothes. Had she really fallen asleep that way? She rubbed her eyes, her eyelashes stiff from dried tears. Sun spilling through the window forced her to adjust to the time, the morning, the—*shit!* She shot out of bed. *No!* She ran to her phone and pulled the crumpled ball of a napkin from her purse—because she'd deleted Ben's number and text string out of rage and hurt.

Ben.

She'd explain. How she understood now, and hadn't yesterday. How she'd been completely emotional and irrational. Because of who her mother turned out to be. And who her father had never been. And how horrendously sorry she felt for Ben for having to watch his wife, who he'd loved with an endless and absolute value, like Preeya's love for Prana…and she dreaded the day…that her sister might wilt and shrivel and die.

Damn it! It rang and rang. No answer.

No. Please, no. The excursion. Early. *God, no.*

She jumped in and out of the shower in under a minute, threw on a sundress then ran to the elevator, the lobby, the curb. A cab came on cue from the flock of them across the street. "Conchas Chinas, please. 434 Calle Adamo."

On the way she texted Gigi: *How's my remote-aura looking now? FYI, should be void-black. Me, making hell out of heaven. Call when you can. Please.*

*

She rang Stacy's doorbell like a crazy woman and when Ben's sister finally came to the door, the woman looked almost pissed. But Stacy's face softened immediately.

"Preeya? Come in, come in."

"I'm so sorry for coming unannounced. I just never got your number and Ben didn't answer and I was so scared that he'd—"

"Already left? The bastard that he is…" She turned toward the kitchen, expecting Preeya to follow. "So dumb for such an intelligent man. So pig-headed. He just wouldn't listen to reason."

"Wouldn't? So he's gone?" But with an irrational and childlike glimmer of hope, "Did he go back to Seattle? For the medical convention he was waiting to hear about?"

"Convention…umm, no, Preeya. No convention. But my voice to God's ears, don't I wish he'd gone to Seattle. Oh, sweetheart, don't I wish." She pulled the tissue box closer to her, pulled a few out, and handed them to Preeya who didn't even notice the tears diving from her eyes. Then Stacy slid the Doctors Without Borders info card across the counter.

"Oh no, Stacy. Oh God…oh God. *I* did this. He wasn't gonna go. But I…we…fought, and he changed his mind. To spite me. This is all my fault." Preeya clenched her jaws to the point of pain. "How long ago did he leave?"

"At the crack of dawn. Before the kids and I were even up."

"Stacy…I'm…I'm…gonna be sick," she said and ran to the powder room at the far end of the kitchen.

When she came out a minute later, Stacy had a glass of water waiting for her, then walked her out to the sofa, arm around Preeya like a good mom. Like Ben accused his sister of always being. And that Preeya couldn't have needed more right then.

*

She left Stacy's after an hour of much-needed comfort and cabbed it back to the hotel.

But she didn't go to her room. Sitting in the lobby, she zoned. She felt empty and aimless. She had a blank sheet of a day and it almost paralyzed her. Also in her rage, she'd arranged a flight out the next morning—back to her ever-glorious job. So now she had twenty hours to kill. Alone. Trying not to think about Ben.

The Marietas. Not exactly the way to *not* think about Ben. But he'd said how he'd gone there on his own. And how centering it had been for him.

She ran up to her room for her swimsuit and the sunscreen bottle he'd forced on her. She grabbed the sarong, slid her phone and some pesos into a plastic bag from the hotel's empty ice bucket, and got back down to a cab. She was doing this. On her own. To center and to reflect and to goddamn *be*.

*

She sat at the pristine beach all day under the hovering crater hole and bright blue sky. No rocketing enigma or revelation hit her—no magic fairy dust or bandage found the fault line in her heart.

But her mind mellowed. Became quieter. And as she walked the length of the shore's silky white sand, her footsteps felt more grounded somehow.

Then thoughts came, a slide show of the past whirlwind of a week. The way Ben had looked at her, spoken to her, almost bullied her at times about her future—his belief in her was so real, almost tangible. And the way he'd broken her preconceived notions about, God, so many things.

Now back at the hotel staring out at the placid bay at low tide, she felt the great unknown at her feet, the next minute, hour, day, future she was so good at flying away from. But it didn't scare her as it usually had. She almost felt like she could meet it, her blank slate of a tomorrow, and conquer it.

Conquer it. Not run from it like her mother had, but face it head-on and attack.

She just wished Ben were there with her to tell this to.

She looked up at the gulls circling overhead, then back down and across the forever Bay of Banderas. She took a deep breath of the clean sea air, filling her lungs to capacity. Yeah. Flying away wasn't the way anymore. It was time to stop flying and delaying and procrastinating. *Get grounded, Pree.* Time to get serious like Ben had said. Time to start living life.

My life.

It is goddamn time.

She looked at her watch, the time still stuck on nine o'clock. Frozen. She unbuckled the strap, pulled it from her wrist, and chucked it as far as she could out into the bay. She could hardly see where it had landed among the white-tipped waves of sea-blue.

Yeah, time to start.

She looked at her naked wrist and laughed. *And maybe time to consider getting this tattoo removed, too.* Or covered up by something new.

She got into the hotel's elevator feeling better. And even slightly proud of herself for having made the choice to get out, have an adventure for herself, on her own. While she could've holed up in her hotel room all day dwelling on Ben. And she could've called Gigi and relied on her friend's voice as a distraction for the day, too.

But instead she'd ventured. And thought. And analyzed. And reflected.

And it had been Ben, his influence. Even now that he was gone—possibly for good, and all because of her explosive and hurtful reaction to his admission—he was still affecting her. Still moving and motivating her. Inside and out and upside down shaking her up to be better. Because he had seen better in her.

*

She made it to her room. A strange feeling overcame her when she inserted her room key card into the door's slot. From her toes up to her head, a sudden surge of joy. Ben would be in there. He'd turned back. For her. She knew it and felt it in her bones. He was inside the room waiting for her. Her pulse raced, her hands clenched and released then she shook them out at her sides.

She drew in a deep breath to bring her excitement down a notch and pushed open the door.

To an empty room.

Her jackhammering heart plummeted to her feet. Now her exhaling breath, an attempt to slow the flood of disappointment, did nothing. She walked in, now robotic, stoic, and shut the door behind her.

Her phone. Maybe that was the vibe she got floating in the air. She moved across the room like she'd been teleported. She grabbed her phone, powered it on, hit her messages icon.

No Ben.

Just a text from Evan. He'd been thinking about her, it said. Seven days ago? Wow, had it really been that long since she'd checked her texts? Yes, it had been a solid week. Why the surprise? Seven days of sweet, sensual, completely sumptuous life will make someone forget about, well, everything else.

Jesus, Ben. Please, just at least call me.

It was making her nauseous, the worry for him, and the lack of him.

Her hand moved down to her stomach. She bent at the waist. "Oh God." And she ran to the restroom.

CHAPTER 33

THE DAYS OF traveling through the jungle, a blur. And when he'd gotten to base camp he'd been relieved that he'd made it. Strange, though. Relief for making it was never a usual thing for him. In the past he'd always felt disappointed somehow, that nature or man hadn't snatched him up. But he couldn't deny having wanted to arrive safely. Maybe it was the pending trial next month. That chapter coming to a close.

Or maybe it was Preeya lingering in his mind. And in his goddamn heart. *But that's over, Ben. Over and done.*

*

Two solid weeks of refugees streaming in by train from South and Central America through the corridor. He'd probably supplied thousands of vaccines during that time, to those souls seeking a better life. Desperate and brave, all with no other choice. He felt their yearning, children and adults alike. How could he not continue and strive on? Like these poor souls had. If not for him, then for Jamie, and for these nameless seekers.

And with or without Preeya in his life, he'd push on for her, too.

But God, he had so thought it would be *with* her.

*

By week three, he'd found one tiny café with a Wi-Fi hotspot. He'd called Stacy, left her a voice mail—"I'm alive and well"—even though he wasn't exactly well, but trying like hell to be. Fighting to put Preeya out of his head. He'd also checked for and got an email from Stanton. The hearing date was set for the last week of June. He'd probably have to leave the project early, out of Mexico City instead of Vallarta, if that was the case. Either way, he was looking forward to finally being done with the medical review board, his former in-laws, and the guilt. He was ready to turn the page. Really ready.

CHAPTER 34

"HEY, PRANA, SWEETIE."

Her sister's eyes lit up and her hands began to clap and wave wildly.

And then, from the corner of the room, a deep voice. "Preeya, *bitay*."

She spun around, breath halted. "Dad?"

He never visited Prana. What the hell?

Also so strange—the way he'd said *bitay*, "my sweet child" in Hindi. The soft lining around his utterance made her ears ring. Throughout her life, his use of *bitay* had always been unearned, unwelcome. He hadn't deserved to call her his sweet child, or anything else for that matter.

"It's good to see you, *bitay*."

Again. She winced behind the fakest smile she could muster.

Hands in his pockets with obvious uncertainty, he didn't move to hug her—maybe he'd caught on to her radiating fury. Instead he offered a warm and intent look, so off-putting that her throat went dry and her palms got moist. She couldn't remember him looking her in the face, in the eyes, since...forever. Or at least since she was seven.

Prana yelped with excitement and impatience—her sister's warning call before an all-out fit—and broke the strange...spell between Preeya and her dad. "Sorry, little sister." Preeya turned from her dad to kiss Prana's forehead. "I missed you, sweetie, so, so much." A spring of fresh tears welled in Preeya's eyes, but she wiped them away just as quickly. Not in front of her father.

Prana pointed to their dad.

"Yes, right." For her sister's benefit, Preeya made the move and went over to her father to kiss him on the cheek. Then Prana yelped and pointed toward the restroom door just opening.

Ah. The real reason for Dad's super-sweet act, no doubt.

"Preeya, *bitay*…this is my wife, Sylvia. Sylvia, my beloved oldest daughter, Preeya."

Beloved? She wanted to vomit from the pseudo-daddy act. But as she studied her father's eyes, the unwavering goddamn warmth, he wasn't breaking his gaze.

Was he kidding with this shit?

Still with the soft smile to go with the slow blinks over round, kind eyes.

No. He wasn't kidding. Not in the slightest.

"I needed my love to meet my loves, Preeya. And here we are." He reached for Sylvia and pulled her in to his left, and with his other hand, trembling, he invited Preeya to stand close, to stand near her father.

Her heart thudded in her ears—replacing the high-pitched ringing—but she was sure that his voice had never sounded so tender. Had his pitch changed? His demeanor, too? Had this *Sylvia* changed him?

Or…had Preeya's hearing changed? Or her brain's filter of his words, maybe?

"It is so wonderful to finally meet you, Preeya." Sylvia held out her hand, slow and gentle. Taking Preeya's, Sylvia leaned in to kiss her cheek. "Babe," she said to Preeya's father, "you were right about her eyes: sharp and brilliant. More so in person than in the photos."

Huh. Preeya just couldn't imagine her shallow, doctor-to-the-stars father having the time or inclination to show anyone photos of her.

But thankfully her sister started clicking her tongue and moaning, wanting attention. A perfect *out* of this awkward interaction. Preeya smiled at Sylvia politely. "Thank you, and please excuse me. My Prana awaits."

At Prana's side, Preeya's brows lifted for effect. She slowly pulled from her purse the thing she knew Prana had waited for. Prana clapped as Preeya sat down on the chair next to her sister. Opening *The Giving Tree* to the first page, she began to read.

*

They strolled through the landscaped grounds in silence for some time, until her father cleared his throat. "I am glad for this coincidence, Preeya, *bitay*."

"Dad, you've always said there are no coincidences."

"Yes. True." He chuckled. "I'm glad, then, that this timing has put us together. I missed you very much at the wedding. But, I can understand…"

"You can *understand*, Dad? Can you really?" She cocked her head at him and tried to hide the shake of her head. *Calm, respect, control.*

But damn it! He'd never showed up for her, her entire life! And had let her live a charade, one that had shaped her and so many choices. But worse, with this new daddy act, she'd had to wait until age twenty-five for her father to, well, be her father and not just some funding source from afar!

"What is it, *bitay*? Tell me."

"First off, this whole sweet father act… Spectacular Sylvia isn't around right now, so you can stop. The usual lectures can resume. Our traditional once-a-year visitation should keep to script."

"I've changed a lot since meeting Sylvia, and I've healed a lot."

Healed? *Jesus.* Okay. Not going there. "Listen—Aunt Champa…she told me everything. About Mom, why she left. Why she *really* left."

"I know. I didn't want her to, and I am sorry for that."

"No, Dad! *You* should have told me. Forever ago! I blamed you this entire time for everything! Thinking my mother was a huge-hearted giver. A world savior, for Christ's sake!"

"I lied to protect you. A white lie, for the best. I weighed all the options, and really, *bitay*—"

"No 'bitay', Dad! Don't you get it? Because of the story you made up, I put her on a damn pedestal. Tried to emulate her, the ever-wonderer, the aimless seeker. Sacrificial and…selfless." She paused her words and her breath. Selfless? Aimless, yes, but *selfless*? Had Preeya really emulated the person she understood her mother to be?

I mean, you didn't finish med school…and you didn't go join the Peace Corps, Preeya. No, she took an always-mobile going-nowhere job as a glorified traveling waitress.

Hey, as a matter of fact, I saved a life just the other day!

Preeya. Truth.

She sighed. *Truth?*

Fuck. She'd just wasted all this time, years, and had used her ghost of a mother as an excuse. Her scapegoat. To put life off, to put dreams off. To wait for life to catch her, instead of her going out and catching life.

"How much time I wasted," she mumbled.

"What's that, Preeya?"

She sighed again, then shook her head. "I…I don't know. Just that… everything. Just everything. I missed having a mother. And I missed having a father. That is what it comes down to. I just missed my parents." Her mind was blank and swimming at the same time.

"Oh, my beloved…" He moved to hug her.

But she backed away. "No, Dad." She lifted her eyes, narrowed, quivering with hurt and anger. Years—God, nearly decades. "Not that easy. You know, you looked at me today…the first time you cared enough to goddamn look me in the eyes since the day she left us."

He sighed. "Your eyes, *bitay*. It hurt too much. I am so sorry, I just couldn't…." He swallowed back emotion she'd never seen in him, not even that day he had to pry Prana from her seven-year-old grip. "Until Sylvia came, I had too much pain in my heart to look into those beautiful eyes of yours," he said, obvious shame forcing his gaze away.

All she could do was shake her head. A father. Human, yes, but Jesus… he couldn't bear to look her in the face, or parent her, or visit or call or, *damn it*, show love in any incremental amount except for monetarily—because it hurt too much?

Well, she didn't ask for her mother's eyes…or any of the shit her parents had put on her. What a fucking cop-out! And now, damn it, she was drowning with new rising rage and it was too much for her to make sense out of. Too fucking much.

She had to sit down. Getting light-headed, she caught sight of a bench across the way. She went without a word.

He followed. And sat down beside her.

"Preeya," he whispered. "You're not your mother. I know that."

She heard words go in and sensed words being prepared in her head to come out, but damned if she knew what any of it was about anymore. "But I wanted to be *her*, Dad, because I didn't want to be like you. Absent, heartless, greedy—"

"That wasn't true, though—"

"Exactly. But Dad, you made it true. With your lie. Your lie about Mom—and *your* complete abandonment to follow it all up—made her the great sacrificing soul and you became the money-hungry son of a bitch who only visited once a year. And even then we had our status checklist of an interaction, Dad."

"Look, *bitay*, I had to support you, but I couldn't be an effective parent, too, so I put you in the care of someone I thought could."

"You thought wrong again."

"I'm sure Champa did her best, but she's human. And you are a strong spirit, a strong soul…"

"Again, just like the pretend mother you created for me, I'm not strong. I'm weak—like her!"

"Preeya. You aren't even making sense. Don't you see the mother I made up stemmed from the person I knew you had in you to become. I still haven't met a seven-year-old anywhere with the capacity for empathetic and selfless love like you had. And *have*. The way you've always been with Prana…your nature is beautiful. You've always had a beautiful, selfless inside. Always."

"No. You're wrong. I am not caring or selfless." God, she'd dropped Evan flat, visited Prana maybe once a month, quit med school instead of sticking it out to become someone who truly helps people, and then there was Ben. She'd been so cruel and apathetic to him. He was a *truly* selfless person. *Shit!*

"How can you even know, Dad? You don't know me from a stranger on the street. Other than these purple curses in my head…I mean, really!"

"You are a wonderful person, Preeya. Your energy is factually…brilliant!

So brilliant, *bitay*, that I worked in an industry I despised so that I could give you opportunities, an expensive college education, and medical school, so that you could soar—"

"And I crash-landed, Dad. Time and time again. All on my own, I failed. Just like Mom…" Her brain and heart were officially clobbered. "I don't… just…damn it, Dad, I don't know who I'm trying to be, or not be…."

"What is wrong with being you, my love? Your namesake, *beloved*. Be love. My smart, beautiful, beloved Preeya. Just be you. Stronger than me, than your mother…just be you."

She couldn't stop it then. The heaving hiccups of emotion. Not brimming over but busting at the seams of her soul. From her chest, her eyes, her head pounding out the years of collected everything. Right there in the pristine courtyard of SafeHaven. And as she gasped for air through her sobs, her father took her in his arms, held her through the earthquake of it all. And if she wanted to shove him away, punch him, cause him immeasurable, infinite pain, she couldn't even muster the strength.

But she didn't want that. She honestly didn't want him in pain. No, what she wanted was finally being given to her. His loving arms. His fatherly security wrapped around her tight, steady and strong.

"I can only say that I'm human, Preeya, *bitay*." He sniffled and cleared his throat. "And thank God that I have changed and learned so that I can be here now for you and with you, my love."

She buried her face deeper into his chest, crying through unknown time and space, there on the cold, hard stone bench while he continued to hold her tight.

*

She wiped her eyes and nose, let her face lift to see her father's, and took in a clearing breath. "Your shirt, it's a mess…from me."

"It's fine," he said through a light laugh. "Sylvia says the mess inside our hearts is the hard thing to clean up. A shirt's a dime a dozen."

"Hmm." She let a hint of a smile form as she sat up to collect herself, the sunshine hard on her swollen eyes, but much needed. Eye opening, warming sunshine. Hopeful, *restarting* sunshine.

"Preeya, I would like you to get to know Sylvia. She's wonderful, and you both have such huge hearts. After those decades of being closed to the world, Preeya, she opened my heart again." He lifted her face with his index finger. "I really was crushed, too, when your mother left us."

"*Us*, Dad." She opened her eyes and looked at him and tried to find a soft smile. "Operative word *us*. Not just me and not just you, and not just Prana."

"I know…now." He squeezed her shoulder. "And again, I'm so sorry for leaving you all alone with your pain, my sweet girl."

Her breath had become shallow but had slowed, eased.

"We're together now. Better late than ever?"

"Better late than *never*, Dad. Thirty-some years in the States now?" She couldn't help but smile. His idioms and figures of speech were always a little off, the one thing that she remembered that had made her laugh when they were together.

And the next thought that flew in was another possible fitting common phrase: *too little, too late.* Was it? Was it too late for them? She looked at his face. Softened. Aged. Kind. Maybe this was real, this change in him? And why didn't she and he deserve this chance, a second chance?

"Dad, she didn't even say good-bye—"

"Your mother was scared. And deeply ashamed. Wherever she is, she's awake at nights with shame."

Moments passed as she considered his words. *Pity* toward forgiveness. Forgiveness? Maybe. But she wouldn't ever forget.

*

Preeya looked up at her father and a slow, seeping warmth came over her—a cleansing, liberating wave. She'd have done anything to be nothing like him. Her anger ruled. Had blinded her. And now she could see him. Her father. Just a man. And yes, a doctor, but a regular man, her blood. A good, decent, human man.

"Sylvia…seems nice."

"She's got a truly wonderful heart, Preeya. And she's a fighter. Two-time breast cancer survivor. That's how I met her. She was a patient. Trying to reduce her risk years ago with a double mastectomy. But her genes had other plans. Cancer found her anyway."

Chills crawled up her body, stunned at her own ignorance. Her own closed-minded default setting had struck again. The superficial wax woman she'd assumed Sylvia to be had transformed into a brave soldier in a blink.

She sighed hard and heavy. "Dad, I'd like to try and get to know her."

"We would like nothing better."

They sat on that cold stone bench for a long while without saying another word. People and clouds and intermittent squirrels and birds moved through their time while Preeya and her father just stayed very still, very *there*. Together.

And like a crisp breeze coming in off the bay on the beach of her Marietas, an image wisped into her mind. And in an instant, just like that, the blank slate, the unknown, her tomorrow, had an answer.

"Hey, Dad, if I wanted to go back, you know, to medical school…would you still help me? If only just at the beginning. I think…yeah, I think that's what I see myself doing. That's the route I want to take."

CHAPTER 35

S HE'D MOVED INTO her quick-find apartment just in time to register at UW's medical program—getting into Berkeley, even with her father's connections, had become too high a hope after so long. She looked out her window overlooking the Seattle skyline. The Emerald City in summer, the only time the clouds break.

But after nearly four weeks and no reply from Ben, her head and heart felt gray-cloud heavy. No updates from Stacy, either. God, Preeya just wanted to know he was safe. If nothing else, that he was *alive.* Not held ransom by one of the competing cartels or some crazy shit like that. *Really, Preeya— ransom?* How stupidly dramatic—not the life-thrills she'd meant. But after seeing the front page of the Vallarta paper their last morning together, this was no stage drama. Real drug lords and guns. And before this newer surge in cartel activity, aside from the safe tourist spots, she'd been warned through her airline and the embassy about random civilian disappearances in the larger Mexican cities. For layovers in Mexico City, all the FAs stayed at the airport hotel.

And she'd chosen to ignore *that* to go with Ben to Somewhere, Central Mexico.

Jesus, Ben, where are you?

Her lungs emptied in shaky bursts. She wouldn't leave another voice mail on his cell; she swore this morning's would be the last. And after this many weeks, she didn't expect him to reply at all. If only Stacy would get back to her saying he was okay…then Preeya'd put him out of her head and heart as best she could.

Right.

She opened her text message string to Ben for the third time since her no-call promise.

Still a reverberating *blank.*

She clicked out of that screen to her never-deleted summary list of texters. Where a new unopened text stared at her. From Evan.

God, I miss you. Channel 4 *anchor or* Good Morning America, *wouldn't matter. I'd still miss you, Pree.*

She sighed. He obviously needed more closure.

No more "easy road," Preeya. She'd have to handle this. Evan didn't deserve to hurt.

After a reunion brunch with Gigi, she would be registering on campus, only minutes from his place. She'd give him a call, meet up for coffee, maybe. She'd explain, help him move on. God, there was so much to say, and he of all people deserved to hear it.

She texted him and got a lightning-fast response: *Yes, our old spot, 3PM?*

Yes, sounds perfect. TTYL.

*

She walked toward Gigi and waved—*always on time, that girl.* She'd always teased Gigi—the most organized and punctual mind reader on the planet. "It's the detective-dad genes I wear," Gigi would say.

And wow did her best friend know Preeya—her friend had even brought along a magazine for the assumed wait. *But no more of that.* Preeya'd gotten hooked on punctuality since Houston those forever weeks ago.

She even got herself a new working watch to celebrate—and to cover the tat until she could figure out what to do with it. "Hey, you."

"Hey, yourself!" Gigi popped up and threw her arms around Preeya and swayed them back and forth.

"It's only been a few weeks, Geej." She felt queasy, like her friend had squeezed all the oxygen from her body.

"Five weeks, Pree. There was a chance to catch each other in the middle there, remember? But you stood me up for Joshie the Hard Rocker."

Ugh. "You mean the not-so-hard rocker," Preeya mumbled, scoffed then swallowed hard, that queasy feeling turning into a spike of nausea from the mere thought of Josh Bolte.

"You're white as a ghost...he was that bad, huh?" Gigi grabbed a water bottle from her purse and handed it to her. "Drink."

Preeya downed it and sighed with slight relief. "Thanks."

"*Welks.* So I never did get the *Josh* details from you...but maybe not worth talking about?" Gigi grabbed Preeya's hand and took a step back to give her some breathing room.

"No, it's not that...I mean, yes, it was *that* bad, but no, I've been feeling sick to my stomach since, well, since...." *Ben.* Since he'd left. Because of *her* dumb ass.

And the bouts of nausea from nerves kept coming daily. But she hadn't really told Gigi anything of Ben since day one in Vallarta. Or any of her family shit, either. She'd really been off the grid from her best friend for a record amount of time. And in that time, more had happened to her than the series of mentionable events in her entire adult life. "Let me just run to the bathroom real quick and then we can sit and chat over chocolate ice cr—oh God, Geej." Bubbling rage just above her gut. "Gotta run." She didn't run but flew to the restroom.

A second later, "Comin' with," Gigi said out of breath. She locked her arm in Preeya's and shuffled along at top speed.

When they got to the mall's restroom, Preeya zoomed into a stall and hurled. She at least came out feeling better—for the time being. She knew as soon as Ben—his deadly expedition, her guilt, her heart hole—entered her mind again, she'd be back to it.

"Preeya," Gigi said, washing her hands while looking through the mirror at a mother changing her infant at the changing station. "Would you be the godmother of my baby?"

Preeya paused in the middle of rinsing her face, water dripping down her nose. "Uhh...when you have one...of course. There's no question, Geej."

"Good. Because"—Gigi hit the explosively loud hand-drying machine which drowned out all spoken word and didn't shut off until Gigi's rhetorical monologue did.

Preeya laughed at Gigi, her best friend's smile wide and glowing like a kid with big news.

"Hey, why are you laughing?"

"I didn't hear you, Geej, that's why." Preeya moved to the quieter paper towel option by the door.

"I said…because Rod and I are pregnant!"

Mouth dry, eyes bugged, Preeya's lungs filled with a rush of air, fueling a scream louder than the jet-powered hand dryer times ten. "Gigi! You're having a baby? A real kid? A real baby person!"

"And, Pree…"

"What, Geej?" she asked, squeezing her best friend's hands with out-of-control excitement and awe and fear, because that's what she'd be if she were in Gigi's shoes!

"So are you."

"Excuse me?" she rasped, mouth drier, eyes wider. Lungs hitched. Because she didn't hear right.

"You, my friend, are pregnant, too."

No. "No." *She's fucking with me.* "I'm not." *Factually not.*

"Yes, Pree, you are. And God, I hope it's not—" Gigi paused, maybe having noticed Preeya's eye roll switch to *death stare* within a baby heartbeat.

It wasn't funny. Visions and feelings and senses from the ethers about, well, just about anything else—*fine!*—but not about this. *A baby?* Everything trembled, head to toe, inside and out.

"Nope, never mind." Gigi swallowed. "It's not *his*…I don't see any fiery flames of *asshole* or anything," she said, stepping back to gauge Preeya's body, her belly, her aura? "Just a warm, golden glow. Yeah, not Josh's, no way is it Josh's."

Preeya felt dizzy and heavy and light all at once. And still quaking, the shock hit her brain and jumbled everything about. *Not Josh's. A baby. Gigi's baby. Glow. Nausea.*

Nausea. *Of course.* Just nerves over Ben? *Jesus.* Her chronic obliviousness toward her life, her body...and her period? *Who actually ever keeps track of their cycle?* She'd always guessed a day on her GYNO's questionnaire. And she'd thought she'd been better about the pill but...*fuck,* she couldn't say for sure. Every night and city and hotel bathroom merged together. She swallowed back another swell of nausea, then turned on a dime and ran to a stall, slamming into a woman on her way. No time to even apologize—the retching took her voice and breath away. Gigi had to hold the door closed for her because she hadn't gotten the chance to lock it.

"You'll see, Pree, it's gonna be great. So, so unbelievably great...us being pregnant together! I mean, it's a dream!"

*

Preeya put her hands on either side of a sink and attempted to catch her breath. *Fuck.*

She leaned into the sink, scared to glance at herself in the mirror of the crappy mall bathroom. She turned the water on, cupped some into her face, her burning cheeks and eyes.

Gigi handed her a piece of paper towel.

"Thanks, Geej," she whispered.

Gigi squeezed her shoulder. "I'll go grab a water from the vending machine outside the door. Be right back."

Water, yes. And breathe. Chill.

And as she mellowed, a small glint of hope crept in.

Because Gigi had been wrong before. Yeah, wrong about...well... there was...

Nothing.

Gigi had never been wrong about any ethereal call she'd made about new life or pending death, at least not in Preeya's presence. Gigi'd known about a chick in high school, an acquaintance of theirs who had gotten knocked up then had an abortion before anyone besides Gigi, and therefore Preeya, knew about it. And then there'd been the wrestling captain their senior year. Overdosed at a house party. If not for Gigi, who knew if they would have ever found him in that unfinished basement? She'd also known about the death of her grandfather weeks before his passing—the man had been an ox.

And every year in school, some teacher was pregnant—Gigi'd called it each and every time, and long before any baby bumps began. Oh, and Preeya's favorite: the ten tiny gerbil babies in fourth grade. The classroom pet, Big Al, had actually been super-pregnant Alice. A snicker escaped her there in the thankfully empty restroom. She ventured a glance up at the mirror then in a foreverblink she hid behind her swollen eyelids.

Please let Gigi be wrong. Because just like her best friend had freaked out their entire fourth-grade class with her impossible gerbil premonition, Preeya felt this close to freaking the fuck out now.

"I need to take a test," she mumbled when Gigi returned with a water. Preeya took the bottle without looking up at Gigi, scared shitless to crush her friend's heart with her doubt—Preeya had never doubted Gigi, she'd been the only one in the world to *never doubt* her.

But on the other hand, this was much larger than a litter of damn gerbils.

"Yeah, I need to get to a drugstore and pick one up." She forced her eyes up. "It's just too much, Geej. It's too goddamn big. I need to see the sign on a stick."

"Of course, Pree. Yes, it's huge, and yes, you should take a test—like at a doctor's. At *my* doctor's. She's alternative, like a midwife but—"

"Gigi, please. No doctor yet." God. "Just a pee-on-a-stick *now* kind of test. Need to be taking one step at a time, here." Gigi's excitement, despite Preeya's dread, was driving her nuts. "One baby step at a friggin' time."

She rinsed her face one last time, pumped the lever of the paper towel dispenser and ripped, then wadded and tossed it. "I need to leave this bathroom now." The association alone was making her gut surge again.

She and Gigi walked down the long corridor and passed ten strollers in a matter of seconds. Fine, two. Two goddamn baby strollers with babies—one cooing, one crying—and their doting, glowing mothers.

"Awww…"

Preeya glared at Gigi then picked up her pace, needing more than anything to get her hands on a pregnancy test, like, yesterday.

Because, *a baby?* Preeya thought of her mother.

Now *she'd* be a mother—*possibly*—to a tiny, innocent baby.

A chance to right her own mother's wrongs?

A soaring gust filled her chest. She'd be the best mother humanly possible, taking all the boiling, buried hurt and spinning it into magic. For her baby.

A baby...

Ben's baby. For certain *Ben's* baby.

Ben's baby...without *Ben.*

"Pree? You okay?"

Am I okay? She'd be raising this baby, *his*—no, *theirs*—on her own. Alone.

In an instant her lungs went airless, shoulders sunk. She felt beaten. Old panic renewed.

Count, breathe, calm.

"Are you? Answer me." Gigi grabbed her hand.

Preeya nodded as she finished a mental one-to-ten in a second flat.

Start over, slow down. She had to find the peace she'd felt that morning. Psyched to see her best friend for fun and epiphany-sharing then to sign up for classes...

Shit!

"Gigi, I've got to register for classes today."

"I think that'll have to wait, Pree. You're completely flushed. Let's take the afternoon to—"

"No, Geej. It can't wait. Today is the summer term deadline. And if I am, you know...I need to get my ass in gear. I mean, a kid?" She was suddenly so thirsty, but she'd left the damn bottle back in the bathroom. "A kid on my own? I need to support it, *us*. And I've got my plan. I need to start my—"

"Your plan can wait."

"It can't!"

"Then it can *change*. But, Pree, you need to stay calm." Gigi squeezed her hand. "You can always hit the fall semester or next summer after the baby's—"

"No. School to residency to career. That's the plan, the *only* plan." She shook her head. Gigi just didn't get it. No more talk; only action would do. It had been decided on the beach in Vallarta—with the sea as her goddamn witness.

And apparently Gigi had Rod, *the father.*

While Preeya had goddamn *no one.*

Don't you dare say it, Preeya. Don't say it out loud and make Gigi feel horrible—as horrible as you feel. She locked her jaw down tight to abide by her inner instruction.

"Did you hear me, Preeya?"

Deer in the headlights.

"I said that your dad won't let you or your child go without."

She didn't need anyone for the money. Well, except for school, but she'd already set it up to pay her dad back. No, going with her plan—*busting ass* in school, then residency, then practice—she'd support herself...and this *potential* baby. *Money's not the missing piece here.*

Ben is.

"...so do you get that your *grand plan* has got to fit a baby now?" Gigi asked, sitting her down at a sitting area they'd come to—across from a fucking maternity outlet.

Preeya sat but pulled her hand back.

No more discussion. No more wasting time.

And no more fucking advice from someone who...who had *Rod* and ultra baby-joy and who had no earthly goddamn idea what Preeya was about to be up against.

Eyes on the ground, Preeya licked her lips—dry and cracking, she just realized, from her ongoing puke-fest. "I need to sign up for my goddamn classes, Gigi." She stood up and stormed off toward the parking garage, leaving Gigi to explore the goddamn Maternity Warehouse.

Or her best friend would sit there on the hard mall bench in sheer shock, crying—but Preeya wouldn't know because she refused to look back over her shoulder.

CHAPTER 36

FOOTSTEPS AND HEAVY breathing echoed against the dark cement of the parking garage.

"Hormones are already going crazy, Pree. I *get* the roller coaster of emotions," Gigi said through gasping breath as she caught up to her in the B2 section.

Hormones. "Not in the fucking mood, Gigi." *Now where the hell is B4?*

Gigi picked up her pace to keep up. "No more swearing, Pree." Practically panting now. "The embryo can hear and *feel* that energy."

Ignoring Gigi, now…and searching for B4. Ah, B3…now where's B4?

"Seriously, Pree. Stop, already, would you?"

Preeya stopped and spun on her heels. "What, Gigi. What!"

Gigi's eyes glistened with impending tears—and mean as it was, her dear friend's loss for words felt like heaven.

Preeya sighed and shook her head. "Sorry, Geej, but…I've just…got to go."

Gigi snatched Preeya's car keys. "I'm driving you, then."

Her best friend took the huff-away-in-ludicrous-anger baton, hit the keyless remote to find Preeya's car, and marched to it in the next row.

*

On the way to campus Preeya scanned each street corner for a drugstore and stayed atomic-silent as Gigi drove and talked. And talked and *squeed.*

That irritating goddamn enthusiasm.

Preeya rolled her eyes.

This is so like us. Either she or Gigi could be scorching pissed—at each other or at the universe, whether justified or not—while the other hit fast-forward to the point *after* making up. It's what happens when unconditional love glues two people together. For them, making up was a given—actually, the only *given* either of them could ever count on. So, per their routine, Gigi rambled on and on despite Preeya's underlying fit of jealous rage, however unwarranted.

Because, damn it, she should've been happy for Gigi. *Happy* that Gigi was happy.

Opposite of her dismay. And terror. But the involuntary fury that flooded her brain sent her mind flying light-years to nowhere.

Because this was too much all at once.

Her hand glided over her belly and tears welled then plummeted down her cheeks. She'd pushed him away. The one good thing in her life—finally, a really good thing—and she shoved him off. To Central fucking Mexico.

Fists clenched, knuckles white, she felt insane. Paralyzed. Her heartbeat pulsed everywhere, pummeling her from the inside out. She had to shelve the jumble—*Ben, baby, lost, found, alone*—because there wasn't a thing she could do to find him and fix this, other than what she'd already done. A sharp heat hit her right temple and began to spread across her skull.

Focus and shove it down fast, Preeya.

But she couldn't. Gigi wouldn't shush for her to *focus* and *shove.* Baby plans and nutritionists and special yoga classes, all the way to cribs and play-groups. And the new head pain shooting across her forehead.

"Gigi, stop! Just stop talking, please. First I need to get through this day." *And maybe be sure that I am carrying my ex-lover's child.* "My plans. I just need to focus on my—there. Pull in there." A big-box drugstore.

Her seat belt hadn't fully recoiled before her feet hit the pavement. "Be right back."

"You know I'm right," Gigi called before she'd reached the entrance.

Yeah, I know you are.

Gigi knew, yes, but she cried anyway when Preeya came out with the pink plus sign showing.

Preeya sighed, swallowed, then gave Gigi the slightest of smiles. Then through brimming tears and nervous tremors running up her neck, she cleared her throat to hear herself say the words out loud. "It's a fact."

The reality had nearly settled in her palpitating chest from the drug store women's room to the register to the car. She was having a little baby girl or boy. Yeah, it nearly, almost, not-at-all-in-her-wildest-surreality had settled in. That she would have two heartbeats within her soon or already…unreal.

Gigi reached over the console and pulled Preeya into her. "Whatever happens, Pree, you will not be alone in this. I am here for you every 'baby step' of the way."

"Until you're a balloon like me…and in labor like me, and sleepless and raw nippled—"

"*Like you.* Yes, but Rod will help—" Preeya could feel Gigi's breath hitch through their embrace. Her friend's guilt hit her like static electricity.

"It's okay, Geej, really. I'm weirdly…not scared to be alone in this now. Somehow, I know it will work out. Before the baby comes, I'll get through a solid eight months of school. Added to the year I'd already finished, I'll only be, what, a quarter of the way through?" She broke down laughing, just from the ridiculousness of it. "Hey, I can leave Baby Nameless with you and your little psychic wonder through my entire residency, right?" She winked.

"Yes! I wouldn't have it any other way. Our girls are going to be sisters."

"Girls? Gigi Donlow, please don't tell me you just told me the sex of my child."

"No, no. It hasn't been decided yet."

"Geej, you *will not* be telling me the sex of my child. I want to be surprised. When you know, you promise me you won't?"

"Sure. Of course. I'm just being *hopeful* that they're both girls, is all," Gigi said, crossing her heart and smiling. "I won't tell you the sex of yours *or mine.*" She hugged Preeya with all her might.

"Listen," Preeya said in Gigi's ear, still stuck in their tight embrace, "I know you're here for me as much as you can be, and I am for you too…I love you, Geej, and your little peanut."

"Oooh, our little peanuts." Gigi giggled.

"Yeah, our babies." Preeya pulled away and looked down at her belly, at the mystery growing inside. She shook her head. How unbelievably crazy. And amazing.

Amazingly scary, yet thrilling.

God, she wanted Ben to be with her now to feel the thrill and craziness of it all. "Gigi…while I don't need Ben here, in this, with me, with us…I really just…want him. I want him in my life, with our child. That…that would just fit. He made me so happy, fulfilled. Want to be better, you know?"

"Preeya, let's find him, then. Let's find Doctor Ben…Ben what?"

"Trainer. Dr. Benjamin Trainer."

"Heck yeah, let's find Doctor Benjamin Trainer." Eyebrow waggle. "Good name…sexy and solid."

Preeya smirked. Yes, sexy and solid. *And sorely missed.*

CHAPTER 37

REGISTRATION WAS A process, and when Preeya finished the papers and lines and all, she was exhausted.

"Home to rest?" Gigi looked tired, too.

Preeya looked at her new working watch. *Two fifty.* "Yes, that sounds—*shit.*" Sudden panic pressed on her chest. "Evan!"

"Preeya…language."

"Sorry, Geej, not gonna happen today." Silence. Then a sigh. "*Anyway,* I'd forgotten that after registration, I'm meeting Evan for coffee. Three p.m."

Gigi gave her a sideways glance. "Evan, huh? Why exactly would you ever want to meet Tight Ass for anything…ever?" Again, Gigi'd never loved Evan, and now they were stuck in one car too far from the mall, with the 405's bridge traffic preventing Gigi's escape.

And while Preeya still wanted to make things right with Evan, shed her guilt—and no, she wouldn't, couldn't stand him up—she wanted nothing more than to go home, crawl up in a ball, and sleep away the tumult of her day, or her life. Even the hunt for Ben, Gigi's new mission, felt heavy and draining to her. Just thinking about the unknowns, the danger Ben faced, and then the possible, probable rejection she'd face if they did get a hold of him. Shivers shuddered through her and she blinked to reset. "Just tying up loose ends, Geej. That's all. Putting it to bed so Evan can move on."

"First off, I never again want to hear the words *bed* and *Evan* come out of your mouth within a minute of each other. I'm pregnant, Pree, and I don't need the stress."

Preeya just shook her head.

"Second...*grrr*...fine, we'll do this. I'll just...read...at my own private table." Gigi gave her a crooked, half-assed smile. "You so owe me." Gigi grabbed a stick of gum from her purse while the light was still red. "I mean, between Josh and Evan, your gamut of assholes is baffling."

Preeya glared at her then laughed. But her laugh was a hollow one. After all those "assholes," she'd finally found her partner in crime, in life—her just-right, brutally honest, sharply intelligent, wholly humble and humbly sensual and loving match.

All she had left of him was a tiny remnant of *them* glowing and growing inside her.

Ben Trainer, damn it... Come back to me. To us.

CHAPTER 38

EVEN WITH GIGI driving as slow as a damn grandmother—"We've got the babies to think about now," she'd said—they got to the Ave. at 2:59 p.m.

She texted Evan—*Just parking*—and anxiously scanned up and down the street for vacant spots.

"Relax, Pree."

"I just don't want to be late."

"He knows you're always—"

"Not anymore, Geej. I'm not like that anymore." She gave her best friend a stern, almost too stern, stare. She had changed. Evan seeing that would confirm it for her.

He was early as usual, coffee already in hand at their table in the far back corner where the aroma of the grinders was strongest. Handsome to a fault—a familiar flash of heat welled below her belly—he stood up and waved to her. Well-built and clean-cut in his sexy rimmed glasses, she wanted to spin around and leave.

No. "Hey, Ev."

"You look amazing. Glowing, almost. And punctual?" He tucked his chin to look over those sexy frames and, once sure Preeya wasn't an imposter, he winked with condescending approval. "Impressive, Pree." He kissed her cheek then pulled her chair out. "Really impressive."

"Oh, thanks. Um…" Gigi had conveniently hidden behind her so she reached and took her arm to pull her forward. "You remember Gigi?"

"How could I forget? Hello, Gigi," he said with an unconvincing smile then kissed her on the cheek as well. They'd always kept a healthy arm's-length distance from each other during Preeya and Evan's short-lived stint. He was a reporter, a news guy, a facts man. And Preeya's best friend, though punctual, was anything but fact-based and black and white.

"Good to see you, Evan. And on the anchor desk now…congrats."

"I didn't know you *watch* the news, Gigi," he said as polite as his sarcasm would allow.

Gigi hunted for a smile, gave Preeya a nod, then spun around, making her way to a table on the other side of the coffee house. "Come and get me when you're ready," she called to Preeya over her shoulder.

"So…" his deep voice hummed new confidence as he sat down across from her.

"So?" She smiled then flicked her eyes down at the table.

"Our old table…weird, right?"

An awkward chuckle and nod filled the next beat.

"Shoot, how rude. Can I get you a latte? No, you're a grande-mocha girl, right?"

"Right, but, um, not today. Already pretty strung out. Registered for classes."

"Classes? Wow, Pree. I mean, who is this newly ambitious and put-together woman?"

Patronizing much? She found her fakest FA fake smile because, wow, she'd forgotten, or maybe hadn't even realized, how condensing to her he was. And always had been. "I guess, you know, my gut was right on, Ev. We both needed to fly our separate ways in order to 'spread our wings'."

Evan's look of shock sent a slight thrill through her—but she was there to tie up loose ends, to help him move on. Nothing more.

She sighed and shook her head. "Listen, Ev, it's been a…day." She puffed a laugh, *such an understatement*. "I have some explaining to do, you know, with how I left things. You deserve—"

"Don't, Pree. No need. Water under the bridge. Seriously, no hard feelings." He slid his hand across the small, round table and took her hand. "I want good things for you, Pree. All good things. Always."

While he stroked and played with her fingers, she felt a tinge of nausea rise up in her gut. Was it repulsion or was it the few cells of baby—or both? Whichever, the thought of fleeing the table, The Bohemian Coffee House, the city of Seattle, all sounded like *good things*.

"Preeya, did I lose you?"

"Sorry." She snickered. "What were you saying?"

"No, I was just saying that I grew a pair and landed the position. But it was you who influenced me to do it. You gave me the wake-up call, you know? And the motivation. I realized that to become the man you need, I had to rise."

"Oh?" She cleared her throat then swallowed. "Hey, uh, I think I will grab a drink, maybe just a water?" She started to stand up. "Can I get you another—"

"Nothing for me, thanks." He patted his trim waistline. "The camera adds enough, you know? But, hey, let me grab the water for you."

She nodded because the queasiness had become more real. "Thanks. Room temperature if they have it please."

He smiled and left her there.

Alone for the moment, she let her mouth relax into a neutral line. This was harder than she thought. But more confirmation of her extremely right call in ending things with Evan Chambers.

She startled when a warm, moist hand gripped her shoulder and squeezed, then a bottle of spring water lowered down in front of her.

She relaxed her jaw. "Thanks, Evan," she said, shifting in her seat from the awkward vibe. She opened the water and pounded it fast. His eyes widened with every loud gulp.

"Like I said, it's been a day...or twenty-five." She smiled and puffed a light laugh without meeting his too-intense, too-close-to-seductive gaze.

"When did you get in?"

"Yesterday, so I am all out of sorts."

"From where this time?" he asked, leaning a few inches closer, playing with her water bottle cap.

"I was in Berkeley visiting Prana and, well, my dad and his new wife… then before that, Puerto Vallarta."

"Hope your family's doing okay, and the new stepmother, huh?"

"Yeah…she's a nice lady."

He smiled at her warmly but with a suspicious look in his eyes. Probably—no, most definitely—not expecting such a neutral reaction to *anything* relating to her father. Evan had known how torrential things were with her dad and her aunt.

"Wow, you really *have* changed." His head tilted, then he reached his hand under her chin and lifted her face to meet his. "And, as if it were possible, you're even more gorgeous than I remember."

Preeya rolled her eyes and sat back in her stylishly uncomfortable coffee-house seat—putting space between her and Evan's not-at-all-subtle advances.

"So…Vallarta? Oh, right! Amy's wedding. You'd gotten that route special. How was it?"

Indeed, *how was it?* She didn't know.

She told him the entire saga except for the *Ben* specifics, of course, and it turned out to be a good way to bring the interaction between her and her ex back to the necessary level of superficial.

And as she recounted her recent weeks' adventures to Evan at their little two-top, something happened. She realized that Evan had always been more of a cardboard cutout of a person. And she would have become one, too, if she had stayed. No doubt in her mind. With every nod and wink and polite laugh he guffawed in his perfectly pressed collared button-down, there was no question in her mind. Even with the totally awkward come-ons, she felt good. Her chest inflated while the guilt eased out her toes. Closing this chapter the right way had been important, as much for her as it had been for Evan. If not more.

Then she actually started enjoying herself. Evan was a total character. Comical, even. His self-importance, his chauvinistic air and his cheesy advances started to make her laugh rather than cringe. *Weird.*

Or not. Magical Vallarta—with Ben and even after he'd left—had transformed her. Made her *truly* go with the flow. Just thinking about the person she'd found there—the more accepting, open-minded, braver Preeya—swelled her heart. Her nausea even faded for the most part. Yeah, her stomach settled and her tensions eased as she ran through the events of the past weeks in her mind as she chose which real-life movie scenes to share with Evan and which precious ones to omit. And God, were there so many—too many—scenes to omit. Mind-blowing, earth-shattering, soul-filling omissions—especially the fake honeymoon, the Marietas, the falls.

The falls.

Oxygen swept in like a gust of warm sea air off the bay. *That's where it happened.* The falls. She and Ben, together, as close as two people could be. Behind the magical cascade of purity and pleasure and perfection. That was when the moment overtook them. She stroked her middle—their baby had been created there and then. At those falls.

*

She had to cut it now, get going. Get to finding Ben. She sat up straighter. *Get to the point and go, Pree.* "I know you said water under the bridge, but still, Evan, I owe you an official apology."

"That's ridiculous—"

"No, I need to." She grabbed her purse from the chair-back and held it on her lap in preparation to go. Because, *Ben.* He took her over—mind, body, heart, soul. "I was selfish and less than honest. I should have shared my true feelings. And you *also* deserve the best. Better than I...was. And—"

"Wait, Preeya. As far as I'm concerned, this is the *better* you. You have changed so much." He grabbed her hand again. "I can see it. Everything about you is lighter, Pree. You are more complete, anchored. You leaving me, taking time for yourself, it seems to be *exactly* what you needed. What *we* needed. And now, maybe this is a clean slate for us? Our second chance?"

CHAPTER 39

DRINKS? NO. THAT wasn't how he wanted to celebrate the close of the medical board saga. He needed to relish the memory of his in-laws' disappointment in crystal-clear lucidity. Standing outside the hospital's entrance, he took Stanton's hand and shook it firmly.

"I think that I'll just...walk. Breathe in the victory along with the fresh Seattle air, Go through campus. Rain check, though."

Stanton gave him a doubting and disappointed glare, then perked up. "Wait, your place?"

"Yeah, I didn't tell you, but I've been offered an adjunct position with the university. Lecturing on pediatric critical care, an associate I worked with back in Nepal and again in Mexico is on the board...so, I'm here for a while."

"Wow, man. Terrific! Glad for you. Really, that's great. And hey, it's probably time to plant your feet for a while anyway?"

Ben nodded as a plane thundered overhead. *Hmm.* Planting his feet— "Yeah, Stan, it's time"—while wondering where Preeya was flying to then.

"Well, shit man, you deserve it. It's been a long, tiresome road, but you made it through."

Ben grinned, knowing Stan meant the hearings, but he had no illusions that the next chunk of time, this clean start—in civilization, alone—would be hard as hell, a next section of *long and tiresome.* But, he was ready. Or *readier,* at least. "Listen, man"—Ben clapped Stanton on the back and pulled him for a hug—"thank you for everything."

"Thank me for real at our celebratory meal. Now that you'll be in town, no excuses. I'm goddamn holding you to this one. And if *I* don't scare you, then my mean, pregnant wife will."

Ben laughed. "How's the mama-to-be doin'?"

"Really well." Stanton knocked his fist on the top of his head. "We're getting ready, as should you, godfather."

"Right, yes...of course. Again, I'm honored...and I am...I'm ready." Strangely, he was. He might not have his own kid this lifetime, but, he'd play a role in Stan's kid's, Stacy's kids, and future patients if he got back into surgical. Ben smiled and reached his hand out again to shake goodbye, ready to get walking, though talking had gotten easier. A lot easier.

"Hey, with this all happening last minute, you know where you'll stay? You need to crash with us, borrow a vehicle?"

"No, man, but thanks." Stanton was a really good friend. "Another DWB associate who's away for the year has a house within biking distance to campus. An awesome Victorian. Too big for me, really, but it's vacant, clean, close to everything."

"When things fall into place, man..."

Ben nodded, hiked his messenger bag up on his shoulder, and grinned. "Yeah." *For the most part.* "They do." He swallowed back the persistent knot that hadn't left him since Vallarta and sighed.

"Okay, so *dinner*...call me this week. And hey, maybe, we'll bring Zoe's sister?"

Ben nearly flinched at the thought, and at the lack of argument to be found. "Uh, yeah, maybe, Stan." He cleared his throat. "Might be good." A distraction to clear his head, his heart.

Stanton beamed. "Great, man."

Ben shifted his stance and dragged his hand over his head, immediately regretting the hope he'd given his friend. "I said maybe, Stan. Maybe." He sighed into a fast topic change. "Oh, by the way, I'm getting a new phone, new provider tomorrow...so I'll be calling you from a new number."

"It's about damn time you replaced that ancient thing." Stan laughed.

It was time. To detach from the association of it...and the device had deteriorated to sporadic static on this last mission. "I'm smart enough now for a smart phone, so my nephew's told me, though I'm scared shitless that I'll be taken over in my sleep." Ben snickered. "Am I old, or am I goddamn old?"

Stanton shook his head and nodded. "Fucking old, man. We're getting fucking old." The other man slapped him on the shoulder. "I'll wait for your new number, Ben. And again, congrats."

Ben threw Stan a wave and headed down the sidewalk for his victory stroll through campus.

*

He filled his lungs then let out a long, liberating breath. He was Dr. Benjamin Trainer again with no stigmas or scars on his record to fight or hide from. He raked his hand over his head…to feel the waves he'd let grow while on the vaccine expedition. It had gotten too difficult to maintain the clean shave—and he'd run out of sunscreen. Plus, he'd been ready for the change.

Change. God, how so much had changed…since Preeya had entered then exited his world. And though it still burned like hell, he knew he had become a better man for having known her. Intimately, deeply known her.

*

Officially settling in the Emerald City was ironic, he knew. But to say fuck you to his past, and to find his future, he thought it poetic. Ben wandered the grounds with Portage Bay to his left, the Olympic Range far out in the distance and sighed. Between the Sound, Rainier, and every amazing island, pine forest, mountain trail and rafting river in between, the landscape was priceless—enough to keep his mind off…things.

No, Ben. To allow him to process those *things.* His past life with Jamie, his start and end with Preeya. With the medical board saga behind him and the university position ahead, he'd look forward. He'd just "go with it". *Thank you, Preeya.*

He hit University Avenue and headed up it. *The Ave.* People-watching to rival the airport. With the hipsters and street guitarists, the backpackers and bikers, and the students fresh out of thrift-store commercials. He smiled—regular American life, Seattle life. Clean air, conveniences. It was… well, interesting to be home, to say the least.

The word *home*—it lacked meaning anymore. Just a word, a syllable. One single sound that had once carried the universe with it, with Jamie—and weeks ago, with Preeya, it had been nearly redefined. But now it carried nothing. Not yet, at any rate. But hell, he could do this, make a home here.

He sighed and shook off the nagging low. *Not today, damn it. Not now.*

With a deep breath in, an aroma of *rich and bold* hit his senses. Sound and scent—fresh coffee beans poured to their heavenly demise into grinders— tugged Ben's attention up and away. He found himself standing at the door of an authentic Seattle coffeehouse with vibe and taste and warmth. One he'd been to before, so long ago, though. When he'd been young enough to almost blend-in—becoming part of the hip and mellow crowd had never really been a possibility.

Go in, Ben. Enjoy and relax, for God's sake.

A real Seattle roast sounded ideal.

A steampunk wonderland hit him like a slow-motion tidal wave as soon as he pulled opened the door. Mismatched sofas and side tables and board games strewn every which way, the smooth strumming of an acoustic guitar and, of course, bold espresso scent filled the space. Cool and warm and gritty, all of it. The *whir-shhh-whistle* of milk steaming became the only disruption of the vibe, yet it played its vital role—punctuation to the sentence. It all made him feel at ease.

He headed up to the coffee counter, smiling at the sippers and chatters and readers, texters, gamers, writers, and thinkers along the way. He snickered at the black nail polish and lip piercings. God, when had he gotten so old? *You've always been so old.* He nodded at the accuracy of his thought as he approached the *very chill* barista with her thick nest of dreadlocks. "Hi there. Just need a second." He grinned glancing at the chalk-art menu.

Behind halved lids, her eyes smiled back. "No rush, man." She grabbed a rag and wiped the counter while humming along to the guitar's take on a nine-ties grunge ballad he'd never been into.

Jamie would have liked this.

Preeya would have *loved* this.

Clearing his throat and his head, he perused the long and wide menu of options above him. How many drinks could a bean or a tea bag produce, anyway? Board one, board two, board three. How's just a black Americano? A double-shot espresso straight up? Or did he want to venture out, try something new? He scanned and debated. At the fourth and final board overhead he'd decided. He nodded, looking to the large hopper filled with the alluring mountain of dark beans calling his name. Telling him what he *really* wanted.

"I think I'll have"—he pulled his bag off his right shoulder for his wallet— "an Americano, please." He put down a five spot and smiled.

Without a word, the so-cool barista got to making his drink.

As he waited for the drink and his change, he scanned the bar for napkins and the necessary coffee paraphernalia, when he caught something. From the corner of his eye. And did a double take.

Hand in hand with a man at a small table for two in the cozy and private back corner next to that huge hopper of beans, was…Preeya? Adjusting his glasses and squinting to be sure, lungs caught—yes…*Preeya*.

On-to-the-next Preeya. His might've-been Preeya. *Preeya Patel.*

*

He'd ducked out—without his drink—before she saw him. And headed home—a storming mile of fury.

What the hell was she doing in Seattle? She was from Northern Cali. Could be a long layover, time-enough for a coffee date? *Desire*-enough for a fucking coffee date. Done so quickly with Ben? Obviously, because there she'd been, holding hands with a guy who could've been in a men's clothing catalog. Button-up shirt and upright and leaning into her with a look. *Fuck.*

Stop, Ben. It was good. That it was easy for her to move on. He didn't want her to be dwelling, lonely, sad. He fucking cared about her, despite her feelings toward him. And those feelings had obviously been only surface droplets. It was just a casual rendezvous for her and nothing more. Just a few-day fling. A deep, intense weeklong tirade of a fling.

That text. The one he'd caught on her phone, from an Ethan or Evan—*I can't stop thinking about you.* Maybe Ben had been a fun and temporary escape from a much more serious something? She'd run back to her past, the next-best option. *Fuck me.* He wanted to punch a concrete wall and create a hole the size of the one he'd allowed to spear through his heart. A hole bigger than the overhead crater of the hidden beach at his Marietas. God, so much bigger. *Just... fuck me.*

He blew hot air from his flaring nostrils, just a bull, ready to...to...do not a goddamn thing. Because she wasn't his. Never had been.

And he'd gone off, back to his old routine, escaping to the jungles, to help faceless people while running from his own demons. Fleeing, hiding.

Not fighting.

Fuck.

With a death grip on his handlebars, he looked up to the clear, strangely cloudless Seattle sky. *No, this is right. This is best.* A clean, stinging pain, a fast rip of the bandage. Officially. She couldn't even tempt him. She was taken, off limits.

And he'd move on, too. Jamie had made him promise to live after her, and live fully. So he'd find someone. Or someone would find him.

Stan's sister-in-law...? His stomach cramped up. From the uphill ride.

Or because he couldn't picture being with anyone anymore but Preeya, damn it.

But that's done, Ben. Done.

Fuck. He pedaled hard, jamming his legs down, quads burning. He got to the top of the hill as if it were life or death, then swung left onto 17th, breathing hard. Lung-and-brain-clearing hard.

The sudden scene change of the neighborhood threw him. The line of Chestnut trees and Victorians leading up to his place made his panting anger seem melodramatic, stark. And people, new and unmet neighbors, were all outside today—again, summer in Seattle. All waving to him as he rode by. An elderly man gardening, a woman washing her car, a professor walking back from campus, a young father tossing a ball with his toddler...

Ben's seething breath halted then, and became one full and easy exhale.

Maybe that *someone* isn't a life partner at all.

Maybe it's a child. A child in need—and he'd seen how many children around the world went without parents, homes, food, a roof. He could adopt, with the connections he now had, he could do that. Why wait to find the right woman? His life with Jamie—and his…stint with Preeya—might have been it.

He took a deep breath to slow his pounding pulse. It was a good plan.

Then go with it, Ben.

*

She slid her hand back slowly from Evan's hold and gave him her most heartfelt smile, forcing eye contact though she died to look away. "Ev, listen. I think—well, I know—that I've made a good decision…for the both of us. And I can't go back. I care about you, but not in that way."

He sighed, looked down at his now-empty hand, and then pushed his chair out. He stood up and paused. A thin, tight line razored across his lips. No more dimples. No more TV-ready glow. "I made a mistake coming here. Reaching out to you. It was stupid…bordering on pathetic. Preeya, I wish you the best. Good-bye." He turned and left her there at their little table for two.

Good-bye, Evan.

Gigi sat down across from her, where Mr. Channel 4 News Anchor had been before he stormed out of the coffeehouse and drove off in his hot-red sports car.

"Was it self-indulgent to meet him in the first place? God, I don't know what I was thinking. I just want him to know that he wasn't the reason for me leaving, per se. That in the end, it was *me*. My screwed-up, aimless self."

"Your intentions were good and, well, you can't help how someone takes things. You did right. He obviously wasn't ready for the truth, is all. If he wants more of the lie, let him find it with someone else. You, Pree, are moving forward. Looking for the real thing. For you and, now, for your little miracle in there."

Preeya exhaled long and slow. She knew now more than ever who the real thing had been. "Let's go find him, Geej. I need to find Ben and get him back."

CHAPTER 40

BEN SLID THE new-in-the-box smartphone into his bag and with a last wave of thanks to the clerk, he left the store. Weaving through a few kids toward the bike rack, someone grabbed and pulled his bag's strap off his shoulder.

"Hey!" He spun around holding tight to his bag with his new phone, his passport—and his wedding band—inside.

In his face, a teenage girl, wide-eyed, frantic. He yanked the bag and stepped back. The girl—helpless, apparently homeless, obviously strung-out—fell forward, then stumbled off.

Shit! He'd never had that happen to him. An attempted mugging. In broad daylight! Not in Mexico, Nepal, or West Africa. Then, *Jesus*, to come back to it? He watched the girl slink into a store but decided to leave it be.

In awe, he situated his bag—his murse, *eye sigh*—across his chest, then got on his bike to head home. He scoffed. Before the attempted day-light "mugging", he'd been having a better day. The bike ride to the cell phone store had been good for him. It had worked his heart, moved his blood, and helped clear away—or, at least, push down—the shock of yesterday's Preeya-discovery. Although the coffee aroma from every other storefront shot flashbacks at him and made him wince.

But really, there was no escape. A kissing couple, an airplane overhead, the fucking color purple, the sunrise. He couldn't help but think of her and their surreal time together. Touching, kissing, caressing, laughing, whispering, breathing each other in, and just *being*.

But then yesterday's image surfaced. Of Preeya up close and comfortable with the prep in the coffeehouse.

Shake it off, Ben.

More easily said than done. Because, how ironic. That yesterday while his dysfunctional phone mocked him from his bag, the one person he longed to tell his news to—about the hearing and his new stint on campus and the house—hadn't been Stan. And it hadn't even been Stacy—who, *shit*, he really had to get a hold of or she'd disown him.

No, it had been Preeya. The first person he thought of when he woke up, the last one he thought of when he shut his eyes. And all through the night in his masochistic fucking dreams, *Preeya*.

And Fate had thrown him the insane opportunity to tell her his life-changing news in person. Face to face. He gnashed his teeth and white-knuckled his bike handles. Yeah, Fate had thrown it right in his goddamn face.

*

"I got it," Gigi announced, coming through Preeya's apartment door like a train to somewhere. "I had to embellish a bit…and omit a lot," she said with a wink, then rubbed Preeya's tummy on her way to pecking Preeya on the cheek. "But for the most part, it was all true. *You are* worried sick about Ben, and *you do* have to get in touch with him right away. Anyway, Dad doesn't doubt anything when it comes to *you*."

Preeya nodded. "Thanks, Geej, and thanks, Detective Donlow!" Preeya laughed, then nodded while staring hard at Gigi. Waiting. "Well? Tell me, Gigi, *Jesus*."

"Oh! Sorry. So, he's safe."

Preeya's lungs filled as if she hadn't breathed in days. "Oh God, Gigi…" Her chest heaved, her lip quivered, her eyes filled. "Thank you. Thank God!" Sobs interrupted her words.

"Breathe, Pree. It's all good."

She counted in her head, and by four she needed to dive back into the questioning. "So, where is he?"

"He flew out of Mexico City five days ago—"

"Mexico City? I wonder why?"

"Into Sea-Tac—" Gigi paused for effect.

After Preeya's mouth fell open and snapped shut again, she widened her eyes to hurry Gigi along. "Please, Gigi, stop with the drama and spit it all out. He's here in Washington? In—"

"Seattle! He pulled money from an ATM just off campus, Pree."

"What the hell?" Not a coincidence. No such thing.

"There was a registration on file my dad found, something with his medical license. It wasn't suspended, but some note was lifted or something. Oh, and he has a new cell phone. Here's the number…"

"Oh my God, Geej. You are amazing. This is amazing." Her heart ramped to overdrive—then crashed to the floor. "But…I can't *call*! With this news?" She held her stomach, woozy and quivering. "I mean, he didn't return my last messages. The ones where I apologized and explained and begged him to call me back…so what the hell am I even doing?"

Gigi put a glass down in front of Preeya. "Drink." Then she sat on the couch next to her. "Maybe he lost his phone somewhere in the jungle? Or got it wet? Or maybe he's technologically illiterate and doesn't know how to check his voice mail? Or the government confiscated it?" Preeya's eyes morphed into sheer annoyance. "Or, or…the cell service there, or even here, is wonky. Whatever, Pree. With something this big, it doesn't matter what the reason. You just have to do it. You've got to call. Arrange to meet up." Gigi grabbed Preeya's phone from the coffee table and shoved it in her visibly trembling hand.

But Preeya just stared at the number. And at her phone.

"I guess you can just wait around that ATM for a few days?"

Then Gigi's phone buzzed from her pocket. Gigi mumbled the text to herself then gripped Preeya's wrist. "Shit, I don't get the paper…who reads newspapers anymore?"

"What? What the hell are you talking about, Geej?"

"My father…"

"Let me see that." Preeya snatched the phone from Gigi. The text read: *Look at today's paper. About Dr.*

Preeya hopped up and slid across her apartment to her makeshift desk of plywood and crates. She threw open her laptop and typed *Seattle Times.*

Midway through page two: Dr. Benjamin Trainer Cleared of Negligence.

She read on. *Globe-trotting nonprofit pediatric surgeon…Cleared by Seattle Hospital's medical review board…Wife, Jamie Trainer, passed away…Stage 4… Doctor's in-laws' claims unfounded and dismissed…*

His confession in Vallarta—and her reaction to it—God, how it haunted her. She'd known his pure nature, his kind heart. It killed her how she'd doubted him and his goodness, his integrity.

Now, though, thank God, she knew he was alive and well, and within the boundaries of the same city. What she needed more than anything was his forgiveness and him—his love—back in her life.

"What is it, Pree? What's the damn thing say?"

"It's an official statement by a hospital board," she explained while making no eye contact. She couldn't tear her eyes from the popping print at her trembling fingertips while a flood of relief for Ben coupled with a surge of guilt boggled her senses.

"Stating what?"

"Exonerating him for any…negligence or involvement in his wife's death."

Gigi snatched the mouse from Preeya and scrolled. "Jesus, Pree."

"I know. And he tried to explain it all to me. I flipped out, Geej. He blames himself, for supporting her wish to end the treatment…and for making her comfortable. But now, this"—she pointed to the article on the screen—"the medical board and the autopsy officially clear him."

Gigi read, nodding and *hmm*-ing until she exploded off the stool. "Preeya, listen! 'Looking forward to moving on, Doctor Ben Trainer will start guest lecturing at the UW Seattle campus for summer and fall terms.'"

"Wait, what?"

"You heard me. You will go to his lecture, Pree. And *get* him."

Preeya couldn't think. Flashes of heat and color and light filled her vision.

"You've got to. It's perfect. Approach him after the lecture hall lets out."

"Too stalkerish…way too stalkerish," she mumbled. Gigi couldn't understand how badly Preeya had hurt him. Insecurity and fear sucked her throat dry in an instant.

"He is the father of your fetus, Pree, and it's not like you didn't try a billion other ways. And…I think you've got all the options you're ever *gonna* get."

"Wait. Wait a minute. Grab that for me. That folder."

Gigi pulled the UW folder off the kitchen counter.

Preeya thumbed through the stack inside the folder as if on fast-forward. She found and pulled out a grid. Her class schedule. Starting at 8:00 a.m. the day after tomorrow. Pediatric Psych. With…her finger followed the dots across…Professor Dr. Helen Mantu. 10:00 a.m. Pediatric Critical Care…*Dr. Ben Trainer.*

"No fucking way." Her own whisper filled her ears with freeze-frame wonder.

"Preeya, please with the language," Gigi said, rubbing her own belly with irritating care. "What, though? What is it?"

Preeya put the paper down on the plywood surface, her index finger tapping the page, the name, for Gigi to catch on.

"No fucking way!" Gigi yelled jumping up and down.

"There are no coincidences, right, Geej?" she said, eyes dazed and damp with tears, completely unbelieving. Because…how the hell? Total insanity.

Gigi hugged Preeya and danced her around the small apartment.

"Okay, okay. I'm gonna be sick if you keep spinning me around like this."

"You're gonna go to that lecture and get your man!"

Light-headed, Preeya went to the sofa and fell into the cushions. Gigi bounced over to join her. "Please, Geej."

"Right, right. Now, listen…you can't tell him about the baby until you're sure that he wants to be with you first."

"I've got to *apologize* first. If he even gives me the time of day." Preeya's pulse double-timed at the possibility that he really wouldn't want to see her. She grabbed a fast breath. Then what?

"Right. *Then* the whole loves-you-for-*you* deal, *then* the baby."

Preeya rolled her eyes. "Sometimes, Gigi…I swear."

"What?"

"You know I've got to tell him about the baby whether he forgives me, loves me, or none of the above."

"Right, but fate wouldn't have brought you both this far just to, you know, have things fall apart."

Preeya fisted the decorative couch pillow in her lap, then swallowed back her words. Boiling-hot anger reached her earlobes and made her ears ring. Anger not toward Gigi, no. It was flaming fury at the goddamn unknown. The unknown she'd always said she relished, craved. Fuck!

"I can't right now, Gigi. I can't think about…that possibility right now." But she *could*—and her brain *would*—think about it. In fact, the thoughts sprinted in, just a mad dash of dreadful hypotheticals to her frontal lobe. *What if, Pree?*

What if he's done with you? What if he was unwilling to accept her apology, her deep, sincere understanding, her love? Knowing in the pit of her being that after the "gamut of assholes," *Ben was it*. Her perfect fit—her thrill and balance and heartbeat. If he didn't let her back into his life, she might as well give up now. Because there was no one else for her. No one but Ben.

So let it be just her and her baby. That's it. *That* love. *The end.*

But she'd gone without both parents. Without that security, that grounded, grown-up love. She'd of course have to keep Ben in their child's life. He'd of course want to be in the baby's life. So she and Ben would play acquaintances, eventually friends? With—what?—shared custody?

Her heart dropped.

Would he meet someone?

Her stomach churned.

And then Preeya'd have to hand off her kid to Ben and another woman? A *stepmom to my child?* Through all the kid's landmarks and milestones. And—

"Preeya!" Gigi shook her arm.

"What, yes!" Preeya pulled her arm away. "Sorry, Geej. What...what is it?"

"You were in a zone, turned pale. Hard to do for an Indian, even half an Indian. Here." Gigi handed her a glass of water. "I'm putting on a movie for you while I make you food. Take your mind off things for now."

Preeya sighed, unfisted the decorative pillow in her death grip, and snickered. Gigi had shifted into mama mode like a natural, a pro. Preeya fluffed the frill pillow and tossed it onto the other couch. "A distraction would be good. But hey...no romantic anything, okay. No babies, either."

"I'm not an idiot, Pree," Gigi scoffed. "How about *Terminator*, the first one?"

A slow, deliberate blink told Gigi what Preeya thought of that suggestion. "I, uh, think I'll take a nap, Geej. Feed me later, okay. Right now I just...need to sleep." *Escape to sleep.*

CHAPTER 41

H E STEPPED OUT the front door to check the weather. He did not miss the thick humidity of Central Mexico, that was certain. Barefoot on his front porch, the breeze blew by him as he grabbed the morning paper by his foot, tucked it under his arm, and headed back inside to get ready then head out to the first day of his lecture series.

He just needed to grab his coffee and a shower, throw on the outfit he'd laid out the night before, and he'd be good to go. He sighed. Yeah, it would be good, convincing himself as he padded his way into the kitchen where the coffee aroma called to him—and filled his mind with an image of Preeya for the umpteenth time.

Jesus, Ben, stop already.

Bring-beep. Bring-beep. "What the—?" His new phone and its unfamiliar ring sounded from across the kitchen, apparently charged and ready for use. Stacy. Who else was there?

*

"Hey, Broth…it's me. Can you…me, okay, because I'm…getting…retreat… Ben?"

"Stace? Can only hear every other word…"

"Is that…ittle…etter? Can…hear me now?"

"Yeah, yeah. I hear you, Stace. You got my voice mail, then." *Obviously.*

"Just minutes ago. Did you get mine?"

"No. I couldn't—can't—access my old messages…don't ask. But new phone in the civilized world…should be all good from here. So…"

"So…the hearing's done! God, Ben, I'm so glad. You can finally move on."

Right, move on.

"And the teaching gig! Means no more missions? Because I was so damn worried about you, you selfish bastard…my fraying nerves."

He sighed. "Sorry I worried you, Stace…I—"

"*You*—nothing. After two weeks of not sleeping, eating, writing, I couldn't take it anymore…"

He wanted to interrupt, take a rain check on her worried rant so he could still get to his first lecture on time—but he knew better. *Just let her fume.* He owed her that much. He'd just have to bike-it faster than he'd wanted to, was all.

"…*so* I went."

"Went?"

"To the yoga and spa retreat—God, Ben, are you even listening?"

"Yes, of course. The connection's still a little choppy, is all," he fibbed then smirked.

He heard her *hmph* into the phone. "Anyway, just got back. Spent a whole week—no phones allowed, no email, no TV, no *nothing*. There weren't even mirrors! It was in the lushest jungle…about an hour south of Vallarta. Pretty awesome, huh?"

He smiled. "Sounds it. Your *very own* excursion into the Mexican jungle," he said, making a slight point.

"Yeah, I guess. Minus the pre-reported *cartel activity*, you stupid a-hole!"

"Stace…I just had to—"

"Yeah, I know, I know. Well, for your information, I wasn't the only one worried to death about you."

"God, please tell the kids I'm sorry. How are they, anyway?"

"Oh, the kids? They're fine. They came with me—24/7 fun for them. But it wasn't the kids I was talking about, dummy."

Silence. Where was this going?

"God, men are so stupid—I'm glad I don't have one." She laughed into the phone. "*Preeya*, Ben. She came to the house two hours after you left that morning, then stayed an hour more crying…that she needed to apologize and stop you from going. She was literally sick over it."

More silence—earth-quaking, deafening quiet rocking his ears, his chest, his gut.

Too little, too late. Way too little, way too late.

"You there, Ben?"

"Yes. I'm…here."

"And it sounds like she's still worried sick—she left several frantic voice mails and texts after that. One from just last night, in fact. After I get off with you I'm gonna call her and—"

"No."

"Whoa, there."

Reel it in, buddy. "Please don't, Stacy."

"Why the heck not?"

"Because." His pulse spiked. "That's why." He poured his coffee and shoved the pot back onto the burner, scalding himself in the process. "Damn it."

"Hey!"

"No, it was the—never mind." He stuck his burned hand under the tap.

"Look, Ben…I don't know exactly what your fight was about, but she felt horrible. She deserves to know that you're alive. That you're okay."

"I saw her," he blurted, almost against his will.

"What do you mean, you saw her? Where?"

"For some reason she's in Seattle. I mean, I know the reason…she's *with* someone. In Seattle."

"Not sure I follow?"

"Stace, she was with a man, in a coffeehouse. The point is, she can't be too worried about me or my welfare. She's got a new distraction now."

"Benjamin Gregory Trainer, will you please grow the heck up?"

"*Excuse me?*" He slammed his coffee cup down hard; black water splashed up and out, pooling on the flecked granite countertop—not before burning his hand a second time. But he ignored the sting. Easily. "Did you just ask me to *grow up*?" Fumes shot from his nose—instigated, condescended. "Because I'm thirty-two years old, Stacy." Who the hell did she think she was? "After all I've…what I've…seen—been through…*grow up*? Just…" *Fuck!* "Damn it, I want to handle this *my* way…that is, if it's okay with you, *Mom*!"

He calmed his breathing while he heard long, purposeful, pensive breaths from the other end; maybe something she learned from her god-damn yoga retreat.

"Ben…" She paused, then sighed. "I get it. I'll back off." Deeper sigh. "But only after I call her back. Tell her you're okay."

"Stacy, *Jesus*." He took off his glasses to pinch the bridge of his nose, a headache suddenly splitting his forehead in two.

His sister was so damn stubborn. He wanted to cut it, move on—like Preeya had already done. And his sister getting involved, dredging things up…*damn it*.

And damn his feelings for Preeya, continually dredging up, no matter how hard he shoved them down. *Preeya.* Who he had cared for—did…*did* care for. Independent of anything else, anything she'd said or done. In spite of himself, *damn it*, he didn't want Preeya in pain—like Jamie didn't want *him* in pain. "Love," his wife had told him. Why wouldn't he wish the same for the wistful woman—his *no-longer-his* Preeya—who'd helped him surface from the suffocating depths of the ocean?

Yes, contacting Preeya was the right thing to do—and God, he hated that his sister was right.

"I'll do it, damn it. I'll call her." Even though the mere thought of her at that table, hand in hand, fingers entwined with that other man, made his guts knot. "I've got my first class which I'm already late for. I'll call her this afternoon. And…I'll talk to you…over the weekend." He pulled the phone from his ear, needing to be done with the call. "Bye," he mumbled as he hunted for, found, then hit the End button to his new goddamn smart phone and slammed the device down on the counter.

*

She waited for the hall to fill up first, students a couple to a few years younger than her filing inside. Her hiatus from school made for quite the age gap. She clutched her bag and her pride, then slipped into a seat in the very back row. At the front podium, no prof yet. She sighed—undetected, safe. And so far, Preeya hadn't felt ill all morning, even got through her 8:00 a.m. class without a hiccup. If she could just hold it together through this, keep her nerves in check, she'd be okay.

Because she had to be okay.

And she had to be okay if he brushed her off. If he'd already moved on, even. Just during those three weeks, maybe he'd met someone? Why not? Good-looking doctor, adventurous, giving. Passionate. *Amazing.* Yeah, none of the worries, the insecurities—*the realistic possibilities, Pree*—had left her. Why would they? Choosing to keep her feet on the ground, she needed to walk through the mud.

Her hands got clammy and her mouth dry, as if she'd eaten sawdust. She took a swig of water. It didn't help.

God, he's not gonna forgive me.

On that reverberating thought, Ben approached the podium from the left-side door. Her heart shifted into fifth gear from first. Seeing him alive, her breath halted, tears welled. Her Ben, tanned, lean, tall and calm, with hair—rich amber waves of it—and the start of a beard, neatly trimmed yet rugged. He stood just a hundred feet away from her. Still too far away. She could lose it and sprint down the aisle to him. Weeping, screaming, laughing past the hundreds of clueless souls and take him, hold him, kiss him, devour him. She worried she would. She gripped the chair arms and swallowed hard to gain control. *Control* like Ben's steady display of cool, calm control—the only nervous giveaway, his Adam's apple bobbing above the knot of his tie.

"Good morning, everyone. I'm Doctor Benjamin Trainer." His voice, deep and rich, sparked her insides with hope. "Welcome to Pediatric Critical Care 201."

CHAPTER 42

I T WENT FINE. Really fine. Some interaction and questions even, a few asking about his travels with DWB, one about the Jetta Air flight—it had apparently made local headlines—and a few questions on the course material. Ben felt in his element, and a new exhilaration drifted up his body. He tingled almost. Alive—in the right place, right context. Just, *right*.

But as the hall emptied, the world's future doctors filing out to their next classes, that feeling began to leave him. These students would move on to a next class, like everyone moved on with everything. And like Jamie had moved on from this world, *his* world. And like Preeya had moved on, leaving him without a picture for himself. An unwritten future.

Jesus, Ben. Get a handle.

He put together his notes, tapping the sheets down on the podium. The noise, and his steady breath, echoed throughout the great hall.

Except for a clank in the far left corner of the massive amphitheater. The back of a female student lifting her computer bag to her shoulder. A jet-black ponytail down the length of her back. It reminded him of Preeya. Jesus, he couldn't get away from the constant damn reminders of her.

He bent down to grab his bag from the podium, stood up, made sure the mic was off, and almost ready to leave the hall, he glanced up.

At the student in the farthest back row. Facing him...

*

His heart halted, frozen in his chest.

Not a reminder of Preeya Patel at all. It was the living-flesh pain, in person.

Fuck you, Stacy. She just had to call her.

He looked down at his hands. They were shaking. From nerves and fury and embarrassment and hurt. He forced them steady, shoved his papers in his bag, then targeted the side exit door.

"Ben, please." Her voice crashed into him, a melodic and unwelcome tidal wave.

But he focused on zipping his bag, difficult with his shaking, betraying fingers. He yanked the zipper so hard that it caught midway. *Fuck it.* He hiked the strap up onto his shoulder with the help of his opposite hand, and headed for the side door with attempted calm and confidence.

"Ben, please."

Ignore and go.

Oh, so no "grown up," Ben?

Shut the fuck up.

Only five more long strides to the door.

"Didn't you get my messages? I went to stop you that morning."

He stopped short but didn't look at her. "I know you went to Stacy's, Preeya," he stated in an ice-cold rasp that surprised him. He sounded foreign to himself, cowardly. "She told me and, well…you see that I'm fine and alive. So"—he turned his head but made no eye contact—"good-bye and take care." And two more steps got him to and through the exit door.

He walked up three steps. Then two at a time after that. Up to the front of the building toward his bike. *Get to the bike, head home.* His mind was blank but filled with scratchy white noise at the same time. *Just get to your bike.*

God, he could choke his sister. Unless Preeya had decided on a whim to reenter med school, and—what?—she coincidently got placed in his class? The thought made him laugh out loud.

Quick-paced footsteps grew louder behind him. But he wasn't stopping.

How inappropriate, Preeya showing up at his work. To tell him to his face that she's moved on? Why didn't she make an announcement *during* the lecture, for Christ's sake?

As if he'd blacked out several steps in time and place, he was at his bike. His trembling hands—*damn it, get it together*—took on the challenge of unlocking his bike lock. Jamie's birthday, 0506—God, he should really change the code already.

And at attempt number three, Preeya Patel was now panting over him, unable to talk but standing close. Too goddamn close. He couldn't help but inhale her scent of sweet coconut and lime. *Damn it.*

Just move the hell away from me—you've already moved on. Now let me!

"Damn it, Ben." She bent forward, hands on knees, even closer to him now. He stood up, giving up for the moment on the bike lock. He just needed to gain some space—Jesus Christ, he needed her away from him.

Then he turned his back to her, and he walked. He didn't know where to, exactly, but he needed to. He had to gain more than space but real distance. A stone bench, fifty paces away. That became his focus.

"I am in love with you, Ben Trainer!" she called out across the courtyard.

He stopped midstride. And from his peripheral, he was very aware of the others who'd heard. Lingering students, a few faculty members, a gardener, and a custodian mid-sweep on a winding garden side path. They all appeared frozen in time.

He spun around, still fuming. *What fucking game is this?* What the hell was she doing?

"I am. I am madly in love with you. I want to be better because of you. I reenrolled in med school because of you, because of your influence, Ben." She looked at her hands, then up at him again. "I mean, I want to be better for *me*...and for *you*. It's the truth." She began to walk toward him, and whether he was mad, moved, melting, or just feeling insane, his feet wouldn't take him anywhere.

She got to him, there in the center of the swirled cement courtyard in front of the triumphant entrance of the medical school's lecture hall, and placed her hands on his chest. Her right hand directly over his heart, which she must have felt pounding its way out of his rib cage.

"I saw you. Preeya, I saw you yesterday." He glared into her eyes—those bewitching goddamn eyes.

"At registration? You knew I'd be in your class? God, Ben, I called your cell so many times, and Stacy's, too. I was so worried…and I am so sorry for attacking you, that morning in Vallarta. What you did for her, for Jamie…you are the bravest person I—"

"No, Preeya." His chest heaved. "I didn't see you here on campus. I saw you with a man. At a coffeehouse." He tried to clear the thick knot of disgust lodged in his throat, but it wasn't budging. "Holding hands. The man who had texted you?"

He watched her visibly swallow and hold her stomach at the same time. Like she was going to be ill. She had been called out by him, and now? Now she had to take this entire melodramatic grand gesture back. Because he was sure that it meant nothing.

He shook his head at her. "Good-bye, Preeya."

"Ben…that was Evan. I was confronting him. So he'd stop trying. I had ended it with him when he'd proposed almost two months ago…but he wouldn't let up. Instead of running like I always do, I met him face-to-face to tell him again that it was never going to be between us. Because I had found someone. Whether you ever returned my calls, Ben, you were—you *are*—the one. There is no other."

He stared in disbelief while his head spun. A rush of what he knew, as a doctor, to be dopamine mixed with adrenaline, shot from his head to his heart, down to his gut, then exploded through his entire body. He pictured it all happening in an instant. An emotional MRI.

Her hand went to his face, slid up his cheek, then his jaw—

But he caught and paused her hand, then glared at her.

"Ben, there is no one but you. For me."

Her hand still held in his against his clenched jaw, his eyes still narrowed, unsure—unclear if this any of this was real.

"Only you. And me." She brought her other hand up to his face, raked it through his hair. "Ben, I'm not going anywhere."

He shook his head…and the next instant he took her. In his grasp. And devoured her mouth like nobody and nothing else existed but Preeya and him, locked together after too many seconds and minutes and days and fucking weeks apart.

He was whole, an entire man once again.

*

Applause finally slowed their kiss. And he let her vibration resonate on his lips, unable to let her slip from his embrace.

"Preeya Patel, you drive me mad. And I want you to do that to me for the rest of my goddamn life. Do you hear me? The rest of my life."

She nodded, her eyes glistening wet, happy—glowing. He wiped away one tear and licked it off his thumb. Salty and real. Not an illusion, not a dream. He sighed a relief he'd never felt before.

Her cell phone rang loud and wide and startled him out of their real-life fantasy.

*

Her heartbeat echoed so loud that her phone hadn't registered until the second round.

SafeHaven. It rang through her do-not-disturb setting, which she turned on for her morning classes.

She hesitated. Just froze in place.

Why? It's probably just Prana, the nurse connecting her through. To chat. On a Friday, late morning?

Their new schedule was every Saturday at nine. Before breakfast.

"Breathe, Preeya, and answer the call."

She wasn't breathing?

"Go on…" Ben urged, his hand thankfully on her back. A firm, strong support. Without it, she thought she'd whither like a leaf down to the hard concrete.

She took a deep breath in, then worked to breathe out that mysterious hovering fear. The exhale lodged in her throat as she accepted the call.

"Hello, this is Preeya Patel." Her voice—it sounded like her, but not. She shuddered again and her shoulders hit her ears. Seven-year-old Preeya. That's whose voice she'd just heard.

CHAPTER 43

SHE WAS SILENT and shaking, and he was honestly worried that she'd pass out like she'd done in Vallarta. Ben took her car keys and got her into the passenger's seat.

"*Nononono*. Please, God," she muttered to herself, eyes closed tight like she was stuck in a nightmare. He took her hand, locked their fingers, and tried to infuse her with all his strength. He felt her pain so sharply; all he could do then was squeeze the fear out of her hand. And she let him.

"We'll get there, Preeya. We will," he said, merging onto the highway. Through traffic, luckily not rush hour, but still. Thirty minutes if no accidents. Then to grab a flight. Jesus. *Just drive, Ben, and get her there.*

Then her phone beeped. Preeya opened her eyes slowly and glanced down at the screen.

"News?"

"A text from Gigi…" She gulped loud. "Oh God, Ben. Oh God."

"What, Preeya? What does it say?"

"Gigi wants me to call her and…to stay calm. *Oh Jesus.*" Sobs erupted.

"What? I don't understand—"

"I told you about Gigi, remember?" Preeya's whisper sounded almost irritated for his confusion. "She sees things…two things as clear as crystal. Oh God, Ben. Please drive faster. Just go as fast as you possibly can."

He still didn't quite follow but wouldn't dare add another questioning word to her obvious panic. "Just hang on for me." He got over to the far left and hit ninety in a matter of seconds.

"Please, Lord, just not yet. Not yet," she whispered as she took her hand from his and raked her fingers through her hair, her entire body rocking forward and back. Lulling herself while he weaved in and out of traffic. He'd get her there. He'd get her to Sea-Tac then to SafeHaven—God willing, in one piece.

He watched her rocking begin to slow and he slid his right hand to her back. She leaned forward then—her hands moving to cover her face, her face in her knees—and just shook her head from side to side. Side to side. Like a young child denying a horrible adult-world truth, not letting it enter or settle in her head.

Then she wailed.

He swerved and the blue sedan to his right slammed on his horn. He recovered and straightened out, white-knuckling the steering wheel.

"She's gone. My baby sister's gone."

"You don't know that..." He glanced at her for a millisecond, then back on the road. "You don't know anything until we hear—"

"I do. In my marrow, I know."

CHAPTER 44

SHE OPENED THE door before Ben could actually bring the rental to a complete stop. Her father was in the lobby. Blinking too slowly. Too damn slowly.

Stop that! And say something, damn it.

Say something instead of just standing there blinking your fucking eyes.

"*Bitay*, come." She ran into her father's arms and screamed her sobs into his chest. Wailing her sorrow so Prana could hear her. To come back. To come back to the world. "She was in no pain, my love. She was in no pain."

She felt her father moving his feet, guiding her somewhere, but he didn't let go of her. His grasp stayed firm and tight.

Please, Daddy, don't let go, or I'll fall. I will just fall forever and ever.

He began to fold himself and her into a seat. Onto a cushiony seat. A soft, velvety one. His whisper in her ear matched the feel of the fabric on her hands and legs. "She stayed in bed later than usual today. Reading." He paused then. And when he resumed, his tone had raw, guttural emotion in it. "And when the nurses came to check on her, she had her book on her chest. She had just drifted out of her body. Poof, just like that." She could hear her father's heart racing, her ear mashed to his chest. Then he swallowed—she heard that, too. A cavernous echo in an endless cave.

Her father shifted, his arms loosened, his hands went to her face, lifting her eyes to his. But she didn't want to look at him. She couldn't. She just kept her eyes shut tight. Like her life depended on it.

"She was reading your book, *bitay*. Yours and hers. You were there with her, and it couldn't have been more perfect. Just couldn't have…and I thank you for being such a beloved heart to my youngest girl. My Prana."

She opened her eyes when a water droplet hit the top of her head. And there on her father's face were a stream of tears plummeting to their death off his hard-angled jaw. She pulled her father in to her. A hard, powerful embrace in honor of their sweet Prana.

*

"I will get you both some water," Sylvia said softly, touching Preeya on her shoulder.

"Thank you, dear," Preeya's father whispered, slowly unhinging himself from Preeya's reciprocal hold.

Preeya wiped her face but kept her eyes softly shut. She took a huge, empty breath in. And there she sat, as if floating in space. She didn't want to open her eyes. To see her surroundings. Not ever. Her world now without…

But, Ben.

Her eyes sprang open and there he was, sitting in the armchair next to her.

"Ben."

"I'm here." He reached for her hand and grasped it tight.

She patted her father's arm and stood up. Ben stood, too, and pulled her in with his strong, decisive arms, and just held her. She had no more tears to cry; she was just an empty reservoir in drought conditions. Not even a well of springs beneath her surface.

He moved his hands to her shoulders to give enough space for him to look her in the face. He said nothing with words. Just the warm love told in his amber eyes made her know he understood. He, of all people, understood her pain.

"Daddy…" Her voice scratched to a start. "This is Ben, Doctor. Benjamin Trainer…" She moved to Ben's side. Not another word of explanation was needed to know who he was to her. Obvious and raw, a blind person could see. "Ben, my father, Doctor Indra Patel."

"A true pleasure, Doctor Patel." Ben held his hand out to her dad. She watched her father—an even newer version of the man—take Ben's hand and they shook. Then, to Preeya's complete surprise, her father pulled Ben into him and hugged him hard. Gave Ben a firm pound on the back.

She let out a puff of a laugh, her heart leaping to her face. But in the span of a breath, it drifted back down into her chest, mimicking her father's glow morph back to stoic. For her—and for her father, it seemed—the introduction of Ben, the man who'd won the heart of Indra Patel's now-*only* daughter…well, it was heart-wrenching and heartwarming in the very same beat.

She sighed and looked up at Ben as he returned to her side. Bittersweet, she thought. With infinitely more sweet than bitter. She melted into his arms and they all stood in silence. A surrendered peace descended and told her it would all be okay. Eventually.

*

Another round of introductions were made when Sylvia came to join them with waters and a clipboard of paperwork for her and her dad to complete. As she stared glossy-eyed at the heading on the first page—*Deceased*—she felt a tinge of nausea.

Fingertips to lips, she sat straighter to try to settle her—*oh God.*

Oh my God. The baby.

Her baby. She hadn't gotten to tell Prana. Her sister left before knowing about the miracle growing inside her. Preeya's breath started racing. Panicked, she felt the greater impact of Prana's departure then, like a firestorm—hot, sharp agony.

Then light-headedness.

"Preeya? Are you all right? You look…washed out and…"

"I didn't get to tell her…she'll never know. And it would've made her so happy. I didn't get to tell h—"

*

Ben laid Preeya out on the couch while detailing the Vallarta fainting-episode to Dr. Patel. "She'd come-to fairly quickly, though."

But in his own mind, he thought her reaction strange, such a stark upris-
ing from what had become an almost floating, slow-motion state of being.
For all of them, it seemed. Strangers, but tied tightly in a web of love and
loss, past and present.

But new beginnings out of that web.

"Preeya. Come back to me," he whispered between light kisses to her
forehead and temple.

What had she forgotten to tell her sister that had upset her so much?

Sylvia came with an ice pack and placed it under her neck.

She gasped awake. "Ever?"

"Preeya, *bitay?*"

"Ever—what, Pree?" Ben took her hand.

But she ignored him. All of them. She just scrambled for her phone in
her purse, and at the same time, as if on cue, it buzzed.

"She'll be okay, Dr. Patel," he said while Preeya studied her phone screen
as if obsessed. He needed to get her grounded. *Alone.* "But would you guys
mind…getting her some crackers or a piece of toast, maybe? Low blood
sugar could be contributing…"

Preeya's father nodded his agreement before Ben could finish, then took
Sylvia's hand and they left him and Preeya in the sitting area to speak with
someone at the front desk.

Still glaring at her phone—a new message?—he wiped a stray strand of
her mussed midnight-black hair from her stunned and flushed face. "Preeya,"
he whispered.

A beat passed, then another. He couldn't rush her. After the next moment
came and went, he cleared his throat.

She finally looked up at him, a slow smile forming on her lips. A wide,
now ecstatic smile.

"Preeya Patel, what is it?" he asked, getting slightly impatient.

"Gigi. It's Gigi."

"No, not who…what? What was bothering you, Preeya?"

"I remembered that I had news—news to tell you, Ben. But then when
I realized that I'd never get to tell my sister the news…God, if fate had just

waited a few hours—but it's all okay now. I know she knows," she said, holding up her phone, near-giggling, tears pooling in her eyes. "She already knows," she said, then took his shirt collar in her grasp and pulled him closer, within inches of her face now. "Ben," she whispered, then swallowed and sighed a light, blissful sigh. "You and I…we're having a baby."

CHAPTER 45

H E ONLY SQUINTED his sun-kissed eyes at her. Speechless. A muddle of emotions waxing and waning across his face all in one forever-moment.

She sat up straighter on the lobby sofa of SafeHaven and searched his eyes. To be sure he'd heard her right. "Ben? Did you hear what I said?"

"I just don't want to wake up. If this is a dream, I'm scared I'll wake up from it." He brushed his finger down her cheek. "Marry me, Preeya Patel. Be my wife. The mother of my child. Of our child…oh God, this is a dream."

She stroked his face, catching a lone tear on its descent, and took his hand to her belly, and held it there. "No, it's not a dream, Ben. You have me—I mean *us*. God, it feels amazing to say that—*us*!" She kissed his mouth with a force he couldn't possibly mistake to mean anything but yes, she'd be his wife.

"To avoid confusion, my Preeya—as we've had some in our extremely short time together—I need to hear you say it."

She laughed hard, from her gut. So maybe he'd always need clarification, confirmation, but she loved it. "I will be your wife. Yes. I am so in love with you, Ben Trainer." She kissed his lips over and over again. "I can't breathe, I love you so much."

He grabbed her and squeezed her tight. Like he never wanted to let her go. "Preeya …I have no words for how I feel about you. But I'll spend the rest of my life showing you. Showing you and our baby."

"Baby?" Dr. Patel asked, standing in front of them with a small, round plate of crackers.

CHAPTER 46

FIVE MONTHS LATER
She put the dish in the dryer rack and looked at her wrist, at the moon tattoo she'd get removed after the baby arrived. "I can't believe how many things the OB says I can't do."

Ben gripped her ass and pulled her into him, spun her around, then nuzzled her neck. "Oh, but what about all the things we can do?"

She giggled then threw her arms up and around his neck, getting his collar wet with suds but neither of them caring. She pressed her lips to his, unable to get enough of him.

"Hey, though." Ben pulled back, his mouth curled. "The doctor also said that you can fly…for another two months."

"I knew you'd catch that." She hadn't been to an OB appointment without him yet. It was sweet how involved he wanted to be. "It's just…an airplane. I don't want to deal with the restrooms, the seats—I mean, look at me!"

"You're perfect." He lifted her onto the kitchen counter and pushed her hair back away from her face. "And gorgeous. I could look at you every second of every minute of every hour, of"—he kissed her neck—"well, you get the idea," he said through incremental kisses along her collarbone while his hand slid down her baby bump, under her blouse, and slowly up to her heavy right breast.

Preeya hummed, then he tweaked her nipple and she squeaked then giggled.

"Mmm, that giggle of yours. And your scent." With his nose nuzzled in the crook of her neck, he inhaled. "And your sensuous, glowing body—carrying *our* child," he said, pulling her into him—into his hard, pulsing need—and moaned into her ear.

She loved that he couldn't seem to control his desire for her.

For her, back pain and exhaustion aside, she really loved their constant and mutual hunger, their foreplay, and, *oh Lord*, their lovemaking.

"I want you with me, is all," he whispered, then noticing the time on her wrist, stepped back with a reluctant groan and pulled a coffee mug down from above their heads.

"It's a conference." She shifted to face him. "You'll be busy the entire time."

His lecture series on campus would end in a few weeks, and as an attempt to keep him connected, if only domestically, Doctors Without Borders had asked him to do some training, speaking, and fund-raising.

"Well," he said, waggling his brows as he filled his coffee mug, "not at night…"

She smacked his shoulder.

He smirked. "Hey, other than working lunches, I'll be all yours for meals, and…you'll be all mine." He nipped her ear.

She sighed, reached for a kiss, then slid off the counter to get back to the dishes. "We'll see," and began to pour the glass of milk she could no longer stomach down the drain. She cringed and flinched from the milk's resonating odor. "Wow. So, forget about the tight squeeze on a plane, just the crazy random smells that set me off, Ben…the food, the people…then the recycled air and colds… " She swallowed and blinked to settle her rumbling gut.

He nodded, took her cheek, and stroked his thumb across her brow. "Well, babe, I'll just have to put it off until after the baby comes." Yes, he somehow had organically begun calling her "babe"—and she loved it. Funny how perspectives and associations changed. "Babe" from Ben's lips had a completely different connotation.

"You're too much," she said before slamming him with a kiss. "But I am fine alone." Her monophobia hardly flared up anymore. Maybe because—she rubbed her belly—she was never really alone anymore.

"I know you're fine alone. I just don't want to be without you."

*

Seattle's sun eeked through the clouds, which it seemed to do more often these days, despite autumn's full swing. Ben locked the door behind him and hopped on his bike, ready to ride to campus, and to scheme.

If he could plan it right, take her father up on some long-overdue fatherly attention and means—though Ben was financially set, pulling in a doable guest professor's salary plus his past savings—he had no qualms about asking Indra Patel to help carry out his plan. With a child on the way and all the traveling he and Pree discussed, Ben didn't think twice about delegating the expense of a private jet and a beach ceremony in Puerto Vallarta to "Dad," as Preeya's father preferred Ben call him.

Yeah, a jet would address all of Preeya's flying concerns. A white sand ceremony on the bay, then off to their hidden beach at the Marietas…perfection for his Perfection.

So, she's five months along now. She can travel through her seventh or eighth. His surprise could actually work.

Now, she'd said again and again that she didn't want the real wedding, the ceremony, the party—but he knew she'd just said that for his benefit. Her huge heart, sensitive to his feelings, thinking he couldn't handle a big, traditional thing, too reminiscent of…his first wedding. But he had already reconciled everything: his love for Preeya, this chance with her—a second chance at love he could have never imagined possible. And there also wasn't an ounce of doubt that Jamie had wanted this for him. *This love.*

The courthouse or a bank notary or, hell, an alleyway would've done it for him. He'd marry her, make her his, any way he could. But this would be her first and only marriage, so help him.

He would keep it small and intimate, immediate family and some friends. He only had Stace and the kids, and Stanton and Zoe…but their new baby? So they might not make it. But Amy and Darren and maybe her

FA friend Amanda, though she just gave birth…and Gigi—who had given him a look or twenty for not insisting on a real wedding in the first place. But Gigi was farther along than Preeya.

So it would be a seriously small gathering. All the better.

Oh. He'd use the picture Preeya kept of her sister, the one on her nightstand, and blow it up, frame it. Set it at the altar so Prana would be *present*.

Perfect.

And with Preeya's father walking her down the aisle, it would be, for Preeya, a closed loop—all the pain of her past culminating in her life, their life, anew. New and beautiful and together.

CHAPTER 47

"OF COURSE YOU know that I—I mean *we*"—Preeya's dad looked in Sylvia's direction and winked—"will pay for it, *bitay*," her father said, his face tilted, a convincing plea in his tone.

Why she and Ben had decided to do the courthouse-thing was beyond her father. She grinned at Ben as she took her dad by the elbow and pulled him to the next row of strollers, trying to keep the topic away from her fiancé and to redirect it to something less redundant and more digestible. She'd been tired of hearing the contests from her father and Gigi and Amanda… Amy, too. "Look at these. They fold up to nothing but open to become… an RV!"

"Your marriage should be celebrated, Preeya." Her dad patted the stroller-supreme but spoke-on despite her distraction attempt. "Yes, it should be celebrated in front of your family and friends."

Sylvia kept up with them, nodding like an overly eager stepmother, supporting her father's genuine desire to see his daughter walk down the aisle. Ben hung back a row, maybe to avoid hearing the tired topic rehashed, and maybe, too, for the allure of toy medical kits for toddlers.

But Preeya might have disliked talking about their "unceremonious" wedding plans more than Ben had. Embers of guilt rekindled in her just thinking on it. She pictured Ben with an inevitable resurgence of grief on the day they'd legally wed. Her chest tightened. That grief he'd feel would be magnified a thousand-fold if they had a large ceremony—with Ben standing at a grand altar in wait of a bride, a different woman in white, a bride different than *his* Jamie.

Other valid justifications covered up this predominant fear. Her family. She had no mother or "mother's side." And she'd hate to have Champa poisoning her day, and she couldn't very well carve her out with her father *insisting* on paying for and hosting it—he'd have the wedding venue bill *and* hell to pay.

Ben's only living relatives were his sister and her kids, then their combined handful of friends, and her dad and Sylvia. How silly to have a grand wedding with hardly any attendees. *And we surely couldn't have a party.*

Honestly, she could skip it all—she and Ben and a blanket under the stars at Gas Works Park would be a dream for her.

Sylvia took Preeya's free arm, natural as could be. Her dad smiled, so pleased. "You know I'd love to go dress shopping with you, Preeya. No children of my own, it would be a pleasure. And having just done the research," she said, motioning to her lacking bust since the double mastectomy, "I know a few places that do custom gowns specializing in rare body shapes." Sylvia winked, now referencing Preeya's belly, though without judgment... just matter-of-fact. Preeya had begun to really like Sylvia, though she'd probably not call to chat or anything.

But thinking on rare body shapes, she rubbed her twenty-five-week-old baby bump. A dress? It gave her heartburn just imagining the fitting and measurements. What, an adjustable wrap for the long, elegant train? And for her ever-blooming breasts? She laughed to herself. She could see the shamed secret-section of some glamorous gown shop—a pathetic sign handwritten in marker: For Pregnant Brides—posted at the entrance of the back mop closet.

"Preeya, what do you think?" her father asked, interrupting her thoughts.

"I really don't want one, Dad."

"You don't want a stroller now? That's what we came here for," he said, tilting his head the other direction.

"Oh," she laughed, "right, the stroller." She looked over her shoulder to find Ben so he could be part of the decision. No longer at the mesmerizing toy aisle, she caught him ogling her more-than-generous backside. It also had grown, and it surprised her how intrigued she was by the preparation her body took. No doubt Ben was intrigued, too.

She glared at him then lifted a seductive brow, followed by a head bob to come and join the discussion. "Hey, you." She took her arms back from her father and Sylvia and patted then squeezed Ben's ass before settling her arm around his trim waist. "I like the joggers, I think. I can get out there and exercise with the baby…but the storage capacity on the standard one, wow. What do you think, babe?"

Her father put his hand on her shoulder. "I could get you both, *bitay*, if you want?"

She glowered at her dad. Ben squeezed her hand, the one situated on his hip. God, she loved how he knew her thoughts, her anxiety at the moment of impact. She took a deep breath. "No, Dad, we're okay." Her father sometimes got carried away, forgetting she wanted her father, not his money. Always had.

And actually, they were more than fine. She and Ben were so on the same page with finances—frugal and conservative, they held most things priority above material wealth. Life and living, travel and impacting the world—oh yes, so "Mother Teresa" of them as band manager Dawn would have said. She laughed out loud at her life then compared to now. A hundred and eighty degrees. *This, now* was the thrill, the adventure she'd been seeking. Ben had helped define it for her.

Anyway, the itch for exploration, growth—it vibrated through them both and made Preeya even more certain of how right they were together. It connected them. *One of many things that connect us*, she thought as she squeezed him to her, his tight, lean waist in her grasp, sending a wave of heat from her chest to her core in a nanosecond. Her cheeks burned the next instant, but her father had been paying attention to *his* better half and so Preeya escaped the bout of embarrassment.

Sylvia fell back to walk with Preeya while her dad went to check out men's ties. "Preeya, would you like to go with me to the café, grab a drink and a snack for the two of you?" Sylvia sent a warm glance toward Preeya's belly. "And we can bring your father back a latte…and something for you, Ben?"

He nodded at Sylvia and smiled. "I'd love a double espresso, thanks."

Preeya noticed how easy the two were around each other. The fact that Sylvia had survived cancer and Ben had intimately understood the fight, must have connected them on another level. Preeya didn't have that with Sylvia. She hardly knew her dad yet, so to build a bond with a new *stepmother* was, again, not high on the priority list.

"Okay, sure, I could use a muffin or two." Her stomach rumbled loud enough for the three of them to hear. Her cheeks heated. "Someone agrees."

CHAPTER 48

"I'VE BEEN THINKING..." Sylvia towered over Preeya by about seven inches; add her three-inch heels and Preeya felt like a little girl next to the woman. Had she been a model? She hardly knew the woman's background at all.

Preeya pulled out a bottle of water from her purse and chugged half of it. "Thinking? What about?"

"I wondered if after the baby is born...well, I know Ben works a great deal and Gigi will be having her little angel at nearly the same time. If you would like, I could come up from Berkeley and stay for a few weeks? I mean, I know we don't know each other very well, but"—Sylvia sighed and held Preeya's eyes with a look she'd never seen before—"I'd be honored to just be there for you. To help."

Preeya inhaled, trying to cover up what might have looked like a gasp, but before a muddle of would-be words fell out, Sylvia cut in again.

"Not as a mom or even a stepmom." The towering woman winked as she pulled out a chair for Preeya, then folded herself into the one across the café table. "Just as a friend. Preeya, I would love to be a part of this in any way that would help you."

Preeya swallowed hard, not knowing how to answer. Moved but unable to picture the woman, essentially a stranger, in her house. For weeks. Helping Preeya adjust? Sore nipples and crappy diapers and crying—both the baby and her, potentially? "Wow, Sylvia..."

Sylvia placed her hand over Preeya's. "Listen, I've been…needy this entire last decade—my treatments made life ugly, really ugly. I selflessly need to be *needed* for once, and for something beautiful, you know? Nothing's more beautiful than a baby."

Preeya felt her pulse in her toes and fingertips. Sylvia had her floored, just speechless.

"And…cancer took away my chances of ever having my own…so it would be a bit of vicarious baby joy. More than that, though, to get to know you, Preeya.…" She got teary and blushed, then dabbed at her eyes with a rough café napkin. "Sorry, so silly…and melodramatic of me." Sylvia shook her head and chuckled.

Preeya patted Sylvia's hand and smiled, blinking away a surprise tear of her own. It was Sylvia's vibe, her genuine desire to help, to be there for Preeya first and foremost…*just surreal.* Her chest felt warm, light, whirling with a distant and faded…something. Like a familiar, long-ago love. "Sylvia, I'd really like for you to stay and help with the baby."

"Oh my…*really?*" Her stepmom covered her mouth, then her eyes, and shook her head for a few beats until she recomposed herself. "Wonderful." And just like that, Sylvia the Sophisticated returned, now with an added glow to her softly aged, high-cheekboned face.

"It'll be so nice to have you."

She didn't have to talk to Ben about it since he and Sylvia had established such a rapport—she knew he'd be glad for the help. Ben liked both Sylvia and her father very much. He'd said he "liked them separately and together, a rare thing."

She smiled, then felt her cheeks heat. Earlier that day as they all had strolled through the department store's crib section, her dad had gripped Sylvia's butt—which swelled Preeya's heart and turned her stomach at the same time. Ben had cracked up laughing, and through his outburst he'd promised to grip Preeya's ass "hard and often" when they got old, too.

She relished the thought.

Strange, how balanced her dad and Sylvia seemed together—a weird but desired model to follow. Even with the several inches Sylvia had over her dad, they looked and acted like a fit. Less like a puzzle piece *fit* and more like two smooth and polished square stones whose surfaces complemented each other in color and design. Two whole and independent beings working in parallel. No overlapping, no one bleeding into the other. They seemed…synergistic. Yes, two souls working in unison toward…toward symbiotic contentment. With a lot of ass-grabbing thrill? Yeah, that's it. What she'd always wanted for herself. Not the Josh Bolte inevitably derailing roller coaster, but rather the fast, splashing boat ride to the Marietas with her Ben.

Her heart swelled.

Sylvia tittered, her head cocked to the side. "You got lost in thought, sweetie?"

"Yes." Preeya laughed then threw her hands to her cheeks, warm to the touch. "Just thinking about Ben. I hope we're as happy as you and Dad seem to be."

Sylvia glowed. "You will be, sweetie. In my heart I know you will be. Which leads me to a question…that you don't have to answer." Eyebrows up, chin down. "Between you and me, Preeya—so that I can help steer your father in the direction you're really trying for—do you want a special wedding ceremony, even if it's small? Or…just legal papers and done."

Preeya nodded, appreciating Sylvia's lack of bullshit. "I see it in Ben's eyes, Sylvia…the ache. He does a strange thing when he remembers a time or an event—like his first wedding. His right eye twitches and he omits her name, just kind of motions with his head like *she's* over his left shoulder or something. He does it more often now, when wedding-talk and questions come up from friends, family…."

Sylvia nodded with an understanding blink.

"But Ben offered—nearly insisted, in fact—that we do the whole aisle parade." She chuckled. Walking down the aisle had never been a picture in her mind—not until Ben, but…"His words don't match, you know, the other stuff, the signs. And I don't want him to have any association, any guilt, any reminders. I told him, and it's true, that all I need is *him*. The courthouse is fine. Just fine. Better than fine. I'm too tired for anything more, anyway." She reclined into the hard wood café chair, giving her belly some space. "Hard enough planning my next meal, our next meal…" She rubbed her baby bump and puffed a light laugh, then reached for a fingerful of pumpkin pound cake.

"I get it, Preeya." Sylvia leaned forward and lowered her chin. "Your father took three years to open up to me about anything, including starting a new chapter of life…with *me*. God, did he cling, you know, to the pain, to the memory of—"

Preeya swallowed, wondered. Would she go there?

Sylvia narrowed her eyes, cocked her head, and studied Preeya, a deep and in-tune several-moment analysis. "Your mom…haunted him…Preeya. But together we turned the *haunting* into…catharsis…and acceptance. So he, and I, could move forward. Not *move on* but *move forward. With* your mom. The *good* parts of her…like you and your sister, and the less than good parts, too—those parts and things and actions that had hurt your father and you girls, his babies. All of it taught and strengthened, right? And it doesn't stop him from *being* with me. He's better for it, *more* for it. He is who he is because of everyone and everything in his life up to *now*—including Jenny, his first love. Yes?"

Preeya could hardly breathe. "Yes." An epiphany. She swallowed it, digested it, let it flow through her bloodstream. "I get it…I do." *How did she do that?*

Preeya hated the delicacy surrounding the topic of her mother…and Sylvia just jumped right in. A big girl now, soon to be a mother with a dependent little girl or boy of her own, for Christ's sake, Preeya hated the tiptoeing, the *dancing*. But Sylvia didn't do the dance, the one that everyone—including her fiancé—had been dancing. Walls and halts and veering off this topic or that plan because Ben assumed he had to be so careful around her—and hell, she had to be ultra-wary around *him*…for his own sore spots.

And Sylvia's perspective on marriage, and about her father—it just blew her mind. Sylvia had woken Preeya up to something.

Something huge.

Preeya licked her dry, cracked lips and inhaled, then tilted her head and leaned back, letting the new understanding fall into the slots of her brain and heart—the infinite categories she held for *Preeya and Ben. Plink, plink, plink.* Only five months of a whirlwind relationship enlightened in five minutes flat.

She stared at Sylvia, so wise—only two decades or so older than her, but the woman's eyes carried lifetimes. Each expression line, every fine wrinkle, told some story. Sad, joyous, and everything in between. And with this woman, this essential stranger connected only by law, Preeya felt strangely... at home. She felt like confiding her underlying fears to Sylvia—about the baby, and not living up to Ben's expectations, and becoming her god-awful mother, and her terrible grief over Prana. All of it snowballed, frozen hard in the center of her chest. She wanted it melted and drained. Her new stepmother's warmth might just be her thawing fix.

"I'm scared, Sylvia. I'm scared that I won't...I won't be..." She cleared her throat, "...be who...ahem...God, excuse—" She coughed then swallowed then cleared her chest, but her parched throat tickled and itched, at the brink of a full-on coughing fit. "Excuse...sorry...water?" Was she choking on her dammed-up emotions, for Christ's sakes? Those she'd been set to purge—finally? Now only wheezing rasps of harsh sound escaped.

Sylvia ran to the counter and snatched a bottle of water from the register's display. "Drink, sweetie. Just go easy and drink."

After several small sips between coughs, she caught her breath and composed herself.

"Better, sweetie?"

Meh. "Yes, better..." Except that she'd just coughed up her dread and couldn't take it back. But redirection's a thing. "You know, though, my bladder's screaming at me pretty loud..."

"Right." Sylvia nodded, maybe even catching the avoidance tactic. "Let's go to the restrooms, then back to the guys."

"Thanks, Sylvia." Preeya might have been wrong. Maybe her new stepmom wouldn't bring up the topic again. Her fear-based confession. Maybe this woman just really...went with the flow.

CHAPTER 49

B EN SAW THE women coming and cleared his throat, a sign for their discussion to end. *Stat.*

"Hey, boys…your hot love in a mug." Sylvia giggled as she handed Preeya's dad a coffee, then one to Ben.

Ben got up from the mall's standard sit-and-wait-for-your-spouse seat so that Preeya could get off her feet.

"Did you get a good nap?" Sylvia asked Dr. Patel, who winked at Ben. God, the other man was bursting at the seams to talk about the surprise wedding. Ben prayed the silvering doctor wouldn't blow it. "Yes, sweetie, we had a good rest together. Parallel snoozes." Another wink in Ben's direction. Did he not get that his daughter was maybe one of the most brilliant minds at one of the most competitive medical colleges in the nation? *Please let her be too tired to notice her father's over-the-top excitement.*

They'd spent the past forty-five minutes going over dates and logistics. Who and how and when the few guests would be arriving in Vallarta, and where they'd all stay so that Preeya wouldn't accidently run into anyone. He couldn't lie, it was thrilling to think about—surprising her, sweeping her off her feet again in the very place they'd fallen in love, where they'd created their baby, and, yes, where they'd split up for a time but, against all odds, reunited.

Vallarta became their unofficial start, and a month from now it would be their official *forever more.* He took Preeya's hand, pulled her up, slid under her, and brought her down onto his lap.

"Babe, I'm too—"

"Gorgeous and amazing to keep my hands off of," he said, cutting her off with a harsh but playful whisper. With a gentle tug, he leaned her back to relax against him, then nuzzled her neck and rubbed her baby bump.

"Ben, we're in the middle of a mall." A return whisper of warning amid a betraying giggle.

Mmm, that giggle.

God, he could not wait. To vow in front of their family that he'd have and hold her through anything and everything, with their Marieta Islands in full, glorious view, their toes in the white sand, their hearts and hands intertwined.

Jesus, how cheesy, Ben.

Yes. But he couldn't give a damn less—and could not *wait* a minute more…for Preeya to be his wife. But he would wait. A month. A month from now, after they'd handled final logistics, he'd make Preeya Patel, Preeya Trainer.

"I like those, Ben," Sylvia said.

"What's that, Sylvia?" He looked up from the crook of Preeya's neck. Preeya's stepmother leaned toward him as Dr. Patel stood up to take a call and Preeya thumb-typed like lightning on her phone—probably texting Gigi or Amy. "Sorry, Sylvia…I got lost in my own little world for a moment."

"Of course, daddy-and-husband-to-be." Sylvia winked and patted his arm. "Preeya was telling me the baby names. Puja for a girl—just lovely. And what was the boy's?"

Ben cocked his head then covered himself with a quick smile. He thought they'd decided that not only would they keep the sex an unknown, but they'd also put off discussing baby names. They wanted to meet their baby face-to-face and let the name come to them. "Uh, yeah, Pree…what was the boy's name we'd discussed again?" To Sylvia, "So many names thrown around, it's hard to keep 'em all straight."

Preeya's thumbs paused before her chin lifted, then a beat or two passed before she met his pseudo-serious glare.

And cue her guilty, and damn gorgeous, smile. "Uh, yeah, no, I had just jotted down Puja and Palav the other day…you know, they just came to me. Brainstorms come when they want to." Nervous laughter fluttered from her lips as her father strolled back after ending his call. "But, yeah," to Sylvia and her dad, "we're waiting to meet him or her before we nail down any names."

"Well, of course you are. I'll call the family priest with the exact date and time of birth, like I did for you and your sister—get the true astrological chart done so you can select the right consonant sounds for the name. The true Hindu way."

"Yes. Oh, that is what we want." Preeya bounced with excitement on Ben's lap.

Ben cleared his throat, then offered a pencil-line smile while his right hand squeezed Preeya's thigh.

"Oh," Preeya said, smiling back at Ben, "we haven't actually talked about…religious affiliation yet, have we, babe?"

Ben gave her a slow, stern blink. "No, Pree, we haven't. The courthouse makes that part easy, but how we raise our baby…gosh, we just haven't discussed our plans yet." He clutched Preeya's hand harder at the *we* and *our* points of his statement.

It stuck in his throat, the principle of the matter—the potential that she had made a decision, *decisions*, without him. Without a thought? No hesitation. And yes, the matter of religion, though big to most people, was really not to him or to her, he'd thought. But again, it was the principle of it. He didn't foresee any big conflict—just that he and Preeya had to put it out there and talk about it. *Together.* A new concept to her, he knew. He got that. And he didn't mind showing her the way, how two people dealt with life matters together. He looked forward to it.

So forward to it.

In fact, he'd been trying to keep things so stress free for her—with her heavy class load on top of all the other crap she'd been faced with…since they'd met, really—that he maybe hadn't set the right example. To protect her nerves, and the baby's, he'd avoided all "big" topics, sparing her the stress.

But he couldn't wait to plan their future, now that he felt excited to *have* a future.

Whereas before Preeya—and after Jamie—well, that void in time was behind him.

Now to a future with Preeya. A dream.

He pictured travel and adventure with Preeya. They'd do the DWB for short stints each year. And he knew many young couples who'd leave their kids with family. They'd leave their child with Stacy, of course. Yeah, when Preeya finished her residency in a few years, he and Preeya could go—make a real difference in the world.

Preeya squeezed his hand to bring him back to the conversation.

"Oh." He smiled, sensing the awkwardness he'd brought on. "But yes, we're excited to bring the baby up with a...uh, wide and accepting knowledge of both our backgrounds. Right, babe?"

She nodded, shoulders eased. "Right." She shifted on his lap and smiled at him, a grin similar to her forced-fake smile on their first flight together. She turned back around. "Dad, the baby will benefit from both our traditions, no doubt. And he or she will be so worldly. We're gonna take this little one all around the world with us." She stroked her tummy. Then to Ben, "Right, babe?"

Ben froze then scoffed in his head. Boy, did they have some stuff to align. He exhaled then nodded. "Uh, yeah...the baby will be well-traveled. Absolutely." He kissed Preeya's cheek and smiled up at them all. "And, of course, infinitely loved."

CHAPTER 50

REEYA *NEEDED* PUNCTUALITY all the time now—she'd become near-OCD about it. "We'll talk later, babe. Promise." She kissed Ben's mouth slow and sweet, then rolled—like the hippo she felt like—off the bed. They'd had it out again about last week's mall incident—but their version of *having it out*...well, it wasn't like their climactic sex life, by any means. Delicate niceties and half-compromises softened by noncommittal touches and superficial caresses. And *laters*. Lots of *laters*.

Result—nothing ever got settled. Not the name, not the baby's faith. *Nothing.*

But she had to go. And so did he. His last week of lectures before finals. Her morning for "yoga for pregos" at Green Lake.

She got to Gigi's in plenty of time to find parking near the yoga spot, that was, if *Geej* had been on time. Preeya tapped her fingers on the steering wheel then texted Gigi a second time. A few beats passed. *Now we're late.* It was like she and Gigi had switched places—Preeya obsessively ahead and Gigi always behind.

But Preeya couldn't blame her. Not after Rod cut out last week. Cut out for good. *Raging prick.*

Preeya's best friend waddled out to the car. "Sorry, sorry...just had two last-minute bladder calls."

"It's cool. You ready?"

"Yeah...sure." Gigi buckled up. "Oh, hey, did you get the marriage license yesterday?" Gigi's eyes were wide with attempted excitement.

"Yes, ma'am, we did." Preeya couldn't even try to hide her enthusiasm, even though she'd been drastically curbing her ups due to Gigi's recent downs. "We can be married within sixty days from the day after tomorrow."

"So great, Pree." Gigi grinned, then turned toward the window.

At the steering wheel ready to go, Preeya took one hand and placed it on Gigi's arm. "Hey, you okay?" Between the hormones, lower back, and, well, the all-over body pain of being five-plus months along—for the both of them—she had to admit that *okay* was relative. Then, add each of their other life hurdles...

"Yeah, Pree, I'm good. Always good." Gigi winked and patted Preeya's hand, reaching for the radio controls.

Preeya smiled at her friend and pulled out of the spot.

How amazing, them being pregnant together, there for each other during the landmark of landmarks of their lives. She flipped on her turn signal and eyed the stunning yet tasteful engagement ring she and Ben had picked out together. *Together. Together* felt so nice. She smiled, then buried it—a pang of heartbreak hit her chest for her essential-sister hunting for distraction on the radio.

"Hey," Gigi said through her gum smacking, happier since finding their favorite Prince song. "I've been anxious about something."

"Huh, what's that?"

"Well, I picked the thing...for you, for the baby shower, but it will most definitely give away the sex and—"

"God, Geej. How many times...we still don't want to know, and that's that." Preeya lifted her brows to punctuate her semi-lighthearted warning.

Gigi *hmphed*.

"Gigi! I'm not kidding! Do not. Tell me."

"Okay, okay. If it's that important to you." Gigi grinned from ear to ear.

"It's important to me *and* Ben."

Preeya caught Gigi's grumble. Ben and Gigi only pretended to get along. But so be it. They were both her life's breath, so they had little choice. And she had a feeling that once the babies arrived, her soul sister and soul mate would bond. No doubt.

"Which do you want, though? A boy or girl?"

"As long as the baby's healthy..." Preeya stated. "But even if he or she isn't..." *Dare she say it out loud?* Unlike her own mother—her vacating coward of a mother—she'd love her baby no matter what. Preeya took a deep breath, remembering her doctor's—and Ben's—concerns. Blood pressure, nerves. So the easiest fix: shove it down for another time. Maybe after the baby comes.

"Hey, Pree, your baby, *my* godbaby"—she waggled her eyebrows—"is beautiful and healthy and already so loved, my dear sister. That's what your baby is. Completely and totally loved."

Preeya smiled and her heart swam. Then her eyes glanced in Gigi's direction. "I'm no psychic, Gigi Donlow, but I know your baby is wonderful and perfectly loved, too. *My* little godchild...he or she is infinitely loved."

Gigi squeezed then kissed Preeya's hand. "Enough sappy stuff." Gigi cleared her throat. "Hey, let's get something to eat. I'm craving a bucket of fried chicken."

"You know we're not supposed to eat before class, Geej. And we're late."

"Can't we just skip yoga this week?" Gigi's eyes got puppy-dog wide.

"Wow, Geej, really? Forget about the heartburn I get just thinking about fried chicken...*and* that it's not great for the babies—but missing class? What about the new breathing exercise?"

"You're right, you're right." Gigi shook her head and glanced at her lap. "I'm so bad. And I'm the one who needs the breathing exercises most." Tears began to well in Gigi's eyes. "Because I'm the one who's alone!" All-out crying now. "And...I can't even keep a man!" Bawling now.

"Oh, sweetie!" She reached over to give Gigi's shoulder a squeeze while keeping her eyes on the road. The sobbing became heaving hyperventilation, so Preeya pulled over—the easiest turn-in was a doughnut shop.

Gigi gasped for air between tears. "You're gonna be such a good mom, Pree." Gigi shifted in the seat to face her. "I mean it. I knew you'd be fabulous at *the thing* awaiting you, and here you are."

Preeya's heart squeezed out a beat. Ben had drilled into her the same message, telling her over and over how wonderful a mother she'd be. But she doubted—God, she held such strong doubt and worry and panic—that she would be. She swallowed back her own tears. "You really think so, Geej? Because"—she looked down at her belly and couldn't stop the building tears...*so much for being strong for Gigi*—"how the hell do I know...what a good mom is? And the odds...they're against me. I've got my mother in me, always have. Skipping out on one thing then the next when shit got hard, just like *her*!"

Gigi unbuckled her seat belt, pulled Preeya to her shoulder, and held her tight. For minutes. Warm, firm, and steadying minutes.

"Hey." Gigi released her grasp.

"Hey back." Preeya sniffled, wiping clean her face—and Gigi's shoulder—of all her leaking...emotion.

Gigi squeezed Preeya's arm. "Oh, please...snot-on, my friend. Snot-on. What else am I here for?"

Preeya cracked up, squeezing Gigi's hand. "Got a tissue or ten?"

Gigi reached into her purse and pulled out a stack of napkins from a fast-food joint and handed a few to Preeya. Preeya laughed harder still and threw Gigi a sideways glance. "Burger Bobo's? Really?"

Gigi shrugged through her own giggle fit. "I'm not strong like you."

"Bullshit." Preeya slapped Gigi's thigh. "Let's get out of this parking lot before we both cave to the doughnut drive-thru."

Gigi grinned with a wink, then got suddenly serious. "Wait. Stop the car for a sec."

"What, Geej?"

Gigi squeezed her hand.

God, too tight! "Ouch, Geej!"

Gigi nodded, narrowed her gaze, and squeezed Preeya's hand again. "About the type of mother you'll be"—Gigi swallowed and slammed her eyes tight, then whipped them open again—"You are *The Giving Tree*?" Gigi asked, tilting her head, slightly out of breath. "Does that make sense to you?"

Preeya choked on her tears and worked to find air. "Prana?" Gigi hadn't known about the one book she and her sister had read a billion times over. "Yes. *Prana.*"

*

Ben had been reading all morning up to Gigi's phone call. Another start-to-*never*-finished fatherhood book. The irony. He had to combat his own sliver—*planet-size sliver*—of parental insecurity spiking in his gut every time he thought about Preeya's secret worries. Her deeply buried fears were only privy to him late at night when she slept hard and deep beside him. His concerns for his own lack of fatherly instinct plagued him still, but he couldn't talk to Preeya about it. Or maybe he could? Maybe that would comfort her? After this phone call with Gigi, maybe it would be the connection they both needed.

He sat on the couch in surrender as he stared at his phone, the minutes from his call with Gigi flashing *42* on his screen. It had been the longest conversation he'd had with Preeya's best friend yet. Gigi relayed the entire episode to him. "Watch her, Ben," Gigi'd told him. "I've never seen her so raw."

Up to that phone call, Ben had pegged Gigi as quite the nut. But the woman had Preeya's back—her mind, her body, her soul—without a doubt. For that, Ben could not be more grateful. He quickly buried the slight pang of something like jealousy for the fact that his fiancée opened up to Gigi about her deep-seated insecurities, and not him. He sighed and raked his hands through his hair. The important thing was that she'd vented it out loud—finally facing her fears in reality.

A huge step in the right direction, the direction toward ripping out the one lingering thorn.

Her mother.

Ben would hunt the woman down himself and hang her if…

Chill out, man.

But it burned him. The haunting ghost of a woman, Ben knew, had been hovering in Preeya's psyche, torturing her soul. Preeya'd started talking in her sleep—and by *talking*, he meant screaming, yelling, wailing—for the past few months. As the pregnancy wore on, she'd expressed her fears and her anxieties about her mother—and worse, about becoming the selfish woman who'd left Preeya without a word. Just a helpless little girl.

Ben had never thought to confide in Gigi about the nightmares, but he did tell her about them on their call. And that his heart screamed out for Preeya. He had, of course, not spoken a word of it to Preeya, herself.

"Why?" Gigi had asked.

He'd had no answer, but he'd said it was his gut instinct. Gigi'd get that, he thought. "And anyway," he explained, "Preeya's fears had obviously not been ready to surface in waking life yet. Suppressing a trauma, such heart-wrenching emotion, it's common and medically necessary, in fact. Especially having idolized her mother for her entire life—all based on a lie." Her father's bald-faced lie.

All in all, everything had been taking its natural course toward the positive. Preeya had come so far with her monophobia, almost excited to be on her own these days—well, not really alone. God, he loved catching her singing to the baby, rubbing her belly with loving intimacy. Chills shot up his neck. *What an unbelievable mother she'll be.*

She had also been opening up about Prana's passing, sharing her grief, her deep ache over her sister's departure. A few weeks ago she'd told him a story about Prana when she was an infant. Preeya took her sister from the basinet and wouldn't let her go. *Really* would not release the child. Preeya laughed as she shared the memory while Ben ignored the thickness in her voice. "Even Aunt Champa and her evil claws couldn't tear Prana from my grasp," Preeya had said. He knew full-well what had preceded the landmark memory. *Her mother's departure, still untold.* That's when he'd jumped on the opportunity, subtly suggesting that she maybe see a therapist—"For the mourning process," he'd said.

But Preeya had flat-out refused, saying she was fine. "Better than fine," she'd declared. "I love you, I love our baby. I even love being pregnant! Nausea, achiness, and all!"

"My case in point, babe"—he laughed—"that therapy's a good idea. I've *never* heard a woman crazy about being pregnant!" He got a good punch in the arm for the comment, but, no, he didn't force the therapy-issue. Because even with Preeya's hormones and emotions on hyperdrive, school, the recent traumas coming to light, she really was doing well. Why was he surprised, though? Preeya proved time and time again to be as solid as a rock.

But the baby. Their tiny miracle. He'd lost a child once and it had been an unyielding vise-grip on his heart. And the amount of stress Preeya shouldered, consciously or not—it was a lot for someone who *wasn't* pregnant to take on. He had every right to worry. God, even free-spirited Gigi worried, hence the call.

But she's fine, Ben. The OB had seen them last week and all was great, on point. And the baby's first kick had been the day before yesterday. Oh man, Preeya's expression—indescribable joy. Their unborn child's sharp kick to Preeya's right side sent her to the next level of ecstasy.

And speaking of ecstasy, even their lovemaking had been pure bliss, a different level of passion. If Preeya's sex drive indicated anything about her mood and state of mind, wow, Ben truly had nothing to be concerned over. Inside the bedroom and out—in the kitchen, Jacuzzi tub, back porch, living room lounger, and on the safe, flat portion of the roof accessible from the guest room—she had been throwing herself at him with all the raging desire of a tigress in heat. But, oh God, so much deeper. Indescribable. He got hot just thinking about it.

When they weren't connecting as if they were reuniting after being apart forever, she was focusing on school and the baby's well-being. Reading every book, blog, and parenting article she said she'd never imagined herself reading. Then weekly yoga, a pre-mommy group, and, hell, he couldn't forget the fact that she'd chosen a pediatric specialty. Yeah, Preeya had every baby-base covered.

"She's an unbelievable woman," he said to himself under his breath as he relaxed into the sofa and grabbed his how-to-dad book from the coffee table. "And she'll be an incredible mother."

"And wife." Preeya's voice came from behind. She placed her hands on his shoulders and squeezed.

He tilted his head back. "Give me."

She leaned down and kissed him.

"Yes, *and wife*. Not-soon-enough wife." They were just waiting out the marriage license process. "Unbelievably sexy, stealthy, and eavesdropping *soon-to-be wife*." He laughed.

"*You're* the one talking to yourself in here."

He rolled his eyes then reached for her. "Get over here."

She made her way around the sofa and surrendered back into his chest.

He slid his hand over her belly. "Hello, my loves."

Preeya purred into relaxation. "Good to be home. Being out with Gigi can be exhausting. Then follow that with Doctor Pelum's lecture. And," she said, looking down at her belly, "I'm five months—"

"Pregnant, yes." He kissed her cheek. "You"—he angled her chin with his index finger to see her face—"are." He caressed her lips with his, drifting over them only to touch and tease. "With *my* baby." His finger slid from her chin and she relaxed into the crook of his neck. He stroked her hair back and sighed. "And I am already in love with…it. Speaking of *it*, did Gigi keep her mouth shut about the sex?"

"Yes. But she screwed with me pretty bad. Hey"—she reached for his book—"what's this?"

He hesitated, then caught himself and handed her the book with a crooked grin and heated cheeks. "I'm a pediatric surgeon who's scared shit-less about being a dad." He took her free hand and played with her soft fingers for distraction. His admission felt good and seemed to lighten her entire being.

And although it relieved his soul to tell her his fear, and he was tempted to tell her another two-ton anchor in his soul—no. Just, no. There was absolutely no need to bring up the miscarriage. That stayed locked away, far from his current life, *their* current lives. His second chance at love with Preeya and their child should and would be untouched, untainted by his past. Done.

He'd focus on them, sharing with Preeya his current apprehension about daddy-hood because that was necessary for the conquering of Preeya's demons. And yes, for his own demons, too.

He swept his gaze from her hand to her near-violet eyes. "Pretty sad, huh?"

She cocked her head, pulled her hand from his, and slid it up to his cheek. "You have no idea how sad and perfectly comforting that is to me." She smiled and gave him a slow, sweet blink. "And needless to say, Doctor. Trainer, you're gonna make an amazing father. Utterly amazing."

He smiled. "You'll be a far greater mother than I will be a father."

"A wager in the making, is it?" she teased.

Wow, isn't this something. His heart triple-timed. Maybe her outpouring to Gigi had opened her up, helped her unbury the doubt and start to really work through her worst fears.

Or was she just wearing an outer shield to hide behind?

Either way, he'd been honest about his fears and the dialogue had begun. "Sure, babe. I'll take your bet." He cocked his head and curled his lip. "The greatest part is that I know I've already won."

She shifted her body so they were face-to-face. "How do you know that?" she asked with a skeptic's eye.

He grinned at her. "The core of a mother, the true selfless core of a nurturer, babe...I've already seen it in you. Not just with my sister's kids and kids on your flights, but I got to see you with Prana—on a video chat, no less. Preeya, you've already been a mother, in a sense. A wonderful, loving mother. And it wasn't even your job to be, but you took the role and you became that child's angel. Yes, you were Prana's living angel, Pree. And you're our baby's angel, too."

She didn't hide her tears or her face. She didn't tuck her head in his shoulder or cover her eyes with her hands. She just kept his gaze and wept. No shame, no sorrow, even. She almost held a glint of pride in her glistening eyes.

He kissed her forehead. "I can't *wait* to see you with our baby, Pree. I just *cannot* wait."

*

She had to be connected with him. *Now.*

Her lips found his mouth within a heartbeat.

Fueled by the freedom flooding her, she kissed him hard, with force. By his words, his voice, his deep insight into her, she'd been energized and liberated. His clarity, his love, had turned a key inside her. And the key rotated faster and faster in her chest, in her core as their mouths spoke to each other without words. Only passion. An impassioned tango she didn't know they knew.

Their tongues tangled as she climbed onto his lap. He was hard, so perfectly hard for her. She hummed as his hands slid down her back to her bottom, supporting her weight and offering balance. Through their kiss, she laughed, then with spliced and mangled words she asked, "Am I killing you with my extra...bulk?"

He lifted his hips into her, grinding, groaning. Then he took a handful of her ass and pulled his mouth away. "You're perfect, babe. You can't know how fucking"—he took her by the nape of the neck and pressed his mouth to hers again, then pulled back, panting—"perfect your body is to me—*you* are to me."

They read each other that instant. She worked the buttons of her top while he worked the zipper of his pants. God, she was so hot and wet for him. A few shared giggles, breaths, then grunts of laborious body-shifting later, Ben filled her with his endlessness. He rocked her gently into swirls of sweet ecstasy. As he did, he slid one hand over her belly, circling, caressing, then down to her mound, then her delicate clit, his thumb twirling her senseless. Bliss leading to bliss.

And when his eyes rolled back behind fluttering lids, she cried out, screamed out, her own release rolling up her body in burning tides of joy. Once the heat reached her chest then her face, tears—new tears—filled her eyes. Through her blurred vision she watched his eyelids lift; gorgeous golden warmth captured her in his gaze. She'd caught her dream. Her wildest dream. The one she'd never been able to picture. She couldn't have. Such pure bliss proved impossible to construct by her mind's eye. Her heart had to wait, search and wait and cling to faith that it would eventually find her, catch her. And it had. Ben had caught her, and she prayed that he'd never, ever let her go.

CHAPTER 51

ALMOST A WEEK had passed in a blink.

The ease and flow between them, in their ever-expanding conversations and in every touch, look, kiss—he'd never known such floating freedom. And Preeya was his cloud—light and soft and laughing and giggling all the time. Manic, angelic, *his*.

She even slept better since the other day's breakthrough—well, relatively speaking, anyway. She still tossed and turned and shifted, seeking the perfect yet unattainable position, but she hadn't spoken, shrieked, shouted in her sleep since the Gigi outpouring, and their day on the couch.

And, oh God, their hunger for each other…as intense as it had been, now it skyrocketed to a new stratosphere of intimate. A new level of *indescribable*.

But he found as much pure joy tending to her while foregoing his own release. He'd just build up to the next time she'd attack him, which seemed to be no less than a day's wait. Anyway, a ritual, so to speak, had been formed. Before bed each night he'd set up a slew of body pillows at certain angles and levels and he'd massage her from head to toe. She'd reach a state that could only be described as tranquil elation.

And, God, it drove him wild. To give her such pleasure. All day every day he'd crave the sensation of her silken mocha skin at the mercy of his fingertips. He rushed them to bed every night just to work out her tensions and infuse her with pleasure.

"Is this good, the long one here?"

She gave him the sexiest coy smile he'd ever seen and nodded.

"Okay." Starting at her long middle toe, he pulled and cracked each one, then pressed and rubbed the balls and arches of each foot simultaneously. Up next to her heels, he rolled and rotated her feet to loosen her ankles. He worked his way up her calves, running his thumbs deep into her muscle fibers. Then to her knees. God, her skin was so soft. Next her quads; he rubbed and kneaded her muscles, pinching and knuckling to unlock the trapped energy.

She moaned her satisfaction. It made him raging hard, that moan of hers.

Continuing up her body, he arrived at her core—his glorious, all-loving slice of heaven. Admittedly his favorite part. That and her earlobes—well, and her round breasts and round belly. Oh, and her voluptuous ass, now more fully fucking fantastic at six months pregnant. So, he guessed he couldn't settle on a favorite part of her. She blew his mind, all parts combined.

Anyway, he set the fingers of both his surgically precise hands to work. And as usual, she was ready for him—wet and hot and so goddamn needy. She clenched her core, lifted her hips, and her bud was engorged and pulsating for him. He kept all his targeted focus on her sex, his fingers twirling and sliding and dipping her into peak pleasure. He sensed her watching him. And as she got close to her edge, she demanded his eyes. With a little whimper and the whisper of his name, she met his gaze. *Gladly.* He glanced up at her, watched her reach her release, swim in that heaven. He'd watch her there forever.

"Ben," she breathed.

"I'm here, babe. I see you, I have you." As she arched into her climax, he slid one hand under her to support her lower back and lay back with her while pulling her writhing body gently toward him. While her body wrung itself out, he felt surges of joy bolt up his spine. As if he was coming, too. A virtual, essential release by proxy. Just watching her come, supporting and holding her thrashing body. Pure empathetic bliss.

She collapsed back into his arms and dozed off immediately. He listened to her breath deepen and slow, lulling him off to sleep as well. Another night of *perfect* with his Preeya.

Sleep had come quickly to him, but it didn't stay for long. He was afraid to move or he'd wake her. After weeks of endless shifting and twisting, it seemed she'd finally found her position. Her spot. And though his knees and shoulders ached, his neck pinched, his bottom arm lay numb, he refused to move an inch with her body sleeping so fully against his.

So at dawn when his phone buzzed him out of his half-slumber paralysis, he swung then slammed his arm down on his nightstand and grabbed the device like it meant to kill him—or he meant to kill it—all without moving the rest of his body somehow. He hit Accept with his thumb just to end the buzzing—he'd worked too hard to have Preeya wake up before the sun. And in answering the call, he wouldn't mind giving the idiot a raking for knowing how to tell the goddamn time.

Before he could even utter his harsh-whispered hello, a too-awake and cheerful voice met his ears. "Ben? Ben, hey, it's me."

Jesus. "Gigi? It's, like"—he squinted at his nightstand clock—"six in the morning." *Breathe, Ben.* He had to remind himself that she, too, was pregnant, and now Gigi was on her own. Preeya, and so Ben, were Gigi's only support. "Gigi, what is it…are you okay?"

"Sorry, sorry, I just had to call. I have this idea and it's been nagging at me all night long. Got no sleep." *You and me both.* "I couldn't wait another—"

"I get it, I get it. It's fine, Gigi. Let me get to a place I can talk." He slid out of bed like a ninja.

He adjusted his eyes to the kitchen light so he could make an early pot of coffee for himself while Gigi began her explanation.

"There's been this idea just clawing at the back of my mind…"

"Go ahead," Ben urged as he added the extra-bold dark roast grounds to the brew bin.

"It's something I stopped myself from bringing up to Preeya a thousand times now because I didn't want to hear her say no. It's just too important— vital, really. And then you told me about her nightmares. That was the final confirmation. I think this idea is the answer, the key."

"The key?"

"Yes, to closing her circle of pain and giving her the ability to open her rightful circle of happiness."

"Gigi—there's not enough coffee in Seattle to keep me awake through your stalling." *Ranting.* "Tell me, what's your idea?"

"Okay, well, I strongly believe that if we help her find—and face—the missing piece to her 'puzzle of pain,' I call it, Preeya would be able to finally and officially move on. No more doubts, no more anger poisoning her baby, poisoning her confidence...."

"Gigi!" he yelled, then checked himself the next instant. He whispered, "Gigi, please...get to your point...in human terms."

"Her mom, Ben."

All of that garbled gibberish reduced to those few words? *Her mom, Ben. Okay, Ben, digest.* Sans coffee? *Yes, Ben, sans coffee.*

Gigi's fast-and-furious, floral crap means...? "Wait...are you suggesting we find her deadbeat mom?"

"Exactly."

"Behind her back?"

"How cathartic would it be for Preeya to face the woman who left her and Prana? To confront her not just in her nightmares, but in real life."

Ben leaned against the kitchen island, stunned speechless.

"Listen, I've gone online to start a search a few times now, but had to quit. Just kept hitting dead ends. I don't have enough information on the woman. And again, if I ask Preeya directly, she'll say no, you know she will—"

"Possibly, probably! Because, Gigi, it's her prerogative. Something this... this...huge has got to be her *choice*. And don't you think she'd take up the search on her own if she wanted to meet the woman?"

"That's the point, Ben. She doesn't want to. But she *needs* to. To heal."

"Your third eye sees this, huh?"

Silence buzzed in his ear.

He didn't mean to be smug or mean, *but Jesus.* She was talking about his pregnant wife. Going behind Preeya's back to find, and then, what...reunite her and her mother? Where would that lead to but more stress, more pain? "Sorry for that snide remark, Gigi."

"No, it's cool. I'm very used to it by now. But, Ben, I do sense and intuit things. With Preeya, the vibe is so intense…because we're so close." Gigi paused then sighed. "She's in pain, she's scared, and it kills me."

It occurred to him that beyond Gigi's true love for Preeya—again, he was so thankful for the role she'd played in Preeya's life up to that point—it was clear to him that *Gigi* was scared shitless. Projecting her own anxieties, rightful worries about having and raising a kid on her own. It was natural, expected, inevitable. He had to tread lightly, knowing Gigi as little as he did, but knowing how much Gigi meant to Preeya.

He cleared his throat. "Gigi, listen. The other night after she came home from her time with you, she seemed different. Open, and light. A drastic change. More relaxed than I've seen her since…since our time in Vallarta. And we even talked, for the first time I might add, about our fears, our goddamn trepidations, about being parents. Thanks to her outpouring to you, her comfort and confidence in you, I've already seen a shift in her. You helped open her heart, Gigi." He paused, almost unsure if Gigi was still on the call—all he could hear was his percolating and much-needed coffee.

"Gigi? Are you—"

"She buries things, Ben. Always has."

"Maybe, but things are coming to the surface now, and they're coming up…naturally, Gigi. Organically. In their own time. I really don't think we need *to do* anything but be here for her."

"Look, I just called to ask if you had or could get a little more information for me on her mom. I don't need anything else but—"

"Gigi. You aren't hearing me. We do not need to force things. In fact, I'm telling you *not* to."

"You're telling me…."

"Yes. You can't do this. Not without Preeya's knowledge or permission, and to tell you the truth, I don't even want you to bring it up right now." His throat got thick and dry. "Not after the baby arrives, either. Not until Preeya's at least done nursing, if at all."

This time there was no buzzing silence. Gigi's huffing fury filled his ear. Then she sniffled, like she'd begun to cry. "I wasn't asking permission, Ben."

Voice quick and quivering. "I need to do this for her. To find her mom, give Preeya the chance to—"

"To what? To scream and yell at the woman who abandoned her so Pree could spike up her and the baby's blood pressure? All to look into the woman's eyes, the eyes, by the way, that mirror her own? Will that help bolster Preeya's confidence, clear her doubts, heal her broken heart? For an intuitive person, Gigi, you're pretty damn clueless."

"Forget it. Sorry I called."

He heaved a sigh, trying to temper his frustration. *Remember, this woman's as pregnant as Preeya is—and seemingly way more emotional. Irrational, really.* "Gigi, please. Just tell me you'll drop this. For the health of Preeya and the baby, *our* baby—mine and Preeya's—you will drop this."

"You know what? Screw you, Ben. Get my best friend knocked up and now *you* know her better than I do? I've been her *family* for nearly twenty years."

"Are we really going there? Jesus." He counted to ten in his head—in three seconds' time. "You're tired, hormonal, and you're not thinking straight, Gigi."

"No, *you're* not thinking straight, and you're not really thinking about Preeya's well-being, either. You're too *scared* to think or see clearly about anything, asshole! Just because you lost one kid, doesn't mean—"

"Whoa, wait." He shook his head and inhaled a roomful of coffee-scented air. "What the fuck did you say?"

"Pregnancies and deaths, Ben. That's what *I* see clearly, clear as crystal. Past and present. And as for future, I *sense*, I *intuit*. If Preeya doesn't face her mother before the baby comes, she'll be miserable. Energetically and physically miserable...and so will my godbaby."

Her slew of nonsense mangled his brain. Where to even start? "*Energetically, physically*? What in the hell are you talking about, Gigi?"

"Ben, I know you're nursing your own wounds, but what I'm saying is that I won't let your *past* hurt Preeya's *future*—her chances for true, essential happiness."

Old wounds. Scared. Life and death. Godbaby? Past, present...future?

This stunning and impossible hoax Gigi had played, it needed to end—*now*.

Because…but…wait…*what the fuck*? No one but his sister knew about Jamie's miscarriage.

No one.

Chills sprinted up his spine and his hands shook. He felt so out of control, out of the realm of reality, he thought he'd vomit and suffocate at the same time.

Get it together. Preeya needed him.

And today and always, he'd be there for her. Fuck yes he would.

And fuck Gigi. Her concern for Preeya's future? No goddamn need. *Preeya's future is with me.* With him and their baby. He made her happy, would always make her happy.

Who the hell was Gigi, anyway? She was the danger, the one he needed to protect Preeya from. Because what horse shit! *Not* meeting her mother will lead Preeya to misery? Again, *what*? Energy and vibes and clairvoyance and the rest of Gigi's psychodrama had no place in his world, or Preeya's.

"You *are* nuts, Gigi Donlow. And by the way, Miss All-Knowing-Psychic who so declares to have my wife's—"

"*Soon-to-be* wife."

"*Preeya's* best interest at heart—you just said you *intuit* the future?"

"Preeya's future. Yes, Ben, I do. Always have. Always will."

Right. "Well, perfect. That leaves me in a better position than you to judge what's best for her future. Basing my argument not on goddamn intuition but on medical fact, none of what you're proposing is good for her blood pressure, her nerves, her or the baby's well-being—my *old wounds* aside. If you care about your best friend—for the record, *my* fiancée, my love and life—and, again, our child's safety, his or her future will not be threatened because of some 'strong *gut* inkling' of yours."

Then nothing. Just more angry breathing on the other end of the connection.

Which gave him time to catch his breath. A few beats passed. His chest heaved as he poured his coffee with trembling hands. He took a sip, burned his tongue. *Shit.* "Gigi, you there?"

"Check your texts, Ben."

His phone chimed. He pulled the phone from his ear and saw one word.

"That's the sex of your baby, Ben. Have a great fucking day."

*

Bitch.

Go easy.

Fuck, though. Emotional roller coaster or not, where the hell did she get off?

He put his mug of coffee down so hard, much of the hot dark roast leaped out over the sides, burning his knuckles. Déjà vu. He yanked his hand back and brought it to his chest. *Just, fuck.* Then after running it under tap water for five, six, seven seconds, he dried it while ignoring the remnant burning sensation, then grabbed his phone with both hands.

Gigi, he texted. *Do not broach this reunion idea again. Not with me, not with Preeya. I mean it.*

He hit Send.

He stared at the ceiling. Then back down at his screen.

And don't you dare tell Pree the sex.

Fuck her for telling him. *Not that she's necessarily right.*

Jamie's miscarriage…*she's probably right.*

He rubbed the top of his head, back and forth, back and forth.

"Hey, you."

He swallowed hard, cleared his throat, then worked to find his smile before facing Preeya. *No doubt she'll know something's wrong.* That he was upset.

A snap decision made, he'd keep the whole Gigi conversation—hell, call it what it was, an irrational and inflamed bout—to himself. Protecting Preeya from unnecessary stress was top priority. He'd put his foot down and that was that. And if Gigi dared push him, he'd work around her—he'd faced Ebola in West Africa, he could handle Gigi Donlow.

He sighed and shifted, throwing his chin up for the best mask of *all good* and *happy* he could muster. "Come here." He reached out his arm to Preeya. "You sleep good?"

"Mmm, yes." Preeya nuzzled her face in his chest. "I was surprised you didn't sleep in, my perfect body pillow."

He snorted and squeezed her tighter to him. "I, uh, felt like getting an early start, grab some coffee, and catch up on work before we run out to find the crib."

"Wow, you remembered."

"Of course I did." He kissed the top of her head. Her hair smelled good, like her jasmine and vanilla shampoo.

"Oh, hey." Her words were slightly muffled, spoken into his robe. "I invited Gigi along. If she finds a crib she likes, I thought we, meaning you"—she giggled and looked up at him with puppy-dog eyes, then buried her face back into his chest—"could help get it up to her apartment?"

On second thought, maybe he *should* tell Preeya about the blowout phone call. He sighed and shook his head. Preeya's cheek still pressed against him so she missed his raw expression of angst and anger mixed with sheer annoyance. "Of course, babe. I can help...your friend with the crib."

"Thank you." She reached up, slid her hands around his neck, and kissed him.

Anything, Preeya. Anything.

"She needs me, *us*, right now. And I owe it to her. Gigi is like a sister to me. She's your"—she pushed away from him to meet his eyes—"your soon-to-be sister-in-law!" She chuckled and lifted her brows, thoroughly entertained by her own witty discovery.

Right. "Yeah, I guess that's what she is." He found a thin grin to mask the rush of pure spite filling his chest. "I'm just thankful that your soon-to-be *actual* sister-in-law has two kids along with the experience and grounding to be our baby's godparent. God forbid anything were to happen to us, Stacy would raise the baby our way, with the right priorities, direction, means, structure, and selfless love."

When he stopped talking, he realized his hand on Preeya's back hadn't lifted and fallen with her deep, relaxed breaths for some moments now.

Preeya lifted her head off his chest and stood back. Her eyes narrowed, face tilted. "I told Gigi already…that she'd be the baby's godparent. Before you even knew I was pregnant. It wasn't even a question in my mind."

Ben's mouth went dry, making it near impossible to swallow the thick knot in his throat. Gigi'd said it on the phone. He remembered now. *My godbaby.*

Fuck that and over his dead body.

Relax, Ben.

How? He couldn't breathe, and he couldn't think in order to initiate his next breath—essential brain freeze.

In and out breath, Ben. In and out.

Oxygen and calm entered his system.

Now he just needed a few moments to formulate a careful, well-thought-out response to this without starting a fight. The last thing Preeya needed. But this is *their* child they're talking about—his and hers.

He'd been married before, knew about the gives and takes, the compromises necessary—money, careers, home, friends, travel, family—just infinite levels of necessary compromise. But the uncharted waters of *joint* life decisions for their baby—now that threw him and his thoughts to the cosmic wind.

And no one has to deal with a meddling…whatever the hell Gigi is. *Fucking Gigi.*

He sighed. Gigi aside, he had to remember that Preeya hadn't ever been in a real relationship, at least not one that lasted more than a few months.

But either way, how could she take it upon herself to make such a call? About their child's guardian. "Without a question in her mind," like she'd said.

As his thoughts whirled, he watched her chest heave with anxiety while her nostrils flared. He willed himself to say something to buy him time… so he wouldn't explode and upset her. But he was floored, absolutely fucking floored, his heartbeat ramming his rib cage. *Just do not explode, Ben.* He rubbed his head while trying his best to slow his breath, then opened his mouth to speak, still unsure of what the hell to say.

But Preeya beat him to the punch. "God, Ben…Stacy lives in Mexico. That isn't where I'd want my baby to grow up, to live, to be educated."

"The" baby to "My" baby?

It's ours, damn it. Our child.

More blood-pumping fury took hold of Ben's throat. He couldn't utter a grunt at this point.

"Ben, listen. Gigi is just…pure love. Don't get me wrong…I like Stacy, God, so much. And her kids are great, so smart and sweet…but honestly, if Stacy lived in the States, close by even, well, I'd still choose Gigi. Her energy, her intuitive and nurturing ways…that's what's best for the baby."

Again—*the* baby?

Our *baby. Our life, our love, our child.*

Calm, Ben. "Preeya." He caught her eyes, held them for a stern instant then shot his focus to the ceiling. *God, what the hell is going on?* What in the fuck had he missed? His heart sank; his stomach floated. How separate, how different, how drastically polar were their perspectives, their experiences? Their stages in life?

He closed his eyes, sighed, then nodded, more to himself than to her. He understood and it scared him frozen.

Don't make this into something it's not, Ben. You are meant to be.

Are we?

We. What a joke.

Was Gigi right? They'd known each other for only a matter of days, really—lustful, electric, and life-inspiring days—before…before Seattle and Prana and the news of their baby. His heart murmured a low moan. Yes, they'd clicked and, hell, seemed to even balance each other, but fuck, how well did they really fit? His practicality versus…her *vibes* and *gut feelings* and…fucking Gigi raising *her* kid? Not theirs, *hers*. He gritted his teeth. Here he thought, breathed, lived, and planned for *them*, while she just couldn't… comprehend it…the idea, the concept of a shared existence—it just flew right over her head.

Granted, she'd never known a model of a healthy partnership, not with her screwed-up parents' example. And again, he'd lived over a decade in a loving marriage. And it hadn't been easy with Jamie. Each day, every day, had been maddening yet glorious work. But Preeya, her *being*, her charisma and vibrancy and positive outlook made him want to do that work again, with her, for her, for *them*. But how can such a learning curve be ignored? Preeya was brilliant, but so damn clueless.

No, he couldn't blame her.

But how *could* he do this with her? How could they get married and raise a child together if Preeya couldn't grasp what *together* meant?

"Ben, are you hearing me?"

"Sorry, Preeya." He looked at his coffee mug—lukewarm, half-empty, *bitter by now*. "Got this raging headache all of a sudden. I, uh, think I'll go lie down again." He sidestepped to the other side of the kitchen and stopped at the open doorway. "You were probably right; I should have stayed in bed this morning."

And not answered the pre-dawn call.

Perhaps, not jumped into…fuck it.

He left Preeya in the kitchen probably hurt and confused and possibly fuming. He headed to their, or rather *his* bedroom. *His* name was on the goddamn lease, wasn't it? *Damn it*, to even think that way made him ill, or *more* ill.

He crashed to the mattress and warded off all thoughts, all worries—all decisions—for another time. *Just escape to sleep, escape. Like old times, Ben.* Escapist Ben.

*

Preeya felt short of breath, heartbeat thumping in her ears, all alone there in the kitchen. For the first time in months, that old panic crept up her body's central column, clutching her heart in her chest. She rubbed her belly, hoping the baby would kick, but nothing.

So, count and breathe? Or call Gigi?

No. No Gigi.

No crutch. She had this.

And she had Ben. Just upstairs.

Ben. God, he'd tried to hide it, but it had been written all over his face, the surprise, the hurt. And how removed and walled-off he'd become the next instant. How upset he was that Preeya didn't want Stacy to be the baby's godparent. She'd chosen Gigi…

That *she'd chosen* Gigi.

Shit. It seemed that not one, but two issues had set him off.

Her thoughts began to war.

Ben is the father.

But I'm the baby's mother.

He didn't trust her instincts?

She didn't trust her instincts.

You should trust your damn instincts, Preeya.

And her choice in guardian—no question, no doubt—was *Gigi.* The only soul she could ever picture caring for her child. Her child and Gigi's would be like siblings, family. Like Preeya and Gigi were family.

Not an aunt just because of blood ties.

She looked at the hand-painted rooster wall tile above the stove. "I mean, Gigi's been my life, my only constant since I was seven. Seven years old." The vibrant backsplash tile didn't answer. Only the ice maker in the freezer rumbled a cryptic reply.

She sighed then rubbed her hard, tight belly. "And your aunt Stacy is great, don't get me wrong," she whispered to the baby, "but she's so introverted, reserved, closed off." The woman was kind to Preeya, sweet in her own way. "But she's a writer, in her own head all the time. You'll see what I mean, sweet pea." The night Preeya had dinner at Stacy's, those kids had been starved for attention, craving contact and conversation. Just picturing her child in that environment, it made Preeya gasp for an extra breath to satisfy her lungs.

And isn't it the mother's choice anyway? To decide who'd care for the child if…if she weren't around? She? *It's "if they weren't around," Pree.* She shook her head, confused by her own logic, her own feelings, her own threatened sense of control.

But no, I am clear on this.

And anyway, Ben wouldn't have known about the baby if she hadn't tracked him down. She invited *him* to be a part of her and her baby's world.

Whoa.

Jesus, Preeya, you're in love with the man. Marrying him in a few weeks.

The father of her child.

She had hoped, prayed, for his safety, his forgiveness over their blowout in Vallarta. She'd prayed that he'd reciprocate her feelings for him. *Before you even told him you were pregnant.*

And he had passed the test.

He declared and committed and supported and reciprocated—*you stupid idiot.*

But, God, zooming-in to this one issue, there wasn't a chance she'd give in—she couldn't be comfortable with the baby being with anyone but Gigi.

And what is the likelihood of you and Ben both...you know...seriously?

Seriously? Ben's young wife died. Prana died. Her mother, she might as well have died. Who knows, maybe she did die. Yeah, maybe her mother's dead? People die. And so this was a huge deal. Preparing for her child. In case.

And if they couldn't agree on this...then what of everything else? *So the tie goes to me. When it comes to this child, the tie goes to me.*

Because, again, the mother knows, she's most connected—she has the spiritually fused bond. The mom's instinct trumps all.

How the hell would you know that, Preeya?

Her heart fell to the floor.

She wouldn't know.

Shit, she wouldn't have a clue about the connection between a mother and a child.

What does your heart say, Pree? Follow that.

Follow her heart? Her heart told her that...*Ben is wonderful.* A wonderful man, friend, partner. He'd be a wonderful father.

He was everything she'd ever wanted, without even knowing it. And thank God she had his love. It made her happy, whole, better, purposed, sated. His love—their love—was different than any she'd experienced before, with any person before. Ben had jumped in with two feet, ecstatic about getting married, growing their love, sharing their lives together—

Sharing their lives together…

*

Oh, no.

She ran up the stairs and down the hallway—and stubbed her toe on the doorjamb upon entering the bedroom.

The empty bedroom.

Winded, she sat on the edge of the bed.

She heard the shower running.

She swallowed hard and went to the bathroom door. She moved her hand up to knock but stopped herself. In a whisper, "Ben." Tears welled but dried up before one could hit her cheek. "I understand."

Her head shook side to side with relentless fury. She backed away from the door and when the backs of her knees hit the bed frame, she surrendered to the mattress, letting her body fall back, sprawl out—exhausted. She reached for her pillow and stuffed it underneath her head. "I do understand, Ben," she whispered. "I get *us*."

She stared at the door, listened to the spray of the shower and the clinking of the pipes from the hot water heater's effort. She'd wait for him to come out of the bathroom. She'd tell him. Her heart still pounded in her ears and now in her temples, too. Yeah, she needed to clear the air. Her thoughts revolved around and around, anxious for the chance to make things right with Ben. And as her mind whirled, her eyelids sank under her heart's weight. So heavy. And though she fought it, sleep overtook her.

CHAPTER 52

THE DOORBELL RANG in rapid-fire succession, as if it were a final attempt.

She sat up and searched for the time through her sleep-laden eyes. *Noon.* Her eyes went wide.

"Ben?"

Of course he wasn't there—he would've answered the front door if he were home. And his car keys weren't on the dresser. He'd let her sleep? So no crib buying today? But he'd gone without a word. She grabbed her phone from the nightstand and looked at the screen. No text, either.

The doorbell's chime filled her ears again. So, not the final attempt then?

She lumbered down the stairs while straightening her ponytail. "Coming!"

She peered through the peephole—Gigi. She flipped the lock then reached for the door handle and drew it open a crack while hiding from the sunlight which threatened a slap to her deserving, unmade face.

"I mean, really!" Gigi rolled her eyes then kissed Preeya's cheek and slid, or rather maneuvered, past Preeya, their two round, pregnant bellies bumping each other.

Preeya closed the door and followed Gigi to the couch. "How are you feeling, Geej?"

"Feeling? Panicked, thank you very much." Gigi threw herself onto the sofa like she'd run a marathon. "You didn't answer my calls or texts. God,

Pree, like I need déjà vu from the *Josh* night. I'm pregnant, too, you know. And it's not like I have only *you* to worry about now." Gigi motioned at Preeya's midsection. Then her own. "And the doorbell, even your next-door neighbors heard the darn thing." Gigi glared at Preeya for a moment, expecting something—a reaction, for her to catch on. "Pree—crib shopping? Three hours ago? You were supposed to pick me up. But if not, maybe a heads-up?"

Right, crib shopping...*with Gigi*. "Sorry, Geej! I was...sleeping." *True, in summary.* "Dozed off, didn't even hear Ben leave." She flicked her eyes toward her phone. "Speaking of Ben, did you try his phone?"

"Yeah—no. Just short of calling my dad to check the scanners for any car accidents, though. Anyway, I took some deep breaths and decided to drive here instead."

"Geej, really, I'm sorry. This time...I kind of, well...Ben and I..." She didn't want to discuss their not-quite-a-fight *fight*, especially not with Gigi— the subject of the thing—not until Preeya smoothed things over with Ben. "We needed extra sleep, I guess. I think he got an early phone call that woke him, and I don't really sleep well when he's not lying next—" *Shit.* Preeya grinned and lowered her eyes to the right. Single Gigi—nearly married Preeya. *Constant tiptoeing all around.*

Gigi sighed and rolled her eyes. "It's cool, Pree. Stop filtering for me— the singlehood stuff. I'm, you know, doing okay with it." She squeezed Preeya's wrist. "Hey, I have all the autonomy here—I can make all the calls for this little one. No compromising or negotiating or settling. Yeah, I'm starting to see the silver lining, for sure."

"That's awesome, Geej." *Compromise.* Her own deeper lesson for the day. And while she liked that Gigi had found the positive in her situation, Preeya wouldn't trade Ben—and all the required compromise and negotiation—for anything in the world.

Gigi reached over and slapped her hand. "Another perk? Shaving my legs...*so* out the window. I've got no man to say a damn thing about it." Gigi laughed.

"Too cold to waste the fur, anyway." Preeya winked then tilted her head with a knowing smile. Gigi was trying so hard. "And also, you don't have to worry about keeping anyone awake...with all the tossing and turning through the night!"

Gigi winked back then nodded. "Exactly." Gigi sighed into a genuine yet stoic smile. "Hey, and I've got you, the best support system a girl could hope for...except when you stand my wide-ass up." Gigi pursed her lips. "Still better than some useless swinging dick."

Preeya smirked. "Totally." Then she sank into the couch. Her *swinging dick*, her Ben—angry, hurt...and always so good to her. Staying up late every night massaging her aches, tending her tensions—*God, did he tend her tensions*. And playing the human pillow so she slept through the night. Her heart splayed thin across her chest.

She wanted to vent to Gigi. But no, *not happening*. Despite Gigi's attempt at a positive outlook, Preeya couldn't. She'd cried to her last week in the car about her fears and worries and blathered on about the marriage license and—no more. Gigi didn't need to hear any more of any of it, no matter what her friend said about "filtering."

"Geej, I'm here for you, no doubt." She took Gigi's hand. "Hey, how have you been sleeping?"

"Haven't been, but I've kept myself busy. I even found a project."

Preeya's phone pinged—a text. Maybe Ben? "Let me get this, Geej. Your project, I want to hear more about it in just a second, okay?"

Gigi nodded and grinned. "Second place takes some getting used to, is all," Gigi teased in an unconvincing tone.

Preeya lifted a brow then waddled around the sofa toward the corner armchair for some privacy. "Hey, I got your favorite cookies yesterday," she said over her shoulder. "The ones with the mint filling. In the pantry."

*

Sylvia, not Ben. *Checking in, sweetie.*

She sighed. This wasn't like Ben. To leave, vanish. Without a word.

Damn it. Her heart rebounded under her ribs, fast and fierce. Could he be more insensitive? Her chest tightened. Like it used to when alone, even with Gigi in the very next room.

Breathe and just call him.

She hit his speed dial, but hung up the next second. If she tried to speak, she'd burst out sobbing. She'd never told him the entire story about that day, the day her mother left, but he knew the gist. *He knew the goddamn gist.* Fury filled her airway, and she coughed to clear the knot of rage.

"You okay? Need some water, Pree?" Gigi called from the kitchen.

"No, I'm good, thanks." She swallowed and inhaled through her nose then cleared her throat again. *Text.* Send a text and defer the conversation while Gigi's here. She couldn't let Gigi in, not on this one. Not on this one.

Where are you?

She hit Send and waited, thumb tap-tapping the screen.

Five beats passed until, *Ping.*

At the office. Didn't want to wake you.

She grimaced and heaved a breath. *No note? And when will you be back? Left note on the coffee maker. Will be home for dinner. Let's talk then ;-)*

She let air infiltrate her lungs. Her shoulders eased down as her next breath seeped out. They'll talk and all will be fine.

*

Preeya returned to the sofa after snagging the note from the kitchen. With the box of chocolate mint cookies ripped open on the coffee table, Gigi beamed from the couch with remnant crumbs at the corner of her upturned mouth. "Cleopatra" had a cookie in one hand while reaching for another. Preeya smiled and winked at her. She was glad her best friend was there with her.

"Good cookies?"

"The best. You're the best," Gigi said through a second mouthful, then laughed, crumbs spewing onto Gigi's lap.

Preeya cracked up, too, then Gigi's phone bleeped.

Gigi glance at her screen. "Oh my goodness!"

"What? What is it?"

"My dad. He got me a stroller—the super deluxe you told me about. He texted a picture. Look!" Gigi rocked her body to upright but couldn't bring herself to stand, and since Preeya had already surrendered back into the cushions…. They laughed and Gigi just held the tiny phone screen up in the air to show Preeya from afar.

Preeya squinted. "Well, I remember it, anyway. Awesome, Geej. You can take the baby running around Green Lake."

"Yes, yes, I can." Gigi looked pleased, positive. Then her friend's eyes sank a bit and she took another big bite of cookie. "I'll have enough extra weight to run off, too." More crumbs sifted off her mouth.

"Please. Our jobs now are to feed these babies!" Preeya wagged her finger then pointed to a cookie. "Throw me one." She caught it midair, smiled, then bit. "So…" mouth full, "the project…tell me everything."

"Oh, yeah!" Gigi sat up straighter on the couch, excited, prepping the buildup Gigi-style. But then she paused and tilted her head with narrowed eyes. "Ben's still sleeping?"

"Uh, no. He…decided to get work done at the office when he found me so deep asleep."

Gigi nodded, seemingly relieved. "Oh, okay…well, anyway," she said, tucking a leg under her, "I started working on a family tree for my little… offspring here." Gigi rubbed her belly and before Preeya could respond with anything more than a nod and a smile, "And I wanna do yours, too! For my godbaby!"

Preeya blinked and gave Gigi a close-lipped grin. Oh God, would Preeya break her heart when…*if* she recanted the godmother title. She couldn't bear to think about it. "Sounds…terrific!"

"Yeah, it's so fun, Pree, and a great distraction for me. But more importantly, it'll be great for the kids to know their histories." Gigi's face froze with glee—for effect.

"Wow, Geej." She was excited to see Gigi genuinely pumped about something. "That's awesome. I love it."

"I was going to surprise you, but, you know, there's some information I need…so I can finish the online genealogy questionnaire."

More information.

Her family.

Preeya licked her bottom lip then smacked both lips together. Her genealogical tree would be half a tree. Her father hated talking or thinking about her mother. And Preeya steered clear of *Jenny Patel*, too.

"We can do the questionnaire now, on your laptop if you want? Since there's no crib shopping…"

"Geej." She looked down at her hands and swallowed. Gigi meant well but, God, she just didn't want to—

"I know what you're thinking." Gigi giggled and slapped her own thigh. "Not like clairvoyant *I-know-what-you're-thinking*, of course…but I know… that your mother's a bad topic. But, you know, confronting your fears… it can only heal, mend. And, Pree, knowing where you come from on *both* sides, and seeing, factually visualizing, that you are your own individual person…that's truly cathartic."

It made sense. But Preeya's turning stomach disagreed. The logic didn't matter. The thought, alone, felt bad. She burped and swallowed a flash of hot acid.

"More heartburn? You want some tea?"

"No, Geej. I, uh, I'm just not sure I want to think about my mom, with my mood affecting the baby so directly." She knew Gigi would understand that—Gigi was the one who taught her those things.

"Right, of course. It's just…buried deeper, Pree, are more negative memories and associations with your mom. They need to be addressed."

"You've seen something, sensed something? Is something wrong, you know, with—"

"No! No, no. Not at all. It's just"—Gigi rocked and shifted to her feet, then came over and sat next to Preeya—"I spoke to Ben. The other day when we had that bawling session in the car…and he mentioned…that you'd been having nightmares."

"I haven't. I haven't at all." She should be happy that her best friend and fiancé were connecting, talking, assumedly about her welfare, but…she wasn't happy. She felt like an untrusted child.

"Not consciously…in your sleep. He said you scream and yell every night. About your mother."

Preeya couldn't catch a breath. She didn't remember any of her dreams…

or rather, *supposed nightmares*. Why wouldn't Ben tell her, wake her, mention it?

"I'll be right back." Preeya scurried through the kitchen to the powder bath. Unsure if she needed to vomit or cry or just splash ice-cold water on her heated cheeks, but she knew she needed to be alone.

*

Gigi had eaten half the box of chocolate mint rounds by the time Preeya returned from the powder room.

"I think it's a good idea, Geej."

"What? What is?"

"Let's do the family tree. My mother's side included. I know where she was born and I know her maiden name. That's about all—I'd never met her parents. Can't ask my dad because, well…doesn't matter. Anyway"—she fell into the sofa next to Gigi and took her hand—"I was thinking…I want to dig a little deeper, and maybe with *your* dad's help, we can locate her. Find her. I want to find my mom. My dad would hate the idea. But, Geej, I think—and feel—that you're right. I have negativity buried and I want to be done with it. For the baby, and for me and for Ben, I want to be done with it, with *her*."

CHAPTER 53

S HE SAW THE headlights soar up the front curtains. *Ben.*

Then her phone buzzed in the center of the table. Both Gigi and Preeya could see the message. *Gigi's here?*

Preeya smiled at Gigi. "Have some more ice cream, Geej, and give me a few minutes."

"No, Pree." Her best friend slammed her last spoonful of ice cream and slid her chair back at the same time. "I'm gonna go."

She'd insist Gigi stay to chill with her and Ben, but she and Ben wouldn't be chilling. They'd be clearing the air. Discussing stuff, a lot of stuff. And without a word of explanation, Gigi already seemed to understand. Her friend kissed Preeya on the cheek, collected up the pages of notes they'd taken, and stuffed them in her purse—a little haphazardly, Preeya thought. "Why the rush, Geej? Relax, you really should slow down a bit, like you tell me to."

Gigi nodded as she brought her empty bowl and spoon to the sink— fast, faster than Preeya'd seen Gigi move since their twentieth week—then moved to the side kitchen door, blew Preeya a last kiss, and left.

She heard the front door bolt flip. The door opened, then shut a moment later. His sigh—a sigh of relief to be home—met her ears, and her chest rushed with pounding heat and soft flutters. Of all the things she'd wanted to say to him that morning, then more from new realizations she'd been hit with throughout the day, the only thing she died to do was hug him. Hold him. Be held by him.

She dropped the kitchen towel she'd wrung in knots and marched out to meet him.

But he was already heading up the stairs. Away from her.

*

Alone, but not by choice this time, not like earlier in the powder room, she got the old chest-squeezing sensation again. Preeya paced and counted and breathed. For what felt like forever. He wasn't coming back down? His note, and his text, said they'd talk.

What the hell?

Don't make things bigger than they need to be, Preeya. Remember, he buries things, hates conflict, hates opening up.

And when he had confided in her about Jamie's death—in Vallarta—she'd exploded at him. Could she blame him now for the avoidance? He had been hurt by her this morning, and hell, the man fled to the third world for more than a year to process his loss, his pain over Jamie.

Just give him space, Pree. A day and a night. And try not to take it personally.

Wait, don't take it personally?

That's all it is—personal!

And it had been—she looked at her phone—twenty minutes. She didn't hear the pipes kicking and creaking, so the shower wasn't running. Had he… gone to sleep?

That's it. She tramped up the stairs, huffing the entire way.

*

At the doorway, she caught her breath.

He'd folded down the comforter for her, a neat triangle, and had placed a fluffed pillow for her head and two long body pillows like she liked along the length of her side of the king-size bed.

He lay on his side, snug under the covers, facing away from her. His chest, the blanket, lifted and fell with every deep, soft breath he took.

Officially asleep.

Sweetly asleep *and home*. In their bed. Only after he'd arranged her pillows for her. She could've just melted to the floor then and cried.

Pretending to be a single light feather as she crawled beside him, she fell into the turned-down bed more like an entire bird—an ostrich, maybe. She froze. He stirred, grunted, and shifted an inch away.

Away?

What is this? And what am I doing?

She *wanted* him awake. She couldn't take another second without clearing things up, opening up. She needed his heart and arms open to her now, and holding her through the night. She just couldn't end the day this way.

She reached over with some effort and gripped Ben's shoulder.

"Ben," she whispered. "Ben...please wake up. Talk to me."

He groaned and rolled over to face her, his golden eyes still mostly hidden behind sleep.

"I get it. I understand. Please, I am so sorry, God..." She sighed and scooted closer to him, then pushed her belly up against the small of his back, took his arm, and draped it over her hip and thigh. He inhaled, his eyes closed, nostrils wide, then he sighed and engaged his arm, pulling her into him tighter.

"I should've... I should've asked you, discussed it with you, the whole Gigi *godparent* thing. I mean, *of course* I should've. But, then again, I had promised her the day I found out I was pregnant... Then, when you and I got back together, it just didn't come up. We've been so busy, I guess."

She waited...for Ben to respond. It took him a second to open his eyes. He swallowed; she watched his Adam's apple bob up and down. A beat, still no words. He just looked at her—no, looked through her. Not from drowsiness, it seemed. His eyes were distant, zoned-out. Resigned.

"Ben...listen, even though I feel strongly about Gigi being the, *our* baby's godmother, I know it isn't solely my decision. It's *our* baby, our decision, our lives. And I love you, *us*. God, so much, Ben."

The corners of his lips lifted to form a half smile while his gorgeous golden eyes remained glazed over with a glint of hovering doubt.

Couldn't he see she was trying here?

And that us *is a two-way street?*

"Ben." Sick of the silence now, her pulse spiked. "You know, while we're kind of, not really talking here, you really should've told me about the night terrors."

"Gigi," he grumbled. His stare shifted to the ceiling.

His first word to her—*Gigi*? So her best friend told her about the dreams. Like *he* should have. *What the hell is his deal?* He still held her tight to him, but God, where the hell had he gone? A fortress stood between them.

"Talk to me, Ben. How long have I been…or, rather, what all did I say? In my sleep?"

He sighed while shaking his head then shifted, and kissed her forehead. "Fucking Gigi."

"Hey!"

"Preeya…you haven't had one of your… episodes in nearly a week. I didn't tell you—and yes, maybe I should have—but I decided not to because you were working through it. You *are* working through it. The natural course of things, Pree—and time—heals all. I didn't understand that when Jamie died. Everyone tiptoed, pretended, skirted topics and conversations and events that might trigger things. I hated it. Fucking despised it. But now I see the purpose. There are stages, Pree, and they need to be respected. Your world was turned upside down with the truth about your mom, then the loss of your sister. Add the start of you and me, the baby. Things this deep can't be rushed—no shortcuts, Preeya. And as for Gigi—she shouldn't have told you about the nightmares. I told her in confidence." He huffed and flared his nostrils, as if ready to punch a wall. He closed his eyes. "That was stupid of me."

"It is my right to know, though, Ben. It's my—"

His fingers pressed her lips. "The nightmares were *your* body's way of working through the trauma. What if I weren't here during your unconscious night-fits, not lying next to you to hear you screaming, your seven-year-old self wailing away? No one would be there to tell you, anyway. And if you were ready, you'd have had waking thoughts, not REM episodes. But you weren't ready. And now they've stopped, Pree. Like I said, you're working through a cluster of shit, and doing it naturally. In *your* time."

She grimaced, nothing to throw back in her defense. *Fine, but...*"What about this morning? You think I'm too delicate for you to voice your anger about my choice of Gigi as the baby's godmother?"

"Yes, Preeya, you're fragile right now. I don't want to argue while you're pregnant and knee-deep with school, on top of the other shit I mentioned." He blew out a stream of air, then lowered his voice to a whisper. "Getting you upset, stressed—babe, that's not okay for you, and it's potentially harmful to the baby. *Fact.* It's just fact."

Preeya had heard every word, let each one sink in, but she couldn't ignore the airy feeling in her stomach, slightly queasy. "Okay, I get it. You didn't want to argue this morning. You don't want to set me off. But our relationship, Ben, it needs to be open and honest. We...we have so much ahead of us...and so much behind us...and just so much going on in our *present*, we can't dance around things, each other, or...or we'll lose *us* in the process. I mean, we're just getting to know each other, really. And, like *I* said...yes, I'm learning to think *us* versus *me*, but I can't have you treating *me* like...like a child with kid gloves. That's also not *us*. If you believe in me, then trust I can handle things...life—especially with you by my side."

"First off, I don't doubt you, Pree. Physics, biology, the science of the body and birth, those are the variables that concern me. I never doubt *your* strength. I—" He paused there.

"What, Ben? See? This is what I mean. Just tell me." She huffed. "Let me in, Ben."

He squeezed his eyes shut. His head shook, holding something back. Keeping something from her...assumedly something that might just *upset* her.

*

"Listen, Pree," he said, then pinched his nose in thought. A beat, then another, flitted by. "Wait a second." He scooted his body up to a sitting position but then made sure to help her shift with him. He needed to maintain a physical connection with her for this. He'd gone over it all in his mind, God, for so many hours. He'd been at the office to check his mail then escaped to Gas Works Park across town for the rest of the day. A perfect distraction. Another people-watching haven, and the entire scene had helped him to both take his mind off and put his thoughts on his situation. His life. The situation from that morning with Preeya, tiny but enormous at the same time, really had him reeling.

Preeya glared at him, reaching her breaking point, he knew. He brought his hand to her face, sliding a loose strand of her silken black hair behind her ear. "I—"

"Benjamin Trainer, I swear. Here, I'll start. You can follow my lead on how to talk openly—a new precedent for *us*, I know." Said with a not-too-subtle hint of sarcasm. "I won't even talk about the godparent thing again… that we can put off for a little while." She sighed. "How's this, a light topic. I'm"—her eyes got wide, like she hoped to incite anticipation in Ben, but he had trouble finding the energy, the mood—"going to locate my abandoning mother so that I…"

The rest of Preeya's words floated off into the room. He could only see her mouth moving, her eyes and head and hands animated, demonstrating her intense enthusiasm. Why couldn't he hear anything? Not even the usual clanking of the wall heater. Foggy, all sound. His thoughts, too. Until his rage settled in, then the beating of his heart thudded in his forehead. A deafening *thump-thump-slam*.

Her mother?

Goddamn you, Gigi.

Preeya said she understood, the *us*. But no. Too young or too naive or too goddamn selfish. He couldn't speak. She'd stopped talking now—just a blank stare into his burning-hot face.

He rubbed the top of his head. His hair, curls now, felt surreal. Like, not his own hair, not his own skull. He blinked to try and reset, to mend the sudden separation between him and his body. And between all of him…and all of Preeya.

"What, Ben? You're scaring me…you look ill."

"You, Preeya, are scaring *me*. This is a *light topic*? You…thinking about your mother, let alone learning about her, finding her—now? Of all times?—is goddamn scary. Dangerous, even! It can only lead to stress. Serious trauma like what you've experienced, Pree? I mean, you can't even talk about it when you're awake—only in your goddamn sleep. Scratch that; you can only scream and shriek about it in your nightmares. Awful things you'd say without the slightest memory in the morning. Like you were seven again, then you'd jump to now, scared of the things…the things you'd do to the baby. You need a therapist, Pree, not your goddamn vacating coward of a mother."

He ignored her tears. He just…just couldn't get logic past her naive bubble, hers or Gigi's. *Gigi.* "Fucking Gigi!"

"Stop saying that," Preeya whispered through her sniffles.

"No. She's selfish, self-absorbed, self—"

Preeya covered her ears and shook her head at him. Like a child. "She's anything but, Ben," she yelled. "She's anything but selfish."

"I told her not to bring her asinine idea up to you. I explained the dangers. I'm not just your fiancé and—*fuck!*—I'm not just this child's father—that jealous, passive-aggressive bitch—I'm an MD for God's sake. A surgeon. Pediatric, Preeya. And I've seen *you* faint twice in the six months I've known you. That's without another human being growing inside you."

Preeya scoffed.

"Okay, you want me to scare you? Fine. I've seen birth defects that would turn your stomach, Preeya. I've seen—"

Her hands flew from her ears to his mouth. Her cynical expression had morphed into sheer horror. "Stop, Ben…about the goddamn birth defects. I am a third year."

Exactly, goddamn it. Why then was she acting like an ignorant moron?

"Fine…*never mind* the medical aspects since you *know* already. Bottom line—Gigi posed the idea and I said no. Absolutely not now, and not even after the baby. Not with the baby breast-feeding, the most dependent on you that he or she will ever be. Communication with—or worse, meeting—your mother could send you into a tailspin, forget standard postpartum depression, Preeya. I mean, God, you're brilliant…and even Gigi isn't stupid. But, well, here we are. She went ahead anyway and you bit."

Dehydrated and spent, he sighed. The worst part? She hadn't fucking thought to talk to him about it…*again*.

"While I love sitting here being called an idiot, you have to admit this is about your ego, your controlling goddamn nature, your pride, flaring up all over the place. All over your precious *us*."

"Goddamn right, my pride." He paused, raked his hair, and growled. *Fuck.* "Pride is what you call it. I call it mutual respect for each other. Because you…you, Preeya, uttering the word *us* is a joke. Fucking *us*? What *us*? You didn't think to discuss the godparent thing—fine, you forgot to bring it up when we got back together. I didn't think about the matter, either. But this morning? Your blanket statement…and now *this*? Scared to ask me about the hunt for your mother while carrying *our* child? Maybe considering what I might *say* on the matter?" He paused and glared at her. "Need it your own way, despite your own welfare, and again, the baby's!" He shamed her with another shake of his head. "More likely, it didn't even dawn on you to discuss it with me."

He pushed her off of him, needing air, space, separation.

She shot him a look of disdain to match her expression their last morning together in Vallarta.

But fuck it. "Here I am, my sole focus on you, solely on you, your well-being, and our child's—to the extreme. It's like I care about you and this child more than you do." His throat got thick, his breath harder to catch. "It rips my heart out, Preeya. You are my life, and you dare threaten…risk… fuck!"

Moments of excruciating silence blipped by.

She reached for his hand.

No. He fisted it in the sheets.

"I…Ben…it didn't…I thought finding her, my mother…would help… me, the baby…and you. Erase the pain."

He swallowed then cleared his throat. "You thought? *You* thought. All on your own, again. And you don't want to be treated like a *child*? Isn't that what you said? Well, stop acting like one, Preeya."

He narrowed his eyes at her, fucking done with it.

"The answer is no, Preeya…you cannot look for your mother, or think about her, or research her, and for God's sake, you can't *meet* her. Not now and not for the foreseeable future. It isn't safe. Just, *no*." His chest heaved. "You know better, Pree. Shit, you're about to enter your residency…you *better* know better—that this level of drama is *not* okay."

Preeya's cheeks shone red, eyes seething, darting at him. She filled her lungs with an enormous breath, as if about to make a grand speech. She held it in, that air oxygenating her body and brain, obviously working hard to prepare that last-minute discourse. He tilted his head and waited, readying for the response, praying she'd meet him on his ground, priorities and hopes matched, like he'd thought they'd been.

Her eyes targeted his. "No, Ben. I will."

She will—*what*? Because while her voice had been quiet, almost soft, her words could've gone either way, and her glare, God, the look in her illuminated violet eyes, was one of stubborn and prideful defiance. *Like a goddamn teenager.*

"My heart tells me that I need to do this. I love you, but I need to find and face her, Ben. Now. Not later." She lifted her chin and pursed her lips, punctuating her final words on the matter.

So that was that? Staunch words ending with her chest puffed up, her superficial confidence bolstering her stand. That she'd do whatever the hell she wanted to do.

A deflated feeling lingered in the room, in the air, sucking the warmth that had been so tangible between them up to now.

He still couldn't look at her. He wasn't sure he knew who she was, or ever had.

That's not true, Ben. This bullshit is Gigi talking.

But the fact that Preeya had it in her, this selfishness, so uncompromising…especially when it came to the well-being of a child, *their* child. It raged fire up his throat.

But if he said any of this to her, what he really wanted to say, he'd devastate her. It would magnify her *awful-mother complex* tenfold. He couldn't.

Preeya drew a loud breath, bringing him back from his mental tirade. He forced himself to look in her face, but she shot her gaze up and away. Shaking his head at the paradoxical clash, the rioting of their egos and perspectives and priorities and the resulting stalemate they'd found themselves in, he knew one thing still—that he...he fucking loved her. And he couldn't see her in pain or in harm's way.

He couldn't just stand by and watch.

"Preeya, I...love you. I do. But I can't see you do this. Risk your health and the baby's." *The baby's.* Rage rocked his heart. "Damn it, Preeya!" he yelled. "I've already lost...lost too much, and *I'm* still grieving." With his index finger he moved her chin to meet his gaze. He hoped his eyes blurry with fucking tears knifed into her while he struggled to find his voice again. Throat cleared, he let a low baritone of admission rumble up from his chest. "Not just Jamie, Preeya. I...I didn't just lose Jamie. And it's taken me so much to let *life* back in again. You, you and the baby, are my life. I can't—" Tears fell like sharp icicles to the thick white comforter they'd made love under just the night before.

"What, Ben? What else did you lose? Tell me, damn it." Her tone was harsh and insistent and furious, but her violet eyes betrayed the auditory armor. He saw her care and love for him, but God, she was torn. So damn torn. Why let this...this bullshit endeavor—and Gigi, and her past—come between them? He hadn't even asked or forced her to choose. He hadn't asked her to forget. He just needed her to trust him, to confide and consult and respect him, his part in...in their family. His only family.

Preeya huffed shallow breaths, nostrils flaring with each in and out. "Tell me," she whispered. He saw her hand near his, but then she pulled away. "Just, tell me."

"My baby, Preeya. My baby...with Jamie. Miscarried, at twenty-nine weeks."

"Jesus, Ben." She closed her eyes. Shut them tight. Glistening tears formed at her eyelashes. Her bottom lip quivered and her control, lost. She cried, maybe for him and his hurt, and maybe for her fear—the exact reason he hadn't uttered the word *miscarriage*. But she cried—while his tears dried up and no more came.

He longed to hold her, touch her hand, her face, her skin, her hair. But the signs weren't there. His admission of the deepest grief had been met with a strange isolation. She didn't lean into him, didn't touch his hand. She just kept her eyes slammed shut. Minutes of agonizing separation crawled by.

Until, like she woke from a nightmare, she shook it off, straightened herself up, and lifted her face to his. "Why, Ben? Why do you close yourself off from me? We're getting married, having a baby, and…you couldn't tell me… *this*?" Spoken in a hush—a hurt, defeated hush.

"If you don't get it by now, Preeya—" He bit his bottom lip. "It's always for you, for our baby. Each and every snap decision and bottled-up goddamn emotion and long-term commitment…I do it for you. To protect you, to love you. For *us*, the *us* you…just *do not* grasp."

One tear rolled down her cheek. "I feel like, like, I don't know you, Ben. How much more have you hidden from me?"

Is she fucking kidding me? Fire burned his gut. A controlled surgeon no more. "God, first the names and the religious affiliation, then how we'd travel with or without—"

"Oh please, like we're gonna leave our kid, abandoned, while we go fix the world! Not over my dead body, Ben."

"But we at least needed to talk about it."

"That's what I'm saying. I'm begging you to talk to me."

"What the fuck is there to talk about when you've already goddamn decided everything for us, Preeya? Fuck! This morning, you *told me* who our child's godparent would be—no, who it already was. God, I sensed it—hah! *Sensed.* Fucking Gigi-intuited"—his head rocked in minuscule tremors, probably looking as crazy as he felt—"that you're just not ready. You're not ready, Preeya, to be with someone else. For all the years you dreaded being alone, your monophobia, attaching to people any way you could…but with all that company, you never actually stepped outside of yourself to be *with* another. Maybe Prana and Gigi are the exceptions…but, well, all I know is that you are not ready…to be *with* me." He sighed. "If you ignore my plea here and you do this thing, hunting down your mother, then I'm…I'm sorry."

"Ben, I need to do this. I just…I need to."

Air flooded his lungs and he held the breath in for one long, surreal second. "You can't play pretend with me while you live your solo existence without me, Pree." He slid out of the bed. "You know what, I just…can't be here to watch this."

Then he froze where he stood. *Hmm.* "Hey, I'll even give you some time to think things out, Pree. Some distance." He grabbed his pants from the armchair and slammed each leg down into the day-old jeans. "Last week I got a call. I've been requested to run a two-week DWB training course in southern Texas over the holiday break. I'd said no, of course." He let a puff of a laugh escape him. "But I've just decided that I'm going." *Take that, lone decision.* "Then I might—no, I will visit Stacy and the kids, being so close to the border."

Preeya said nothing. Made no eye contact. And she stayed perfectly still. Meanwhile, he grabbed his watch and phone from the nightstand and pulled on the T-shirt lying crumpled at his feet. "I'll be back before the birth. Stay here, in the house. I'll leave enough cash, cover all the bills. And—" He snorted, "—have Gigi stay with you…because fuck it, you're going to do whatever you want, anyway. Hell, maybe you'll find your mom, reunite…she can come and lend her support, too. She can crash in the guest room where Sylvia was supposed to be."

He got to the bedroom door and looked back. To his surprise, Preeya was bawling now, close to hyperventilating. She'd been so ice cold. And, wow, had he blocked it out, the sound of her sorrow, deep and hollow and heart-ripping? How in-tune one moment and planets-apart the next.

And fuck, he wanted to rush to her, hand her the half-full glass of water on the nightstand and add a pillow behind her back to support her, then throw his arms around her, sit with her and rock her and talk all night about then and now and forever.

No. He couldn't. He and Preeya…they were just an illusion.

His jaw locked with a level of detachment that scared him. He couldn't help her, couldn't control the situation—why did he think he could control anything? Just like Jamie and her cancer and their dead baby. *Fuck.*

He forced his gaze down to the scuffed hardwood floor. "I'll come by tomorrow to pack. I'll stay…at Stanton's tonight." He swallowed, reached for the door's old tarnished knob, and mumbled, "Call if there's an emergency."

"Wait, Ben." He paused in the doorway, but didn't turn around. "The marriage license: it's good for sixty days. You'll be back, right? Before…so we can, still"—her gasps for air between each few words were killing him—"get married without reapplying again."

He cleared his throat. "I don't know, Preeya." Because he really had no answer for her. Or for himself. Not in his head, and not in his heart.

Or did he? An answer that he couldn't acknowledge.

"Ben." A defeated whisper.

"We'll see." And he walked away, down the hallway, down the stairs, with her trailing words following him. Something about "escaping again" and "running again."

CHAPTER 54

SHE FELL ASLEEP crying.

And she woke up crying. The sun had long risen, midday mocking her out the window.

A rush of blood hit her head as she swung her legs off the edge of the bed, feet to the floor, and a flurry of motivation sent her to the closet. To see. To know if it was all a terrible nightmare, an empty threat, a hollow, angry bluff.

She froze at the closet door, her shadow on the wall from the ray of sun leaking in through the translucent curtains. Like in the hotel, or in the bedroom of her parents, a brewing knowledge boiled in her head and heart. That an answer was only a closet door away.

She sighed and opened the walk-in door. A section of *empty* filled the bar among her clothing. A section of *empty* to match the hole in her chest. She sank to the hardwood floor, rough and worn from decades of whoever had lived there before. Her fingers felt the antiqued planks of wood and thought splinters would be welcome. She sank down, lay back. She'd just stay there for a few minutes, just until her next inevitable bladder call. Even though she knew she'd need help getting up. She and her boulder. She laughed then, through sobs. She and her boulder might be stuck on the floor forever. No Ben to smile sweetly, offer his hand, pull her to standing. Yanking her close to his chest. To his heart. No Ben, not right now. He had sneaked in while she was asleep, packed a bag and taken off. Just taken off like he said he would.

*

She found herself in the kitchen eating toast. She'd gotten there through a haze of robotic routine.

She only knew one thing for certain—that she did not call him or text him.

Her pride wouldn't let her.

And she didn't reach out to Gigi, either, though she died to cry out, yell out to her best friend for help and support and confirmation that she, Preeya Patel, was not wrong. But she was too angry. And pushing fast-forward in her head, she foresaw blowing up at Gigi without meaning to. *It's not Gigi's fault. None of this.* Although Ben certainly thought it was.

Too much. Too much to think about and no one to help her untangle it. And no one to wrench the vise grip from her heart. Because, damn it, Ben left. Took a temporary leave of absence. *Maybe* temporary, is how he made it seem. *Jesus.* Her blood raged through her. What man just up and leaves when shit gets rough? Like in Mexico. Was she not worth fighting for? This was all too reminiscent of someone. Up and leaving her. Too goddamn close.

His words, his meaning—*she* was selfish? *She* wasn't putting her child first? Goddamn him. She snatched her phone, thumbs at the ready. One beat of contemplation, then they tap-pounded the virtual keyboard with rhythmic angst.

Just fuck you, Ben Trainer. Fuuuuuuuck you!

She paused, her chest heaving, her thumbs—like leashed pit bulls ramping up to enter the fight—hovering over Send.

Fuck! *Hit Send, and then what, Preeya?*

In her constricted chest, her heart knew he wouldn't answer her, not unless her text included something to the effect of, *Yes, I will abandon my hunt for the woman who left me stumbling through the world alone.* And, *I've been selfish, self-absorbed, not considering your feelings.* Even though, counter to his belief, she *had* been thinking of her unborn child. Of the buried negativity plaguing her and everything and everyone connected to her, namely the baby. See, she had not been thinking of herself alone. She and her baby, *her baby*, remained the priority.

She slammed her hand down on the table.

He wanted her to give in? Bend to his whim?

It's not a damn contest, Preeya.

No, but this was her life, and would he or their baby want only half of her? A pained, fucked-up version of Preeya Patel? No matter how logical and practical and, yes, medically based Ben's reasoning had been, Preeya's gut and heart and instinct told her to follow through.

Now, Gigi being the godparent for their kid…how would she feel if Ben insisted on someone she didn't trust to be their kid's guardian? Like, say, Kelly from Denver? But he'd picked Stacy. And counter to Gigi, though also a single mother, Stacy seemed grounded. And she'd practically raised Ben, and was doing a fine job with Beth and Peter.

Maybe Preeya could bend…and let there be two godparents, Gigi and Stacy. Maybe that would balance things out for Ben and her, but more importantly, their kid's upbringing. School in the States, summers with Stacy? But, fuck—all just thoughts in a vacuum. She needed Ben here, now. To talk to and make decisions with. *Together.*

But he'd decided to leave. No answer on their marriage license; no answer on their future. Which meant, what—no future?

Yes. That was what it meant, at least, that was what she needed to be prepared for. Abandoned again…officially alone.

But this time, so help her, she wouldn't play the helpless, floating soul. Now, her feet planted firmly on the ground, her legs and body, mind and soul all had gotten strong and sound and solid—like the tree in Prana's favorite book.

And like that tree, Preeya would give and give to her child. She'd give everything.

CHAPTER 55

SEVEN DAYS SINCE Ben had left. The junk mail pile on the kitchen table had become more of a tower. She tossed today's bit on top, and the whole thing fell. Preeya sighed, dropped the groceries on the center island, then surrendered into one of the hard kitchen chairs.

From the top of her purse—no longer a pit of despair, but rather a giant organized billfold with handles—she grabbed the sonogram. The little 3-D image of her baby. She beamed, then felt her heart free fall. "You were supposed to be with me." *Holding my hand, Ben.*

Shut it off, Pree.

Hard as hell to do toward the end of a long day. Especially after seeing the baby on the monitor. Moving, waving, kicking. *Heart beating.*

She could've called Gigi. Preeya had gone to *her* sono.

But, no. Ben, or no one. She chose *no one.* She needed to get used to it, anyway.

Because she *could* go this alone—without Ben.

She put the baby's image to her chest, over her aching, wrenching heart.

The fact, the truth, the unchangeable reality? She wanted him. *Ben.* In her life. *Always.*

She should have felt joy today as she watched her child in real time. Her out of sight but so in her heart little blessing. More than relieved and grateful for the baby's good health, but the joy? The culminating depth of ecstatic, united joy? Without Ben there, it was missing. The journey felt more like a trip to the next room.

But he's not in the next room.

The raw ache that had simmered below the surface all week long—her fight to prove she could do this without him—it morphed in an instant to hot red spite.

Instead of being here with me, he's in goddamn Texas. Not returning her calls, or the voice mails she'd left, or the texts she'd broken down and sent. She planned no apology, just a plea to talk. To hear his voice, to gauge their future on his tone and mood and the length of conversation he was willing to hold with her. But so far, he'd been willing to do nothing. The silent treatment like a damn child.

And now, despite her anger, she was so tempted to shoot him the sono, to tell him all the doctor had said, that she and the baby were fine—fine, despite her sleepless, high-stress week from hell since he'd left.

While he'd been so hell-bent on relieving her stress? *What a crock of shit.*

But she resisted the temptation to reach out again, especially with the status of the baby. A high-point card she held. He must be dying to know how their little creation was doing, right?

If he even cares, goddamn it.

Of course he cares, Preeya. You know him; you fell in love with him. He cares.

Yes, and his need to know about this week's checkup would be the impetus for a phone call from him. He'd probably reach out today.

But the day's near over, Pree.

That son of a bitch....

She should send the sono image. He accused her of being selfish—she should send it to show him how unselfish she was. Just like the search for her mother wasn't for *her*—it was for the baby, damn it. The *uprooting* of Jenny's poisonous roots was for the baby.

So yes, despite their rift, she should send Ben, the father, the image of their child.

She took a snapshot of the sono and got ready to hit Send. But her trembling fingers stopped her. She put the phone down and shut her eyes. What-ifs filled her head. Maybe—even as she prayed for a call or a text…snail mail, something—they really were…over? Sonogram or not. Baby or not. *What if?*

Her chest tightened and a sharp, stabbing pain in her right side made her wince.

A kick.

Preeya grunted, then giggled without meaning to. It was as if the baby wanted her to buck up, wake up—stop pouting, sulking, dwelling.

Another jab, same spot.

Let it go for now, Pree. The baby says to let it go.

She patted her belly. "Thank you, little one." She let out a long, measured stream of air like a leaking, overinflated balloon. Her mouth dry, her eyes now, too, she got up for some water.

Yes, focus. Do, move, be.

She finished the glass, conquered the four grocery bags of frozen and refrigerated items, then refilled and took her glass back to the table to sit, her feet already throbbing from the four-minute stint.

She propped her feet up on the opposite chair and sighed, ready to breathe and hydrate and distract herself with the coupon mags, brochures, and BS promos strewn across the kitchen table. She sipped her water while sifting and sorting. Putting her mind on diaper brands warmed her heart rather than constricted it. She smiled through the glossy pages of baby food and tush cream. Then she came to baby meds—and lodged in the crease were two, no three, letters. She flipped them over. Two credit card promos for Ben. And…a letter addressed to *Preeya Patel?*

In the five months living at Ben's rental on 17th , she'd received not a single stitch of mail. All her stuff went to her PO box close to Gigi's place since she'd become a flight attendant two years ago.

But this letter—she held it up to her face—was definitely addressed to her. With no return address. *Of course.*

*

A check fell out of the handwritten letter.

A check made out to her. From…DP LLC?

For eleven thousand dollars and change. Memo line: Gift.

What the hell is this?

She pushed the paper and the check away from her now-trembling hands. Swallowing hard, she racked her brain. Because who knew what to expect? Had Gigi's search for her mother gone farther than she knew?

She hadn't spoken to Gigi since Ben left. In fact, Gigi didn't know he'd left—Preeya knew, *stupid*. Maybe even unsafe, especially with Ben fifteen hundred miles away. But she didn't want to think or talk about it or anything stemming from it. Not the godparent thing, not the hunt for Preeya's mom—which she'd maybe subconsciously halted in its tracks—and not Gigi's *situation*—pretending not to be alone and depressed even though Gigi no doubt was both. Just like Preeya was now alone and depressed, but not pretending otherwise.

So avoidance had been the name of the game. She even skipped out on prego yoga the other day for a "mandatory exams study group." Gigi bought it. She'd texted Preeya later that day, saying she'd gone to class anyway and then had gone for ice cream with a bunch of the women from class, "the single ones." Oh God, *single*. Preeya's heart cringed at the thought. It almost seemed like Gigi had found friends, other friends, single friends, all with positive goddamn outlooks on being alone. Alone and pregnant.

Get used to it, Pree.

She laughed to herself. In a subconscious way, she had been...getting used to it. *Single and alone*. No calls or texts or social media. She'd boycotted it all, except for her one-sided *Ben* text string. Why? No, not only because she didn't want to say what she knew had to be said: that she and Ben...they were, well, for all intents and purposes, over.

No, the reason she'd chosen to wall up and cut off and hide away was because, damn it, Ben was the only person she wanted to speak to, see, hear, touch, breathe in or wake up to.

While he was the only one in the world who wouldn't speak to her.

She reached for the water glass to her left—an inch from the letter and the check. She watched the note as she drank, like it might flit up and bite her. But it lay still, silent, keeping its contents secret.

She put the glass down away from the letter.

Look at it.

What if it was from her? Her mother. *Jenny.*

Ben's warnings crept in and scurried around her head like venomous fire ants, furious and mean and biting.

Look at it or don't, but Jesus, do something.

Decide something.

Her right hand slapped the letter and grabbed it between her thumb and fingers.

She inhaled then blew out.

Preeya. Preeya Patel.

The handwriting was horrendous.

You are a hard woman to find…if this letter actually did find you. I messaged you a bunch of times on a bunch of your social media channels for the past few months, but no luck there.

Huh. Thinking back, Preeya guessed she'd been ignoring her social media for far longer than the past week. With the baby and Ben and everything, it made sense.

So I used my pull, or my prior pull, that is, having since parted ways with the band…

The band? She shot down to the very bottom of the page. A signature, hardly legible, like the rest of the scribble. A large *D*—not an *M* for Mom or a *J* for Jenny.

She sighed.

But…*the band.*

Dawn.

Preeya shook her head and laughed, a belly-bouncing laugh that both hurt and delighted…until her bladder leaked. Then she laughed harder. Dawn—Josh's helpful little lesbian band manager, Dawn.

She ignored the spot of pee in her panties and kept on reading.

…to find this address (the airline led to the UW campus.) Congrats if you did go back to school to heal the world. LOL. Anyway, here we are, Pretty Preeya with the "near-violet" eyes. Yes, you intrigued and captivated me that day. The day of vomit puddles and memory lane. Whether you're single and still searching…or

not, you seemed like a sensitive soul, and if you are in Seattle, which is where I've parked myself since leaving Carnal Knowledge, I do hope to see you again. Coffee at minimum.

Anyway, the sensitive-soul subject leads me to the point of this note and the explanation of the enclosed check.

As soon as I put out the metaphorical fires inside the house that morning (Josh did wake up, only to snort a few more lines before proceeding toward Otto's room for a shower, where he subsequently passed out, ripping the shower curtain and its pole from the tile surround, flooding the damn master bath) I went back out to see if the cab had scooped you up. It had. I almost wished it hadn't. Selfish, I know, but we are…all of us humans are…selfish, self-preserving assholes.

Okay…where the hell was this going? She snagged a sip of water before returning to the note, or rather, the damn *novel*. The handwriting wasn't only bad, it was tiny. She rubbed her eyes and got back into the thing.

Anyway, stranger than strange, I stood on that porch with only one thought in my head: Sandpoint Way. Weird, I know. But the stupid road name wouldn't leave my head. I walked to the end of the driveway thinking maybe I'd find your cab broken down a ways? Shit like that, thoughts or dreams leading to reality, have happened to me before, as freaky as that sounds…

Preeya chuckled. Not so freaky. Not so freaky at all.

…but anyway, no, there were no cars in sight. Nothing. I looked straight ahead of me, across the street toward the lake, which, to follow the strangeness of the happening, had been glimmering in the sunlight through a break in the cloud blanket above. Still, the road name scrolled across my brain like a ticker tape. I looked at the roadway (at the ruts and random potholes, at the yellow double line) and there, six feet from me, was a flattened piece of paper embedded into the road. Why I had to go out and get a piece of goddamn garbage from the middle of a 50 mph road, I don't know. But I just had to.

Preeya lifted her eyes from the note. *Trash in the road?* She licked her lips, chapped to hell as they were, and bit down on her bottom pout before resuming the read, her curiosity piqued. She had a strong feeling she knew exactly where this was heading, though.

Wouldn't you know, as I peeled the paper up from the blacktop, a car nearly hit me…yeah, that's how totally stupid but compelled I was. Anyway, I leaped back to the safety of the driveway, unsmashed the wad of paper, and opened it.

Preeya took a breath. *The letter.*

The original handwritten love letter (and yes, lyrics to the number one top hit of my now former band, Carnal Knowledge) from and by Josh Bolte to you. To Preeya Patel, the inspiration of it all.

I intelligently brought it to show Josh a few hours later (you know, once he'd come down.) I was thinking I needed certification that it was really written by him. All I had to do was insinuate that he'd plagiarized the words to his awe-inspired "Sun and Moon in the Guest Room," and it worked like a charm. He snagged the page from me, held it to his face, pointed at it (all while my phone's video record function had mysteriously turned itself on, ahem, so strange) and went on to state for the record that the words, the handwriting, the letter to his very first love (on that paper) were indeed penned by him.

Yeah, so, for once, just to see how it felt to do something for no reason but to see justice done for someone else, I popped the video up on the Carnal Knowledge fan site and put the letter up for auction. I sold it to the highest bidder for the net amount which you see in the enclosed check.

"Wow, that's unbelievable." Preeya stroked her belly. "This woman…she hardly…hardly knew me. To…do this?"

The only thing that caught me up? A little bit selfish…(see, almost nothing can be done with pure and total selflessness LOL.) I just had to punch Josh in the virtual face for being such a goddamn prick to me, to you, to countless women, people, animals…for as long as I've known him. So…I added a little "bonus material" to the auction post.

Oh no she did not. Did she?

Our little water-pouring video snippet. It felt so good, Preeya. Embarrassing the shit out of him, even though it potentially risked the value of the letter, making the "great Josh Bolte" less desirable…but the fans jumped on it anyway. And, yes, the whole incident got me canned. Worth it, though. Totally worth it.

So that's the story. I'm hoping to hell you're holding the check instead of it being in the hands of some new prick in your life who's not worth the crud underneath your fingernails.

No…no new prick.

No prick at all.

Her mind spun. She has, or *had*, an unbelievably amazing man, one whom she'd pushed away. Alienated. Selfishly goddamn alienated and hurt and had only *considered* when the decisions were simple. She hadn't let him in—not really. Not with any of the vital choices or parts.

God, how different was she than Josh-fucking-Bolte? Center of the Universe, Josh Bolte.

Because here she was, center of *her* universe, alone, Preeya Patel.

Maybe never to be Preeya Trainer. And it goddamn served her right.

And while she'd played for control, Ben had been busy assuring her health and well-being. He'd been so focused on her fears, on protecting her, that he locked away his own hidden pains. Beyond losing his wife to cancer, Ben had lost his first baby! How could she not know that? He held it back for her welfare.

Jesus, she'd been a horrible partner, person, friend. How lonesome Ben must've felt.

She hadn't been there for him.

Like her mother hadn't been there for Preeya's father.

Then her thoughts shifted to the soothing balance struck by Sylvia and her dad. And, in contrast, how muddy and murky and downright blurred she and Ben seemed, had become. Or had always been?

Because of Preeya's officially apparent one-sidedness. Opposite of Sylvia…and just like her mother. But she'd end it here. She'd change the tides. She wanted to share her life—truly share it—*with Ben.*

She wiped a rogue tear from her cheek while she stared at the letter in her hands.

God, what a prick—Josh Bolte. How many times might she have gotten pregnant by mistake with Josh's kid, as that stupid teenager she'd been—that teenager who Josh Bolte had convinced he'd loved, and set to be with forever. So convincing that, goddamn it, they "didn't need protection." She gagged. *"Let's make true, raw love—no barriers, no shield."* And gagged again. No fucking condom? And she'd caved. Thank God the universe didn't teach her a lesson by planting *that* seed—a *sure* path to hell on earth. Goddamn coke-snorting Josh Bolte as the father of her kid. Full-blown nausea now. The idea of having a baby, a life with that man, *Jesus.*

She winced then slammed her eyes shut, forcing an upsurge of bile from her stomach back down her esophagus. A flash of Josh's empty eyes in that guest room that regrettable morning met her mind—thank God again that he couldn't get it up or keep it up because who knows if she'd cave again, that the baby in her womb now really could have been that asshole's. She flushed the memory away as fast as it had come.

Replaced by a soothing realization that the child growing inside her was Ben's. God, what she'd taken for granted. All he'd wanted was for her to share her life with him. The decisions about their family. Ben just wanted the best for her. The best for the baby, and the best for *them.* Ben Trainer set the bar—not a selfish bone in the man's entire body.

She felt numb, frozen in time.

Read the rest and be done—so she could...*do* something. Change something. Fast.

Her finger traced down the muddled page of scratch to find her place.

In closing, Preeya Patel, some things have changed...while some have not. Undoubtedly, Josh is still a cocksucker. A selfish prick. And that may never change. But here's to people like you and, now me, acting otherwise. The way you spoke of your mother, the woman who'd left you and your sister to help the children of the godforsaken world. That struck me, man. It truly did. For a child to take such a hit, and not to be bitter and sour and ugly, but instead to show love and compassion to your helpless little sister. I hope to find more selfless people like you...

Other words based on illusion followed. Then, *Truly yours. Dawn.*

And a cell number.

How insane.

And motivating.

She stood up. Things were clearer than ever. She spun around, nowhere to go, but, God, she had to do or go or say something to change the course of things. Like Dawn's compulsion into Sandpoint Way, she needed to fix what she'd broke, and she had to do it now.

CHAPTER 56

A N AVALANCHE OF truth buried her.

Time to dig out.

Call Gigi. Tell her that what Gigi'd done—going against Ben's wishes—it wasn't okay. And that she's sorry, but Gigi couldn't be her child's godmother. And she understood if she didn't want Preeya to be Gigi's baby's either. Though it hurt her heart.

And it would rock Gigi's.

Bad timing. Okay, maybe she'd wait. To upset her best friend in the same state, farther along, in fact. She would not do to Gigi what Gigi had done to her. She loved Gigi like a sister, always.

But she was ready to prove to Ben where her loyalties lied.

With him.

And she needed help to do that. To prove to Ben that *he* was it.

She picked up her cell.

And dialed Sylvia—more of a mother to her in six months than anyone else had ever been.

"Sweetie, we've been trying to reach you for days, and to be honest, if we didn't hear back by the end of today, we were booking a flight up to you."

"I'm sorry to have worried you."

"I'm just glad to hear your voice, that you're okay…but, Preeya, are you? Okay? Because Ben called your father. Told him to hold off on…well, he was planning—"

"Planning what?"

"The day you and I had coffee Ben had apparently brought your father in on a secret. Ben arranged with his sister to surprise you. In Vallarta. A beach wedding, a tiny ceremony, right after you guys became…'courthouse legal'. But the other day he called to ask your father to hold off on buying the tickets. He wouldn't say why…just that we should call you, make sure you're okay because he had to take a long-distance long job in Texas? Why didn't you guys ask us if money is an issue, Preeya?"

"It's not, Sylvia. Money's not an issue." She snorted, holding the eleven-thousand-dollar check in her hand. "No, it's not money, and it's not Ben. It's me, all me. I screwed up royally and now I need to make it right. I need help, though. I need your help to fix this…please." No panic, just stoic surrender.

"Of course, sweetheart." Sylvia paused. "Indra, I've got Preeya on the phone. Come!" Back on the call. "Can I put you on speakerphone, sweetie? Your dad is here. We're both here."

*

She couldn't believe he'd planned a surprise wedding for her. And one so vastly different than his first wedding, like he'd read her mind, her soul. Jesus, it made her heart hurt worse than it already did.

But it was more confirmation that she'd found the *one*. And *lost* the one. Again.

She'd correct what she'd nearly destroyed. Sylvia and her father were on it. She'd left Stacy a voice mail and waited on that return call, also.

Now for Gigi. A delicate version of the truth, but it had to be done.

Preeya sat down on the sofa and threw her swollen feet up while she found and tapped Gigi's image on her phone screen.

She waited for Gigi to answer while a jumble of words bubbled in Preeya's mind. Her eyes shut tight as she tried to prioritize what to say first. Gigi didn't know that Ben had even left. And how would Gigi take it, being the root of the most major issues?

But bottom line, Pree…Gigi had only burst the bubble, while you had blown it up in the first place.

She sighed. *Truth hurts.*

"Pree, it's like we haven't spoken in ages! One second, though…over there, Dad, in the left drawer under the plates. Sorry, Pree. Lord help us, my dad is cooking dinner tonight."

"That's rarer than an earthquake," Preeya chortled, then felt a sudden worry prickle her arms.

"Yeah, I, uh, had a bit of a…thing today, Pree—"

"What? Geej, what is it—you okay? Why didn't you call me?"

"I didn't want to scare you, especially when I was too out of it to really put it in perspective…" Clanking pots in the background. "Sorry, one second, Preeya."

Teeth gnashed, Preeya huffed her irritation and dread. She didn't want to even imagine the matter. And she needed to shove down her impulsive fury at Gigi for not calling her. Hell, she would have done—has done—the same thing…keeping her own scenario close-lipped.

"I'm back. Dad's about to burn the place down, but lucky he's got an in with the fire chief." Gigi laughed.

Preeya didn't. "Tell me, Geej. What's going on?"

Gigi exhaled into the phone. "I had my weekly exam this morning, and, well, it's nothing horrible"—Preeya had already stopped breathing—"but the doctor says I have placenta previa, which is—"

"I *know* what it is, Geej." Enter oxygen. *Placenta previa—okay… it's manageable.*

"Right, of course, med school."

Yeah, med school, which, as Ben had pointed out during their blowout fight, should have corrected her own screwed-up stance on her own pregnancy. Finding her mother? After all this time? *Really, Preeya?* The realization of her over-the-top stupidity now played like a broken record in her head. Previa is only one of a thousand complications that a woman could face. And Ben's Jamie had miscarried….

"You there, Pree?"

"Yeah. I'm here, Geej." *My mind's just unhinging, is all.* "Partial or complete previa? What did the doctor say?"

She heard Gigi sigh. "Complete. The cervix is completely covered, and at this stage, six and half months, my OB says I'm hereby on pelvic rest. No intercourse—*check*—no more vaginal exams—*yay!*—and no other activities that may promote bleeding. Basically, I need to take it really easy."

Preeya swallowed back her lack of words. *Complete previa.* She cleared her throat of the new knot of worry. "Not just easy, Geej…*complete* bed rest. Err on the side of caution here. I mean it." And Preeya would do the same. Her own saga would remain completely off the table. Gigi shouldn't, couldn't handle any of it right now.

"Which is why my dad is here. I know you can't juggle any more than you already are, even *with* Ben, so Dad took time off."

With Ben…right.

"Oh, Geej, I'm so sorry—"

"Hey, quit it. I'm fine. Dad's here. The baby's healthy, which," she said, exhaling deep relief, "is the most…important…" Sudden sobs broke through her best friend's shield of calm.

"You're right, Geej. The baby's healthy. That's what matters. It'll all be fine."

"No, Pree," Gigi nearly shouted, "that's not all that matters." Her long-time friend gasped for air. "Your baby. Your baby's health, my God…and *your* health, it's equally important, Pree, and today with my feet in the stirrups and the doctor's face paler than it should ever be, I could only think of how goddamn selfish and downright…horrid I've been."

Helping her find her mom was less than prudent, but Preeya wouldn't go as far as to say Gigi'd been *horrid.* "Geej, I think you're overreacting just a—"

"Pree," Gigi growled, "let me talk. Tell me, did you see my text…from this morning? Because you usually answer right away and you didn't so I'm praying you didn't. Either way, I just need you to erase the damn thing. Don't look at it—delete the entire string of…"

But Preeya had already put Gigi on speakerphone two-rambling sentences ago to see the text. From Gigi. With an address and a name.

Jenny Freedman.

Gigi's frantic talk buzzed like flies around Preeya's head while she read the text again and again: *522 Dawson Street, Tucson, Arizona. Jenny. Jenny Freedman.*

She felt a dull kick then a follow-up rumble on her left side. From the baby. *Jenny's your grandmother's name, little one. Your blood-only grandmother.*

Alive. In Tucson. With a new name. Not her maiden name.

Gigi's voice still hovered like radio static—overshadowed by inner sounds, deafening noise, namely Preeya's pulse. It squeezed up the side of her throat and sent reverberating throbs of heat the rest of the way, to her fore-head and eyes and ears. Wonder and questions pulsed through her thoughts with each wax and wane of the slow-motion pounding. "Gigi, are…are you sure it's her? Are. You. Sure."

"Preeya, listen to me now. Ben…he told me not to bring her up, not to mention my idea now or ever. He was concerned for you, for the baby. I ignored him, the fucking idiot I am. I ignored him and it…it hit me, with today's news. This condition, the previa, it's a warning. You have to put this whole thing out of your mind, Pree. You just…just have to delete the text; delete the thought. Facing her, erasing the negativity, won't matter a damn if…if there is no baby. My godbaby, Pree. Please…do you hear me? Just leave the whole thing alone."

Curiosity to numbness transitioning to irritation rooted in her dia-phragm like she'd been sucker punched. Then it all snowballed into hot fury and erupted into her chest.

"I will do what I need to, Geej." *No remorse. No guilt.* "And, sorry, but Ben and I have decided to choose Stacy as our baby's guardian, the godparent—"

Beeep-beep. Her call-waiting. Preeya didn't hear Gigi's reaction over Stacy's incoming call.

"Listen, Gigi, I gotta take this call. Rest, and I love you. I'll be in touch… next week. And I do…I do love you so much."

She answered Stacy's call with her chest heaving, hands shaking, head still throbbing along with her feet and ankles.

Ben. God, Ben. I wish to God you were here.

"Stacy." Preeya held back a river of tears.

"Preeya, honey…what? What is it? Are you and the baby okay?"

CHAPTER 57

THE CABBIE PUT Preeya's carry-on in the trunk while she lumbered into the backseat. "Jetta Air Departures, please." She hugged her purse to her chest and exhaled until she was empty. Nothing left to do. She'd gotten Amy's wedding planner in touch with Stacy who reserved the beach behind the Airington—the ceremony *after* the turtle release, which had been Ben's niece's idea. Then on to Las Caletas for their celebration by torchlight under the stars. They'd head to their Marietas for their honeymoon the following day. Their *real* honeymoon.

The only unplanned, unpredictable variable—Ben. God willing, *Ben*.

Her pulse spiked, teeth clenched. Wasn't this what she asked for, the thrill? The unknown? Yes. *Sky's the limit, Pree.* And her limitless love for Ben, her sky—he was worth everything. Worth it *all*.

Screech. The cabbie slammed on the brakes. Her equilibrium got thrown to Sea-Tac while she and her fetus remained in the cab.

"If you could take it easy on the stop and go"—she rubbed her belly and worked to catch her breath—"we, uh, just ate…and you seem to keep your cab in mint condition." She lifted her brows and smiled.

He winked in his rearview. "Will do, ma'am. Sorry. Due in, what, three months?"

"Just about, yes."

"I'm having a little one in just about that time, too. Exciting times."

"Yes." Her eyes shot down to her lap as she swallowed a tremendous knot of anxiety-coated...excitement. "A thrilling roller coaster ride, for sure."

*

"Ben, I just feel like you ran again."

His nostrils flared.

His sister threw her hand up to her jutted hip.

"I actually flew, Stacy, and it was absolutely not the same thing."

"As what? The last time you ran from her?"

Fuck. "That time she...she cut me off, out, up and down, when I told her about...it doesn't matter. She figured it out, found me—"

"Alive, thank God. You *do* and *act* and *go* out of...spite. That's what it is. First, to spite Jamie for dying, then her parents for that whole medical review fiasco—"

"Hold it..."

"No, I don't blame your anger there, but...let me finish, little brother. Now you take this job in Texas, leaving your pregnant fiancée *out of spite*..." Stacy shook her head at him. "Thank God she's as rock solid as she is for all she's been through. But you know, the one you always end up hurting most is *you*. You don't give yourself the time or space to...to..."

"To what? Dwell and rot? To settle? Look, past is past. Marriage is something I cherish. And my marriage was cut off, stolen from me. My next one has to be...worthy and...different, but better. And Preeya doesn't want a husband. She wants...a follower, a support when it's convenient."

"I was married, Ben, and sorry, but it was as close to perfect as Mexico is to Canada. And—"

"And you, my dear sister...ran."

"Whoa!"

"What? You did. You quit, took the kids, ran here to Puerto Vallarta, holed-up in your paradise cave. Max didn't fit, so—"

"Max didn't earn or help or care or—"

"Or what?"

"Or love us, Ben. Preeya does love *you*."

"How do you know that?"

Stacy growled, literally growled. "She hunted you down to see if you were alive in Central Mexico, found you in Seattle, and now…now she's alone in Seattle. While you're here escaping. Again. Instead of, hey, doing one of a billion proactive things to work this out with her."

His chest tightened. But he said nothing.

"What about a therapist?"

"She won't see a therapist."

"You wouldn't, either. You are both so alike it hurts."

"Well, last month I offered, for her own stuff, I offered, Stace. To go with her. I bent over backward, forward and through, damn it."

"You can't stop there. Why am I telling you this? You already did the long haul once, but that marriage…had an expiration date. Well, you gotta do it again. Push through again. Even if it's hard."

"I pushed, Stace. And she stopped me. I can't do any more than I've done. It's not fair to either of us." He raked his hand through his hair and yanked for the pain. "Maybe we…we fell in lust instead of love…I don't know." But he did—he did know, and that's what burned so bad. He far more than lusted for Preeya Patel. He loved her beyond and back…while she maybe, probably, seemed to have only lusted for him. An idea, an image, a dream.

"What about the baby?"

"I will be in that child's life, Stacy. I will be that baby's father—to the fullest extent of the title." He swallowed back a knot of hard angst, picturing Preeya opening the front door, that little news anchor Evan or some other schmuck holding her waist while she held Ben's baby. Handing him over for the weekend.

Fuck.

His voice cracked. "We can work out custody…and be friends."

"That's insane, Ben. You love her."

"I know I do, Stacy." His chest heaved. "I know I do."

He paced the room. His breath shallow, his spine staunch. "Bottom line, if she can't come to me and discuss vital things, little things—everything—then it's done. And I will…go through the courts. And I will…be fine."

He ignored Stacy's clucking and head shake of shame.

"Look, I still get a second chance at having my own kid. That's more than I could've ever hoped for." His chest lifted with a new fuller breath. "Preeya's given me that chance. I'm thankful. For that, I'm so grateful."

His eyes sank with his heart to the floor.

"She and I, though, we just…don't know—and didn't know—each other well enough."

Stacy began to tear up. He grabbed the tissue box and handed it to her, then squeezed her shoulder. "It's just better this way. It is. Why put a kid through inevitable heartache? Starting out honest, separate…it's fair. It's real."

"Ben. You two are too…" Stacy's eyed widened, tears broke free.

"It's best, Stace." His heart racked his ribs. Jamie really might've been his *one and only*.

"This is *not* best." Stacy's sorrow morphed into a death glare, and it began to penetrate his cheek until a text—*thank God*—pinged her phone. "Shit—I forgot. My meeting with Phyllis."

Ben narrowed his eyes.

"My editor. You met her a year ago? Oh, never mind. But"—she looked around the kitchen—"I didn't make dinner. You and the kids—you're comin' with me."

"I'll make them food here, no prob—"

"It's at their favorite spot…so move your butt!"

He looked down at his swim trunks, no top. "You guys go. I'm fine to lounge here…in my sloth-wear"—he opened and shut the fridge in a flash—"with a beer."

"You need to get out of the house, Ben…and I'll drive so you can get a drink at the resort. Kids! We're going to the Airington. Wear your nicer outfits!"

Ben rolled his eyes and fumed. "Fine, but—"

"The baby turtle release is tonight!" Beth yelled as she trampled down the stairs in a white linen dress.

Ben found his smile. "You look very pretty, niece. Very grown-up." Beth winked at her mom. "Thanks, Uncle Ben." She smiled. "You should brush your hair and change...and then I *might* return the compliment."

Stacy smirked; Ben huffed and shot a look at his sister. "I appreciate your honesty, Bethy." He reached for Beth to knuckle her head.

"Stop, Uncle Ben! *My* hair is nice."

She smoothed her hair as Ben hugged her—*carefully*. "Fine, I'll change. But I'm wearing shorts if we're doing another turtle release."

Stacy cleared her throat. "Pants, Ben. The restaurant requires it." He watched Stacy scurry for her purse and her laptop bag. How she forgot such important meetings, he didn't know. "Yeah, just roll your pants up when you're at the water. Oh, and a tie. You need a tie."

"A tie? What the hell, Stace?"

"It's their favorite place, Ben." Her eyes got wide, imploring. "I saw one in your luggage so buck up and put it on. And please don't bring that awful man purse."

"You know what...I'm boycotting all women, you two included." He heard Beth and Stacy snicker as he walked toward the stairs, then he glanced back over his shoulder. "And I'm bringing the *murse!*" He headed up to change. "Thank God I'm having a boy," he muttered.

"A boy, Uncle Ben?" Beth bounced over to him. "A little boy—awesome! I can take him surfing and digging...a boy! It's a boy, Mom!"

"I heard, sweetheart." Stacy pulled Ben down from the steps for a hug. "Congrats, little brother."

"Yeah, thanks." It felt amazing. *And not enough.*

"So you've been in touch with the doctor?"

"Yes, actually, I have, to make sure she and the baby are good...but, I knew a couple of weeks ago...long story. But hey, tick tock, right?"

"Right, right...well, go—get dressed."

Ben trod up the stairs, passing Peter on his way down. "A boy, huh? So, PJ or Peter, Jr.—just sayin'."

Ben laughed. Yeah, a boy. *A baby boy.* He couldn't wait to have and hold and love his *son*. Even though it would be without his Preeya.

*

Hidden from view, Preeya watched from behind the concierge partition as Stacy sent Ben to the reception desk—under whatever pretense—to be handed the letter.

It was her turn to bestow a handwritten message of her deepest sentiments to her truest love.

God willing, he'd read it.

*

Dr. Benjamin Trainer (aka Babe),

You.

How have you done it again?

Made me see?

See inside myself.

Given me a new lens. A lens that, hopefully, I am not too late in finding. You left it for me when you went away, when you escaped me, the one who is supposed to be your safe haven. I have failed you. I failed your heart, your ever-open, loving heart.

So here I am (don't turn around yet, just keep reading), with reshuffled priorities. You and our child, our family, are my priority, the priority. All others need to wait in line.

Gigi (my best friend, my sister) included.

And as for my birth mother…I woke up to reason and logic (and to your wisdom) just in time. It turns out she's alive in Tucson, but I don't know anything more than that. Not worth our family's well-being to find out.

But my mother by choice (and by law), Sylvia and my father are here, as is Stanton, and of course your sister (our child's godmother) and our niece and nephew. They are all here to witness and celebrate our union (the union, I pray, you will re-agree to).

In other words, I am asking you, Ben Trainer, to marry me. With our Marietas and our families as witness—today, now (in a minute, you can turn around) on the beach behind this resort.

I want to walk through this life, this world, with you, and with no other.

Hand in hand, heart in heart.

Together.

Side by side.

I promise to choose us, Ben. I do. You—my escape artist, my heart—and me—the one at the bottom of the steepest learning curve ever known.

I choose us, if you'll still have me (you can turn around now).

Marry me, babe. Make us, us.

Please.

For always.

All my love,

Your Preeya

*

Unsure about his grasp on reality, Ben took off his glasses then folded the letter with slow and precise care, blinking the emotion from his eyes. A lone tear rolled off his face and hit his hand. *This is real, Ben.*

And if it's not...if just an illusion...if, when he turned around, she stood on a cloud of haze and pretend, he might disintegrate. Be done. If only a dream, he'd give up right here, right now.

Please. Please, let this be real.

His eyes shut tight as he forced his feet to pivot, turning him around to face...

*

His Preeya, in his arms—tight. Probably too tight. "I do, I will…take you for my wife, Preeya Patel—and I won't let you go. Not again. I promise that I won't let you go ever again."

When he pressed his lips to hers, the world went away, pulled out from under and around him, *them*. A floating balance had been struck. Symbiosis. Blissful, pulsing silence filled his chest. Their kiss rolled in and out like the nearby tide—and anchored him to earth at the same time. And no one else existed…

Until Beth's and Peter's titters tickled his ears as they fled the "sickening scene."

With Preeya's tender, sweet lips still pillowed against his, he laughed then sighed, inhaling her in.

"You ready?" he asked, bringing his hands from her face to her hands.

She winced then dug out a smile. "Hmm. Yes, babe, we are *both* ready." She pulled her hands from his and held her side. "Me and our little soccer player here."

He laughed as he knelt down while holding Preeya's hips in his grasp. He put his ear to her belly and listened. Whirling perfection. "I hear you, little one. I hear you." He kissed her belly then rose to his feet. "I missed you both. Too much." He planted another deep kiss on Preeya's mouth, unable to resist.

"*Mmm*, babe." Preeya giggled while obviously reluctant to break their connection. "The wedding planner wants to start before we lose the light." But her lips remained skipping and dancing over his, as if unable to pull away.

"Oh yes, right." But Ben wouldn't let their lips' entanglement end, either. Her taste, her softness; he needed this, his Preeya-replenishment. He'd left her for too long. God, too damn long. And he swore he wouldn't fucking run again. *Never again.*

"You'll have your lives, guys. Your entire lives!" Stacy called from the patio.

"And the honeymoon's only a few hours off, buddy!" Stan shouted from the open doorway to the beach, the bay's rolling tide echoing behind him.

They all laughed, Sylvia and Indra, Stan, Stacy...their witnesses. Their family.

"Hey, Mom, Uncle Ben, Aunt Preeya!" Beth yelled from the sand. "The baby turtle release, it's happening! Hurry up, everybody!" Beth was gone again in a blink, before Stacy could catch her to tell her some motherly instruction.

Ben winked at Stacy then mouthed a thank you for her part in this "grand plan." His sister nodded and blew a kiss to his bride-to-be, then headed off after the kids.

Ben took Preeya's hand in his, their fingers woven together, a perfect fit. "Turtles, first...*then* we tie the knot?"

"That's the plan," she said with a coy smile, blinking those eyes of heaven-and-sea. "Then the party by torch light at Las Caletas." She grinned, so proud of herself.

And he was proud of her, thankful for her, amazed by her. Hell, the woman hunted him down twice, for Christ's sake. That's a strong woman. And a strong love. A love that he'd work his ass off every day of his life to *eventually* deserve.

"Sounds amazing, babe...but"—he nipped at Preeya's ear and squeezed her close to him as they dug their toes into the white, silken sand—"I'm all about our Honeymoon. Our *real* honeymoon."

Preeya smirked and licked her lips. "Yes, our *real* honeymoon." She beamed. "In the morning, Pedro is taking us, and only us, to our hidden beach, then to our falls."

"Oh...no Sun Hat and Charles?" Ben cracked a smile. "It just won't be the same without our old friends."

Preeya, in her white flowing dress and free-flowing hair whipping in the wind, broke out laughing and giggling—God that giggle. "I think we'll have enough company this trip to the Mareitas"—she rubbed their baby bump—"don't you? Just the three of us..."

"You, me, and the baby, Pree, is perfect. Always."

*

Perfect light, sunset ushering in dusk. She stood at the start of the petal-lined aisle of white sand softness in disbelief. She'd never thought it could be. *This. Any of this.*

With the tide's soft roar behind him, Ben stood glowing under the lattice altar laced with vibrant purple-and-pink bougainvilleas—Amy's wedding planner, Isabel, had pulled together a last-minute miracle. While Stanton and Peter, Ben's groomsmen, took their places next to her groom, she watched Ben pivot to face the bay.

Her chest locked. *What?* What was it?

Before she could heave a breath of panic, he pulled his arm back behind his head and flung something. She squinted her eyes. A gold ring trailed by a chain. His wedding ring. His and Jamie's. It flew through the air like a comet out into the glistening blue bay.

She watched his shoulders lift then fall as he turned again to face her. Her chest warmed with his amber gaze, and the liberating smile on his face made her heartbeat pulse throughout her entire being.

When he disengaged his gaze once more and moved to the rear post of the altar, she bit her bottom lip, wondering what he was doing now, wanting whatever he'd planned—during *her* surprise wedding ceremony for *him*—to be fast. She needed to be his wife already. To have his arms around her again, his firm forever-hold, his mouth and lips and breath entangled in hers.

He stepped forward with an easel, placed it next to Stacy and Beth—her bridesmaids—and began to unroll…a large…photo of…*Prana.*

One quivering hand to her mouth, the other to her chest, Preeya let out a gasp as tears and laughter escaped her. She shook her head, just overwhelmed. With it all.

"Your maid of honor," her father whispered in her ear, then held her arm to steady her.

Preeya had no words. It was perfect. With both Gigi absent and her sister gone…it was just too perfect for a single word.

For composure, she pulled in an enormous breath of sea air, of Prana, of family, of Ben, and nodded that she was ready.

More than ready.

To be with Ben—*and his golden gaze*—forever.

"Are you 'good to be gone', *bitay*."

She glanced up at the man beside her and laughed while wiping one last tear away. "Good to *go*, Dad." She gave him her hand and squeezed. Not in a million years, a half a year ago, could she have imagined being ushered anywhere by her father—let alone down an aisle. "And yes, I am very good… to go."

On her other side stood a woman, a friend, a *mother*—Sylvia—tearful and proud.

Preeya's heart swelled. She gave her parents a final nod and a smile of her thanks and love. "I'd say I've never been so good in my entire life."

Soft music from somewhere lifted above the rolling waves.

Time now. Her chest grew hot and her temples and eyes burned.

Keep it together, Preeya—Ben's right there.

Waiting for you.

She lifted her eyes to meet his—that soul-searing gaze that tore through her heart and made her whole at the same time. Dr. Ben Trainer, tall and strong and solid and gleaming-proud, waiting for her to reach him, to marry him—*to love him forever.* And she would; she'd love this man with all her being. Her Ben, the man of her wildest dreams.

The End

AUTHOR'S NOTE

I really hope you enjoyed Ben and Preeya's story—it was a dream writing it for you!

Now, are you ready for more good stuff featuring Ben and Preeya and the other couples in the Paradise South series—**for free**?
Just go to [www.RissaBrahm.com/Join] and you'll get deleted scenes from each of the Paradise South books as they come out:

Tempting Isabel — (Isabel & Zack)
Taking Jana — (Jana & Antonio)
Catching Preeya — (Preeya & Ben)
Satisfying Ali — (Ali & Dev)
Freeing Kyla — (Kyla & Liam)

And…
You'll receive 1 Free Novelette called *P.S. in Paradise* — (Epilogues for all 5 Books which will only be sold as part of the Paradise South series Box Set) — for FREE! So, head to [www.RissaBrahm.com/Join] and get your free stuff on!

Also reserved for my newsletter subscribers: first-to-know news on release dates, fabulous giveaways and other cool bonus material like character sketches and interviews, failed flings, and more! So, go check it out! xo~Rissa

P.S. Your candid review of Catching Preeya posted on Amazon helps other romance readers know if my stuff is for them, makes me a better writer, and supports and spreads the word, allowing me to continue writing! Your opinion really matters and is so appreciated! [www.RissaBrahm.com/Catching-Preeya]

P.P.S. I always love hearing from you directly! Please, reach out to me anytime…

e: me@RissaBrahm.com
p: www.RissaBrahm.com/pinterest
f: www.RissaBrahm.com/facebook
g: www.RissaBrahm.com/goodreads
t: www.RissaBrahm.com/twitter

BOOKS BY RISSA BRAHM

PARADISE SOUTH SERIES
Tempting Isabel, Book 1
Taking Jana, Book 2
Catching Preeya, Book 3
Satisfying Ali, Book 4 (2016)
Freeing Kyla, Book 5 (2016)
P.S. in Paradise (The series' Epilogue Novelette Collection, 2016)

All five soul-deep and sensual romances of the Paradise South series include diverse and alluring heroes and heroines to love and lust for throughout their impassioned journeys toward their happily ever afters. Enjoy them all: [www.RissaBrahm.com/Books]

ACKNOWLEDGEMENTS

Infinite thanks:

To my content editor, Tessa Shapcott; copy editor, Michael Mandarano, and my proofreaders, J.F., and Markham Correct.

To my beta readers: June M., Saleena C., Lady P., Penny L., Kirsty F., Sandra L., Kerrie K., Gretchen H., Tiffany S.

To my Launch Team: June M., Saleena C., Lauren S. and the rest of the crew for their time, feedback, and energy.

To authors Jessie G., Kimberly Llewellyn, Lynn Carmer, and Joanne Rock for your expert guidance and support.

To romance bloggers and reviewers who share their love for romance with the world!

And to authors Tamara Lush, Desiree Holt, Rebecca Brooks, Jay Crownover, Gail McHugh and Laura Kaye for spreading the word.

To InkSlinger PR, Nazarea Andrews, KP Simmon for their support and time.

To the RWA TARA chapter for such solid support and encouragement.

To my Mom, who is always there for me.

To my husband for all the brainstorming, covering for me, and the inspiration.

To my daughter, for driving me to write the best, truest depths of smart, strong, enduring women that I can.

To VK and GRP, for backing me and for their endless love.

ABOUT THE AUTHOR

CONTEMPORARY ROMANCE WRITER Rissa Brahm grew up in New York and has since lived in all four corners of the United States, and beyond. The beautiful paradise of Puerto Vallarta, Mexico—the core setting of her hot and heartfelt debut series, Paradise South—is Rissa's most recent and beloved home.

When not chained-by-choice to her MacBook, she is embarking on outdoor adventures with her husband and little girl, laughing to tears with a good rom com, eating amazing Indian food with something chocolate for dessert; reading good, hot scorchers in bed; biking, long walks, and yoga; zoning out to killer music from across the decades and the globe; and getting lost only to discover a new exciting route home again.

You can connect with Rissa on Facebook, Twitter or by email anytime by heading to http://www.RissaBrahm.com.

www.ingramcontent.com/pod-product-compliance
Lightning Source LLC
Chambersburg PA
CBHW030545180626
46816CB00005B/1411